'THE INCREDIBLE ACHIEVEMENTS OF BORING JOHN'

Aka

'Réalisation incroyable de Ennuyeux Jean'

Michael J. Cooper

For Mum

Prologue

A rough estimate was three hours. That was the amount of sleep I guessed I'd had throughout the night. It was still early, five o'clock in the morning; I didn't have to arrive at work at the bank until nine, although I was always there by eight. This way I was amongst the first to arrive and I didn't have to do the walk from the front door to my desk past the trendy young cashiers who teased my appearance. Eight o'clock fit with my self-inflicted invisibility; I could be at my desk hidden in the back of the office and not move until six thirty, hence benefiting from the same lonely journey back to the same door. Now, when I say 'not move' from my desk, I exclude the sixteen trips a day to the gents restroom which was conveniently situated only ten feet to my right, this allowed the frequent trips to be as subtle as possible but, unfortunately, by no means unnoticed.

Back to five o'clock on the day in question, and it was this same necessity to frequent the lavatory that meant I had awoken in the bath, the water had all but seeped away through the ill fitting plug and my hands, and no doubt feet, were wrinkled to a prune like texture. I laboriously pulled myself from the bathtub, instantly feeling desperate to urinate again; I stood astride the lavatory, which was ridiculously close to the bath in my miniscule bathroom. I'd tried sleeping on the toilet prior to resorting to the bath, however, this had as always, proved impossible.

Prostatitis had tortured me for almost four years, an infection of the prostate gland, the side effects of which I believe I have explained; although I should add that the sixteen trips to the gents a day resulted in the passing of urine a maximum of only twice. They say the patient becomes the doctor, and it is true that I, John Bore, knew everything about my disease that was available to know. Although I had indulged many of the suggested treatments it is true to say that I had not rigidly managed to adhere to any. I had tried to massage my own prostate as suggested in one book, however found it impossible to twist my hand to such a fashion that allowed me to insert my finger into my own arse. I had begun a diet of broccoli that included drinking the water that it was boiled in; this had helped a little but the results were probably cancelled out by the amount of junk I ate on top of the tiny green trees that my books call 'superfood'. This in turn led to my three hundred pounds weight which truth be told, was the most likely reason for the problem in the first place.

At six feet four inches tall, I think I carried that weight as well as anyone could, but I was fat, huge, no avoiding that. I could not be clear on when I took the steps from slim to average, from average to chubby, from chubby to fat and finally obese. I had been quite the athlete until at least the age of thirteen, I remembered winning the cross-country race and coming second in the sprint at school sports day. It was around this age that my father died, this probably had something to do with it. Not my mother, she had died giving birth to me so I never knew or even met her, other than briefly for two minutes I understand before she passed away. However the death of my father not only affected me emotionally as expected, I adored my father and knew that I had been the apple of his eye. His parting however, had left me in the custody of my stepmother, the financial inheritance she had welcomed, and the thirteen-year-old boy not so much. A plate of chips, a bar of chocolate, anything that kept me quiet with minimum effort, strange then that she had constantly taunted me about health, weight and appearance.

My appearance did not bother me now, other than making the invisibility tougher, I knew I was no oil painting. As I stooped to shave I barely even noticed the huge mole that sat to the right of my nose above the corner of my mouth. In all honesty I could not remember when that started to appear either. I carefully shaved around it before picking up a pair of small nasal scissors and trimming the hairs that protruded from the brown lump itself. I cleaned my teeth, which due to the diet I mentioned, well you can imagine were not the best of shades and every one sported a large black filling somewhere about it. I slipped my underpants over the incontinence pad, which I had lost the nerve to leave the house without, although I had never actually needed it. I finished dressing in a black suit, the only colour I would wear so that should I have an accident it would not show, as it would on say a grey or a blue suit. I completed my ensemble by pulling on my necktie bringing the buttons of my shirt as close as they would go at the neck. I huffed and puffed to pull the Velcro straps on my shoes and left my flat on tiptoe in an attempt to elude my landlord who lived in the flat below. I failed.

There was no sound of an opening door or footsteps, so as I noticed Mr Tsang standing in the hallway by the front door I couldn't help but wonder if he'd been there all night simply waiting. As was the norm and in fairness with good reason, Mr Tsang was not in a good mood.

"RENT!" was the expected first word. Mr Tsang was a bitter man at the best of times, a wealthy doctor forced to move into one of his own dilapidated tenancy investments during a messy divorce from a wife who wanted everything. "I don't know what the hell kind of life you're used to 'Bore' but a life in this house is paid for. Don't give me the bullshit line about the bank making errors either; I know you cancelled your direct debit." Mr Tsang was right; I had cancelled it knowing there was not enough money in my account. I had put a selection of my fathers' old Beatles albums on Ebay convinced I would get rent money there, however, they remained unsold.

"Mr Tsang it was the bank I promise, I'll have it sorted in the next day or so", even through my panicked excuses I was aware that my hand rose across my face, an involuntary gesture to hide my bad teeth, if only my hand was big enough to cover my entire frame. Obviously, an oriental man as his name suggests, Mr Tsang was not tall, but he squared up to me even though I towered over him by well over a foot.

"You are full of shit Bore, I know you lie, and that's why you hide behind hand. I should phone bank, I know where you work. Not so good for you if they know how bad you manage own money". I squeezed past him and opened the door.

"No need for that Mr Tsang I promise I really do, the next day or so honestly", I never looked far from my own feet as I pulled the door behind me and shuffled down the outside stairs trying to breath and relax my pelvis as suggested in another book I'd read, the angry tones of Mr Tsang faded behind me as I approached the bus stop at the end of the road.

At this stage it was impossible to know, as in fact it always is, where that day would go, the events that could mould a life and change a future, possibly destroy these two things but possibly, just possibly, something else.

Chapter 1

A Particularly Shit Day

The journey to work that morning was un-spectacular, a nervous forty minutes on the bus, slowly rocking from foot to foot trying to focus on the fact that urination was impossible as no liquid had past my lips for at least twenty-four hours. I pretended that I did not notice the school kids giggling at my expense and acted as though I was oblivious to the leader of the pack whose reflection I could see in the large glass door, dancing behind me, puffing out his cheeks and arching his arms outward in a mock emulation of my size. All in all a particularly shit start to the day, however, no different from any other day in recent memory so nothing to complain about.

"Nothing to complain about", but then the rage, inside I was boiling, I wanted to snap the little fucker's neck, smash his face against the window, and knock his teeth out before throwing his limp body on the floor in front of his shitty friends, see if they kept laughing. Yes, I confess I wished for that 'Hollywood movie-hero' ability to perform a horribly aggressive act but somehow make it cool and acceptable. Unfortunately, I was a pasty, fat English bloke on the number forty-four bus from Holloway to Euston, and the teasing kid had a Nike sports bag and trendy sneakers, along with a gaggle of adoring fans, so he was far cooler than I.

I got off the bus before my teenage tormentors, so as you would expect, with the added protection of a soon to be moving bus which I was no longer on board, the chants of 'you fat bastard' echoed through the narrow windows as the bus pulled away from the stop where I alighted. I again pretended I could not hear, or rather convinced myself I could not hear. I jogged across the road to the large black front door of the bank, I say jogged, I actually shuffled my flabby legs slightly quicker than usual as the crossing light was flashing and I wanted to be at a distance where I genuinely could not hear the insults directed at me. Knocking on the huge door I went through my routine of praying it would be Roy who opened the door. The cashiers and admin staff took turns at arriving early, doing a quick security check of the building and then waiting at the door to allow arriving members of staff access. This meant they had to be up at the crack of dawn; however it came with two hours overtime each day, which was a much-coveted bonus. Now Roy, who I specified as my preferred doorman, although like the rest was at least ten years younger than me, was a small, balding, chubby guy from the North of England. Although he was incredibly popular throughout the bank for his Northern wit and friendly demeanour, I think his knowledge of his own physical appearance stopped him being cruel to me. Not that he was nice by any stretch of the imagination; my entrance would simply be easier, a nod and a mutually mumbled 'good morning'. Alas, this particular morning, the door was opened by Gemma.

Now, when I tell you that Gemma was by far the most pleasant person in my life, you may well assume that she would be my preferred encounter at the beginning of a working day, especially after such a shitty start. If I were rational and fully excepting of my appearance and position in the world, then you would be right. Yet it would appear this was not quite the case, for somewhere deep inside, some ridiculous crevice of my mind allowed a thought, or a dream to hide itself. Gemma was in my eyes the most beautiful thing that I had ever seen, be it compared to other girls or to natural wonders of the world that I had seen in encyclopaedias, alas never visited. She was tall, for a Chinese girl, maybe five foot seven? The most breathtaking smile one could imagine. She had the smallest button of a nose, the darkest, friendliest, sexiest eyes imaginable. Her perfect face was set with high and angular cheekbones, full lips and the whole package framed by the long, straight, black, shinning hair of an angel. I am far too Picard to comment on her figure, her legs, waist, breasts, needless to say, 'OH MY GOD!'

"Good morning John, how are you today?" I hated her seeing me like this, I knew there was someone else inside that she should be seeing. A rugged, six foot four, toned, hero that would make her swoon, a guy she could fall in love with. I dreaded her opening the door to me even more than the most vicious of my other colleagues who would great me with things like, 'morning Chunky, how many times are you gonna piss today, do you think we should just move your desk into the toilet? Do you wank in there?' All this is going through my head as I am staring at Gemma and realise I have still not responded to her greeting.

"How is my uncle treating you?" Ah, I should probably point out my other issue with Gemma as my greeter, Gemma Tsang's uncle was my landlord, the very one who'd screamed at me only an hour earlier, and the other thirteen mornings before that. I knew a point would come where my financial situation would reach Gemma and make the fantasy of her and I even harder to conceive of, if that was indeed possible. So, I did what I always did, I sweated, tried not to piss myself, went as red as a radish and mumbled some incoherent bollocks as I sped past her as fast as my beastly frame would allow, all of this through tightly pursed lips, my alternative bad tooth disguise to the hand across the mouth.

"You have a nice day John" were the beautiful words that followed me as I tapped the security code into the keyboard by the door that allowed me into the staff section of the banking hall. I went redder, I sweat harder, I grinned, I waved and I accidently let out a fart that I am sure she heard. Bloody marvellous, I bet she was gagging for me!

Safely at my desk, after a quick toilet stop, nothing came out and nothing had leaked, I did my best chameleon impression as always. Doing all I could to blend into the environment I sat low in my chair, I made minimal movement. I watched the rest of the staff arrive one by one, the small cluster of the young cool cashiers gathered as always and I watched them as they looked at Gemma through the glass that separated them from the customers when the working day started. I watched them giggle at their own obscenities, joking about what they would like to do to her. When Craig, their illustrious leader, entered and stood behind Gemma, thrusting his hips to mimic sex when she turned away, they broke into hysteria in a demonstration of their adulation of him. In my mind for the second time that day, my internal 'Hollywood hero' vaulted across the desk and began throwing them around the room with an effortless violence that was acceptable and cool. Alas, as my fantasy focus had been on the small group that were staff side, I did not see that Craig had progressed through the banking hall and entered through the security door which had been the scene of my ill timed fart. Despite my invisibility skills that ensured most people never said a word to me in any given day, Craig always seemed to pick me out. It was as though he could not start his day unless he had humoured himself at my expense in some way.

"Good morning Mr Boring", was his classic opener, "or is it just Bore I am sorry, maybe it is Boring? Boring John? Seems to make more sense", I pretended that I found it as amusing as his support group who were now beside themselves; I smiled and even chuckled a little through my finger shield, slowly nodding as though I found his assault to be no more than friendly banter. I didn't, my internal hero was ripping his throat out. "Boring can I ask you, it's what? Nearly nine in the morning, just how many pies have you eaten so far today? Give or take a hundred." He slapped me on the shoulder and walked towards his followers with his smug grin ready to accept their praise.

"Are you okay John?" I spun in my seat to see Gemma standing by my desk.

"Err what? I mean, huh? I mean, sorry?" Her face showed a genuine concern and she didn't smile at my blurted nonsensical words.

"I see them picking on you all day and you just sit there, if it gets to you, then you should complain to someone, it's disgusting of them" At this point it felt like it was a thousand degrees around my desk and I could feel my shirt starting to stick to me. I realised I was exposed and instantly raised my hand to scratch my lip, this was actually a better plan when Gemma was around, as well as the teeth it was a desperate bid to hide the mole that paraded across my face.

"Oh it's just the guys having fun, they're young they don't mean it, I guess?" My God I had managed to get a full sentence out, it was bullshit but fifteen words one after the other is a sentence and that was progress.

"I was going to talk to you today John", Jesus Christ, she was what? "You know that I do the pay roll each month", shit, her Uncle had talked to her I was just starring at her like a disciplined dog stares at food before the owner snaps their fingers to indicate it's time to eat. "Well I couldn't help but notice your birth date", what did she say? She paused.

"Notice my what?" Did she say mole? No she said something else, "Notice my what?" I repeated again, the full sentence was obviously a one off. She smiled at me and I melted that bit more.

"It's your birthday today John. Listen I know how shy you can be so I left a little something in your drawer. I didn't think you'd want a fuss or those guys teasing you. It's not much, but happy birthday anyway". With these words and one more smile she turned and she was gone.

She was right, it was my thirty-second birthday, I had totally forgotten. In fairness, so had everyone else in the world, not that I think anyone knew to forget. I remained frozen for what seemed an age, when I eventually came too and my eyes focused it was on the condescending face of Craig.

"Oooh 'Boring', a girl talked to you, what is she, a feeder?" my face of mock amusement returned. "Don't go kidding yourself that she likes you 'Boring', it's pity and that's just embarrassing, you've got no chance you do know that right?" I turned to my computer screen and tried to vanish as he walked away speaking over his shoulder, "mind you none of us have a chance once princess fucks off to Hollywood, she wishes".

Two things sprang to my mind at that moment. The first, maybe it's not just me young Craig takes issue with, Gemma was perfect and nothing but sweet to anyone she met, the venom in his tone when he spoke of her, easily equalled that of when he spoke to me. The second was the accidental reminder he had given me as to my date that evening. I say date but allow me to explain.

Gemma, at this stage we can call her the love of my life, was heavily involved in amateur dramatics. She had been an active member of the 'Islington Players' since she was young. Now the 'Islington Players' are what you would imagine, a small group of amateur actors and actresses who put on around three shows a year out of a small theatre near Caledonian Road. They are amongst the most talented of the amateur dramatics set and their shows regularly have over two hundred people, maximum capacity for their small theatre hall. Now the previous year they had made the bold move of stepping into Shakespeare territory, well as the only member of the players who was remotely within the age range, Gemma had been cast as Ophelia, opposite Peter Jennings playing Hamlet, Peter owned a butchers shop on Upper Street.

Well, the first Chinese Ophelia was born and to rave reviews, the Islington Gazette gushed. Within journalist circles a friend of a friend, of a friend talked to someone at 'The Times' and before you know it the Islington Players had their first national review. To shorten the story, people who may not have normally attended a small theatre in Islington turned up in droves, one of these being the Chairman of the Royal Shakespeare Company. So it came to be that, the very night of my thirty-second birthday, Chinese Ophelia would be appearing at the Grand on Shaftsbury Avenue and this was her last day working at the bank. I guess "fucking off to Hollywood" as Craig so eloquently put it, was a way off but it was very likely that a career outside the public banking system beckoned my love.

Anyway, what am I thinking, she'd left something in my drawer. I can't believe I let myself ramble on this long. I looked around before sliding my drawer open, as if for some bizarre reason anyone may be paying any attention to me. There it was, a small package around two inches square, wrapped in red wrapping paper with a gold ribbon holding it in place. The package was sitting on top of an envelope, also red, with my name written on it. I looked around again before reaching for it.

'Okay, now at this stage you may be asking yourself, 'what's so shitty about this day? I mean yeah, the landlord, the kids on the bus & Craig but that happens every day. He just got a present of a hot girl he is besotted with who is an up and coming actress.' I fully understand this reaction I really do, please bare with me and join me in enjoying the next small part of this day before the title of this chapter becomes all too obvious'.

I reached for the package and slowly lifted out this prized bounty, slipped it straight underneath my polyester suit jacket and made my way as discreetly as possible, which by the way was impossible, to the gents toilet. It was after all ten past nine so it was about time for my second visit. Once in my haven, I sat on the lavatory, seat down, and trousers up, and paused. This was a rare occurrence, no unbelievable, and I wanted to enjoy it. I first opened the envelope; taking so much care anyone observing would assume I were diffusing a bomb. I slid my pudgy fingers inside and retrieved a small red card with a single Chinese symbol in black ink printed on it. Before I opened the card, I turned it over and looked at the back, again simply trying to make the experience last. At the bottom of the rear side a short sentence was printed, 'The symbol printed on this card depicts confidence'. I frowned, not sure why, took a deep breath and opened the card. The printed message read, *'There is something special in everyone; it just takes courage and confidence'.* Followed by hand written text, *'Happy birthday John, love Gemma'.*

Wow! 'Love Gemma', let me say that again, 'Love Gemma'. At that moment, sitting in stall one of the banks' toilets, I was my Hollywood hero alter ego. I suddenly remembered this was not all there was to the adventure I was going through. Gently tucking the card back into the envelope and then the envelope into my inside pocket, I retrieved the package that was balanced on my left thigh. In all honesty, balanced is a stretch, it had more than enough room to firmly sit on my huge leg, I could have lined up three presents, she could have bought me a bike and it would have fit on there. I tugged at the ribbon making sure nothing could possibly tear and then, with the care of a surgeon, I unfolded the red shiny paper to reveal a small red cardboard box. Tucking the paper I had caringly folded into my pocket alongside the card, I lifted the lid to reveal the contents.

Inside was a small bracelet of polished dark red stones. This at first surprised me; the bracelet had a small tag attached, this told me it was, *'Carnelian', a genuine precious stone that promoted courage and self-confidence in its wearer'*. It was without doubt the most beautiful thing I owned. After trying and failing to roll it over my swollen hands and wrists I returned it to its box and deposited it with the rest of my things in the jacket pocket. I sat there, I smiled, I breathed and I thought of Gemma, she had obviously thought of me in choosing such a considered and kind present. Sitting in my state of bliss it occurred to me that I had not worried about wetting myself during my present opening ceremony, could Gemma's affection be the cure I had needed?

'Bore, are you in here?' was the screamed sentence that returned me to both the present moment and the desperate need to piss.

'Err, yes Mr Riley, I'll be right out'. Paul Riley was my boss, the assistant manager of my branch. He was a bear of a man; he'd obviously played rugby all through school and university before discovering beer. This resulted in a hugely muscled man wrapped in a layer of fat, not nearly as impressive as mine of course, but this gave him the hugest of arms, chest and just general presence really.

"Thought as much, come to my office as soon as you finish doing whatever it is you do in here", 'Shit, this cannot be good', I thought.

I spent a further few minutes in the gents toilets, focusing on my breathing and relaxing my pelvis as much as possible, another impossible task suggested in one of the library of books I was building on my ailment. Several times I checked my pockets to ensure my gift was initially not simply a dream and secondly still in place. I eventually re-entered the main floor and focused on Mr Riley's office way on the opposite side of the room, an impossible journey to make invisible. Options, do I stick to the wall and go the long way around the room, or simply head down and as the crow flies just get my ass in there? I quickly realised both options were futile as my invisibility cloak was already in tatters, although not with blatant stares, without doubt everyone was looking at me already. The heat returned to my brow and the crippling desire to piss doubled with intensity. The only option left was 'plan b', as the crow flies; I waddled as fast as I dared toward my destination. Eyes followed me from every direction, swiftly fleeting away should I dare to risk a return glance, which in honesty I didn't so that observation may be my memory compounding the situation.

On reaching the mock wood panel door I gently knocked and

entered on the command barked from inside. The solid door had always struck me as pointless, baring in mind the rest of the office was entirely made of glass. I stood in the office trembling and noticed for the first time the only thing in the room that the door had obscured from view. Sitting in a chair looking extremely sheepish as she stared at her knees was Gemma Tsang. Oh my God, I'd somehow imagined the whole thing and stolen the package that was in pieces about my pockets, I knew it was just too good, well, you know the rest of that sentence.

"You know Ms Tsang from Human Resources I assume Boring?" She spoke next

"Mr Riley, that is hugely inappropriate, you know Mr Bore's name", the slip had barely registered with me but her reaction too it made me feel a little better about whatever the hell was going on. "What? Oh of course! I'm sorry Bore it's just that I have heard your friends out on the floor teasing you with that, harmless banter, good for moral and all that". Friends my arse, harmless banter my arse, this whole situation my arse, my arse, my arse, my arse. He paused for me to acknowledge the apology and although it registers pretty low on the bravery stakes I saw my refusal to give it as a huge victory. I stood in silence.

"Well, anyway, moving on", I could tell he was flustered because crumbs from his morning biscuit had fallen from his moustache due to his twitching, "Ms Tsang is here to represent Human Resources and your interests in this difficult time". He paused for what seemed an awkward period.

"Err, difficult time sir?" I prompted, not because I was taking control, more because if I didn't get out of there soon I was surely going to piss all over his office floor. I shifted from foot to foot and focused on my breathing as much as possible.

"Ah yes", he continued as if I were being demanding, "Bore please sit down you're dancing around like you have ants in your pants", I took the seat against the glass wall and hated that this meant I was staring directly at Gemma. The wooden chair creaked under my weight. "The thing is Bore; the thing is, well, you are probably aware how challenging things are in the economy at the moment". It was true, the country seemed in melt down and although I cannot claim to have been politically or commercially aware enough to understand a recession, I was assured from all angles that we were indeed slap bang in the middle of one. Maybe it didn't register with me so much as I'd been in a personal recession for sixteen years, since my sixteenth birthday when I left school I guess. "Well, we need to cut costs", he continued, "look there's never an easy way but I'm going to have to make you redundant, instructions from head office, we have to save money, I'm sure you understand". As a matter of fact no, I didn't fucking understand. I must have been the cheapest employee on the books, I worked the longest hours of anyone, albeit forced on me by my condition, I came with no extra costs I didn't even use the tea bags and I bothered nobody.

"But Mr Riley I..." I was going to enter a speech and tell him about my prostatitis, explain my weird behaviour and try and win him around. I looked to my right just in time to see the entire body of staff spin around or drop their heads so as not to look at me. I stared through the clear glass for a second and as my focus changed, Gemma's reflection came into view as she sat now looking directly at me. The giving of her wonderful gift seemed an eon away. I turned to look at her but spoke to Mr Riley without moving my gaze from hers. "No Mr Riley its fine, I understand and I'm 'CONFIDENT' something will turn up".

"John I didn't know about this until two minutes ago I promise", she noted my emphasis on the word 'confident', a quote from her oh so generous gift, obviously designed to soften the blow she was due to participate in that day. I turned back to Mr Riley and made it easy for him.

"When do I go?"

"Well", he pounced on the opportunity to end this quickly, "we of course want you to have every opportunity to find another job, so no reason you can't head off now", the bank have been very generous", he offered an envelope, "there's a cheque in here for two months wages, take this and I am sure we'll manage if you want to get straight off". Bloody hell after all this time, two months wages and fuck off John, unbelievable. One month was already spent; the second months ergo would be gone in a month so in reality I was no better off. At least I could give Gemma's uncle some rent straight away. I slowly stood without a word and turned to the door, surprised to realise it had been open throughout the entire performance, I stepped through onto the main stage to be viewed by my audience.

"I'll walk you out John, is there anything you want help carrying", I turned back to face Gemma just in time to catch Mr Riley and young Craig sharing a smile and a wink through the apposing glass wall.

"I'm fine", there was nothing in my desk I was worried about, a million vitamin supplements designed to clean or flush my prostate but nothing worth enduring any more time in this place like a circus freak. Luckily, I hadn't even unpacked my cheap briefcase so I scooped it up as I passed my desk before rushing to the door, holding my breath until I was outside on the street, that place behind me forever. What the hell was I going to do now, another job? I couldn't sit still long enough to get through an interview. Who'd interview me anyway, I was thirty-two, that very day I remind you, and a bank clerk, most my age would be well into management roles and people wanted trendy good lucking young clerks, like bloody Craig.

I was brought back to the now as a red London bus sped past within an inch of my face, I had wandered far to close to the curb. At this point, I realised there was one thing I had left in my desk that I could have really done with, my bus pass. I spun around and looked at the large oak doors, now with a steady stream of customers entering and leaving, it was nine-thirty. Nine-thirty and my rollercoaster of a day was unfathomable, the one high I'd experienced, my gift from Gemma, would pale further in significance as the day progressed. Well, there was not cat in hells chance I was going back in there for my bus pass. It was only three miles, and I could walk that.

Two hours later, I sat on the small wall at the end of my garden path. It was the fifteenth time I'd sat down in the last one hundred and twenty minutes and my heart was trying to climb through my ribcage, dragging my lungs behind it. I heaved my chest to try and take in more breaths, my head rising and dropping in an attempt to swallow more oxygen; my shirt was almost transparent with sweat. I sat there for at least twenty minutes before I was anywhere near a reasonable distance from a heart attack. I was still breathing heavily when I was snapped back into reality by the voice of Mr Tsang.

"Bore, is that you Bore?" He barked the words and I stood and turned so I was in full view and no longer hidden behind the sole conifer that grew in the small garden. "Phone for you, make it quick you're out of here, they say urgent, last phone call for you". The full sentence didn't register as my ears were still ringing from the exercise, I slumped one foot at a time toward the door but my entry was blocked. Mr Tsang simply pushed his cordless phone toward me, I took it and the door was slammed in my face. When I had moved in Mr Tsang had allowed me to give his number out in case of any emergencies, I didn't have a phone in my apartment, yet the only person who had that number was my step mother who I hadn't spoken to in at least a year. I put the phone to my ringing ear, ironic huh?

"Mr Bore?"

"Yes."

"Ah, my name is Doctor Singh; I'm at the Royal St. Michaels Hospital with your mother".

"My mother", initially this did not compute.

"Yes, I'm afraid your mother was brought in early this morning having suffered a heart attack. The only number we could get an answer on was this one, it was in her directory", the good doctor paused for a response.

"She's not my mother", I stated in a matter of fact tone, still out of breath and with half my mind still in the room at the bank with Gemma and Mr Riley.

"Oh, we have the wrong Mr Bore" I shook myself back into the conversation.

"What, oh no I'm sorry, she's my step mother, what's the problem again?"

"Mr Bore I'm sorry to say your step mother has had a heart attack, could you possibly come to the hospital? We really couldn't contact anyone else." What else could I say, and what else did I have to do?

"Sure, did you say St. Johns?"

"No St. Michaels, Chelsea, ward eleven."

"I'm on my way." The door opened, Mr Tsang snatched back the receiver and, leaving me standing on the step, slammed it back in my face. I paused for a short while trying to comprehend what had just happened, eventually deciding not to worry about it. Maybe

Mr Tsang had a weird daytime routine he didn't want me to see; hell, he was probably inside hosting a cockfight or torturing puppies. I plodded back toward the gate trying to figure out how to get to Chelsea. Pausing on the street, I reached into my pocket to retrieve the envelope that Peter Riley had handed to me before banishing me from the bank. I tore it open and took out the cheque, three thousand pounds and some pence. Not much to show for myself at thirty-two years old after sixteen years in the work place. I owed Mr Tsang almost half of it.

The next thing that struck me was what I should do with it? No way was I going into one of the banks branches to embarrass myself further by paying in a redundancy cheque. Anyway, having walked all the way home, I didn't cherish the idea of returning on foot to another branch of my former bank, they were all in town. After some thought, I wandered to Holloway High Street, only half a mile but on top of the excursion of the walk from town this nearly finished me.

"Are you okay?" was the question from the young teller at 'Cheque Busters', where I had decided I would exchange my redundancy cheque for cash. The small room was somewhere between a book keepers and a homeless shelter, the only other occupant being a guy resembling the old man at sea, precariously poised at one of the small tables for people to rest on whilst signing the back of their cheques, gifting away ten percent of its value in exchange for instant cash. The man in question seemed to be hovering over his grubby cheque with no intention of signing, he certainly didn't move throughout my transaction in the store but nobody seemed to mind.

After six minutes, I left the building with just over two and a half thousand pounds in my pocket, a small price to pay for avoiding the humiliation of a visit to my former colleagues. I wandered back down Holloway Road, nervous at the wealth I carried in my pocket, though figuring nobody would think for a second that I looked like someone who would have this kind of reward in his possession, so feeling safe from muggers. Especially as at this stage, it was noon, and I smelt like I had run a marathon through a kennel where the dogs were fed on cabbage and no one ever mucked it out.

At Holloway Road tube station, I purchased a ticket and boarded the Piccadilly line all the way to Green Park. Switching to the Victoria Line, I went one stop to Victoria Station itself and then on another line, the yellow one I think, I don't know it's name, to Sloane Square. I emerged into the world of the beautiful people and ignored the looks that acknowledged my obvious lack of belonging in this trendy neighbourhood.

After asking a few people, who gave whatever direction they could with incredible haste in order to avoid being seen talking to me, I was soon standing outside St. Michaels hospital, ward eleven. I took a breath, tried to collect myself and wandered inside to see a woman that hated me, constantly wondering why the hell I'd even made this journey; after all I'd just been fired and needed to find a job.

Now, as little affection as I had for this woman, I could not help but be affected by the sight that beheld me that day. Even at ten years old, the age I was when my father had married her, I could see why he had. She was a stunning woman, a former model that'd worked until her fifties, simply switching to other sections of the catalogues as she aged. I'd seen her less than two years ago, close to her seventies, and she was still what you might call a handsome woman, striking. In front of me now lay an old woman, thin and pale with an almost transparency to her skin. Her hair was almost completely grey and as she lay sleeping her mouth lulled open and she exhaled a rasping sound before struggling to fill her lungs again.

"Is it Mr Bore?" As I turned to see who had addressed me I noticed the frail figure in the bed stir a little. "Mr Bore I'm Doctor Singh, we spoke on the phone".

"Yes", I said "I'm John", Doctor Singh was an impressive man, at least as tall as me but obviously rugby had been on his curriculum at medical school as he had huge shoulders sitting atop a long lean frame. I reflected on my own appearance and wondered if he was analysing me in the same way, I wondered if he was disgusted.

"Boring John", the breathy voice came from the bed behind me, but both Doctor Singh and I paused for a second before we realised that, when we did we both turned our attention in the same direction.

Having managed to drag herself ever so slightly more upright on her pillow my stepmother was now recognisable. Even as ill as she obviously was, the look of disdain, which I always inspired, was painted across her drawn face.

"What was that?" asked the good doctor, I knew exactly what she'd said.

"John Bore here, 'Boring John' was what they all called him at school because he was good for nothing and useless. Isn't that right, Boring?" It was right, but I should point out that she had introduced this nickname. She would stand by the car on the odd occasion she took it upon herself to collect me, should I be talking with a school friend she'd yell, 'Come on boring'. This was probably around the time my confidence plummeted, the activities stopped, the weight gain and the tooth rot began. "They still call him that at work now"; this produced something between a chuckle and a sneer to appear across her chapped lips. Again the work situation had been down to her, she'd called me only once in the time I'd worked at the bank. Unfortunately Craig had answered the phone to be asked, 'Can I speak to Boring John, oh sorry I mean John Bore'. Ergo, the name had stuck at work. Interestingly, I was in the toilet at the time, well that's not interesting, but what is interesting is the fact she never called back so I can only assume the sole reason for the call in the first place was to introduce the nickname to my colleagues.

"Now then" said the Doctor in his best bedside voice, he stepped closer to the bed and adjusted her pillow slightly, "is that anyway to speak to your visitor, John came straight down when he heard you were here".

"Who bloody called him?" She gasped as she started to cough, the coughing got worse and she struggled to breath.

"Now you just relax and lay back", the Doctor had dropped the bedside voice, he grasped a small clear oxygen mask from beside the bed and placed it over her nose and mouth, it misted as she began to inhale deeply. Slowly her breathing became shallower and her eyes fluttered closed. "She'll sleep for a while now", the attention had turned back to me, "don't take anything to heart, she's a little delirious". The hell she was, this was she on top form. "It probably won't be long now". I stared at the Doctor.

"Won't be long? You mean?" I left the question dangling.

"Oh Mr Bore, I'm sorry, I assumed you were aware of your stepmother's situation", he shuffled his large muscular frame uncomfortably, "I'm afraid this is her third heart attack in as many months, as I understand it she had been having problems before that. Her heart has simply given up, and when that happens the body soon follows suit" I simply had nothing to say, I think I've made it clear I had no bond with her but the thought of the way she was ending her days instilled me with guilt. My father had loved this woman no matter what; I should have been there for her whether she wanted me to be or not. "The best thing is probably to just sit with her". With this he placed a huge hand on my shoulder, delivered a brief pause, a reassuring squeeze and a comforting smile, before heading off down the ward. Sit with her, probably the last thing she'd want but probably the last thing I could do for her.

I found a restroom and sat on the loo for ten minutes doing nothing but just making sure. I then made myself as presentable as I possibly could in the small mirror before returning bedside and sitting in a grey; plastic chair that seemed more befitting a dolls house, my flanks bulged around the edges as if my body wanted to consume the squeaking chair. I sat for what felt like hours, just thinking about my day thus far, what I would do for work; at least I had rent for a month or two. I was then for the second time that day surprised by the same voice.

"It was his idea you know", I was dragged back to the present moment and looked at the face staring back at me from the bed. Her eyes narrowed and even under the oxygen mask I could see her grimace.

"What?" I asked.

"Boring John, the nickname, your father made it up" I just looked, "he was so embarrassed by you, he had such high hopes when he found out he'd had a son"

"That's not true, my father loved me more than...." I was interrupted with a surprising increase in aggression and authority as a bony hand pulled the oxygen mask away, so it sat under her chin.

"Rubbish, you never achieved anything. All his dreams and the first thing you do is murder his wife, as soon as you're born. He'd talk about how ambitious you claimed to be as a young child, only to turn into a nothing by the time you were ten". In my head I said a thousand things but so many that just one couldn't come out. It simply couldn't be true my father adored me; before he died I was a good student, I mean never top of the class as he'd been but never bottom, and I was a good athlete as I've already said.

"You're lying", was all that came out.

"I think it was his embarrassment that killed him eventually, he always wished he'd had children with me instead" Now that was crap, well, at least half of it.

"He died of cancer," I mumbled, but she pounced

"He died of shame; you killed your mother first, your father just took a little longer." I felt like I had been shot through the heart. Could this be true? The only good memories I had of my life were those with my father, so many of them and all full of love, she knew that, it's why she feigned pleasantries with me when my father was around. Still, could it be true? Why would anyone say this no matter how much they hated me, if there was not something to it?

My chest felt tight and I laboured with my breathing, I felt emotion rise in me, my eyes dampened and then filled before tears poured down my face.

"It can't be true, please take that back, please", I was begging, I needed her to tell me this was not true. I stumbled from the chair and knelt by the small steel bed on the tiled floor. "I know you hate me I do and I understand, but not my father, tell me your lying, tell me this is just to hurt me". Her eyes were suddenly alive inside her dying body, just for a second, and then they closed. The corners of her mouth slowly curled to form a smile of pure contentment.

Throughout the time I'd been at the bedside the beeping machine on the opposite side of the bed had not registered, and now as the beep turned to a single, long, flat tone it again went unnoticed. It was only when two Nurses rushed to join me and hastily flung the green curtain around the rail that framed our scene that I realised what was happening. They did not fuss for long, after all they were expecting this, one of the Nurses looked past me at someone I could sense behind me, then she looked at me.

"I'm afraid she's gone", were the words she used. I looked back at the body in front of me.

"No, no" I didn't yell but my voice sounded as desperate as I felt, "please tell me the truth". I almost whispered to her as a desperate after thought. The familiar large hand returned to my shoulder and Mr Singh spoke.

"These things are never easy John, but at least she is not suffering anymore, and look John, you made her smile."

Less than an hour later, still before two o'clock on that same damn day, I was standing back outside my apartment block in North London. My shirt was yet again drenched with sweat however at this stage that was more comfortable, I had soaked it so often that when it dried it was to a firm crust that scratched the skin under my arms. I breathed heavily and looked at the selection of boxes and bags piled around the bins in the small garden to the front of the building.

Something was so wrong here, what first made me realise this was the old suitcase to the left of the dustbins. At first it was familiar, it was small, maybe two and a half feet long and one and a half feet high, it was a faded green tartan fabric with a steel buckle attached to a leather belt which was wrapped around the entire circumference holding it closed, not quite fully closed as items of clothing were protruding all the way around the side where the top and bottom halves met. I realised it wasn't just familiar it was mine. I hadn't used it in a while but it definitely came from the small shelf above the old boiler in my kitchenette. I took a step closer and realised that everything there was mine. One box had in it some cheap plastic plates and cutlery, a pasta jar less a missing cork top, a knife block for eight knives containing only the four I'd ever had, basically the contents of my kitchen. The second box held my small radio, my father's Beatles albums, a few more objects and so on and so on. What the hell was going on? Knowing the answer in my heart I shuffled to the front door and gently tapped, half hoping I'd done it either quite enough for no one to hear or even better that no one was home. The ancient intercom system buzzed to life.

"Yes?" Came the simple statement.

"Mr Tsang?"

"Bore? Bore you don't live here anymore, evicted". It was stated so matter of fact.

"But Mr Tsang, you can't." The intercom went dead and I heard the rustling of keys, first the internal door from his apartment into the communal hall, then the door in front of me.

"I can do whatever I want Bore", he thrust a leaflet into my face entitled 'Landlords Rights', "two months no rent, I can evict, so I evict. Apartment has already gone". I looked at the leaflet now in my hands, I was sure he was telling the truth, he was too confident for it to be any other way. I plunged my right hand into my pocket but thought again before withdrawing the cash; he may well snatch it and still leave me on the street.

"Mr Tsang I have the cash, I told you I only needed a little time", the gravity of the situation was hitting me, where the hell would I go?

"Fine, give the two months you owe, apartment has already gone Bore, take your things or bin men will throw it all away", he then paused and looked me up and down filling his nostrils, "you stink Bore"' the door was slammed in my face. I raised my hand to knock again but stopped myself, what was the point. I slumped back toward my belongings and looked at how pitifully little I had to show for the last thirty-two years. There was nothing there of real sentimental value nothing I desperately needed. I placed the suitcase on top of the wall to my right and opened it just about all my clothes fit in here effortlessly; they had been badly packed that was all. I refolded things as best I could and pretended I did not notice the mother and child groups returning from school and giving me confused looks as they past the gateway, pulling their giggling children closer.

With a little more space in my case, I went to the box containing my bathroom items and retrieved a small tin of deodorant and after a quick worthless spray over my shirt I placed it in the case. I added a razor, my mole scissors, a flannel and a small bottle of store brand shower gel. I then set about the other boxes to see what I might make use of; I wanted to take no more than the case, although I had no idea at this stage where I was taking the case or myself.

Held in place by a worn rubber band was a pile of old bills and papers, these I knew had been simply tossed on top of the pile as an afterthought, they had been on a small shelf by the door. They were next to my father's records that I had already decided I would have to leave, far too heavy and impractical. There was one thing in this pile I wanted and I sorted through each piece of paper hoping it was still there and Mr Tsang had not taken it as part payment. No there it was, I looked at it for a few moments, my theatre ticket, 'The Royal Shakespeare Company presents Hamlet', further down the text written smaller but far more important, 'Introducing Gemma Tsang as Ophelia'. The ticket was for opening night, tonight. Ironic that I had forgone paying rent to her uncle so I could buy this ticket. I wondered if that would have made him feel better or worse about the situation. It was a bad seat, on purpose, right at the back buy the aisle. If I was a little late I could sneak in under darkness and frequent the toilet unnoticed, if I left right on the final curtain my whole presence would be clandestine. I'd thought that should this go well and I was financially frugal I could go once a month for as long as the play ran, still see Gemma even though we were no longer banking colleagues, we had both left the bank, of course, for very different reasons. If my new bracelet worked maybe one day I'd knock on the stage door and tell them I knew her and would like to pass on my congratulations, unlikely. I tucked the treasured prize into my inside pocket next to the gift Gemma had given me that morning. I returned to my search around the bins.

Right at the back of the small pile my things had made, wedged between two of the bins was a smaller box, I cleared a path and reached for it, slowly dragging it to the front. I stepped back to make more room and, as I looked over my shoulder to watch my step, I noticed Mr Tsang whip the net curtain of his bay window closed to hide him as he watched. Back to the box, which I recognised instantly as the collection of my old school books. I had no idea why I had kept them for all of these years, maybe as they contained the only evidence that I had ever done anything well. I flicked through the pages of an old geography textbook and noticed the odd smiley symbol or 'well done, nine out of ten' from old teachers. I placed the box on top of one of the bins and for no reason started to randomly leaf through each book and almost managed a smile at some of the memories induced. I still remembered what each book was, orange was geography, green was history, red math etc. I then took a blue one, English, the only possible confusion, as this could be either literature or language. It was language, Mr Newton, I remembered that old bastard. I say old, I was ten so he seemed it but at the time he was probably a trendy thirty-year-old teacher, I recalled his close-cropped ginger beard and swept back hair. He had a swagger of confidence and loved to make a class laugh by isolating one pupil and mocking them. In fairness, he did that to me no more than anyone else but one of those times stuck out in my mind as I picked my way through the pages of the book in my hands to relive the time in more detail, the memory was making me angry. There it was near the back of the book, I remembered this day so well, we'd been set a simple task but I had given it such careful thought and consideration. The task was this, 'make a list of everything that you want to achieve in life'. A loaded question for a classroom full of ten-year olds. Most had played it safe; most of the guys had said they wanted to be professional footballers, some of the girl's Nurses or actresses. The odd person had stated that going to Australia would be on their list and one guy wanted to swim with dolphins. This question for me however had really pushed a button. At this point I was, or so I had thought, my father's little hero, I could achieve anything I set my mind to, and I knew I would.

Back to my 'shit' day I glanced down my list, my anger slowly ebbing away replaced with bitter regret as I realised there was not one thing I had achieved. Now, in fairness, it was a pretty far out list, developed in the mind of an excitable ten-year old but again, none of them and in reality not even close.

My anger returned when I got to the end of the list and read Mr Newton's note, 'a delusional dreamer, poor'. I recalled him strutting around the front of the class like an over-confident stand up comedian, reading each of my goals one by one and adding a witty quip, 'oh and after *this* young Bore is going to do *that*, well *that* should be easy for someone who's done *this* and *that*" The hysteria he produced fuelled his show and he became more theatrical in his gesturing, until he eventually dropped my text book back onto the desk in front of me with his final line,

"Marvellous Bore, what an imagination, if you do any of that stuff maybe they'll stop calling you boring!" with this the class collapsed and the real me died a little more inside, "people that aim too high often turn into nothing", that was his final word on the matter, all whispered, just for me.

'Nothing', that's what he'd said; exactly what my stepmother had said my father had thought of me. I was nothing, I achieved nothing and I never would. Everyone I'd ever met thought I was nothing and that day they were right. Standing there, jobless and homeless, nowhere to go and not a friend in the world I was a big, fat nothing.

A rage consumed me that was like nothing I'd felt, I could change, I had time, I was going to do something, be someone, I was going to prove anyone who had ever called me nothing, a failure, a loser wrong. I was going to prove anyone who'd ever called me 'boring John' wrong. How though, I looked back at the open page in my old textbook sitting atop the dustbin. There was the answer, back to age ten, back to where everyone had made up their minds about my fate, I was going to take this list and I was going to achieve everything on here, all of it. One by one I will tick things from this list and everyone will know my achievements and just how incredible I am. I tore the page from the book, grabbed my ancient suitcase and strode through the gate without looking back, I felt like a million dollars, my plan was a simple one, I had my list and I had the will. Before I tucked my list away I took a quick look at it to re-confirm my first mission.

"Shit", I said out loud, "this might not be that easy after all".

Chapter 2

Achievement number one.

The French Foreign Legion

Yep, you read that right, number one on my list of things to achieve was to become a 'French Foreign Legionnaire'. I recall well the opening line to Mr Newton's improvised stand-up routine, designed to titillate my peers and humiliate me.

"Well, let's just look at this list of yours in a little more detail shall we young 'Bore'? First things first, you're going to run off and join the 'French Foreign Legion', how will you get to France 'Bore', will you fly there on a pig perhaps?" The class burst into fits of hilarity that simply succeeded in motivating the condescending prick to continue.

Truth is, I knew little about 'The Legion', and even now it seems like a perfectly normal thing for a ten year old to write. I had seen it in movies, always portrayed as an elite force of hero's and what ten-year old doesn't fantasise about these things, the S.A.S. and such? While we are being honest, I should also admit that having made the decision to take on my list, standing there by the dustbins with schoolbook in hand, I still knew nothing about 'The Legion'. However, that wasn't going to stop me. At that moment in time, I experienced sheer determination for the first time in my life. I was going to France and I was going to be a Legionnaire, and after a stint at that, I was going to get on with the rest of my list. First though, I had a date. Okay, you all ready know I, of course, did not have a date but in my mind it was the closest I would ever get, the fact that the girl in question wouldn't even know it was happening seemed a moot point. I was going to use my theatre ticket and I was going to say a silent goodbye to Gemma on her debut night.

Well, I looked and, as informed by Mr Tsang, I smelled a state; I had to try and improve that if for no other reason it would make invisibility a damn site easier if I didn't smell like a horse's arse. I took the tube from Caledonian Road to Piccadilly Circus and sat myself amongst the tourists at the steps around the Eros statue. As people edged away, a circle soon developed around me but the light was fading and I didn't care. The show started at seven o'clock and I planned to get there five minutes later so I could sneak into my seat at the back of the theatre unnoticed, after my bathing plans. Bang on seven I walked the hundred yards to the relevant theatre and looked at the posters around the door, her picture had not made the promotional literature but every piece had the words, 'introducing Gemma Tsang as Ophelia' at the bottom in small italics. Inside I asked a concerned looking member of staff where the gents was and after proving I was supposed to be there with a flash of my ticket, I shuffled across the plush red carpet in the direction he had indicated. I was distraught to see there were still several other occupants using the urinals and washing there hands, and I was further perplexed that they were in no rush to get to their seats, chatting away as though they had all the time in the world. Well, I wasn't going to strip in front of them so hugging my case to my chest I squeezed into one of the cubicles, turned and sat, weighing up my options. I only came up with one, I stood and put my case on the loo seat open, I turned and hung my jacket on the hook on the back of the door, acutely aware that every time I turned my fat arse banged on one of the flimsy plywood walls making it rattle on it's small metal feet with alarming volume. I took off my shirt and placed it on top of the cistern and opened my case. I had salvaged a couple of shirts and although they were creased they were clean, as they had simply been forced into my case and luckily not straight into the bin. I paused before I stretched the bed sheet sized shirt over my vast girth. I still stank, this new shirt would stink the same in seconds. I had heard no body leave the gents, in fact the new found silence outside my cubicle made me think they were all simply stood watching my door quizzically, trying to figure out what the hell the fat bastard was doing in there. Too late to worry about that now, I hung the fresh shirt on the same hook as my jacket and placed the old one underneath my case on the cistern. Opening the seat I was pleased to see nobody had left a nasty surprise and the water looked quite clean. I did a cautionary flush and then I delved my hand into the water and began to wipe my armpits and the area beneath my man boobs with my palm. I did the best job I could though the effort alone was making me sweat again. I dried myself with toilet paper and used the salvaged deodorant to cover myself as much as possible. Shirt and jacket back on. I left the cubicle and my earlier observation was proved correct, I simply nodded to the audience staring at me, dropped the old shirt in the bin and headed out of the door with the words, 'enjoy the play' offered to my fellow attendees.

With the help of the same usher that had directed me to the gents I found my seat and squeezed into the miniscule gap between the armrests. I was please to see, that as promised on booking, I was in the seat write at the back by the aisle. Even better, the seat next to me was free but, even with this gap, the middle aged lady in the seat after that looked offended by my arrival and I'm sure, even in the half-light, she was staring at my centimetre wide mole. The joy of the gap seat didn't last long as I had to wedge myself free to let her husband take the seat, her husband who had just observed my shenanigans in the toilet, bloody marvellous.

I watched the first twenty minutes of the play; this is when Gemma made her entrance. My God, she was the most beautiful thing I had ever seen. I only watched for a further five minutes but it was obvious, even to my untrained eye, that the girl could act as well. All around there were mutters of, 'she's amazing' and the like. So why did I leave? I could say that it was embarrassment at the disturbance I proved to be to my neighbour, I was shuffling and fidgety, desperate for a pee even though as always that was impossible, I had taken on no liquid that day. That wasn't it though I expected that, it was a realisation, an obvious one that I should have made a long time ago. That vision on the stage, why would she want me here, she was the most beautiful girl in the world, no doubt at the beginning of a life changing exciting journey where she would mingle with others of her standing. I was a fat, homeless, unemployed slob, with a list of fantasies in my pocket, who just had a wash in the shitter. Maybe this list was my route to being on such a standing, maybe if I did these things I would belong in a room with these people, I had to get to France.

I ignored the statement from my neighbours as I again forced my arse out of the seat.

"For crying out loud," he whispered harshly.

Then I was out; free to embark on my adventure. I delved into my worldly wealth and took a cab to Kings Cross, approaching a ticket booth I learned the first available seat on a 'Eurostar' train to Paris was the following morning and would cost me ninety-nine pounds. I wandered next door to a 'Travel Lodge' I had noticed and paid a further fifty-nine pounds from my stash for a single room and then asked the night porter through teeth hiding fingers if I could use the business centre which was advertised on the reception as free to all guests. The business centre transpired to be a desk next to said reception with a computer on it, it also came with a fee of three pounds per fifteen minutes for the internet and a more confident type may have challenged the advertising. I decided I should do some research into my new planned career and I tapped the words 'French Foreign Legion', into the Google search bar.

I spent hours reading that night, starting with the fact that the Legion was established in 1831, specifically as a unit for foreign volunteers, primarily to protect and expand the French colonial empire during the nineteenth century, all interesting but not helpful or comforting to a fat English guy planning to join the ranks. I was most surprised to find that the Legion is actually a division of the French army, not the mercenary gun ho operation I had imagined, this made me feel a little better, they would be professional and have rules and boundaries. They had been involved in every Major conflict around the world since their inception including both world wars and more recently the gulf and it was even said they may be going into Afghanistan if the current conflict lasted, not so comforting but my mind was set, as it never had been before, I was going to achieve something amazing.

The training schedule didn't make for easy reading for someone in my physical condition. Fifteen weeks of which only the first four sounded remotely within the scope of my abilities, these weeks would basically be an initiation to military lifestyle and learning the traditions of the Legion. After that I would be letting myself in for an intimidating schedule of technical and practical training, followed by mountain training in the Pyrenees, exams, marching and machinery training. I was terrified, no question, but I was in a trance, I felt dead or close to death. My life was flashing before my eyes all the time and it sucked, an obese, timid, giant, mocked by everyone perhaps, even my own father. I still could not believe what I'd been told beside that hospital bed earlier that day, she just wanted to hurt me, she was jealous of my fathers love for me it had to be that. I went to bed that night and as you can imagine slept very little, when my eyes did close for more than a minute my head was filled with dreams of being a Legionnaire, a honed machine capable of those things I had fantasised about while being verbally abused all those years. I was terrified but I was excited and filled with anticipation, most of all I was desperate to prove the world wrong.

The next morning, I freshened up as much as I possibly could in the tiny bathroom, I had rinsed some underwear and shirts leaving them to hang on the shower rail overnight, they were still damp but better than they had been. I took my ticket and boarded the train where, realising I had a carriage to myself, I hung my damp cloths on the backs of the chairs about me. I soon realised that it was only me who boarded trains an hour before they were due to leave and as my fellow passengers arrived at their seats I flushed bright red and apologised as I gathered up my underpants, socks and shirts before forcing them back into my small case. The trip was in silence as no one spoke to me the entire trip. Although I was feeling a desperate need to pee, I grit my teeth and kept my eyes closed, not moving from my seat once on the two and a half hour journey. I disembarked at 'Gare Du Nord' station in Paris realising this was the first time in my life I had ever left England, and I felt new, anonymous. Nobody knew me there and nobody cared, I could be anything, a banker, a lawyer, a salesman or maybe even a Legionnaire awaiting his destiny. The web site had told me that there was a recruitment office at 'Fort de Nogent' and that this was near Paris. It transpired to be only fifteen kilometres away and after changing the remainder of my cash to Euros at a small booth inside the station, I had no intention of heading back to England anytime soon, I grabbed a taxi and we were on our way. After giving the address to the driver he pulled into the flowing stream of traffic before looking at me in the rear view mirror and asking, "vous joignez la Legion?"

"err, sorry?" I enquired, as I had spoken no French whatsoever since I was twelve.

"vous voulez être un Legionnaire?" Oh great, he said it differently like now I'll understand. However I picked out 'vous' which I knew meant 'you' and 'legi'naire' of course explains it self

"Yes' I said, and then in a burst of confidence added, "oui, un Legionnaire" pointing at myself with a reversed thumb. With this my driver burst into hysteria that rivalled Craig's supporters at the bank and I swear it lasted the whole bloody journey.

To distract myself from his amusement I looked out of the window at the Paris streets and the people who lived there. We turned left onto a street called, 'Boulevard de la Villette', before continuing along, 'Avenue Jean Jaurès'. It occurred to me that was my name here, 'John' in French was 'Jean', Maybe I'd stick with that, new country, new life, new name?

I liked the look of Paris; it seemed calm despite obviously being a bustling metropolis. It was full of contradiction; on one corner was a guy who looked like a stockbroker screaming into a cell phone while his free hand forced a pointing finger into his spare ear to drown out the noise of a passing truck. Within yards of him, an old man in brown trousers held up by braces over an off white vest was sitting on his stairs smoking a pipe and taking in the morning sun. It seemed quite around him as though the stockbroker and the truck were in another town miles away. I watched him scratching his grey stubble, that adorned the lower half of his leathery face, and wondered what his story was. We suddenly crossed another busy intersection, with blaring horns and stressed out drivers, but within seconds we were back on a small cobbled street. Suddenly we were on a three lane highway and, as this appeared to be like any other motorway, I allowed my mind to re focus on what I was actually doing here. My doubt came in waves interspersed by the fantasy of a future that I had created in my head, yet underneath the waves and the fears was a solid current that knew it's path. I had experienced fear before and wherever possible tried to get out of those situations, be it a meeting with a customer at the bank or a 'monthly report' presentation to Peter Riley, I'd often make up outlandish excuses or even take sick days. This was different, what

I was going to do would strike fear into anybody, but right there and then I knew I was going through with it, I knew I was going to do this, 'Exciting Jean' that's what they would start calling me. We'd turned off the 'Périphérique' and I'd seen signs for 'Lille' and 'Montreuil' but the next sign I saw was for 'Rond-Point du Fort de Nogent', it had been around twenty-five minutes so I knew we were close and as always happened when nerves got the better of me my prostate was on fire. To be safe I had to find a toilet before I went into the recruitment office.

The driver seemed to know where he was going and we pulled into a long, thin car park with a field to my left and the 'Fort de Nogent' itself standing to my right. I was surprised that it seemed a low building, it appeared to be only one story high and not the grand structure I had imagined, certainly from the back where I thought we were. I paid the driver and stepped from the taxi, transfixed on what I thought would be my new home. The driver managed to stop laughing long enough to yell, "bonne chance" as he sped away, I had no idea what that meant.

I turned to face the fort, but before I had the opportunity to observe in more detail, I was to have my first encounter with a real life Legionnaire. I saw him striding toward me and was instantly awestruck by his appearance. He wore a crisp, white, short-sleeved shirt; it was open at the collar but nonetheless looked very formal, adorned as it was with green epilates leading to a row of red tassels at each shoulder. He had a row of medals on the left of his chest and the shirt was tucked into a blue cummerbund around his waist underneath a green utility belt, from which hung a vicious looking bayonet. His sharply pressed beige trousers were tucked into black military boots and he walked with a sharp, authoritative step. He stamped to a stop right in front of me, looked me up and down once and demanded, "nouvelle recrue?" It was said as a question and I figured 'recrue' to be 'recruit' and nodded my confirmation. He looked me up and down once more and then pointed of to his left, "à la gauche"; I immediately headed off in the direction he had pointed. As I commenced my trek my second Legionnaire encounter occurred which was slightly more bizarre, there was no interaction; in fact the soldier in question did not even seem to notice me as he jogged past. His dark face was set in stone, the huge scar on his face would usually have held my attention, were it not for the fact that he carried on his back a large green rucksack that contained nothing less than an exhausted looking chocolate colored Boxer dog. Unlike his master the dog did pay me some attention, albeit through glazed eyes, just it's head and front two paws protruded from the top of its makeshift carriage and it's panting tongue lolled from the side of it's mouth, seemingly desperate for breath. The dog and I stared at each other with equal confusion, until he was carried around the corner by the jogging Legionnaire, unsure what to make of the spectacle I continued on my way.

My driver had indeed dropped me off at the wrong location and I had to circle the whole structure before I reached a large stone arch with the words, 'LEGION ETRANGERE' emblazoned above it. It struck me later that the Legionnaire could just as easily have sent me, 'à la droite'. Once through the arch a third soldier gave a similar glance up and down before beckoning me with an out stretched finger and walking me across a small courtyard, then ushering me through an unimpressive plastic door. Inside was a small room, half of which was a waiting area containing several plastic chairs that reminded me of school chairs, the other half had an office area where two further Legionnaires sat at desks looking through a variety of papers and files. A long reception style desk split the two halves of the room. Looking over my shoulder, I realized the soldier who had guided me there was now gone and when I turned back into the room one of his comrades had stood and approached the reception. He stared at me as I stood holding my suitcase in front of me with both hands. He wasn't the only one staring at me, his colleague from behind the counter as well as three further faces, three other recruits filling roughly a third of the plastic chairs surrounding the walls. The terrifying observation I made was that the faces on both sides of the dividing reception all looked the same, not in the brotherly sense but in the eyes. These were all soldiers, confident, chiseled soldiers; their auras just stank of it.

"Pardon?", my head snapped to the right at the man behind the counter who had spoken, seeing my confusion he continued in accented but flawless English, "Can I 'elp you?"

"Er yes thank you", I dropped my case to just one had at the side in an attempt to appear more confident and suited to the environment, also to free a hand to hide my mole and teeth, I stepped toward the desk, "I'm here to join up". To their credit no one laughed, but the smiles that appeared on every face spoke volumes. I suddenly realized that I had not found the loo I needed and began to panic and sway slightly from foot to foot.

"Oui? You wish to join the Legion?" His grin broadened a little.

"Oui, but I was wondering if there was somewhere I could have a wee first?"

"'Ave a oui?" His grin was replaced with a confused frown.

"Oh sorry, not oui, I mean wee, a pee, the toilet?" With this the restraint in the room broke and two of my three fellow recruits laughed out loud, receiving vicious looks from the man helping me at the reception. One of the guys on my side of the room stood and explained in what sounded like perfect French, the situation, he then turned to me.

"Just ootside 'n t'n reet, y'll see a wee door, if yuv any sense lad, once y've bin for a piss y'll get yersen oot ov 'ere. All respec' like, this is no place fo' someun in yer condition". Following his excellent French I was surprised to hear the strong Scottish accent; he was at least as tall as me, with huge muscled shoulders and a neck that was wider than his shaved head. He smiled at me with his mouth and his eyes and I realized he was not taking a shot, he was simply stating a professional observation. I looked around the room again and his words hit home with their full meaning.

"Are you guys all soldiers already?" I feebly asked.

"Tom and I f'sure, aye" responded the Scottish chap in front of me, he pointed with his thumb at an equally muscled but shorter man still seated; Tom nodded and smiled at me. "Ney sure about the otha fella", he added nodding at the third recruit, "doesna seem to speak English o' French but lookin' at 'im ad guess so". The whole room was looking at me now. The Legionnaire had placed a clipboard with a pen and what looked like some kind of application form on the counter, I noticed that all had one of these filled in on their laps. My prostrate burned and without a word I backed out of the room and quickly found the loo that the Scotsman had directed me to. Once in a cubicle I sat and cursed myself, 'stupid, stupid, stupid', what was I thinking? They were right I had no place here. At this stage, I realized that other than a Mars bar & packet of crisps in the hotel the night before I had eaten nothing in over twenty-four hours. 'Typical', I cursed myself further, after all your bold self promises you are sat in a toilet having cowered from your first achievement thinking about food, 'you useless fat bastard', I said out loud to myself, 'I'm so ashamed". 'Shame', that was exactly what my father had been accused of only yesterday in the hospital, of being ashamed of me, 'he died of shame' that's what she said. I clenched my fists and put them on my bare chubby knees, I straightened my back as I sat on the pot and I set my jaw, 'NO, I am not a failure yet, I can do this'. I stood and pulled up my pants, marched out of the toilet and straight back into the recruiting office where I picked up the clipboard and pen that were still on the counter. Without a word, I sat down in a spare chair that I barely fit on, curled over like a child in class who didn't want the others to copy, and began filling in my details. The room was in silence, but I could feel all eyes on me, "Gotta try" I whispered half to myself and half to answer the quizzical stares I knew I was receiving.

"Well god bless ya laddie" said my new Scottish friend slapping me on the shoulder, "an all luck t'ya".

I had just finished my form, when in walked a formidable looking man from a second door at the back of the small room. He was more casually dressed than the other Legionnaires, wearing green fatigue combat trousers tucked into the same black boots as the men I had seen outside, the same green utility belt suspended a long scabbard containing a bayonet, but above the waste was a simple white t-shirt stretched at the sleeve around bulging biceps. My three companions instantly stood so I followed suit, my nerves back in force, making it impossible for me to stand as still as they were. The new arrival stood with his back to us talking in French to the Legionnaire behind the counter, the air of authority he commanded and spoke with led me to believe he was a senior officer. I realized at this stage he was the first man I had seen wearing a Kepi, the signature white circular hat of the Legion. After several minutes he spun around and I saw his face for the first time, I can honestly say that I think this is the first time in my life I have felt fear from a pure appearance. He took one look at the people stood in front of him from left to right, looking each potential recruit up and down. As I was last I got to really observe our inspector, he was not tall, five feet ten at most, but his large barrel chest was supported by a ramrod straight back. His skin was the color of aged leather and stretched around a chiseled jaw. The shade of his skin magnified his electric blue eyes, and the scar that ran from the right of his forehead straight through one of those eyes, before finishing at the corner of his mouth, seemed to give him an almost demonic grin. It was this scar that identified him as the man I had seen just moments earlier, running with a dog in a rucksack. He removed his Kepi and held it in his left hand as he looked at the parade in front of him with what seemed like disgust. His piercing eyes finally rested on mine and he sighed, rubbing a vast hand over his shaved head. I swallowed and he paused before taking one solid step toward me and speaking in broken English, "merde, what ze fuck is zat on your face", with a cobra like movement he whipped his bayonet from its scabbard, touched the tip of its blade just beneath the mole close to my right cheek, before slightly pushing and flicking his wrist upward. I could tell that the huge arch of blood that projected from my face surprised him as much as I. In a crimson mist, the mole exploded forward, striking the intense man directly in those blue eyes. My head started to bob as I began to feel nauseous; the spray followed the movement of my head covering his pristine white t-shirt. "Merde!' he yelled again. The world became blurred and vague as I felt myself falling and sinking into a deep darkness.

I still to this day have no idea how long I had been unconscious when I awoke; when consciousness did come I initially kept my eyes closed. I knew I was awake because I could hear myself breathing; I kept my eyes closed because I was comfortable and it felt strange. I was definitely laying on something very soft that felt like a bed, and a blanket or cover of some sort was pulled up around my armpits. My arms were outside the covers and I allowed my fingers to brush back and forth, it felt like my blanket back in the London apartment. It seems crazy to say, and personally I hate it in books and films when people say 'was it all a dream?', I don't believe that's possible, if something this intense is happening there is no way anyone would ever think it was a fucking dream. In summary, I would say I was praying with desperation that it had been a dream, initially the last forty-eight hours but in reality the last thirty-two years. I squeezed my eyes tighter and realised I was doing it to hold back tears. What had I been thinking; I let out a small sob before the reality of my now came crashing in on me.

"Jean, sont vous éveille?" I didn't know what had been said to me but I knew who it was, I prayed harder, I didn't want him to be here, I didn't want me to be here.

"Jean" was repeated, "you are awake, oui?" I slowly opened my damp eyes and was surprised how dark it was; I glanced around me to see I was in a single steel framed bed in what appeared to be a small hospital ward. There were just five other beds and although the room was, as I said, dark I could make out that only one other bed was occupied at the far end of the room. I turned to my left and my eyes came disturbingly close to another pair, of the most intense pale blue

"You feel good? Okay?" was the question asked by a mouth, which was connected to those eyes by an angry looking scar. The events that led to me collapsing flashed through my head, and I remembered looking into those eyes as their owner, essentially, stabbed me in the face. Still, in silence I raised my hand to my face and felt a thick piece of gauze attached with a kind of tape. I was surprised by the amount of bandage that was covering almost half of my ample cheek.

"Your mole it is gone, I am sorree about surgery but I think you 'ave piece ov merde on your face". I re focused on his eyes.

"Why so big?" I said in a slight panic, my hand going flat across the entire surface of the dressing.

"Ah oui, it is true. I did not get it all and I make a mess I think? le chirurgien he say you 'ave grandes raciness, er how say raciness? Mmm, roots I theenk? Mole had roots. You 'ave a big scar Jean, look like me". With this he smiled as if he'd done me a huge favour and sat back in a small wooden chair that he had pulled beside my bed. He was looking very proud of himself. I allowed myself to contemplate what he had told me for a second and then to my surprise I smiled too. A scar, a big, cool scar right across my face. That's gotta be better than a hairy mole right? In anybody's book? The facts were I'd been stabbed in the face by a battle hardened Legionnaire, at least that's how I saw it. It was by far the most exciting thing that had happened to me, it definitely wasn't boring.

"How big?" I asked the question like a kid asking how many presents he was getting on Christmas morning.

"Ah, la très grande cicatrice énorme!" I was clueless but that sounded big and to me even cooler. He leaned forward again.

"Jean, take theez scar as a momento, une experience. Leev 'ere now, theez place, it is not for you". My smile vanished and I looked at him, what was he saying, I was born to be there, I had a scar and everything. The truth is every fibre of my being knew he was right, I'd known that all along but it didn't matter, I'd rather die there than achieve nothing once more in my life. Besides,

"I've nowhere else to go", I feebly whispered. The old soldier frowned and looked a little sheepish, but I understand he simply had to be honest.

"You cannot be 'ere, votre physique, the training. Maybe you go git fit, maybe you come back?" How the hell was I going to do that, I also knew he didn't mean it, he just wanted me gone. I took another look around the ward and tried to weigh up my options of which, as far as I could see, I had none. We both sat in silence and I could see him twitching with discomfort, he just wanted both of us out of there, him the room, me the country I imagine. I looked up again only when the double doors that appeared to be the only entrance to the ward swung open. I realised the room was brightening and decided it must be dawn. I was thirty-two and two days and on the edge of nothing again. A slight man in a white coat, who I assumed to be the doctor, walked towards me in a brisk efficient manner. He had an uncontrollable mop of mousy coloured hair that trailed behind him like smoke, he appeared to be at least seventy and his thin pale face was lined with deep wrinkles. As he got closer I realised that each eyebrow was a mock miniature of the hair on his head, and they rested on top of a pair of round tortoise shell glasses. He nodded to the soldier but barely acknowledged my presence, simply grasped my wrist and looked at his watch. After around a minute he decided to speak.

"How are you feeling? Mr Bore isn't it?" I was amazed to hear such a flawless upper class British accent.

"You're English?" It was intended to be rhetorical

"Well there's no pulling the wool over your eyes is there Mr Bore", was the sarcastic retort, "My wife is French, wanted to move home so here I am".

The door opened again and a young Nurse stepped into the room

"Médecin, Monsieur Jean est ici"

"Ah yes" said the doctor looking frustrated, "thank you Nurse Picard" Hearing my name from the Nurse, and seeing the response it commanded, raised concern.

"Was that about me? Is something wrong?"

"What? Oh no, not at all, the Nurse was just telling me that my next appointment is here, a Mr Jean. For some God forsaken reason I am interviewing a janitor for this place, how I was roped into it I'll never know?" With that flippant sentence a plan was born, I sat bolt upright surprising both my bedside visitors as well as Nurse Picard, who still lingered by the door. They all stared at me.

"I'll do it," I explained probably too loud.

"You'll do what?" asked the doctor, I could see the blue eyes of the Legionnaire begin to register where I was going, I focused on him and began to lay out my plan.

"You can get me fit! I might not be ready to be a Legionnaire yet but maybe soon, maybe the next time or the time after that. I can work here as the janitor and you can get me fit". He stood and his mouth began to open and close, but his mind was not telling his lips what to say quickly enough and I had to close the deal. "You stabbed me in the face!" I tried to sound as authoritarian as possible. "You owe me," I then whispered as a follow up, "You can do it, please, make me a Legionnaire". Okay, any authority had vanished from my voice by the end of that sentence I admit. I repeated "please" and simply stared at him as the flummoxed doctor and Nurse looked between the two of us like they were viewing a tennis match, wondering who would speak next.

"Oui!" he finally exclaimed whilst slamming a foot to attention, "Okay, I make Legionnaire ov you, may kill you trying but oui" He turned and marched from the room, his departing words "one day you will walk my dog", I had no idea what this meant. He left just the doctor the Nurse and I. I realised I had another person to win over.

"I'll work hard" I shrugged and smiled, "I can sleep here and if there are ever six people sick I'll find somewhere else", I glanced around the beds to confirm the number, "it will save you interviewing Mr Jean?" I felt bad for Mr Jean but bigger things were at stake here. The Doctor turned and headed toward both the door and the befuddled Nurse.

"I am not sure you know what you have just let yourself in for Mr Bore" he shouted back over his shoulder, "Sergeant Petit is quite a different animal". He raised his voice again; I'm not sure why as he was addressing the Nurse and was getting closer to her by the step, "Nurse Picard, send Mr Jean home, the position is filled". She turned and ran ahead of him, and they were gone, the double doors flapping in their wake.

I lowered myself to the pillow with a satisfied grin on my face for all of a second, before the same doors once again burst to life and back into the room stormed a focused Sergeant Petit. In his arms was a bundle of clothing, combat trousers and a utility belt, a white t-shirt, thick socks and a pair of the black boots I had seen all the Legionnaires wearing.

"habillé et dehors", he barked at me, "cinq minutes", with this he was gone. I looked at the clothes that he'd thrown on the bed in front of me, as he'd spoken. He had obviously grabbed the biggest size of everything he could find.

"He wants you outside pronto mate", it was a thick Australian accent and the voice made me jump, as I had forgotten I was not alone. I suddenly remembered the other occupied bed and looked down the ward. My roommate was sitting up using toned arms to keep himself that way; his equally muscled torso was visible, as the sheet had dropped, revealing that he was covered in bright tattoos. In contrast to an aggressive looking frame the face on top of it was amongst the friendliest I've ever seen. Large smiling eyes created deep crows' feet and matched his grinning mouth, that revealed almost all of his perfect white teeth. A short crop of frizzy red hair completed his image.

"For what it's worth mate, I think you're flat out fuckin' crazy", with this he smiled once more and lay down pulling his blankets back over his head and adding, 'I'm Pete by the way'.

Missing my five minute deadline, it was probably eight minutes before I found myself standing in front of Sergeant Petit outside what I was to learn was the medical wing of the fort, my new home. My tardiness was confirmed as the back of the Sergeants hand smashed across my face, "Legionnaires are never late", was screamed within an inch of my bandaged face, bollocks and I thought we'd bonded.

I stood trying to take it like man and ignore the aching sensation that told me I had to pee. The clothes provided fit as well as they could, the trousers were tight at the waist but all the buttons fastened, albeit with my immense gut hanging over the belt. Unfortunately the t-shirt was not quite as roomy, it looked as though it was painted directly on to my body and its whiteness was not much paler than my alabaster skin, it finished just above my naval leaving a band of fat around my midriff between where the t-shirt finished and the combat trousers started.

Sergeant Petit spent some time explaining what our routine would be, he had his own duties that took him from eight am until around six pm each evening, and these duties included drilling the actual recruits as well as their physical training. His intention was to wake me at five am each morning and spend three hours, 'turning me from this useless fat bastard into a machine that could be a Legionnaire', some of that may have been lost in translation but I got the gist. He would continue my training for two hours each evening leaving me to conduct my janitorial duties during the hours whence he was soldiering. He assured me that one day I would be fit enough to walk his dog, this still confused me but I feared to push the matter.

Now on that first morning it was already seven am when I was standing, face bandaged in my ill-fitting kit, we had little time to start a real routine. Sergeant Petit span on his heals and yelled, "me suivre", he was walking away so I took it to mean, 'follow me', and waddled after his brisk military pace.

We stopped near the gate of the fort where I had entered the previous day. Piled there were a mountain of sacks, crates and pallets all brimming with different food produce. Every fruit and vegetable one could imagine was bagged or piled high. The pallets contained tins and jars of corned beef, soup, pickles, pasta and tuna. My Sergeant, forgive me, as I am writing retrospectively, I instinctually call him my Sergeant now, an indication to you of the relationship that was to develop. My Sergeant hoisted one of the hessian sacks onto his shoulder and pointed at the pile indicating I should do the same, it took me a little longer but eventually I ended up standing next to him, mirroring his appearance with a sack of potatoes across my right shoulder. I say mirroring, I was at least a head taller but we were attending the same task. I followed him around the perimetre of the fort to a large steel door, next to this was a flight of stairs that led to a basement I was told was beneath the kitchen, a food store. This was already three quarters full but that led me to believe that the stockpile I had witnessed at the entrance to the fort was delivered to fill this store. The Sergeant and I deposited our burdens in the store and in his broken English he explained that the stock that was there, was to be moved to the front of the room next to the stairs that lead into the kitchen and that everything else we had seen by the main gate must me stockpiled behind it. I frowned and enquired why we had simply not had the delivery trucks drop the supplies by the kitchen. Sergeant Petit informed me that this usually was the case, however that morning he had managed to intercept the delivery after leaving me in the hospital to acquire my kit, so now it was for me to transport the entire delivery from the main gate to the kitchen. With this he smiled, patted my shoulder and was gone.

I was approximately half way through my ordeal by one pm and convinced I was going to die, my clothes were drenched with sweat and my muscles ached like nothing I had experienced, though you will learn a little later as I did that the following morning made these pains seem like feather strokes. At this time a stream of soldiers in combat fatigues began to file past me into the mess hall itself. Some sniggered, some pointed and laughed out loud and some yelled jocular insults in a variety of languages that drew an all too familiar chorus of laughter, from those who understood each dialect. I was by the entrance to the storeroom with my thirty-ninth sack of potatoes; I had decided to take a mental ledger in order to add some mental stimulus to my task, when one member of the group heading for lunch broke away and approached me. It took me a little while and for me to hear his voice before I recognised him as the Scottish guy from the recruitment office the previous day.

"Afternun t'ya laddie, Jean's ya name isitna? I'm Andy" I had descended down a couple of stairs with my load so he bent, hands on his knees to be at my level.

"Er well it's John actually", I regretted it immediately as I much preferred Jean, it was what the Sergeant called me and it made me feel like someone else. It made me feel like a soldier, or at least a little less like a useless fat wanker.

"Well Sergeant Petit ses ya names Jean, I reckon ya shud stick with it pal, new start 'n all that, do ya gud", perfect I thought, "listen pal, one a the fella's was in 'ospital with ya, Pete, and he told us ya plan", my mind flashed back to the Australian who had called me 'nuts', Andy pointed over his shoulder with a thumb extending from a clenched fist, "ignore somatha tossa's, a few of us think yar a fuckin' hero ya'na, balls a fuckin' steel Jean". I have to take a moment here to express the pride I felt, hardened soldiers, men of action thought I had 'balls of steel', at this point, that was the highlight of my life.

"Are you all in training now?" I thought maybe he could tell me what to expect once the Sergeant had me ready.

"No yet Jean no, just three days first, make sure werall fit n' all, sign papers, shit like that". I glanced at the last few men entering the mess hall, all trim and toned, and I then looked down at myself.

"How fit do you have to be?" I asked wondering if it was a level I could ever reach.

"No as much as yer may imagine at first", that sounded promising. "Once yer in y'll be pushed tya limit mind, but ta join the's just some basics yer nid to doo, run eight kilometres with an eighty pound pack in under n 'our, thirty push-ups, fifty sit-ups, climb a twenty-foot rope without ya feet, eight chin-ups, think that's about it?" He obviously read my expression well as I acknowledged the fact that any of those things would be impossible for me right now.

"D'na worry y'sen Jean, Tom n' some a the boys and I a gonna help yee, I recalled him introducing Tom as his friend in the recruitment office, "way we see it we all joined together and we'll get ya through. Listen, t'morra yer gonna ache like a b'stad, when I finish up t'neet al come give ya a rub dun, try and git blood flowin', it'll 'elp. After that wi can top up whatever Petit 'as yer doin', al get yer through Pal, d'na worry".

"A rub down?" the term was alien to me and I wondered what he meant.

"Aye, a massage like, sports massage yer knows. D'na worry pal am no an ass bandit or not'in. Yer muscles are gonna need it. With all respect Jean, if I was a poo pusha yer'd no be top a the list at the moment". With this he winked and thrust out his hand, I paused and then reached out to shake it. To do this I had to remove my right hand from the sack that was still balanced on my left shoulder with my other arm looped around it, as I did the contents of the sack seemed to roll to the back shifting the weight, my balance wobbled and before I shook my new friends hand I began to circle my own hand desperately trying and failing to regain my centre of gravity. I slowly went backwards seeing Andy's face turn from a smile to a frown, as it got further away from mine; I let out a yell as I disappeared down the stairs into the darkness of the store room.

"Jean! Jean! Jesus H! Is ya ok Jean", the concerned voice echoed down to me from above as I lay on the piles of vegetables I had spent all morning carting from A to B, I was laying there with a smile on my face larger than any I could recall, "Jean!" repeated my new friend.

"I'm fine", I yelled back from the darkness.

"Thank God man, thought 'ad lost yee already. So Jean, wiv got a deal yeah?" "Yeah, it's a deal", I allowed myself another few seconds of happy contemplation before I decided to get on with the job at hand, after all, I was in training.

True to his word that evening Andy walked into the hospital ward that had become my home, I was alone my Australian roommate gone. I was already in agony and every inch of me felt as though it were slowly setting in concrete; I could not imagine how this could possibly be worse the following day as predicted by Andy. He greeted me with a smile that bordered somewhere between sympathy and entertained and sat on the small wooden chair by my bed.

"Okay pal, this is 'Tiger Balm'", he held up a small plastic tub with a blue label centered with an orange and black striped tiger. "It'll bern but ney t'bad n' it's only way yer gonna be walkin' t'mora sunshine". With this he pulled my sheet to one side leaving me lying there in my vast y-fronts. I was in too much pain to move or complain. "BeeJesus yer a bigun Jean", my cheeks flushed with embarssment in front of the toned machine observing me, "yis ney as fat as yer look though, yer a big boned bugger, we'll whip yer ta shape". With this he placed a large dollop of the 'Tiger Balm into each palm and rubbed his hands together in aggressive circles to heat the substance, he then started to kneed my thigh at first sending shooting pains to the bone but gradually releasing a comforting burn into the flesh that did seem to ease the growing ache. Another peace also came over me generated by Andy, 'I was not as fat as I looked, I was big boned' that made me feel pretty damn good.

At some point during my rub down, I must have dozed off and when I awoke it was to the beeping of a small radio alarm clock that Sergeant Petit had gifted me. It was five am, the same time I had awoke in my bath back in London only a few short days ago; however on this occasion I had slept like a baby, dream free and deep. I focused on my crotch and realized I was not desperate to be on the toilet, there was a dull ache, an extremely mild version of the sensation that had tortured me for so long, but certainly bearable. I realized that in those few days I had eaten pretty damn healthily and during my task the previous day had drank water by the gallon, could it really have been as simple as that all this time? For this reason I awoke as I had fallen asleep, feeling pretty good, then I tried to move.

As I said the details of the deal were that I would be up at five and spend three hours training before commencing with my choirs, mopping the floors in the hospital and all the other communal areas as well as any other caretaker duties that came up. Luckily before my father's death I had had many years watching him perform his DIY skills and I could carry out most minor tasks.

I swung my legs to the floor and sat upright in one motion, a huge mistake. Lactic acid burned through every inch of my body, a move of any kind sent pain through the relevant muscle and I grimaced and yelped as I tried to lie back down on my bunk. I lay there contemplating the failure of Andy's rub down before it sank in that without it I likely would not have been able to move at all. Then something else occurred to me, something I would never have expected and I suspect may surprise you, I liked this feeling, it felt good. The pain coursing through my limbs and torso was an achievement in its self and it was sending me a message, 'you are getting stronger, you are getting fitter, you are becoming a soldier'. I allowed my eyes to close and a smile spread across my lips but it was short lived. Suddenly, from nowhere I felt a hand grasp a clump of the hair on top of my head, I opened my eyes in time to see Sergeant Petit's furious face as he tugged me from the bed allowing me to drop to the floor, my already aching muscles exploding.

"Do I waste my time?" He screamed at me, the veins at his temples and thick neck looked set to burst and his face was the colour of a freshly boiled lobster. I desperately tried to scramble to me feet trying to ignore the resistance that every muscle in my body gave.

"What?" was all I could muster before I pushed myself to all fours, smashing my head against the cold grey steel frame of my bed and sending myself back onto my stomach. I felt the huge strong hand of the Sergeant grasp my ankle and then to my amazement I was effortlessly dragged along the floor toward the double door exit, my skin squeaking as it stuck to the vinyl tiles.

"Cinq heures, cinq heures", he repeatedly yelled, "You think I wait for you?" it suddenly fell into place as we burst through the double doors into the half-light of dawn, me wearing nothing but those ample Y-fronts from the previous day. The Sergeant had said five o'clock and this is the time I had set the alarm for, of course I should have understood that five o'clock meant out front in kit, ready to go.

My shoulders, and then head, bounced from each of the three steps that led down from the medical wing, before I was released from the grip and lay in the dust trying to scramble to my feet.

"As you 'ave no time to dress, today we exercise in underpants", by us I assumed he meant me, but I did have a secret fear he was going to undress and join me in my state. I finally got to my feet as the Sergeant turned and began a slow jog across the yard in front of me. I followed the best I could, but the pain from the previous day doubled at the movement, though still, a part of me liked it. I was pleased when after just one hundred yards he drew to a stop, as I caught up with him he turned and faced me.

"Never again will I wait", I nodded and mouthed the words 'yes sir' incapable of actually making the sounds that went with the movement of my lips.

"Until you are fit, we run one hundred paces, we walk one-hundred paces", with this he turned and began to march at a brisk pace toward the perimeter of the fort, I waddled after him my body wobbling in time with my untrained march. So there I was, day two and I was marching behind the Sergeant in nothing but my underpants with agony already penetrating my whole body. Even at his walking pace I struggled for breath and my chest heaved, but I kept up and believe it or not, a smile returned to my face. This was soldiering and this was how I was going to become a Legionnaire. The Sergeant kept the increase in pace to a minimum when we reached the one hundred yard running sections and somehow I managed to stay within a reasonable distance. The pain in my body subsided slightly as adrenaline replaced the lactic acid. After just under an hour we stopped outside another grey, single storey building that I knew to be the barracks of the new recruits. I was ordered to attention in front of the door before Sergeant Petit burst inside, screaming as loud as he could in French. I listened to the echoes of his voice and the chaos it seemed to cause inside as people were abruptly woken. My breathing started to calm but sweat drenched every inch of me and I looked down fearing my y-fronts may have gone transparent, I was safe.

One by one the occupants of the block we had come to scurried through the door, before standing in line to the left of where I stood. After realizing it was not my imagination, I was amazed to see that they were all in the same state of attire as myself. After only a couple of minutes there were approximately twenty-five recruits in a perfect straight line, standing to attention in their underpants. Many of them were looking at the fat semi naked sight they beheld with the same gob smacked expressions. Sergeant Petit exited the building with the last of the men, which happened to be Andy; he joined the end of the line smashing his foot to attention before looking at me with a Cheshire cat grin. Several of the men were now smiling at me, some trying to hold back giggles, and then the Sergeant addressed them.

"From today, you take exercsees in the same attire az our friend 'ere", he motioned to me with his hand, before explaining to them that, 'I could not be arsed getting out of bed so the whole unit would be punished'. To my amazement he then went on to explain the deal he had struck with me and that everyone in the lineup shared the responsibility of getting me fit enough to walk his dog, still no clue what this meant. They were to take it in turns at meeting me at five am each morning in order to take on this duty. This suddenly made sense; maybe it was a bit crazy of me to think that the Sergeant would be outside my door at that hour every morning. He then barked some more commands and the unit turned sharp left and began jogging away on the route the Sergeant and I had taken, looking I am sure as ridiculous as I did, in nothing but underpants. Andy gave me a nod and thumbs up as he joined the run.

It was indicated that I should follow the Sergeant into the barracks and once inside my next task was explained, I was to empty the barracks. Let me explain, every single item in the building was to be removed and placed on the parade ground outside. The room was around fifty feet in length and maybe twenty five feet wide, thirty beds lined the walls, fifteen each side and each with a footlocker at its foot and a taller matching grey steel upright locker to its left. Without repeating his explanation the Sergeant left me alone.

It took me almost three hours to move all the contents of the barracks outside and I felt like it had taken six, I was way past my allocated time for exercise each morning. My head pounded my body screamed with every movement, but unbelievably, I was still enjoying myself, I simply cannot explain this but I loved the challenge, the sense of achievement and in honesty the exercise.

Around every half an hour the scantily clad unit would pass me on a circuit and I envied them and longed for the day when I could run for that length of time. They would look at me, incredulous at my appearance but after the second pass they began to cheer, not mocking me as you might expect but chants of encouragement and support, this only added to my euphoria. On their sixth pass, as you may have calculated, they found me standing to attention beside the entire contents of the barracks. They drew to a stop at the Sergeant's instructions and most of them lent with hands on knees drawing in precious oxygen. The Sergeant marched past me into the barracks for just a couple of seconds, returning he stood no more than five inches in front of me, his head tilted right back so he could look up at my panting face, he paused for an uncomfortable period of time before issuing his next command.

"Remettre", he said it with a flippant under stated tone and turned back to the men who, after a round of sighs and moans, fell in line behind him continuing their underwear streak. The sun was now higher in the sky and warmth prickled my salty skin, I squinted up at it briefly before looking around at the departing runners. Andy's friend Tom was the last to join the pack and he seemed to understand my confusion. As he spoke in a thick Yorkshire accent I realized it was the first time I had heard him speak.

"He wants you to put it all back Jean".

"Huh?" was all I could muster.

"All of it back where it was Jean, chop-chop lad we're all knackered"

It was mid afternoon before I had completed my task, and the platoon of men were allowed to stumble back into their lodgings, in order to finally get dressed. I was pleased that none of them seemed angry at the morning's events and those that did speak to me mumbled words of congratulations to my efforts, one or two even slapping me on the back as they passed me, all still in their underpants. I dragged my feet back to the medical block in order to shower and finally get dressed myself. I was filthy and coated with sweat, my hair sticking up almost vertically and my underpants hanging baggy around my thighs, it was probably this sight that made Nurse Picard scream and run straight past me from the ward when I entered the room, I was too exhausted to speak and I couldn't blame her in fairness. The rest of the afternoon I spent performing a series of tasks that had been left on a list by my bed, I assumed by the appalling handwriting it was from the doctor, don't they always have bad handwriting? I mopped floors, I unblocked a toilet in the main office and changed some light bulbs, as I did all of this I enjoyed the aches and pains that were the proof I had exerted and pushed myself, on some level I craved more exercise. My only meal that day had been a plate of steamed chicken and broccoli which I had eaten alone in the mess hall after wiping down the tables, the cooks had been briefed on what my diet was to be while we were trying to move fat more than build muscle. The strange looks were a plenty when I asked to have a glass of the water over which the broccoli had been steamed. My prostatitis had subsided immensely over the last few days but I was taking no risks and the psychological paranoia the problem induces was still deep set, I decided not to try and explain my actions, simply smiled and returned to my seat with the glass of green bitty liquid.

At around five pm I wandered back to my digs to find a young recruit in fatigues waiting for me. He introduced himself as 'Ivan' by simply stating the name and offering me his hand, it soon became apparent that Ivan spoke no English. He was one of the smallest of the group I had seen, probably why I had not noticed him before. I would guess he stood at no more than five feet seven inches and he had the wiry physique of a long distance runner, however I was to learn that this was not his area of expertise. His hair was shaved to nothing all around the sides with a centre-parted mop of mousey hair left on the top. His thin face constantly smiled as he continued to speak despite the obvious fact that I understood nothing he was saying. Eventually he paused and seemed to contemplate how best to get through to me, he frowned and rubbed his chin before a 'eureka' moment seemed to come over him; he rolled up the right sleeve of his t-shirt and pointed to a tattoo on his sinewy muscled bicep. It appeared to be a fully body portrait of Ivan himself, in a fighting stance, black boots, red shorts and a pair of bright red boxing gloves, underneath this was some lettering which I again did not understand but the appearance of the letters added to my first suspicions that Ivan was of Russian origin.

"Boxing?" I asked, with shock or fear I'm not sure.

"Ah" Ivan slapped his head with the flat of his hand as if chastising himself for being stupid

"Ah, boxing!" With this he beckoned me to follow and led me to a large gymnasium the floor of which I had washed earlier that day. As we entered the gymnasium I felt a little nervous, I had never boxed or anything remotely like it. Surely I had nothing to worry about; Ivan was a good nine inches shorter than I and probably weighed half as much.

In the gym I was put through my paces skipping, hitting a punch bag and a variety of other exercises true to the sport that was Ivan's passion. After forty-five minutes of this I was more exhausted than I had ever been in my life, an amazing fact considering I could have said that at least six times in the last seventy-two hours. After a fifteen-minute rest break the five foot nine, one hundred and twenty pound Russian gave me a pair of gloves, donned a pair himself and proceeded to beat the shit out of me.

Aching, bruised and beaten I half walked and half dragged myself back to my bunk that evening, I allowed my clothes to fall off of me onto the hard floor and collapsed face down onto my narrow hospital bed. I lay there partially grimacing at the messages my body was sending to my brain and partially smiling at the sense of achievement the day had brought. I had achieved more that day than in the previous thirty-two years and at that moment in time if I had fallen asleep forever, never to see my list again I would have been content. I barely heard the clipped footsteps on the ward floor; I barely felt the huge hands turn me onto my stomach, and true to his word as Andy massaged my muscles I was mentally and physically numb to his good doing. I recall his words, as he told me that the whole platoon had made an agreement between themselves to get me into the best possible physical shape, that they had challenged each other as to who could push me the furthest. It mattered not, as at that moment in time; I did not believe anyone could physically, mentally or in any way push me further than the small Russian man had that evening. How wrong I was. As these thoughts played around my mind a recollection became a question, even speaking was an effort so I have whispered to Andy

"What's the deal with walking the Sergeant's dog?" I asked

"Ah that", Andy replied through a suppressed laugh, "you must have seen the Sergeant off running with that boxer dog yeah?" I had only seen the dog once when I first arrived at the fort, it was in a rucksack on the Sergeant's back and I relayed this to Andy, "that's the one" he continued, "well you see the good Sergeant takes that dog off running every day with a rucksack full o' bricks, he runs until the dogs so knackered it can run ne' more, then he off loads the bricks, shoves the bugger in the rucksack and runs back"

"You have got to be kidding me," I urged

"No at all Jean, thus far no body else has ever been able to out run the dog and a few of us 'ave tried", his smile continued.

"You've tried?" I asked

"I 'ave I" he confirmed, "after four hours I was fit to drop so I dumped the bricks and tried to force the dog in the bag. The shit nearly tore my hand off and then ran back 'ere. When I got back I was given half rations and double drill for trying to cheat". I smiled at the thought and as I fell asleep I vowed to myself that one day I would 'walk the Sergeant's dog'.

The next four weeks all passed in a similar vein, every morning at five am a different soldier would arrive at my door. I never kept anyone waiting; I had taken to sleeping in my clothes on top of the covers and setting my small alarm for ten minutes to five. I was always stood to attention on the tarmac outside the hospital wing before my trainer of the day arrived, no matter how bruised or battered I felt from the previous day. The same was true in the evening when I would finish my menial chores for the day and await my physical instruction with the same, almost self-masochistic excitement at what my body could achieve. They all had their own views on how I could be pushed, challenged and possibly broken. If it was Ivan I would box, several other individuals would concentrate purely on cardio, making me run until I vomited, do star jumps or run up and down the twenty-six stairs that led to the roof of the main admin block, amongst other challenges. If it was Andy, his friend, and, I guess now, my friend Tom, it would be muscle work with weights. Now and again it would be Sergeant Petit himself who, despite his age that was probably double that of my other physical educators, would push me harder than anyone with a combination of everything that the others concocted. These were the mornings or evenings that I cherished above all, despite the aggression with which the good Sergeant addressed everything during our time together; I could see something in his eyes when he looked at me. When I was broken, when I was beyond my limit, I would push myself. There was never a time when I would not be trying to drag myself to my feet or do that one more sit-up, box that extra round or run that extra step. I never gave in, I never stopped until whoever was with me, even the Sergeant, said 'enough', I would always try to leave them as exhausted as I because I was loving it. The look I mentioned earlier, the look that came from the steely blue eyes of the battle scarred Sergeant's face, it was respect. I had never been looked at like that before, especially not by someone like him, it was like a drug to me and I craved it.

I have no idea how much weight I lost that first month, I was never encouraged to weigh myself nor had the inclination, but I was aware of changes. It was only one calendar month, so do not get me wrong, I was still a 'fat bastard', but the three t-shirts I owned now touched the belt of my combat trousers without showing a band of white fat between the two garments. I could now run three hundred yards before I walked at a brisk pace the one hundred yards in between and I could do this for at least half an hour before the sweat broke out in force. My appetite had reduced to what was delivered to my stomach; although I ravaged every meal that was put in front of me I never craved anything in between those meals. Most of all, my desperation to constantly piss had all but gone, now when something new or intimidating was before me the fear of it would return, but I came to terms with the fact that this was a psychological scar, it would be there forever but I would deal with it. The scar that was not psychological was the one my face, the dressings long gone this was now an angry red lightening strike down my cheek, this I also loved, my first badge of honour, the first thing that happened that could have made me give up, the first thing I had beaten.

It was around this time that my new group of friends were sent away for mountain training, amongst other things. I was left alone and for the first time tried to walk the Sergeant's dog, when I collapsed in a heap the dog was still springing around me like an excited puppy and I began to wonder if the task was possible. The fort was quiet; without enough recruits for another internship the few that arrived were sent away to other recruitment centres or told to return later in the year. Sergeant Petit remained at the fort and with his responsibilities diminished by the absence of trainees he focused his efforts on me more than ever. Even arriving at my post by ten to five each morning he would often be there before me, he would push me to my limits but I would never actually allow him to reach them, always arriving at a stage where he would say 'enough', before I gave in.

The main change came in the evenings when he would sit with me and share stories of his past exploits in the legion. He had served in every conflict I knew of in the last twenty years, as well as several I did not know of. Now and then he would arrive with a bottle of cheap French brandy which we would share, on these nights he would eventually talk of his absence of family, the one love he had ever had years before and the hole he felt at never having had sons, all this he had given up for the legion. No matter how drunk we got on these evenings, five in the morning we were back on point, pushing ourselves and getting stronger, even my Sergeant looked slimmer and more toned.

One evening, after a particularly gruelling torture session, at times my Sergeant would be extra sadistic, I lay on my bunk my body effectively dead to the world, when I felt hands on my body. I was too drained to react and as the hands massaged my calf I first assumed I was dreaming and then decided that Andy must be back and resuming his nightly sports massages. However something was different, the hands were smaller and less aggressive, and these hands were gentle and warmer to the touch. My daze continued as the massage came along my leg, as the hand suddenly grabbed my cock I sat bolt upright and let out a sudden cry,

"Jesus fucking Christ Andy what are you doing?" I must have elevated myself three feet above the thin mattress and as I came to rest, my initial relief that it was not Andy grabbing my manhood was replaced by a cocktail of emotions at whom it actually was.

"I am sorry Jean, I did not mean to shock you", I looked into the deep brown eyes of Nurse Picard with not an inkling of what to say, nothing but bedlam going on in my brain, I just stared at her as she continued to massage my thigh before once again taking hold of my throbbing cock by running her hand underneath what was now becoming, as with all my clothes, my baggy y-fronts. Her other hand she placed on my chest pushing me back onto the bed and in the absence of any reasonable thought I simply let her.

"I 'ave watched you Jean", she said to me in hushed tones as she proceeded to stroke her hand up and down, having now pulled me out through the pee hole in my underwear. "You are very impressive man", 'I am?', was the only thought in my terrified mind as I began to get hot and my body filled with a feeling I could not describe. Before I knew what was happening the beautiful young Nurse had straddled me and dropped herself down taking me inside. It felt warm and tight; all the air left my lungs as I experienced a phenomenal sensation. As she sank all the way on to me I felt every muscle I had tense and a fire shot through me as I screamed out and exploded inside her almost instantly. Just as instantly, embarrassment followed the erotic sensation, as I recalled an article I had once read in a doctor's surgery magazine about premature ejaculation. The Nurse sat upon me and stroked my chest before giggling and climbing off of me. She stood next to the bed and straightened her starch white uniform before leaning in and kissing me gently on the lips, she giggled again, "do not be embarrassed Jean", she said in her heavily accented English, " this I think is your first time, no? We will improve with practice" With this she skipped down the ward and through the double doors leaving me there in a world of confused feelings, one thing she had right, at thirty-two years old I had just lost my virginity, that wasn't even on my list.

The following day 'the gang' as I now called them returned. The old routine continued, every morning and evening a different person would arrive at my door and add their slant to my training routine, Sergeant Petit's regularity increased constantly and when it was he punishing my mind and body the exercise and the pain would be dispersed with conversation. We covered a lot of ground and talked about most topic's from world affairs to our personal lives. I shared with him as much as I have with you to date, dear reader, he reciprocated this and I learned much of my Sergeant in those early weeks and months, it is not a stretch to say we were becoming close. It was obvious to all, and regularly commented upon, that he wanted me to succeed more than anyone including, if possible, me. My guess, I was filling a void in his life, he had traded everything for the legion and I was becoming the son he had never had. Now I didn't need a father, I remained convinced in the main that my original father had doted on me, for me it was different, for me he was 'another' and his praise and encouragement felt to me like it was coming from both of them. Every compliment, every enthused encouragement and subsequent look of pride was my father speaking to me. This is not to belittle the pride I felt at Sergeant Petit's input, it simply felt to me that the positives were coming from two sources, both my old and my new father. By this time, when I walked the dog it was looking decidedly knackered by the time I gave up and unloaded the bricks.

So we continued, by day a band of hardened soldiers taught me to run, lift, endure and fight, by night a young beautiful Nurse taught me another set of skills. Though over time I would come to see all soldiers as equals, my nocturnal prowess would never come to match that of Nurse Picard I am sure.

I hope I am not jumping ahead too far when I tell you that eighteen months flew by with astonishing pace. That year and a half saw my first 'gang' come and go and a second take their place, at this stage my Sergeant still considered me unfit to go through the training. The truth is that my appearance had changed beyond comprehension as well as the fitness level that went with it, in hindsight after just nine months I could probably have walked the initiation into the legion. I once read that anyone could run a marathon with only three months of training if done correctly. I was spending a minimum of four hours a day in training with some of the toughest soldiers in the world, my diet was monitored and I had more support and encouragement than anyone could need. The truth is that both the Sergeant and I wanted our journey to continue, we said we just wanted to be sure I was ready but we both knew the truth.

So it was on the third round of recruits that I crossed over and stood in line with the Legionnaire 'wannabe's', moving from the hospital that had been my home into the barracks that I had regularly unfurnished before refurnishing. As with the previous eighteen months, the training flew by. Of my peers, I was among the fastest and the strongest. I worked the hardest, now addicted to the burn of exercise and pushing my body to its limits, I would continue to rise at five am alone and run ten miles before breakfast whenever possible. At this point in my life, the fat bank clerk, who was only up early through the burning in his prostate was a distant memory. I had been known as Jean for a long time now, and it had been used with pride and respect. The other recruits assumed I was an old soldier like Andy and the friends I had previously made, I was eight stones lighter, I was strong, defined and lean, John Bore was long dead and long gone, Jean Ennuyeux was a different kind of animal all together.

The formal training I had now entered into added variety and I thrived upon it, the mountain training in the French Pyrenees was exhilarating and I learned to survive from the land and disappear into it if needed. I learned the same skills in the desserts of Morocco and Saudi Arabia where the dry, arid landscapes and searing heat burned what little fat remained from my body and darkened my skin to such an extent I would never drift back to the paste of my past. My scar had now settled to a sharp jagged line just slightly lighter than the rest of my complexion and when I looked at the stranger in the mirror I could see why the others in the troop thought me an experienced soldier, this always made me smile, if only they knew.

One morning shortly after returning from the desert I stood within the confines of the fort at the foot of the stairs to the medical block that had once been my home. On my back I had a pack which was completely full of bricks and sat on it's haunches in front of me was the Sergeant's infamous dog, it looked at me with challenge in it's eyes and barked once.

"Come on then you shit" I said to it, "let's see what you've got". I had attempted to 'walk the dog' several times, failing each one. Like Andy before me I had tried to cheat in many ways but the dog could not be fooled, even if I simply emptied the bricks early to lighten the load it would run back to the fort alone barking. This morning as I set off on our run I noted my Sergeant watching me from the gatehouse with a knowing smile, I exited the fort with the Boxer at my side. Over three hours passed, I was soaked to the bone with sweat and my legs felt like lead. My pace was slowing but as I entered a wooded area I had not reached before I realized my pace was slowing so the dog could keep up, it was getting tired. The realization gave me a lift and I added a stride a minute to my speed. No more than five minutes later in the depth of the wood there was another low bark, I stopped and turned to see the chocolate brown dog, as soaked in sweat as I was, laying on it's side panting heavily with it's tongue lolling from it's mouth. Twenty feet to the right was a huge pile of bricks that marked the place where the dog's limits were reached. Smiling to my self I added my load to the pile created by the Sergeant alone, until now, and threw the empty rucksack onto the floor, where the dog managed to slowly reverse itself inside. Just under three hours later with my new lighter load I ran back under the sign that advertised the Legionnaires entrance, I was greeted with cheers from my fellow recruits and embraced by my Sergeant.

"I knew today was the day" he informed me, "I see it in your eyes". He embraced me again but as I released his dog from its confines I couldn't help but feel he gave it a look of disappointment as if it had let him down.

Throughout out all my training I also demonstrated an incredible aptitude for weapons, my first experience on the firing range confirmed to the others, their theory on my military past. The truth is, shooting just came naturally to me, and it made sense. I lay in the grass some five hundred meters from a mannequin dressed in an old brown uniform and positioned the crosshairs of my scope on its chest slightly to the left of centre, as instructed I drew in a large breath, let half of it out and began to squeeze the trigger. Just before I let the round fly I noticed the grass around my target swaying in the strong breeze and it occurred to me that this may carry my bullet slightly, again it just made sense to me. I moved my sites around an inch to left of the red circle that was drawn on the scarecrow's tunic and then watched as the bullet I let fly pierced the centre of the fake heart. Repeating the process immediately I put a second round right between the eyes. My gunnery Sergeant was ecstatic and with his technical training ingrained I rarely missed a bull's eye, or a heart, or a head.

In between training assignments we were back at the fort where Sergeant Petit would always join me at five am for training and we would often dine together in the evening when he would drag me away from my comrades and share brandy with me in his quarters, I would tell him about my efforts in training and he would take all the credit, reminding me that it was his vision and training that had prepared me, I would remind him that I had essentially blackmailed him into it as he had stabbed me in the face and then we would laugh it off and drink more brandy. By now all our conversations were in French and it felt to me like my first language as it was what I used daily, again these lessons had come to me easily due to the interaction with my Sergeant and of course my Nurse. You will be relieved to hear I will now avoid trying to write in an accent to demonstrate their dialect, as I no longer heard it.

At the end of my time I stood in line with others and was sworn into the ranks of the French Foreign Legion, I had done it, I was a Legionnaire. After chanting the 'code of honour' in unison we each hurled our new white Kepi's into the air and cheered our joy. I returned to my bunk to pack my belongings but before I did I removed a small red box from my footlocker, I opened it gently and took out the red stone bracelet that I cherished. Even in the absence of all my fat, it had not fit over my hand but Nurse Picard had restrung it for me on a length of thin leather, it now rolled onto my wrist with just a one inch gap of the leather knotted at my pulse. I then took a small pencil from the pocket of my shirt and retrieved the only other content from the box, a faded, crumpled text page, my list. With an emotion I still cannot explain, a cocktail of pride, melancholy, nostalgia, elation and regret I drew a thin line through the item detailed as 'number one'. I smiled to myself and looked up and down the remainder of my list, all written in the hand of a ten-year-old boy who thought anything was possible. Sure some of these things I could do, some I should have always known were simply ridiculous. The memory of both the boy and the fool who had rediscovered the list two years earlier turned my smile to an internal chuckle, I realized at this point I did not need to complete my list, I had already achieved more than I or anyone else ever thought possible. I had friends, a career, and a life I thrived upon, I was happy and that I realized is all I had ever wanted. As I tucked the list and bracelet carefully back into my box I heard footsteps and turned to see Sergeant Petit. He reiterated his pride before handing me an envelope with my deployment orders, I was to be posted to, 'Compagnie d'éclairage et d'appuis', the 'Reconnaissance and Support Company'. The next day I would leave for Africa to join maneuvers with the division, or so was the plan. My Sergeant hugged me and kissed both my cheeks before abruptly turning on his heels and marching from the room in the hope I had not noticed the tears that had developed in his eyes. The parting comment yelled back over his shoulder was, "joyeux anniversaire", and he was gone. My God he was right, the day I officially became a French Legionnaire was my thirty forth birthday, two years exactly since my 'particularly shit day'.

Chapter 3

Achievement number two.

Become a hero

Please remember that I was ten years old when I made this list and I have not altered it to make myself look more mature or wise to you, dear reader. Anyway, as I said at this stage, I had decided the list was no longer a necessary quest. My age was also something that had not registered with my old English teacher Mr. Newton, as he had continued his one-man show to the delight of my classmates.

"So young Bore, he is then going to become a 'super hero", he was embellishing with the word 'super', but to his credit he knew his audience, who were now holding their stomachs and crying with laughter as I continued to shrink into my chair. You can imagine the following narrative about learning to fly, 'maybe with the pigs taking me to France, underpants on the outside of tights' etc Jesus he was a prick, but anyway..........

I slept soundly that night and was surprised when I didn't awake by my own body clock just before five, but with the bark of my Sergeant's voice. Instinctually, I flew from my bunk and began to make my bed, ready to stand to attention by my footlocker for one of his surprise inspections. On this occasion however, as soon as we were all standing, he simply turned on his heals and indicated that we should follow him with a further bark in French. There were only eight of us in the room. Of the twenty-five recruits who had gone through basic training with me, ten had failed to make it all the way and another seven, who were to be posted on domestic duties in France, had already left to join their new units. Those of us in the room who were expecting to be heading to Africa in a few short hours, simply looked at each other blankly for a couple of seconds, before hastily dragging on fatigues and rushing after the Sergeant who was waiting impatiently at the entrance to the barracks. We followed in single file, through ingrained habit, as Sergeant Petit marched us across the parade ground and into the mess hall, which was a wash with activity. People I knew, people I didn't know and people I had seen around were rushing, sitting and in some instances openly weeping.

The room was in a mass of emotion, panic, anger and grief ebbed through the air and instantly affected those who would enter, me included. I looked around and noticed the flames that were displayed on the large television that had been placed on a table at the front of the room. It felt like an hour but was probably a minute before the cause of the bedlam registered with me; everything went into slow motion as I glanced from the television to those around the room and back again. Throwing away the secrecy of our relationship, Nurse Picard appeared and hugged me, her tears instantly soaking through my t-shirt. I placed my hand on the back of her head and looked back at the unbelievable scenes that were been displayed on the screen in front of me.

It was several years since terrorists had flown planes into New York's World Trade Centre's, slightly fewer since smaller attacks had devastated London. The effects of this and the emotions created I am sure you all remember as did I, but how could this happen again. It was around four am in France and I listened as journalists around the world explained the devastation created by three bombs that had initially detonated in Tokyo's main commuter rail stations. Now this alone, as horrid as it was, would probably not have made people on the other side of the world wake colleagues, friends and loved ones to hear the news, however it was not alone. The Tokyo explosions had occurred at eight am local time, in the height of rush hour creating maximum devastation and death. An hour later in Manila, Shanghai & Beijing a further twelve explosions in similar key commuter stations had left an instant death toll estimation impossible. Now it was nine am in Tokyo as the fires still raged and eight am local time in the latter three cities. An hour after this when it was nine am in Manila, Shanghai & Beijing it was eight am in Malaysia & Singapore and four devices exploded on Kuala Lumpurs LRT system and Singapore's MRT, an hour later the central station in Dhaka was levelled by the largest blast as yet and the hemisphere burned.

Four hours of reprise followed as the sun, which seemed to be creating these acts itself, passed over the Middle East. At this point someone decided to take credit for the madness that had been unleashed on the world. It was released on the Internet so fast and furious that keeping it from the TV was not an option, and soon a grainy video was been constantly repeated on every station in between revisited news footage of each burning city. I stared at a man who looked no older than me, despite a long black beard that dropped to his chest. He was dressed all in white including a kind of turban that wrapped around his head. However over his pristine garb was a camouflage combat jacket and across his chest, below the beard, hung a Russian made AK-47 assault rifle on a leather strap around his narrow shoulders. He paused for a while and seemed to be fleeting his black eyes between the lens of the camera and someone who I am guessing was directing the filming, it seemed he wanted to be sure they were rolling, that he was ready for his world debut. When he did speak it was with perfect, only slightly accented English. The dark skin seemed to be suppressing a smile, more so as he spoke, he radiated with pride at what he was no doubt about to take credit for. I will summarize what he said but no more than that, even now after all these years I do not want to entertain him by redelivering his message and adding any further immortality to his little speech, this speech quickly became the most watched clip in history though in under two years it would be knocked from the top spot, we'll get to that.

He introduced himself as 'Bda Nam Sadden Oboe', the leader of 'Al Qaeda's' new 'Brothers of God', I can't recall nor care to remember the Arabic name he also informed us of. This group basically transpired to be a bunch of guys who found 'Osama Bin Laden' a little too fluffy and hands off since 9/11, so had decided to go their own way with a splinter group. In reality at this point we didn't know if 'Bin laden' was dead or alive and his command over news headlines had diminished.

He gave their reasons, their motivation and detailed the guidance they had from God to destroy infidels, you've heard the same old shit before so let me set my stall out now on the subject. These guys were murderers plain and simple, thousands were dead because this man and his followers had decided they should be, of their own violation, not God's by any name. I understand the west has committed some atrocities and continued to do so, much of this I think is wrong but I distance myself from any man, religion or God that would address this with mass indiscriminate murder. Again not to overdo his coverage here, just what he would want, he talked about the sun dawning in each country and unleashing God's fury, and the beautiful light it radiated on the beloved land now from where he spoke. This is where it got concerning, 'soon the light would pass over his land and it would again see the corruption of the infidels and become angered, with Gods will the destruction would continue and he and his pure', he called them, 'would celebrate in our fate'. Basically he was telling us we were not out of the woods yet.

Sure enough when the sun came up in Egypt and the clock crept to eight am, the main station in Cairo followed in the same vein of the previous six cities and seventeen explosions. The world was in panic, it was now seven am in Europe and I am sure there was not a living soul who was not fully aware of what was happening, and the fact that we may be only an hour from this madness reaching our own doorstep.

Milan, Rome, Berlin, Barcelona, Madrid, Athens, Genève as well as cities in Poland, Norway and Sweden. We were now getting reports that many devices had been located and defused yet over thirty explosions had followed each other around the globe. Casualties were been minimized as the world stayed at home, but estimates were already reaching thousands dead. Then it happened, Gard du Nord Station, as you may recall from my journey to the fort, was a little over twenty miles away from us, but it seemed we heard the explosion as if it were in the room. There was a hole in the ground where Paris most famous station used to stand. The room fell silent for a second that felt like an hour, and then our little part of the world reached chaos. Some ran outside to see the mushroom that was clearly visible to the northwest, some grabbed cell phones and desperately started trying to place calls despite the fact that most, if not all, civilian communication networks had crashed globally due to overload. Most of the Legionnaires had nobody to contact, it's why we were there, so in the absence of anything to do and in complete confusion and fear, I went outside for a run. After an hour of this I went to the gym and lifted weights for a further hour, I then ran again and kept going on the cycle until I was told to stop and ordered to one of the Fort's classrooms for my new orders. This was almost six hours after Europe was struck and although those in time zones behind us had taken all possible precautions, many more had died and the destruction had continued.

Eight am in London and Victoria, Paddington, Euston and Kings Cross were crippled only one device at Liverpool Street station had been located and stopped. Five hours after that Grand Central in New York ceased to exist, a device was removed safely from Union Station in Washington DC. By the end of our day as the clock reached eight in California where four bombs detonated and four were prevented, over fifty massive explosions had rocked the very planet, the death toll was estimated by many and varied from twenty–thousand to as high has seventy-five thousand.

The TV stations were all now filled with various world leaders pledging sympathy to each other's nations as well as guarantees of revenge, it felt like we were for sure at the end of the world.

I was sitting in one of the classrooms with just my fellow, new Legionnaires and Sergeant Petit, who in the absence of anyone more senior, as they had all rushed to Paris, gave us our new orders. Those of us who were due to have headed to Africa had a different calling thrust upon us, 'Compagnie d'éclairage et d'appuis' was to be instantly reposted to the Middle East, exact destination to be confirmed, and as the unit's new blood we were to meet them there, at that point we did not need to know why. Although the obvious was looking us in the face, we would not find out for sure until the rest of the world at large shared the knowledge.

Two hours later, I was riding in the back of a military transport vehicle toward a small air field just five miles from central Paris, the Charles De Gaulle airport as with all other forms of domestic transport was completely locked down and would remain so for some time, only military facilities were permitted to launch aircraft and only the most secure facilities at that.

One thing that may seem trivial in the scope of what was occurring, seems worthy of a mention, something that I witnessed as we skirted the southern suburbs of Paris en route to our dispatch point. As I looked from the rear of the truck in which we travelled, I was still in a daze at what had happened, what it would mean to the world and what it would mean to me as a soldier, which I had barely come to terms with. The vehicle stopped at what I can only assume was a red light or intersection, through the canvas flaps that represented the door and entrance to the seating area where my comrades and I sat in contemplation, I saw a familiar face that took the air from my lungs with twice the ferocity of anything I had seen in the last twenty-four hours. On a nondescript bus shelter that resided empty at the side of the road sat an advertisement, it was standard fare for a new movie, it carried a striking resemblance to every other movie advert I had ever seen. Across the top of the poster was the title of the movie in bold, gold capital letters, 'Chinglish', a confusing title that tried to explained itself as one continued down the remaining text and images. Directly underneath the title we were informed that this particular movie was staring, 'Kent Reeves', Hollywood's man of the moment, beneath that a picture of the man himself, leaning back to back with another individual who was obviously also a star of the film. They both looked jauntily at the camera, or in this case at me, and his female costar held onto the end of his burgundy tie which was cast over the shoulder of his crisp white shirt. Cascading down either side of the text book commercial were quotes from a variety of entertainment industry publications, 'Variety Magazine' stated that it was, 'The Romantic Comedy of the Decade', and gave it five stars, 'Entertainment Weekly' informed me that I would 'laugh and cry like never before' and finally, 'Movies.com' told me that, 'Gemma Tsang, made the most amazing debut since Audrey Hepburn'. My eyes returned to the central image and I looked at the girl who two years before had given me a bracelet that she hoped would give me confidence, and was now sitting in a red box in the kit bag at my feet. As our transport vehicle pulled away I dipped my head so the sight could remain in my vision as long as possible. So many things went through my mind, first and foremost she was still the most beautiful thing I had ever seen, it would be crazy to say she had 'aged well' after just two years, she was still well under thirty, but she was shrouded in a confidence. Now I know this was an airbrushed photo shoot to sell a movie but these things can't be faked, her smile, the look in those amazing eyes, she had arrived somewhere that she fit. I thought back to my 'shit day', and recalled Craig's comments about her 'fucking off to Hollywood'; pushing away the distaste he still brought to my mouth I acknowledged how right he had been. The bus shelter now out of sight, I looked back to the floor, my eyes flitting around a small area between my feet as rapidly as my mind was processing thoughts. What would she make of me now? She had been so right, I recalled the message she had written in the card that sat with the bracelet in the kit bag I just mentioned, *'There is something special in everyone; it just takes courage and confidence'*, I had shown and now possessed both of these traits, however I doubted she would conceive the evolution I had been through and I again and again wondered, what she would make of me now. I realised I was touching the jagged scar at my cheek and I felt the square jaw that my palm rested on as I did so, with my other hand I touched my solid slim waist and allowed myself to comprehend the transformation I had put myself through, my God she would not even recognise me, not that she would remember me for a second anyway and this thought led me to frustration when I realised how often my mind had drifted to her over the last two years.

As our truck pulled to a stop and I heard the engine die, I shook my head and returned to the moment. I could kid myself that I would not think of her again, but at this point, I decided to simply be happy for her and see where my adventures were taking me next. It appeared to be to war.

The transit was uncomfortable and boring so I will not waste either of our time detailing how I got there; the facts are I did not know where I was going until I arrived, which would make the description of the journey even more pointless. As I jumped from the back of my fifth mode of transport in two days, a familiar voice yelled out to my comrades and me in French,

"accueillir aux garçons d'afganistan". I turned to look at the smiling eyes of Andy; my Scottish friend who had kick started the platoon's involvement in the project to make me a soldier. When my eyes met his, he froze for a moment and I realised that he had not yet recognised me and his mind was placing me as a familiar face. Last time he had seen me, I had lost a considerable amount of weight and was relatively fit, he had never seen the finished article and I think it was only the scar that put the final piece to the puzzle, "Jesus H Christ, Jean? You made it", he looked nothing less than gob smacked.

"Hey Andy, it's been a while" I beamed back at him. With this he grabbed me in a bear hug and laughed out loud.

"Bloody hell Jean, you feel like a fucking tree, look at you man". He continued to laugh as my companions gathered around us surprised by my acquaintance with the hardened soldier who greeted us.

"Well, what the fuck are you lot looking at", he turned his attention to them with a change in manner that surprised us all. "Get your shit together and find the Staff Officer, Santa will bunk you and we'll brief you later". With this I placed myself back with the new recruits and ignored Andy waving me in another direction. Despite my joy at finding Andy at my new post, I had no desire to distance myself from my fellow recruits or take any privileges; Andy seemed to understand this and pointed us across the baking sand in the right direction. We agreed to catch up later that day and parted company; I wondered who 'Santa' was.

As I strode toward the Staff Officer of the days tent, I glanced around the landscape that I had just arrived in. My immediate surroundings were no more than a small military compound that covered around an acre, mostly tents with a few more permanent looking prefab style buildings that I would learn were ammunitions stocks, strategy and briefing rooms. I could see around fifty soldiers though there were of course more who would be resting, out on patrol or performing indoor duties. What surprised me was the fact they seemed to be from a multitude or regiments and indeed countries, in fact I could see no more than a handful of Legionnaires dressed in the darker, plainer desert attire that my comrades and I displayed. A group of British Marines kicked a soccer ball around just outside the perimeter of the compound, their distinctive light coloured dessert uniforms identifying them. Four US Rangers carried wooden boxes from the back of a utilities vehicle to the ammunitions building I mentioned, they all looked like Rambo, bulging muscular frames, cool as ice and not sweating despite their labour in the hottest sun I'd ever, or ever would experience.

Beyond our small outpost the land looked barren and inhabitable, there genuinely appeared to be nothing, in the far distance I could make out a mountain range that I was to learn was the Pakistan border and out of bounds, though of course our location and proximity was no accident. Neither now, nor in the text to come, will I become embroiled in politics for two reasons: firstly, as I do not possess the knowledge of the intricacies politicians fabricate, and secondly, when I have tried to grasp an understanding I have inevitably found it to be bollocks, a minute percentage of the population with their own goals and agendas in mind.

We met the mentioned staff officer and the nickname with which Andy had addressed him became immediately obvious. 'Santa', was around 5 feet 4 inches tall and possessed a mop of uncontrollable white hair, although his beard was cropped close it was that same dazzling snowy white and it helped to frame a round chubby face with ruddy cheeks that dictated too much whisky. He wore no uniform so where he came from and any unit he was affiliated to was a mystery, one that would never be solved as it became apparent that the inviting appearance was no more than that, an appearance.

"What the fuck are you pussy, no nuts, soft ass, cockless wankers looking at?"

Everyone in the tent was struck motionless and stared in

uncomfortable silence. It genuinely felt like 'Father Christmas' himself had turned up Christmas morning only to prove himself the most foul mouthed, unpleasant creature on the planet.

"Can any of you fag, low life, pieces of shit, mother fuckers talk? What the fuck is your problem?" The script still did not fit the vision that beheld us. "Jesus fucking H Christ, get in a line, give me your stats so I can tell you all where you're gonna fucking die and get out my fucking tent so I can get back to my bunk and wank myself to death". The next hour continued in this vein, we were allocated to different sub units within the camp we had arrived and directed toward our commanding officers, it was no surprise to find I would be part of Andy's unit under the command of a fellow Brit, ironically called Major French which was actually his genuine given name. Before we departed to be with our new comrades we were also inundated with camp rules, timings for meals, reconnaissance detail and a whole plethora of other activities and duties. Most things would have to be learned as we went along because separating the useful information from the unending repetition of expletives was pretty much impossible.

Around our base there was the same confused, mysterious air that had arrived in France with the images of the attacks that the world had borne witness to. Unfortunately such travesties have been all too common and many of you will be aware of the impending sense of unknowing that I'm talking about. However this was global, now all tragedies carry that tag in that they have an impact on the whole world of course, though these attacks had physically been global. The World Trade Centre attacks had left the world in turmoil for a period of time, yet the impact on Americans, especially New Yorkers, undeniably was tenfold. On this occasion, the sympathy and sorrow that most major populations felt for their counterparts on other continents, was doubled by the mirrored disasters that had occurred on each individual doorstep.

The exuberant greeting I received from Andy was a small spike in a flat line of emotional joviality around the small base. Soldiers discussed repeatedly the immediate world events and how they would influence our lives and actions in the coming days and months, possibly years. The truth was none of us had a clue, or in Santa's words, 'none of us incompetent, arse wipes had a fucking clue so why waste the sweat on our bollocks worrying about it', eloquent as always.

I was ecstatic to find that, as well as Andy, my old Russian sparring partner, Ivan, was in my allocated unit.

There were two units compromised of Legionnaires, a group of ten and my team of nine. I was to learn that there were eight other units of ten made up of a variety of global forces, some of which I have detailed, it came to my attention that the other regiments from around the globe seemed to looked down on us slightly, saying this it didn't bother me then and never has.

Ivan embraced me at the entrance to our makeshift barracks in the dessert and indicated my bunk. After briefly settling in I sat with the rest of my new unit and was introduced to Major French. He was a tall, sinewy man, looking more like a long distance runner than the boxer I had come to resemble. He had a thin moustache across his top lip and his slicked back, black hair led me to believe that he was living the fantasy of been in the Legion more than the rest of us, he actually looked like the black and white pictures from the twenties that I had seen whilst on the internet in my hotel, the night before I left for France. Couple this with his endless stories of battle and bravery, also the fact that he constantly carried with him a leather bound portfolio which he claimed were his 'rules of engagement', one might think he had been in the regiment since the twenties, one could, of course, equally surmise that he was full of shit? That evening, we were filled in on our duties and what would be expected of us. The following morning at dawn, and every morning after that, we were to do a recognisance sweep of a hundred mile area along the Pakistan border. I wasn't really sure why and as a dutiful soldier who had no clue what he was doing I didn't ask. So, as I stated, the next morning we loaded up in a jeep and drove for an hour through a desolate wasteland dessert until we were much closer, however not that close, to the mountains I mentioned earlier. We then unloaded ourselves and as Major French slowly drove the vehicle in a straight line, flipping through the pages of his 'rules of engagement' binder, we fanned out in front of him and slowly walked for another four hours, eyes scanning and alert, though I was not sure for what? Each trip would be narrated by the ever-present Major French, cruising along in first gear with one leg hanging over the low driver's door outside the jeep. He would tell us of the places he'd been that were hotter than where we were, drier, more desolate and more hostile, often quoting from the beloved leather book. All in all I think I speak for the whole gang when I say our leader was really starting to fucking grate. However it took our newest recruit to finally silence the ever-boastful young Major and his magic book. As I mentioned we were a unit of nine among other units of ten. It was around two months into my tenure in Afghanistan when I returned from the mess tent one afternoon to see the reassuring figure of Sergeant Petit barking orders around my unit's tent as if he had been there forever. As I approached him I smiled to myself at the sweating Major French as he stood by the impervious Sergeant simply nodding and repeating 'yes, quite, splendid idea' as he strangled the 'rules of engagement' which he had inadvertently rolled into a tight tube in his hands.

I stood in the heat as the dust of the dessert swirled around my boots motivated by the warm breeze that rolled over the distant mountains. I loved this man like a father and I watched him with the pride of a young child. He had brought me into a whole new world and cultivated me into a man that could survive in that world, belonged in that world. When he finally turned and looked at his creation I saw the returned pride create a lump in his throat that he swallowed back before he smiled and grasped me kissing both cheeks and stating,

"I could not let you have all the fun Jean!" he said it through laughter before placing is arm around my shoulder and marching me away from the silent Major French without a word or a glance in his direction.

The next few months were considerably more entertaining. Somehow through experience and sheer presence the Sergeant seemed to bring the camp together, he mixed up the units on some days so we got to work and train with other nations forces. I learned advance hand to hand combat skills from British Marines, a US Ranger started to give myself and Andy helicopter flying lessons and in the unlawful environment we controlled I was nipping off on solo flights within a month, occasionally taking Sergeant Petit who would share a bottle of French brandy with me, yes as I piloted a heavily armed battle chopper. Competitions were also initiated, a crude boxing ring was constructed and Ivan continued to beat the hell out of any challenger once he had been crowned camp champion, despite been the smallest man at the post. I came in seventh in the boxing and was happy to be so far up the table considering the company I was keeping.

Where I continued to excel was with the rifle, as I mentioned earlier marksmanship just came naturally to me. I loved the way my rifle felt in my hands, it became part of me as I pulled it to my shoulder and simply placed a bullet wherever I wanted it to go at almost any distance, it seemed, at risk of been arrogant, easy. The shooting competition soon became a chase for second place and people seemed frustrated that I did not have insightful hints and tips on how to improve their proficiency.

Senior officers around base seemed happy to let the Sergeant pretty much take over. Major French masked his envy poorly and constantly moped around in the absence of an audience for his tall tales. Sergeant Petit's stories of past action were written all over him without the need for narration, and I feel sure the Major knew his bullshit would be transparent to the hardened Legionnaire. Doubling the frustration for him was the practical jokes that had swept through the camp, many of which seemed to be focused on him but could never be traced back to the source, which was inevitably the good Sergeant.

Don't misunderstand, he was by no means the recipient of the lion's share of these pranks, I myself received my fair share as did everyone else including my Sergeant, though even then the Major often played a role.

There was, of course, the obvious and somewhat juvenile pranks, hair removal cream, God knows from where, placed in shampoo dispensing bottles. Itching powder, again I've no idea who the hell was sourcing this stuff, placed in underwear before drill parade. The classics, as they became known, did however revolve around myself as the recipient of such a stunt and the revenge that I took on the man responsible. Alas, at the butt of both these jokes was the same man, our very own Major French.

Due to the rotating schedules that Sergeant Petit had organised on his arrival, I had alternate mornings free during which time I fell straight back into my morning routine of rising at five am and running until my body said 'enough', my body seemed to say 'enough' slightly quicker than I was used to in the middle of the Afghan desert.

On the morning in question, I stumbled back into camp at around six forty-five to the usual 'odd ball' looks from those with similar free time who chose to lounge around. No sooner had I passed the outer boundary, en route to my bunk to collect my wash bag, when the Sergeant's barking voice began to directed orders at me.

"Jean! Quick, move the helicopter", it was said with a nonchalant wave of the hand though I knew this was not a normal request.

"Huh" was all I could either think to say or muster through my exhaustion.

"The helicopter, I want it on the North side of the camp, we're going to lay out a soccer pitch and there's only enough flat space to the South where the chopper is". The gaggle of soldiers around him, one of them was clutching a leather soccer ball adding credence to his story, though I had no reason to doubt him anyway. True enough, the chopper-port had been mapped out to the south around twenty metres from the camp in an area that would be perfect for a soccer field, there was less flat space to the south but ample for the chopper to park.

So it was that without giving it much thought I hot footed it to the 'HH-60G Pave Hawk' helicopter, truth is I had come to love flying so much that I needed little excuse. I fired her up and waited for the rotor blades to reach full speed before grasping the control stick and pulling back, I was oblivious to the length of rope that was attached to the undercarriage as I once again cherished the sensation of taking flight. As I was simply to set down again no more than two hundred meters away, directly over the camp, I decided to take the chopper vertical until I was confident that I was high enough to head to my destination as the crow flies without the downward force of the propellers disturbing the camp, as much as I loved flying I was still in need of a shower and wanted to get up and down as soon as possible.

As I ascended I did not see the rope follow me into the air, nor did I acknowledge the crowd that had gathered to watch the other end of the rope.

Now, between the camp and the make shift heli-pad were the latrines, the latrines where every morning the good Major French would visit for what one can only assume was his morning dump. The units were set away to the right, a row of ten crude wooden cubes approximately five feet apart, each no more than three feet square, six feet high, rising to a point where an iron loop was attached in order that they could be loaded from a flat bed truck with the use of a small crane. On this morning, as I am sure you have guessed, the rope underneath my helicopter was attached to one such loop. I am sure you have also gathered who the occupant of this particular cube was. Sure enough the ever entertaining Sergeant had spent some time removing the screws that attached the base of the Major's favorite stall to its walls, desperate for the hilarity that would ensue once I flew away leaving our exposed Major sat on the pot taking a shit in the wide open dessert. Now this in itself could well have been funny to a bunch of bored, adolescent soldiers, I am not sure what reaction, emotion or memory I now attach to the actual outcome.

As I said, I was rising fast and as soon as the rope reached its complete length I felt the jerk and allowed myself a fleeting but definitive panic before the bulk of the vehicle ignored the flimsy weight of the temporary commode. Down on the ground I was told with great frequency over the following weeks, the Major's only separation from the outside world was whipped away like a magician tearing away a handkerchief to show a stunned audience the vanished object was back, such was the speed with which it was gone once the Pave Hawk took hold. It occurs to me now that nobody considered the effects had I not gone straight up, had I decided to stay low at skirt the perimeter of the desert base I could have dragged the latrine along the floor and the unfortunate Major with it. As it was, all below whom were in on the stunt, most of the camp, stood around in anticipation of the hilarity that would follow when the unwitting victim would be left with his pants around his ankles.

It quickly transpired that the Major's pants were not around his ankles, nor was his shirt on his back, nor was he taking the assumed dump. The sight I had magically unveiled was that of Major French, my official commanding officer, sitting completely stark bollock naked on the harsh wooden toilet seat, bar an all too tight looking dog collar, his clothing neatly hung on the interior door of the unit dangling beneath my chopper, his cock in one hand furiously masturbating to the true contents of the leather clad 'rules of engagement'. Open on his knees and tucked between the pages of his 'battle guidelines' was a well warn copy of a magazine I learned was titled 'Be His Bitch', which carried the tagline, 'if he's not hurting you he doesn't care', apparently our Major was quite the homosexual masochist. A million Google searches performed around the camp over the following days would show that this was a magazine targeted at those among our gay friends who liked to dress up in latex or a variety of other garbs and be 'disciplined', for want of a better word by their partner or partners of choice. His other hand was franticly tugging on a leather lead that led to said dog collar bringing a strangled flush to his face and no doubt deafness to his ears, as it took him a good thirty seconds to realize his new public status. It must have eventually been the breeze that made him stop his actions and gradually open his eyes that had been clamped tight shut above his wrinkled nose and gritted teeth. It could also be that it was when he opened those eyes to remind himself of his stimulus, that he realized his predicament.

The dramatic switch in stature was reflected in both the audience and the involuntary entertainer, the audience burst into laughter at what they expected to see for mere seconds, before settling into a shocked and uncomfortable silence at what they had actually witnessed and then returning to a laughter that was as uncomfortable and stifled as it could possibly be.

The one-man show froze; this was followed by an eternal period of frozen silence as his brain did somersaults in an attempt to offer a viable and absolving sentence from the quivering lips. Eventually for the wanker on the toilet it clicked, he joined the laughter and spoke.

"Did he fall for it? Sergeant Petit, did he fall for it?" Obviously thinking at a hundred miles an hour he had surmised that it was Sergeant Petit behind the prank, but knowing our bond and the fact that someone else had to have been in the chopper, he had linked this to me. He was now effectively praying that given the potential destruction of his status, his nemesis Sergeant would save his face and pretend that this was all part of the joke and they had in fact been in it together from the beginning. Everyone froze and looked from Sergeant to Major and back again, as I, still clueless touched down on the opposite side of the camp. The Major's eyes pleaded the Sergeant's eyes considered. Seconds felt like minutes before the Sergeant burst into a beaming smile that glowed through his entire face. He strode toward the Major with his arm outstretched.

"He did Major French he did, the idiot totally fell for it and so did all these morons", the Sergeant waved his arm around at the confused crowd, the Major looked more than relieved and accepted the out stretched hand shaking it vigorously.

"Brilliant Sergeant, a genius plan", he positively shouted with relief. A blanket appeared and was wrapped around the Major as I appeared into the group of soldiers. On landing I had obviously realized what was attached to my helicopter but was clueless as to the why, where, who and how, I just knew that a naked Major was wrapped in a blanket wearing a dog collar and a lead.

An hour later my Sergeant and I were stood to attention in the private tent of Major French.

"What am I going to do with you two?" was the grim opener we received from our senior officer.

"Well" replied the Sergeant, "I'm kinda hoping you're not gonna dress us in leather and stamp on our bollocks". With this I instantly let out an involuntary sound that was half grunt and half laugh, drawing a glare from the Major that could freeze fire. Understandably, with no idea how to deal with this situation, his grimace eventually settled to a forced smile.

"You are lucky that on finding out about your plan I decided to go along with it and even add to the amusement", he really was going to go down this line. "Having been in so many combat situations, and been as battle hardened as I am, I truly understand the importance of humor and…"

"For Christ's sake" exclaimed the Sergeant standing next to me, "you're not battle hardened, you're a perverted freak! I'm sorry you were exposed and I'm happy to play along with the cover up but I'm not gonna stand and listen to this shit". With this he turned on his heels and marched from the tent leaving me alone with the Major. As you can imagine, I basically took the brunt of the blame as the submissive Indian among the chiefs, I was put on daily cleaning duty of the latrines where the event I was been punished for had taken place, and I was also to be a permanent fixture on the evening sentry duty, which was usually rotated about all the soldiers at the camp. All in all, I got off light considering, the hardest part was that I had to stand and listen to the shit that Sergeant Petit had so indignantly walked away from. The facts are the whole time I was listening to his stories of bravery in the field I had one thing and one thing alone on my mind, revenge.

It was three weeks when I returned the favor to the Sergeant Major who I also thought of as my father. A notorious heavy sleeper who could wake people several tents away with snoring that Satan would be proud of, Sergeant Petit provided the answer himself. It took me some time to talk Andy into being my accomplice but eventually the night came. Keeping myself from sleep on pure schoolboy adrenalin, I shook Andy awake at around four in the morning, after personally adding the icing on the cake to the stunt I was initiating. Still an unwilling accomplice, Andy grumbled as I ushered him to one end of the Sergeants small wooden bed frame. Placing myself at the other end, between us we easily took the weight and began the gradual journey out of our make shift barracks and toward the private tent of Major French. As quietly as physically possible we made our way inside and placed the Sergeant's bunk side by side with that of his foe. Andy and I spoke in signals and froze every time one of our victims moved or grunted something in their sleep; I was amused to see the Majors famous 'battle' book by the side of his bed with his favorite fetish magazine between the pages. Taking a pair of handcuffs that I had managed to steal from one of the American Rangers, who was doubling as the camps Military Policeman, I carefully cuffed together the Sergeant and the Major. I then slipped a note I had prepared earlier into the space between cuff and the wrist of my Sergeant, it would be the first thing he read when he awoke in his new predicament, it simply said 'the key is in YOUR latrine', it had been placed there earlier by my good self. We silently exited the tent and awaited our results.

Long before six that morning rumor had spread, thanks to the uncontrollable mouth of Andy who was suddenly proud of his part in the charade. Trying and failing not to look obvious a gaggle of soldiers from various corners of the world were loitering in the vicinity of the Major's tent and the route between there and the infamous latrine. They were not disappointed for their wait.

"What the fuck!" was the first noise to explode from the tent where we had set our trap. The harsh tones of the Sergeant were followed by a scream that could have come from a twelve-year-old girl. Mere seconds past before my Sergeant burst through the beige canvas flaps that represented the door of the Major's tent.

"Jean, you mother fucker" he screamed in French as he marched as naked as the day he was born through the camp toward the latrines. In his left hand he held the note that gave the clue to his release, the other hand was cuffed at the wrist where it shackled him to Major French who was practically dragged along in the Sergeant's wake, desperately trying to stay on his feet in nothing more than a pair of ridiculously tight red and white polka dot briefs. As I had prayed and hoped the Sergeant was thus far oblivious to the dog collar and lead that I had fashioned from a rifle sling and attached to his neck before I woke Andy to assist me.

A few minutes later, the camp in hysteria, Sergeant Petit marched back from the latrine where I had hung the key to the handcuffs on the door of the very cubicle I had previously torn from the earth with a helicopter and had to repair myself. As he reentered our tent he screamed over his shoulder, "Jean, in here now", I headed toward the tent to applause from the entire compound as a confused and still half asleep Major made his way back toward his own tent with the cuffs still attached to his wrist.

I took a deep breath and headed into my canvas barracks ready to take what came, what did come I was not expecting. My Sergeant was sat on my bunk, his own bed was still in the Major's tent, he was holding his stomach and laughing like nothing I had ever seen. As I approached he looked at me through tear filled eyes, "Jean that was fucking genius, how in the name of Christ did you do that". With that comment I joined the laughter and I swear it was twenty minutes before we stopped long enough to actually converse. Wiping his eyes my Sergeant eventually calmed himself long enough to speak, "okay you got me, but come on we still have work to do", with this he stood and finally pulled on some underwear and a pair of combat trousers. "Let's get outside before the whole camp thinks it's fun day".

"Well okay" I said hesitantly.

"What's wrong with you?" asked the Sergeant looking at my confusion.

"Well don't you want to take that off?" I pointed to the dog collar and lead he was still wearing. He looked at me confused for a nanosecond before looking downward at where I was indicating. His eyes went wide and his mouth dropped open.

"You son of a bitch", he yelled as he marched toward me, I didn't hesitate and ran from the tent, as the leashed Sergeant chased me and the entire camp fell into complete hysteria, even the ever miserable Santa was clutching his rotund stomach as he joined the laughter, this made him look even more like his original namesake.

Weeks and months dragged by with little change to our status and I couldn't help but wonder what benefit we were providing to the war effort. We received updates and we had Internet access so we knew the world remained in turmoil after the events that had taken place. It was suspected that 'Bda Nam Sadden Oboe' was hiding in the mountains of Pakistan, which meant our geographical presence made sense, however it was just that, a presence. Major French, in an attempt to rebuild his reputation, had started taking troops much closer to the border on daily recons, much to the annoyance of my Sergeant, other than that little changed.

I continued to clean the latrines on a daily basis but the camp had empathy and I was never short of help. I actually enjoyed the fact that I was getting to know all members of our commune so well, more so because of my sentry duty of an evening. Each evening at sun down three soldiers on rotation would circle the camp, two clockwise and one in the other direction, spaced out as such that one would pass another around every fifteen minutes or so. As the night wore on these 'passes' would lengthen and turn to conversation and inevitably mid shift the three of us would sit and pass around stories and a hip flask.

As I was still undergoing punishment and on permanent duty, I would meet two new friends every night, soon it would come full circle and I gradually started to get to know people better.

One evening, my last at the camp as it would happen, I sat with two of my favourites. Tim was with the Royal Marine Commandos, he was my height and build and many in the camp had asked if we were brothers during our time there, something I took as a huge compliment as in my eyes he looked like a bloody super hero. He had a scar very similar to mine, which was probably the main reason for the observation, though he had received his in Bosnia a few years earlier from shrapnel and of course mine was reminder of the Sergeant slicing off an unsightly mole. Tim loved this story, as did many others, myself, my Sergeant and Andy were asked to repeat it a lot. Our other companion on the night in question was Jayesh, a US Ranger of medium height and solid build, as a Muslim, many in the camp would try and engage in political and religious conversation with Jay, as he was known. I made a conscious effort not to figuring it must piss him off.

I was surprised Tim was there as he had been with me only two nights before but he told me he was also been punished as he had failed a kit inspection, I suspected this was deliberate as he enjoyed my company and the solitude of sentry duty too. The three of us Tim, Jay and I huddled in a small circle wrapped in our full combat attire to ward of the desserts night chill. Tim and I shared a hip flask of brandy that Jay waved away as always.

"Feels like we've been here forever" Jay spoke almost to himself.

"It does," offered Tim, "I suspect we'll be here a lot longer though"

"You're kidding, surely once they catch 'Bda Nam' they're gonna send us home, or at least somewhere different", Jay was pleading for a positive response.

"Well, yeah, I guess" Tim responded, "but catching him is a whole other matter. If he is somewhere in those mountains", he indicated the direction of the Pakistan border with an incline of his head, "getting hold of the bugger will be easier said than done, as I understand it the Pakistani government are not playing ball. That in itself could make the whole situation spiral into all out war, the White House, Downing Street and wherever all those other countries big wigs live, are desperate to make something happen". Tim was right, so far soldiers like us had been positioned all over the Middle East and little seemed to have happened to avenge the deeds that had sent us there.

"But come on" continued Jay, "there's a two hundred and fifty million bounty on this guy's head; someone has to get him surely?"

"Two hundred and fifty million pounds?" I exclaimed, "Jesus we should wander over there now and have a look around". My companions grinned at my shock and subsequent statement, Tim was the next to speak.

"Well, it's dollars but still it would be nice and from what I've read on the Internet it's going up weekly. Maybe we wait a month until it's nearer say half a billion and then we'll go get the prick", we all smiled and spoke in unison, "Deal".

The rest of the night passed in idle banter interspersed with the occasional circuit around the camp. As the sun rose and the chill disappeared faster than snow melts in hot water, we began to wander back to camp in search of a couple of hours rest, or in my case to go for a run, I was still obsessed.

"Jean, over here", the three of us all looked to see Sergeant Petit loading up the truck with a variety of soldiers for the morning recon of the Pakistan border. The Sergeant approached and nodded a good morning to Tim and Jay. "We're a few bodies light for patrol, some of the techs have been called to another base, do you boys fancy jumping on the band wagon?"

"Yeah why not", for me it was easy, I just loved soldiering and feeling useful, I'd also seen Andy and Ivan climb on board and I was keen to spend more time with them. My two companions not so much and their faces showed it, they had been up most of the night. As I headed for the transport vehicle Sergeant Petit turned back to them.

"Come on then chop, chop. I'd heard you Rangers and Marines were little girls if you didn't get enough sleep". That was enough for both of them, unit pride is strong in all elite forces, their jaws stiffened and they followed me to board the truck just as Major

French appeared.

"Ah good, I see you have replacement volunteers Sergeant Petit, I think we'll take it a little closer to the border this morning, see if we can source some more intel", with this he bound to the jeep parked in front of the waiting truck.

"Sir, I'm not sure that's such a good idea", interjected the Sergeant, "we have no idea..."

"Wasn't a request Sergeant, load the men", with this he slammed shut his door and started the engine; an exasperated Sergeant joined us in the rear of the truck.

"Okay men", he instantly whispered to us, "were tackling new terrain this morning, it seems Major Prick has got his ego back. Keep it tight, constant contact and watch each other's backs, God knows where this idiot is taking us". Wherever it was, it was much further than we were used to. As a rule we only travelled fifty minutes or so from the camp yet we were close to two hours of driving before we screeched to a halt that morning. Disembarking, I was stunned to see how close we had come to the mountains that had always been a relevantly distant spectacle, we were practically standing in what you might call the foothills. The Sergeant insisted we stay gathered at the trucks loading point and disappeared toward the Major's parked jeep. We could hear low angry tones but eventually a flush faced Sergeant returned and repeated our need for extra vigilance this morning. The Sergeant's demeanor and apparent concern cast a definite cloud over the whole group.

In the usual formation but slightly tighter knit, we headed from the truck under the gaze of the vast mountains and I wondered if we had actually ventured across the border. The silence was eerie and our boots scraping the hard sand seemed to echo in our haunting surroundings. The Major confidently trundled alongside us in his jeep, apparently speaking to himself in hushed tones, the gentle wind carrying the odd word far enough for me to hear.

"You see….. This is soldiering….. Battles won and lost…… I'm brave enough… Don't need orders…. Kill 'em'", his apparent rambling concerned me and we had wandered far enough to be out of site of the transport vehicle. Jay was closer to the Major's jeep than I and apparently had heard more of the babble that was been spewed. Jay stopped dead in his tracks and turned to face the rest of us, focusing his attention on the Sergeant.

"Jesus Serg, this guys fucking lost the plot", he directed his thumb over his shoulder toward Major French who was rising to a standing position in his jeep.

"How dare you! You insolent son of a bitch, I'm a bloody war hero I'll have you up on a charge…." The approaching Sergeant cut him off.

"Everyone in formation, not a fucking word. Jay that includes you", Jay was looking more concerned by the second.

"Serg you should hear what this prick is saying to himself"

"Enough' yelled the Sergeant. Major French looked like he simply could not speak for the fury building within him. He jumped from the jeep and began marching toward Jay who stood his ground and watched his superior approach. The Sergeant made to intercept and

I also noticed Andy break formation and head toward the scene. Gusts of wind stirred up loose sand and I squinted and looked to my right at the mountains from where the breeze had been delivered. Ivan was in my line of sight some twenty-metres away and he frowned and shrugged at me as if to ask what was going on, I shrugged back and offered a smile before I noticed something in the distance. I turned and spoke over my shoulder as I already started to walk backwards. Ivan noticed my change and my concerned look and turned to the direction I had been looking, "Serg", I said in a rising tone.

"What is it Jean?" everyone seemed to freeze and focus on me, sensing my urgency. Under half a mile away behind Ivan I had seen a reflection, as a shooter I knew the importance of avoiding glare from a scope or another piece of equipment, but before I had chance to deliver this information, hell opened its gates.

"Take cover," I screamed on hearing the first harsh crack and whistle of rounds been fired. As I turned to run I saw Jay on the floor, little more than a stain where his head had been seconds before.

The sounds were deafening as mortar fire joined the bullets that were raining down on us. A shell struck the jeep behind the Major who was the only one not moving, simply stood frozen to the spot. I saw Tim run toward him and tackle him to the ground in order to minimize the target mass and attempt to save him, and then I saw holes appear in Tim's back and he simply collapsed on top of Major French. The truck was flipped onto its side and I doubted the wisdom of Andy and the Sergeant whom I saw disappearing behind it.

"Jean take fucking cover" I heard Andy yell at me. I looked back toward Ivan and notice he was laid flat behind the smallest of mounds created by a desert brush and I decided to do the same thing, diving to my left I lay flat behind a similar spot with my rifle pulled to my shoulder. As the designated sniper I carried a 'M40A3' seconded from the US Rangers who were with us, everyone else carried a variety of automatic weapons from the famous M16 to an AK47 that Ivan had somehow gotten hold of. I focused on the source of the attack through my high-powered scope but saw nothing to fire back at and decided in that terrain simple blanket fire would do nothing but give away my exact location. To my right I could see another three of my comrade's spread across the sand in bloody tatters. That meant at most there were four of us alive assuming the bullets that had hit Tim had gone straight through and killed the man that brought us here. It felt like hours though after probably minutes, if that, it was quiet. I lay still knowing their snipers would be examining the area to reevaluate. Seconds ticked by and then a quiet voice reached me from behind the flipped jeep.

"Jean are you hit, talk to me Jean?" I didn't want to talk it didn't feel right or safe. "Jean, tell me you're good?" I heard a slight scuffle and guessed Andy was trying to stop the desperate sounding Sergeant from venturing away from shelter to find me.

"I'm good I'm good" I barked back, "Ivan looks okay too but

everyone else is fucking toast, they're dead, all dead", the reality of my words struck me and I dropped my face to the floor and gritted my teeth in fear and frustration.

"We're gonna have to move Jean, can Ivan hear you?"

"Ivan" I yelled as loud as I dare but got no response, "Ivan are you okay?" Looking ahead I saw Ivan slowly turn his head and look back at me, I thought I saw a nod. "We need to move Ivan, back up toward me", again a brief nod and then I saw the Russian boxer slowly start to crawl backward on his belly in my direction. I watched his slow progression and spoke again to Andy and the Sergeant behind the jeep. "We're coming to you, I'm waiting here for Ivan". As I spoke, I saw more movement beyond Ivan closer to the mountains. I dropped my eye back to the scope and saw that three vehicles were approaching fast and even, through the haze created by the rising heat of the day I could see that they were fully occupied. At least one of them had someone standing up right in the back manning a high caliber machine gun on a tri-pod. "Speed it up Ivan, speed it up", I began my own retreat but they were approaching too quickly, it was impossible to reach the truck unnoticed so it needed to be done quickly. The approaching enemy was under a thousand yards away now so I lay flat, tried to control my breathing and took aim, "Ivan fucking run" I screamed as I started to lose ammunition. The 'M40A3' was a high-powered sniper rifle so each shot I took mattered, unfortunately the magazine only carried five rounds, and I couldn't rush this. As I prepared to squeeze the trigger, Ivan jumped to his feet and began running toward the up turned jeep. I saw the guy manning the tripod that I could now see carried a Kalashnikov PKM Tank machine gun. I had become quite the gun expert, he braced himself ready to fire on his new quarry and then he took my first round in the centre of the forehead and was catapulted backward from his perch.

I'd killed someone. Unfortunately, as you will learn, if you choose to read on it was not my last; however, it was my first and to this day of all the things I've done that keep me awake at night, the memory of that soldier's head exploding is among the most potent images.

Right there and then in whichever damn country I was in, I still wonder if we had ventured over the border, I did not hesitate to keep killing. The truck carrying the tripod spun to a halt and I saw the driver and passenger duck down. Machine gun fire opened from the other two vehicles as they continued to advance but they were not close enough to be accurate or overly effective, hitting me would be luck. It was three seconds from my first to my second shot that went through the windscreen of the second vehicle, hitting the driver high in the chest near the base of the throat. The whole vehicle rocked as his foot fell from the accelerator and the four men in the back firing were briefly thrown off balance and ceased fire. Three seconds again and I let a bullet fly at the third vehicle, not at the driver who took my fourth shot in the face but the passenger who I noticed screaming into a walkie-talkie, last thing I wanted was him calling for back up. As my fifth shot struck the chest of a man back at the first vehicle, who was attempting to reach the idle tripod gun, I heard Ivan shout my name. I took a glance and saw that Ivan had reached the cover of the truck and, as I ejected my empty magazine and rammed home five new rounds, I ran to join Ivan, Andy and Sergeant Petit. We all sat breathing heavily and looking amongst ourselves, nobody speaking. Then I realized I had hit the man with the walkie-talkie too late. Mortar fire returned to our scene from the mountain range further away, the first hit was twenty-feet from our jeep, the second was ten-feet, the third was going to hit, no doubt. Andy grabbed Ivan by the arm as the Sergeant grabbed me and started to drag me away from the cover of the vehicle, "We've gotta get out of here" was Andy's desperate scream. Keeping the vehicle between us and the enemy we simply started to sprint, looking ahead of us it was apparent we had nowhere to run to, all that lay ahead was barren wasteland and all we could hope for was back up, but we knew that was a pipe dream. The attack had been fast and lethal, I was sure none of us had radioed for help and due to our overzealous Major I am not sure anyone knew where we were. We only got ten-feet from the jeep before it was hit, the strike must have been full on the opposite side of the vehicle as it was catapulted toward us, it struck the four of us like it had been hurtling down the autobahn, Andy and the Sergeant pushing Ivan and I ahead took the brunt but darkness instantly filled all of us.

When I awoke I was on my stomach uncomfortably close to the

burning jeep. I was totally deaf and only partially aware of my companions spread about me. I saw Andy with his hands tied behind his back and on tensing my arms realized I was in the same state of bondage. Boots stamped around me and two men in non-descript khaki uniforms grasped Andy and lifted him to his feet before pushing him toward a vehicle, I could see from the blood spattered windscreen it was one of the vehicles I had been shooting at. I could feel pain in my back which I was to learn was pieces of steel from the bodywork of the jeep; I learned this by seeing the same wounds on Ivan as he was also dragged to a waiting vehicle. As I was then dragged to my feet, my hearing started to return and through a ringing sensation I could hear people shouting orders in a strange language. I still hadn't seen my Sergeant and I desperately looked around but couldn't see him. What I did see was Major French, maybe thirty-feet from me but, clear as day, he lay motionless underneath the huge muscled body of Tim, motionless but alive, Tim's mass had stopped the bullets, saving the officer's life. His eyes were wide and terrified, his mouth agape, we locked stares for mere moments and he shook his head at me with a pleading look. I tried not to judge, I can't possibly know what I would have done had I been in his situation. I was hauled onto the flat bed of the truck next to Andy who smiled and winked at me, before the butt of a rifle was smashed into first his skull and then mine, I drifted back to darkness thinking that I had still not seen my Sergeant since I'd come around.

I have no idea how long it was before I came around again, but the sun was at its peak so it was hours not minutes. I was pulled from the floor to my knees and looked around to see I was in between Ivan and Andy, "Sergeant Petit?" I asked of Andy but took a boot in the stomach for my trouble. I doubled back to the floor and a hand took a clump of my hair dragging me back upright. As you'll have surmised from my comment about the sun we were outside, though in contrast to the scene of our capture, low mountains surrounded us as though we were in a valley. We appeared to be in a camp of at least similar size to our own and with just as much weaponry and resource. The majority of equipment I could see was covered by a variety of mesh, camouflage canopies on stilts, and under the nearest of these structures sat a large oak desk that would have looked at home in a London solicitor's office. It was on an ornately decorated red rug with black tassels and on top of it was a lap top computer with electrical cables leading from it in two directions, the first led to what appeared to be a generator, I guessed the source of any power out here as it was similar to our own back at base. The second led to what appeared to be one of the earliest domestic satellite dishes though I guest this was not the case. A squat dark figure sat behind the screen staring intently, he was constantly chewing and would occasionally hack and spit a mound of black phlegm just beyond the parameters of the impressive rug. His skin was dark and leathery making him look like he had been here in the desert all his life, and the grimace he carried beneath his loosely turbaned head made me think he had been angry since birth. It was not so much he, in his blank garb, that caught my interest but the familiar looking man dressed in white perched on the edge of the desk in conversation with him. I was sure I recognized him but why I would know anyone in this place was beyond me. The man who had kicked me in the stomach approached the man in white and he turned and glanced toward us, at that moment the pieces fell into place. I had seen this man before on television, explaining to the world why it was suffering its just desserts, as bombs he had arranged shook the very planet. He dropped some papers he was holding onto the desk and removed a pair of thick-rimmed reading glasses. On standing he delivered a few orders to those surrounding him and they in turn seemed to forward those instructions on. As 'Bda Nam Sadden Oboe', casually strode toward us the rest of his men began filing toward the opening of a large cave that I had noticed at the foot of the nearest cliffs. He stopped a couple of yards in front of his three captives and we were each dragged to our feet in front of him. On reaching my full height I was surprised to see he was almost as tall as me, at least six-feet two but of much slimmer build. He looked younger in the flesh and despite his long beard been flecked with grey his eyes looked youthful, alive and intelligent. He seemed to notice us watching his men as they started to disappear into the cave mouth; he watched his own troops for a second and then turned back to us.

"It's a real inconvenience but we have to retreat to the caves a couple of times a day, just for an hour when the American satellites pass over", his English was absolutely flawless and he explained the situation as if he were telling us why he had worked through lunch that day. The US had satellites in orbit looking for camps just like this one, however 'Bda Nam' was a step ahead and used the dish I had noticed to track the US Satellites, twice a day they would pass over but an hour before, when warned, the troops and anything with a heat signature that could be traced was hidden within the coolness of what apparently was a huge cave system. When he finished his explanation he looked at us as if expecting a response or even praise, we sat in silence. "Ah" he continued, "I suspect you are surprised by my English, you see I studied at..."

"We cudna give a fuck where yer went to school yer prick", Andy offered with undisguised venom. Two guards grasped him but before they had time to punish the insubordination 'Bda Nam' stopped them with a wave of the hand, he stepped toward Andy stopping little more than a foot in front of him.

"Do you know who I am?" he asked in a genuinely inquisitive tone. With this, Andy slammed his forehead into Bda Nam's. The terrorist's nose exploded in a spray of blood and bone, as he fell to the floor and the two guards began to beat Andy relentlessly, though he did manage to speak out.

"I'm Andy from Glasgow, y'll remember who I am will ya?" With this, I was once again struck on the head with the butt of a rifle and knocked to unconsciousness; that was really starting to piss me off. When I came around again I was cold. I was sitting upright on a small four legged wooden chair that was bolted to the floor, it had a high steel back that I could feel was in the shape of an 'X'. The cold metal running from each shoulder down to the opposite hip, passing in the middle of my back, I was naked. My ankles were bound to the front two legs of the chair, my hands were tied behind the steel back and a thick rope around my waist ensured I could not struggle free. My head was pounding like nothing I had ever experienced and I was struggling to clear my vision as I rapidly blinked to try and make things clear. When my vision did begin to clear an image began to form in front of me, as if emerging from cloudy water my eyes finally rested on the smiling face of Sergeant Petit. The relief that washed over me was amazing considering our situation, like me he was tied to a similar chair stripped of his clothing which was piled with mine, Ivan's and Andy's to the right.

"You're alive," I said coming as close to a smile as I could.

"Happy Birthday Jean", he returned my forced smile. Christ he was right, I was thirty-five that day. I'd been a Legionnaire a year and in Afghanistan almost all of it. I couldn't believe the time that had passed since the attacks around the world and now I was in a cave, no doubt inside Pakistan, and a captive of the very man who had orchestrated the global explosions. Dried blood matted the Sergeant's hair leading me to believe he had also been on the receiving end of a rifle butt a couple of times.

"Where were you?"

"Jeep I was in had a flat half way and the bastards made me change the wheel. I just got here".

I looked around the room where my three brothers-in-arms and I were all bound in the same way. We were facing inward as if we were each at the point of a compass, Sergeant opposite, Ivan to my left and Andy to my right. Andy was in the worst state and still unconscious. After his head butt 'Bda Nam's' men had thrown him a real beating, his face was swollen, his nose broken and bruises were all ready turning viciously black all over his body.

"Jesus, what did they do to Andy?" asked the Sergeant who like me was studying Andy's injuries. Before I could answer there was a noise at the heavy steel door. We all froze focused on the door but at this point nobody entered. I surveyed the rest of the room, or should I say cave. The floor was flat, leveled out with concrete but the walls were the jagged interior of a cave. In its entirety the cave was probably fifteen-feet square, around us were a variety of white clinical looking tables that contrasted strangely with the dark, cold, rock walls. What was arranged on those tables made my blood run cold and fear began to absorb me. Two tables held a variety of bottles, jars and test tubes and looked like they belonged behind the counter in a pharmacy. A white cloth lay next to the chemicals and potions; it was piled high with syringes.

The other two tables were far more chilling; these were covered in other medical looking equipment, scalpels and a variety of other blades as well as a plethora of tools that I couldn't identify. All were chrome and gleamed under the florescent light cast by a single strip bulb hanging from a chain in the rock ceiling, they looked well maintained, clean and cared for, and they looked sharp and terrifying.

"This place looks like a hospital", I said it half to myself, maybe to add something to the deafening silence. Andy had obviously come around and had a response.

"Well Jean, much as I'd 'ate t'ave to watch it. Given the alternative I'd rather it be Nurse Picard come through that door and give yer a blow job". I spun to look at Andy, who was gradually creeping toward laughter, then the Sergeant and Ivan joined in and the laughter grew stronger and louder.

"You knew!" I exclaimed. As ridiculous as it sounds, for that moment I forgot where I was and my mouth fell open. Through his laughter Ivan managed to speak

"What! Jean she screamed like a bloody hyena, I reckon they knew in Paris". With this the three of them erupted into absolute hysteria and seconds later I joined them. I have heard that this happens in extreme situations as a safety mechanism, however to this day the intensity of humour we were enjoying at that moment seems bizarre. Even when the door flew open and 'Bda Nam' stormed in with two of his guards the uncontrollable laughter continued.

"What is this?" he yelled looking furious. He was wearing his thick reading glasses sitting on a hugely swollen red nose that Andy had given him; his bearded was wild and bushy. Our eyes watering, the laughter was diluting to chuckles when the Sergeant looked up at him.

"Jesus Christ" he said, "you're 'Bda Nam Sadden Oboe'", with this Bda Nam seemed to thrust out his jaw almost with pride, "well

I have to say" continued the Sergeant, "that really is a shit disguise!" with this the four of us erupted back into hysteria and I was literally crying as if I were at a comedy show.

The two guards looked furious but confused as they looked from us to Bda Nam and at each other; unfortunately their leader knew how to stop the hilarity. Stepping into the centre of our circle he withdrew a side arm, pointed it and shot Ivan between the eyes at point blank range.

"Nooooo" I screamed and began convulsing as I strained to release myself from my bindings and my tears turned from those of hilarity to pain. Bda Nam turned and smashed the heavy pistol across my face breaking my jaw. The Sergeant sat in silence just staring at 'Bda Nam' with a look that should kill, Andy stared at Ivan also in silence, and there is no other way to describe the look on his face than heartbroken.

"You will have little to laugh about in your coming days", 'Bda nam' and his men left the room and the heavy door slammed behind them.

I genuinely don't want to talk about the following days, weeks and what transpired to be months. I don't think you would enjoy reading about it and to this day it remains hard for me to think about it, which I still do often on an involuntary basis. Some bits are relevant and you will need to know as we proceed with my story, I should also provide glimpses that will hopefully give an indication of what we went through, but spare you the graphic details of the horror that haunts me still. Everything that did happen was right there in the room I described, Ivan's body was never removed and he stayed with us over the months as he decayed before our eyes, when the inevitable delirium of torture came we began to include him in our conversations.

The first day, again I will touch on it only because its relevance will become clear, electrical cables were attached to the backs of our chairs one at a time. What felt like a million volts seared through my system and I felt the 'X' of the chairs back grow hot and burn into my skin. This was the most regular act performed on us, as it didn't require the effort from our captures that basic beatings did.

At first, the two of us who were observers would scream and shout for the punishment of the third to stop. I am ashamed to say this soon stopped and when I was not the one receiving the attention I would sit in a lifeless slump, the screams of my brothers seeming distant as if coming to me through water and, in honesty, part of me was glad each time I wasn't the recipient. The reason for our treatment also became obsolete in reality; they were asking me questions about placement and strategy that I genuinely did not know the answers to. Eventually I did not even try to respond with a denial, as it made little difference and speaking was an effort. My mouth was sore and full of blood where they had torn some teeth out with pliers. The teeth were scattered about me on the floor and, I would occasional look at them and marvel at how white they were at the root, compared to the visible tooth that had darkened due to the diet my step mother provided. Ironically, we were well fed and watered. Also, after each session a doctor would spend time with us, treating at least the physical damage that had been done, truth is they wanted our bodies to live for more torture, and for another plan they had.

In the evenings, we would drift in and out of a half slumber and at times even try and lift each other's spirits. We would take it in turns to tell stories of where we wished we were, and the listeners would close their eyes tight and use a developing imagination to travel to those places. I was often called upon to tell the story of the day we all met despite the fact that we were of course all there, when we got to the part where the Sergeant thought there was shit on my face and stabbed me with his bayonet, we would all come as close to laughter as was possible.

Time passed and things got worse, each torture became almost tolerable as I learned some kind of immunity, but variation is the key to a good torturer and our hosts were very talented in their craft. I did not know how long I had been there on one particular day when 'Bda Nam' visited us and stood speaking with the men who were tasked with our treatment. My head was drooped and I could feel my beard against my chest, when I tried to look up I was peering through a matted fringe, where as my hair had been only an inch or so long when I was captured. The conversation between 'Bda Nam' and his men was laced with frustration and he pointed at us one at a time and made observations in a language I still didn't understand. He then seemed to settle on Andy and he stood behind him with his hand on his shoulder as if a selection had been made, Andy just stared at me as if he knew what was coming. A guard stepped behind the Sergeant and me and our heads were grasped in a vice like grip as we were held looking directly at Andy. I started to weep; I had been praying to die for some time, I'd been praying for us all to die, but something changed in me as 'Bda Nam' slipped a thick clear plastic bag over Andy's head. He took a roll of gaffer tape and tightly taped its bottom around Andy's neck, at first Andy tried to smile at me in defiance but that changed and we watched the inevitable conclusion. Attention was then back on us and more questions I did not know the answers too were followed by more punishment. That night I began speaking to the Sergeant in painful whispers, when I first started talking the cold air stung my gums and I licked them and inadvertently knocked out my last tooth that fell to join its previous neighbors on the floor.

"Sergeant", nothing, "Sergeant", he raised his head and looked at me, somehow forcing a grin.

"Sergeant we've gotta kill these bastards, we've gotta get out of here", miraculously his grin turned to a smile and he spoke to me clearly and strong.

"You will Jean, I know you will. There's a reason we met Jean and this is it, I know that now. I made you into a soldier Jean, an amazing soldier and I'm proud of you, I love you as a son. You fucking kill these guys for me, then you finish your list and I'll be smiling over you".

"No, I'll get us both out of here, I swear. You have to help me with that list, without you pushing me I can't do anything". He continued to smile at me but no more was said that night, I'm not sure we spoke again before our last day as 'Bda Nam's' guests

When that day came I was torn between a realization that I had failed both my beloved Sergeant and myself, and desperation beyond explanation that I must deliver on my previous promises. I had to prove my promises were not hollow and we were not both going to die in those caves.

It transpired that I had been in that one cave for nearly eight months, eight months of hell, sitting in my own waste watching people I loved being slowly killed. Then I had to witness their bodies' rot away in front of me. Despite everything on that last day fear gripped me like nothing before; the change of routine was petrifying. 'Bda Nam' entered barking orders at our all too familiar torturers. Both the Sergeant and I had canvas bags placed over our heads and then tied at the neck. They were threadbare and damp and I could still make out some movement through the patchy weave of the fabric. I felt handcuffs placed on my wrists before the ropes that previously bound them were cut.

"The first one of you to struggle or cause me a problem will see the other instantly executed. Am I clear?" I saw movement that indicated the Sergeant was nodding inside his bag so I emulated that I understood what 'Bda Nam' was saying.

The rest of our bindings were cut and I was dragged to my feet where I instantly fell having not stood for so long. I was hauled back to upright three times before I finally and steadily managed to support myself. I was walked slowly through the iron door, the opening of which had been a sign of agony to come for as long as I could remember. The Sergeant had not recovered the ability to support himself and was dragged along by his arms, his legs beginning to bleed as the stone floor cut in. From what I could see we were walked down a narrow passage illuminated by an intermittent line of halogen lamps that flickered constantly. As I walked along I tried to focus and subtly test at the new force that held my wrists together. I could tell by the texture on my skin that the handcuffs were rusty and my hands were around four inches apart allowing some movement unlike the rope that had bound them solidly together. After a few minutes we entered another room not dissimilar to the one I had just left, though this one looked more like an armory, piled high with boxed weaponry. The top box on each pile was open and a sample of its contents displayed on top making the whole place look like a sales showroom. I was roughly forced onto another chair, that was also bolted to the floor, my hands were placed around the upright back and a leather belt wrapped around the back of the chair at my waist held me still. My hood was pulled from my head and my suspicion was confirmed, I was in an arsenal. Rocket launchers, ground to air missiles and what looked like actual rocket mounted war heads were around me, as well as a multitude of firearms, grenades and landmines. As before the Sergeant was sat facing me but further away, maybe eight-feet instead of four. His hood had also been removed and he looked at me blankly, his jaw set. One of the two men who had been tasked with our torture stood in front of me slightly to the left, he was dressed in desert fatigues and he had a side arm attached to a belt about his waist. His colleague stood to my right and I was confused to see that he was getting ready to operate a video camera that was focused at present on the Sergeant and 'Bda Nam' who was standing behind him, with one hand on his shoulder. The man at the camera nodded that all was well and then he walked to the Sergeant and attached a thick piece of tape across his mouth, a realization began to dawn and I was about to start my protests when a similar gag was attached to my face. The first guard remained in front of me with his back turned watching 'Bda Nam' as he lifted a long bladed machete and rested its flat side on the Sergeant's right shoulder where his hand had previously been. The second guard retook his position behind the camera and waited for a nod from his leader, when the nod came he counted from five to one silently with the fingers of his left hand, finishing with a thumbs up at which point 'Bda Nam' commenced his well rehearsed performance. His words were a verbal haze in my ears but as I have said before, even if I recalled the shit he was spewing I would not grace his memory by repeating them now. You get the gist I'm sure, evil west, atoning for our sins, one true God etc, the weapons I detailed provided the backdrop to the scene that was being filmed. I followed a cable that ran from the camera to a new looking laptop computer and a second cable running from there up through what looked like a man made hole in the ceiling of the cave. I knew what was coming and it engulfed me with fear, desperation and rage. I gritted my teeth behind my gag and I pulled my wrists apart using every muscle in my body, the handcuffs would just not budge but as I watched 'Bda Nam' become more animated in his grotesque performance I dug deeper and willed more strength to flow through my arms. 'Bda Nam' was getting louder and any resemblance to humanity was gone as he raised the machete high and to the right ready to sweep it down on my Sergeant.

Something gave, I didn't feel it but my hands were definitely a couple of millimeters wider apart than before, I was sure of it. I reapplied my efforts, physically I gave it everything I had, ever had or that was ever to come and mentally I was praying to anything that might be listening whilst purely trying to will my freedom. I did all this silently; teeth gritted behind the makeshift gag so those who had applied it would not hear me and turn to look. I ignored the pain of the rusty handcuffs cutting into the outside of my wrists. The two guards were mesmerized by their leader and the man behind the camera, the one who's face I could see in profile, looked borderline euphoric.

'Bda Nam's' blade reached the top of its arc as his words reached crescendo, for a brief second he paused, looked at the Sergeants neck, took aim and began bringing the lethal blade toward its target. The sharp edge hit its mark and my Sergeants eyes doubled in size, whilst still fixed on mine that freely wept. Even with all his force 'Bda Nam had only been able to bury his machete less than two inches into Sergeant Petits neck. The instant and continuous spurts of crimson fluid left no doubt he had penetrated arteries and it was simply thick muscle that had slowed the cut. 'Bda Nam' looked frustrated that he had not delivered to his audience the precise execution he had wanted. He began to look clumsy, as his strength did not allow him to withdraw his blade from the muscles that had now gone into spasm in his victim. Seeming almost embarrassed he attempted to begin a sawing motion that allowed the incision it had created to go deeper. The huge eyes of the Sergeant grew smaller and as they finally closed and his head lolled to the side away from the direction of the savage attack, my handcuffs came in two. I heard the weak link land on the stone floor below me. Without hesitation, I began to undo the leather belt about my waist as I looked around the evil in the room; no one had yet noticed my escape. Free, I stood behind the first of the men who had tortured me for what felt like a lifetime and helped to kill three people I loved. I was no more than a foot behind him and I realized for the first time how slight he was. I reached forward putting my right hand forward and clamping it firmly across his mouth, looking back now I am ashamed to say that Like 'Bda Nam' I had lost any semblance of humanity. I inverted my left hand and put it on the back of his head facing my first hand, then without pause or hesitation I used the same force that had broken my handcuffs and I snapped his neck like dry kindling. I had never noticed before how young he was, what brought it to my attention now was his youthful unlined eyes, such was the rage of his murder, his head had turned a full one hundred and eighty degrees and for the last second of his life that boys eyes were looking directly into mine. I suspect that it was the sound of the cracking neck bones that drew his attention, but 'Bda Nam' was suddenly looking at me and screaming orders at the cameraman, having reverted to his native tongue. I looked back to my right to see the second guard scrambling desperately for his side arm, but my bloodlust for revenge had made me calmer and quicker. I let go of the head of the boy I had just murdered and grasped the handle of the pistol he wore at his side. His falling body did the job of unsheathing the automatic weapon and without pause I raised my arm and put two rounds straight into the skull of his colleague, catapulting him backward to hit the wall before slumping to the floor in a bloody heap.

'Bda Nam', who was unarmed, stood frozen to the spot, looking at me mouth agape, struggling to comprehend his predicament. I kept the stolen pistol low at my side and took the three steps required to be standing in front of my Sergeant. My thoughts then, were some of those that still haunt me to this day, why didn't the cuffs snap sooner, if I was strong enough to do it why didn't I do it quicker, I was seconds from saving him, seconds. I switched the pistol to my left hand and although I was somehow aware that 'Bda Nam's' eyes had began fleeting around the room for help, I kept focus on the Sergeant's still form. I put my right hand on his head and closed my eyes for a second, almost in the hope that when I reopened them my nightmare would be over, it wasn't. 'Bda Nam' seemed set to move, but when my eyes did open they locked on his and he again froze. I was surprised by the terror that projected through those eyes and I could see he had begun trembling where he stood. The stench of the dead began to fill the room and it reminded me of my previous cell and those I had lost, my hate doubled. I took my right hand from the head of my Sergeant and, reaching around, I took hold of the handle attached to 'Bda Nam's' machete. It was another effort for me to bunch the muscle in my bicep and free it from the deep tear it had made in flesh. Flipping it around I turned the blade and lifted the point, pressing it on the sweating neck of the man who had tried to destroy the world. Our eyes remained locked.

"Why would anyone want to worship a God who wants him to do these things to other people?" although distorted by the pain in my mouth, the steadiness of my voice felt unnatural. 'Bda Nam' swallowed and eventually struggled to speak.

"You deserve it, Infidels like you have ravaged my lands for...", I wasn't going to let him finish.

"Like me? You know nothing about me, or any of my friends that you killed. Friends of all faiths including Muslims", he tried to continue.

"A Muslim who fights alongside the infidels also deserves..." again I cut him off.

"They deserve to be tortured and killed too? It seems to me that you are making these decisions, not your God." Suddenly arrogance seemed to come over him and his eyes turned back to the eyes of the man who had executed my Sergeant.

"I am my God", he declared defiantly, "to go against me is to go against him, as he and I are joined in total unison. So yes I decide who will live and who will die, as God himself requires it of me. If my thoughts tell me to kill they are just, as they are God's thoughts", there was a pause and his nerves seemed to reappear, as I twisted the machete in my hand, drawing a small spot of blood at the tip where it touched his neck.

"And what do you suppose my thoughts are telling me to do now?" Fear was back in his face but he managed to speak again.

"Killing me will just magnify my cause, martyr me and my rewards in paradise will be magnificent, I cherish this end as if I were ending it myself". I can't explain my next actions, only to say in my head and heart I was already dead, and I did not really care what outcome came from this cave as long as 'Bda Nam' was dead also.

"Then take your exit", I spoke the words as I nodded toward one of the boxes stacked behind him. Lowering my blade slightly and dropping the pistol from my left hand, I continued as it clattered to the floor, "take both of us to our respective hell or paradise, prove your faith", he paused for a second before rapidly taking a step to his right and returning to his start position with a hand-grenade in his left hand, the forefinger of his right hand already in the ring, which was attached to a pin, that would arm the small bomb. I stood and watched him in silence; somehow I knew what his actions would be, as I'd seen it in him. He began to shake aggressively and then tears began to run down his face, I left him in silence and waited, his finger came away from the pin and he looked at me with desperation.

"Go on" I pushed

"I, I don't think my God wants me to die yet", it sounded pathetic and terrified, it was.

I held out my left hand and he weakly handed me the grenade that could have killed us both.

"You should know, I don't care what your God wants, you're going to die today", he swallowed again and stared at me harder, relieving himself in his trousers. I brought my right arm across my left shoulder and with a backhand swing I used every fiber of muscle in my body, and emotion in my heart. My blade took his head from his neck as if he had been made of warm butter. At the end of my swing I felt steel smash against steel as the camera, that had been rolling the whole time, was shattered to pieces. "Bda Nam's' body remained standing for several seconds before collapsing next to his decapitated head, which still had the same terrified expression.

I stood breathing heavily. I was finished. I had already decide my next plan, I would sit with my Sergeant until one of 'Bda Nam's' men found us and hope that in their rage they would kill me quickly. I dropped to my knees and took Sergeant Petit's hand in mine, as I stared at the floor a broken whisper of a voice spoke to me.

"Did you kill them Jean?" my head shot upright and I looked into a pair of glazed eyes. With the effort to speak the blood flow again machine guns, hand grenades as well as one reusable Bazooka with a box of ten missiles at the end of the corridor, just out of sight of my quarry. I would use the Bazooka as a last resort, I did not want to set fire to the jeeps and block the enemy's exit and I had also never fired one and was not sure how, or even if they were powerful enough to bring the whole bloody cave down on us. On each trip, I risked another peek into the main cave and was relieved each time to see them relaxed and paying little attention to their surroundings. This made me think maybe they had no idea what had been happening in the camera room that morning. On my last trip I collected something else I thought I might need should I escape and kept it by my side. Then I stood with my back against the wall at the corridors entrance, an AK47 assault rifle hanging around my neck and a grenade in each hand. First I needed to cause panic, to minimize retaliation, but I also realized, to my surprise, I had no desire to kill two hundred soldiers. I wanted my attack to be close to me so they would all run in the direction of the caves exit and not in all directions, including toward me. On that basis I withdrew the pin from each grenade and then simply dropped them around the corner to bounce down the three or four steps that led to the main cave. There was no reaction at first; no one could hear two small, steel bombs plink down the stairs over their heated debates and laughter. Then, in the same way they had to me eight months earlier in the open desert, I unleashed hell on them.

The explosions echoed around the cave and were deafening. I

had a multitude of levels following the natural carvings of the mountain and scattered across it appeared to be no less than two hundred of 'Bda Nam's' soldiers. They sat all over the cave in smaller groups chatting, laughing and in some cases playing games with cards or dice. I eased myself back into the recess of the corridor for a moment thinking and coming up with nothing before taking a second furtive glance.

I could see the exit to the cave opposite me, therefore placing every single man between freedom and me. The entrance was also bigger than I recalled when I had seen it from the outside, big enough for several of the jeeps that did not have camouflage nets to drive in and these were parked in a row to the left of the gaping cave mouth. Then it hit, the nets were there to hide things from satellite view, the only possible reason that every Tom, Dick and Harry was in the cave must be that a satellite was passing over and they were hiding, I recalled 'Bda Nam' boasting about two passes a day and the fact that they were ahead of the Americans. Somehow I needed a heat signature that a satellite could recognize outside that cave, I had to drive the Toms, Dicks and Harry's back into the open valley so my allies could see them and come to my rescue.

I tiptoed back to the camera room and tuck a quick survey of what I had; well it was pretty much enough to start World War Three on my own. I gave silent thanks that 'Bda Nam' had proved to be such an egomaniac and had wanted his arsenal on display whilst he murdered us for the camera. Three trips placed a stockpile of ran to the door, nothing but adrenalin fueling every movement. Pulling it slightly open I saw that the dim, rock corridor outside was deserted, although I could hear loud conversation that sounded like it came from many men. I tried to recall my hooded journey from earlier and guessed that my previous abode must be around twenty feet in the opposite direction to the crowd I could hear. Staying low, I ran along the hard floor and soon found the iron door I sought still standing ajar. I crept in and found the room still only occupied by the empty corpses of Ivan and Andy. Trying not to look at my friends' bodies, I ran to the clothes that had been piled against the cave wall for eight months. Finding mine was not a problem and I was not surprised that they still fit me, as you know at this stage I had no fat to lose and again they had fed us well to keep us healthy for prolonged torture. I pulled on my combat trousers and t-shirt and quickly fasted my boots over my standard issue desert socks, I grabbed the identification tags for all four of us and tucked them into the thigh pocket of my trousers, as I did my fingers touched the small red box that contained the bracelet I cherished and my list which I felt I was going to need.

With one last look around the hell that had been my home, I slipped back into the corridor and stealthily headed past the video room. I allowed myself a discreet glance around the corner when I got to the corridors end, what I saw hit me like a nine-millimeter round in the heart. The cave was larger than I could have imagined, at least the size of a professional football pitch and its cathedral like ceiling was as high as the cave was wide. The floor increased from the mortal neck wound. I reached to the first dead guard and tore the turban from his head; kneeling up higher I pressed it hard against the bleeding mess causing a wince from my Sergeant, he was alive.

"Did you kill them?' he repeated

"I did Sergeant I did", tears poured from my eyes, fear, relief, disbelief, "I'm going to get us out of here".

"Not me Jean", his voice was barely audible and I leaned in close. "This is it for me", he took a rasping breath and blood ran from his mouth, which I swept away with my free hand, mouthing the word 'no' I was unable to actually put volume to it. "It's okay Jean I'm ready. I am so proud of you Jean, so proud" he somehow managed to offer me half a smile, "your list Jean, get out of here and finish it for me, I'll be watching. I love you Jean, my son".

Those were his last words; I stayed with him for several more minutes before his pulse actually weakened to nothing, and the inevitable groan of his last breath left his lungs. He kept talking to me though, in my head his voice was still there and it was the strong voice of the Sergeant I had met years before, when he was barking orders at an obese dreamer who had achieved nothing.

"Now get the fuck up and get out of here", the familiar voice yelled in my inner ear.

Looking at the bodies around me, I realized that none of their attire was going to fit me, so I had to get my own kit from the torture cave. I leant forward and kissed my Sergeant on the forehead.

"Get the Fuck out of here NOW", he repeated louder in my head. I ceiling, sticking to my sweat and blood soaked face and arms. Return fire continued but it was less accurate and more sporadic, I guess those left were retreating. I loaded a second missile and sprang to view again confirming my suspicion, the last twenty or thirty men were running toward the exit giving each other cover fire as they staggered their escape. I let one more missile fly and strike the ground some distance behind them purely to eliminate any second thoughts they might have. Once my second Bazooka explosion faded, I was left in the silence of the cave, nothing but the voices of my crazed enemy reaching in from the distance outside.

I hesitated and looked around the cave again, seeing nobody alive or moving I hung a belt of grenades across my shoulder, placed the freshly recharged bazooka across my back and retrieved the other item I had taken from the camera room. I began to head down the steps with the AK to my shoulder. I had to make sure my plan would work and I assumed, and prayed, there would be radios in the jeeps just inside the caves entrance. I carefully made my way in that direction. The noise outside seemed miles away in another world, and the cave itself had the eeriness of an empty church. As I neared the entrance, and the jeeps, one guy's head peeped inside to look back toward the carnage they had fled. He was rewarded, by losing that head in a hail of bullets. I took advantage of the retreat I was sure I'd just caused by sprinting the last twenty-yards between the vehicles and me. I crouched tight behind the rear wheel of the first jeep and edged my way along to the passenger side door, stepped into view taking shoulder high aim with the AK, I had the full intention of firing over their heads to simply drive them out. Unfortunately, many of these men were braver than their former leader. Despite the first group of men being at least ten feet from the bottom of the stairs where the grenades had detonated, they all lay dead or mortally wounded, at least six of them. Beyond them, a few were running in the direction I had intended, most were frozen to the spot confused, the closer ones holding their ears, alas a good number were retrieving weapons and running in my direction. I lowered my aim and began to mow down human beings, sweeping my muzzle side to side to defend from all angles. Bodies fell and more men ran toward the safety of the sun in the valley, yet more still ran toward me and now fire was returned. I dove back to the corridor and the box of grenades that I had retrieved, as quick as possible I began ripping out safety pins and hurling grenades around the corner, five, ten, twenty. Screams were now intense but the bullets kept pouring toward me, chips of hot rock showering down on me; I feared I would be killed by a ricochet but it was a little late to think of that. I squatted to my haunches and dragged the Bazooka toward me; I read the instructions printed on the long circular tube, which for some reason seemed a stupid place to put them. I waited until I was convinced there was a lull in the fire and sprang around the corner. In a heartbeat, I saw the largest group of men had taken refuge behind a small ridge in the caves floor. I pointed, aimed and pulled and was back in my corridor before the next heartbeat. The entire cave rocked and dust fell on me from the keeping the vehicle between the threat from outside and myself.

I saw immediately that the vehicle that I had my back to didn't carry what I was looking for. Through the window of the very next one I saw the mic of a walkie-talkie hanging from the rear view mirror, the spiral cord leading down to the tuning console. As I reached the handle and slipped inside, I was concerned that the voices outside had hushed and seemed more organized, I had the feel they were planning, and I had to be quick. I grasped the mic and looked down at the consul, it looked pretty simple to use, a green button that switched it on and a tuner wheel that guided a digital display through the frequencies. The problem was I had absolutely no idea what frequency to look for. I simply started to slowly swivel the knob and listen for a response as I somewhat pathetically repeated the word 'Hello' into the mic, whilst holding the speak switch down with my thumb. The first voice to scream back sounded just like 'Bda Nam' and in panic I quickly twisted the digital dial past that one, then the first bullets started from the mouth of the cave. I held the gun in the air to lay down some cover fire and hurled two of the ten grenades that I had left into the entrance, before continuing with my frantic radio efforts. My friends outside remained quiet and my 'hello's' were accompanied with, 'please help me' by the time a voice eventually replied in a Southern American accent.

"This is Alpha Red US command two-twenty-six, please identify yourself", thank Christ echoed through my head.

"Hi, it's Jean, I need help", after all I had been through it was all I could muster and things such as the phonetic alphabet had left my head.

"Please identify unit code and password of the day", crackled the voice, as a barrage of bullets once again exploded toward me.

"What?" I screamed back down the mic, annoyance overtaking my pleas "I don't know what the fucking password is I've been in a cave for eight months", more rounds hit overhead and I threw two more grenades to try and delay the inevitable.

"Unit code and password of the day" was barked like an order but with a wavering authority, as he must have been able to hear what was happening.

"Are you fucking deaf? Can you hear what's going on here? We were captured by 'The Brothers of God' months ago, four of us but they're all dead. I'm trying to hold a platoon of their men outside a cave so you can see them on your satellite. I think just inside Pakistan maybe, I don't know but I need help", the silence seemed like an age. When the voice returned, after I had hurled a few more grenades, it was a completely different tone.

"Are you the guy on the internet?" The Southern accent was now stronger and sounded almost apologetic.

"Huh?" it had never occurred to me that what was been filmed in that cave was been transmitted live around the world, "if you mean did I just decapitate 'Bda Nam' then yeah, that must have been me".

"Jesus H Christ, I don't know who the fuck you are son, but if you are telling the truth I suspect your location is gonna be incinerated in about eight minutes. Satellite picked something up, fire is go and launch was successful". What did I just hear?

"Are you shitting me? Call it off", all this and I was gonna get killed by my bloody allies.

"No can do son, I suggest you get the hell outta there quick sharp".

I didn't wait for any more conversation but delivered a return barrage of fire, threw another grenade and reached in to start the engine of the first jeep. Placing a nearby rock on the accelerator, I aimed it at the entrance to the cave and let it go. As I reseeded further behind the second truck I took aim and released the last of my Bazooka shells, hitting the first truck just as it passed the entrance of the cave. Before that explosion had even began to subside, I burst through the flames in the second truck, steering with one hand and pulling the pins from grenades with my other before throwing them toward any gathering of men I could see, also trying to figure out my surroundings.

First, I just concentrated on getting as much distance between the cave and me as possible, figuring their main focus would be there. Bullets seemed to riddle the jeep, and the radio I had used exploded inches from my hand. The only gap I could see in the steep valley walls was to my left around quarter of a mile away, and praying I was right, I gunned the small jeep toward it, keeping my head low as bullets continued to strike all around. As the opening became nearer, I could see tire tracks worn deep into the sand indicating regular use so I knew I was heading in the right direction. A few more seconds and I'd be home free. Well, I'd be in a shot up 'Al-Qaida' jeep somewhere in Pakistan with an army chasing me, but certainly in a better situation than I was a couple of hours ago. Then the earth shook, the first ground missile struck the heart of the compound putting a wall of fire between my pursuers and me but also throwing my vehicle into the air. It landed high on its front wheels and my face smashed forward into the windscreen breaking my nose so that fresh blood mixed with the sweat, rock dust and dried blood that already covered my face. I was in luck, (bizarre statement at this stage I know), as the jeep smashed back down onto all four wheels, but the tires were ablaze and the vehicle was struggling as if it were stuck in a low gear. I gunned the accelerator and prayed to anyone who might be listening. I finally rounded the base of a steep hill and disappeared from the view of anyone in the valley. As I heard more powerful strikes I risked a look back seeing mushroom clouds forming into the sky behind me, I could hear nothing as my ears numbed for the force of the blasts. Ahead of me was just desert, nothing but endless heat searing desert, I didn't care I just drove, my body and mind as numb as my ears, I was incapable of thought.

In time, my ears lulled to a dull ringing and then they started to hear other things, a slow dull beating that felt like it was sneaking up behind me and getting louder. I ignored the hallucination until it became all the more real, and as a shadow cast over me kicking up the earth all around in a violent sand storm, I again prayed for death. The black helicopter gun-ship rotated overhead to face me before landing around twenty meters in front of me to the left, then its twin took a symmetrical station to the right. I came to a stop and sat with my hands on the steering wheel just looking out at my new visitors. When I saw figures in full combat gear jumping from the intimidating airborne tanks, I reached into the foot well on the passenger side of the jeep. The last thing I had retrieved from the camera room in the cave had been thrown from the seat that it rested on when the missile had catapulted me forward. I picked it up with my left hand, exited the vehicle and walked straight ahead to a point just in front of the jeep and between the two helicopters. As the blade atop each vehicle began to slow, and the dust and sand slightly settled, I saw the teams of elite forces soldiers who had exited their transport, and formed an arch in front of me, all on one knee weapons at the ready.

"Hands in the fucking air", was directed at me from one of them, I'm not sure which. "Do you speak English?" the voice from the storm followed up with, 'do I speak English?' Then I realized. I had hair to my shoulders and a beard almost to my chest, my skin could be any color under the filth that also made any distinguishable attire I was wearing unrecognizable. My clothes were matted with blood; my own where wounds had reopened during my struggle, Sergeant Petits and that of the man who had murdered him. "Raise your God damn hands" rang in my ears and this time I slowly obeyed. The chopper blades came to a stop and eventually the sand finally settled to give my fellow desert dwellers and me the ability to see each other more clearly. I saw a team of US Rangers, no doubt colleagues of Jay, they saw a broken, blood and mud soaked vision of death, a cross between the old man at sea and an after battle Genghis Khan. They saw an unrecognizable man on the edge of death, standing in the desert, his left hand held in the air, his right hand just above shoulder level as his strength was gone and that was as high as he could lift 'Bda Nam Sadden Oboes' head, which dangled from fingertips that grasped his thick black hair.

One by one the Americans stood looking for the world like they did not believe what they were seeing, one by one they dropped their weapons to their sides and one by one they walked toward me. As the first approached he drew close and spoke,

"Who are you?" he asked. I collapsed in his arms and he grasped me around the chest, "don't worry son" he said, "I've got you", in my head, to this day; I swear that my Sergeant whispered the same words.

The last few times I have stated that I 'awoke', it was each time a little closer to hell, this time things seemed to have improved considerably. My mind was still in hell; images of what I had seen, what had been done to my friends and me and what I had done to others still consumed my mind and body, even as my eyelids fluttered open. I was on a small but comfortable bed and although my hearing, sight and in fact none of my senses were one hundred percent, I seemed to be surrounded with people who were trying to help me, who cared. Nothing had complete clarity, images became clear and returned to blurred, and likewise sounds developed detail only to once more become vague and slurred. I was comfortable, a completely alien sensation so I did not want to move, yet I was still afraid and wanted to know where I was so I strained to understand more of my surroundings. People leaned in close and lights were shined in my eyes, I was aware of a plastic liquid filled bag hanging by my side with a tube running to my right arm. People observed and commented on my movement as I let my head roll side to side and noticed my blooded fatigues on a chair next to my bed.

"Do we know who he is yet?" asked a tall black guy in a white coat.

"Not a clue, he's been talking in his sleep and we think he's French", it was another white-coated man who offered the reply, stimulating further questions from the new arrival.

"His clothes gave nothing away?"

"Pair of combat trousers and a white t-shirt, European issue boots but nothing to tie him to a regiment or even a country".

"Well make sure we take care of him, everyone on the planet is talking about what he did on that video and, whoever this 'soldier X' guy is, the world is calling him an absolute hero". With this he left and over the next few minutes his colleagues followed one by one until I was left alone to rest.

It took almost as much strain as my efforts in the cave but I managed to lean slightly and stretch out my arm, grasping my war stained combat trousers I pulled them from the chair onto my chest and then paused to regain my breath. Reaching into the thigh pocket I retrieved my red box and rolled my bracelet over my wrist, I then took my list and the small pencil I kept in the box. Trying to focus my eyes on the warn page I remembered the doctor's words and I gently drew a line through the words 'become a hero'. I then laid back and thought of what it had taken for me to draw that line, and as I cried myself to sleep I wished to God I had not reached that achievement.

Chapter 4

Achievement number three.

Win an Olympic Gold Medal

(& achievement number 4)

Yeah, I know you'll just have to bear with me on this one, but before your mockery loses control, ask yourself, did you really believe I'd achieve the first two things on my list? No? Neither did I. Now, I have to admit that this one really was a stretch and I never really took it seriously, of course the first time it was read from my list all those years before it was not really taken seriously either. I don't want to constantly honour the memory of the sanctimonious arse who took such pride in humiliating a child in front of his peers, so essentially I'll leave his narration to your imagination, needless to say it went along the lines of, 'is there an Olympic medal for fantasy or day dreaming' etc and my class mates continued their uncontrollable belly laughing at my expense.

Anyway, where were we? For three weeks I only saw people in white coats. A variety of them that merged into one hybrid through my blurred eyes, which only seemed to open when one of these caring ghosts appeared in the room, even then only for a second or less. I always tried to keep my eyes open as when they closed, be it to sleep or even just to blink, the visions that filled my mind were of the horrific experience that you and I have already revisited. My hosts seemed to have given up on trying to identify me. I had not managed a coherent sentence during my stay; despite this they all seemed intent on waffling on to me in friendly tones that I could rarely segregate into words. For some reason they all referred to me simply as 'X', or Mr 'X' in the case of some of the younger looking images. It was, I learned, some time toward the end of that third week, when words and images began to clear in my mind. I was able to think and focus on more than the nightmares that haunted me day and night. At this time, my body and mind finally allowed me to actually respond to one of the regular visitors who, as always, chatted away aimlessly as he mopped the wooden floor around my steel framed bed.

"You really are missing out 'X'", his Southern American accent almost singing the words and reminding me of the first westerner I had managed to speak to, on the radio from the cave. This new guy worked away with a smile across his face, "world's still wondering who the hell you are but I reckon if you'd just tell us, me and you could hit some bars and pick up some girls, toothless as you are I reckon you're gonna find it pretty easy to get laid from now on". I ran my tongue around my bare gums and fought to suppress the memory this evoked, when I remembered how they came to be this way. I didn't feel strong enough to raise my head but questions had started to formulate inside it.

"Where am I?' the room seemed to freeze as the Southern chatterbox dropped his mop and stood for a few seconds, motionlessly staring at me. His red hair reminded me of Pete, the Australian who had shared my last hospital room with me back at the fort, and that felt like a million years ago. The resemblance ended at hair colour, the man in front of me now had a face which shone as red as the hair due to the sheer quantity of orange freckles that peppered his skinny face. His eyes and mouth seemed equally as wide as he simply gawked at me through a pair of wire rimmed, round glasses.

"Well?' I urged, "Where am I?"

"In bed", was the information he eventually offered, I intended to push for a little more detail when he turned and bolted from the door like his arse was on fire, I was not alone for long.

Minutes later the companions and visitors who had previously been blurred images swarmed around me in their multi coloured glory. My eyes delivered them to me in a sharp and clear quality they had denied me for so long. I tried to ask questions but they all spoke at once, mostly to each other, about me not to me, with a few of them answering every question except the ones I was actually asking, where was I? How long had I been there? Where were the rest of my unit? Was anyone else alive? All of these were ignored. This ruckus seemed to last an age before it was replaced with an altogether different atmosphere, one that made me uncomfortable, very uncomfortable.

"Which one of you is Doctor Carter?" the voice came from one of two suited men who had entered to the rear of my room, it was a monotone voice of authority that effortlessly commanded attention from all in the room who fell silent and looked toward the two men.

Now the next several weeks were a blur, it may seem to you I am jumping ahead again which in fairness I am. I do this partly because, well as I stated it was a blur, but mainly because I think it might be lengthy and tedious to go over the detail I do remember, and fill in the gaps that became obvious with hindsight.

So it was that on my thirty-sixth birthday I found myself aboard a U.S. military Lear jet touching down at Dulles airport in Washington DC. Wait a minute that was a little too much of a jump. Let me summarise as briefly as I can the events that took me from the introduction of the suited men to this situation.

Back to the day the two suited additions arrived in my hospital room. They quickly ignored any protests as they speedily ushered everyone out of the room before introducing themselves as Agent Briggs and Agent Wilkins. Agents of where or what I was never to learn, mainly as I never cared to ask. I instantly didn't like either man as they each possessed an air of arrogance and self-righteousness that I had experienced in the company of 'Bda Nam' and his colleagues. The hairs on the back of my neck were on end, apprehension surrounded me and an all too familiar sensation returned to my loins, forcing me to tense my stomach and bowels. Following the frosty introductions, I was entertained with pleasantries that seemed to make both men uncomfortable before more forthright questions began to flow. The Picard expression is 'debriefed', but although it lacked the physical prompts delivered by my previous torturers, for several hours a day over the next week or so I was once again interrogated. I tried to take control and set a tone from the beginning and to a certain extent I think I did, when a particular phrase touched a nerve near the start of our first session.

"I don't need to tell you that we expect your full co-operation", started one of the agents, I could not separate them, at this point they had merged into one arsehole already in my mind, "if you are not totally forthcoming we…." That was enough for me.

"What?" I interrupted with as much subdued authority and aggression as I could muster. The two government employees hesitated and looked at each other briefly, "just what exactly do you think you can do to me that hasn't been done?" Although I was well on the road to recovery I still looked broken at this stage, toothless and drawn with my pain etched across my face, I continued, "you don't know it yet because you've were too fucking arrogant to ask before you tried to flex your authority, but I'm a British citizen, that makes me an ally and couple that with the reason you are here I'd say a bloody good one wouldn't you? Now ask me your questions and I'll do my best but you'll do it with respect and then no one else need lose their teeth, am I clear?" Evidently I was clear as the mood changed dramatically. Not to say that anything was pleasant at first but there was an understanding between us. It was an understanding that, unbelievably, developed into a friendship by the time the three of us boarded a plane heading to Washington to meet the President of the United States.

Yeah I'm jumping ahead again but hey this was an exciting time despite my initial discomfort with Carl and Bill, previously known as Agent Briggs and Agent Wilkins.

Our conversations were initially cold, monotone, to the point and of the substance you would expect, who, how, what, when and why? I told them all that had happened the day we were captured feeling no guilt at laying the blame as firmly as possible at the feet of Major French, who I learned had confirmed me as dead along with the rest of my unit when he had been rescued. He had portrayed himself as the only surviving hero no less. They became patient with me as I detailed the events between the day of capture and that of escape. Then their curiosity grew and for one of the very few times in my life I shared the story I am writing now with an audience. I started where we started a few short chapters ago and on their encouragement I gave chapter and verse on the adventures of Boring John up until that moment. I guess it was at this time that I decided, should I ever get anywhere near completing my list I may one day write it all down, such was the level to which they were enthralled in my story. They asked questions, they laughed and made me laugh, to my surprise they informed me that Gemma Tsang was fast becoming a member of the Hollywood A-list with a string of box office hits as well as acclaimed West End and Broadway performances to her name. It is more than a little strange that I actually felt a pang of jealousy when they told me about the chain of Hollywood heart throbs she had been linked to in the tabloids and gossip magazines, I obviously still had some kind of fantasy issues here that I had to shake off at some point. Over the days my new friends began to visit me in exercise attire, and between our Q & A's they helped me with my health and fitness. By the time I was on route to Washington, we are getting there I promise, I was almost back to full strength.

Near the end of our time together, we sat in a small room that we had taken over at the rear of the hospital wing, where I had remained my whole visit. All the questions had been asked, my identity had been established and proven then we mutually agreed it would be hidden and would remain so for the rest of my life, until now of course. I had no desire to be hounded, cursed or praised for my actions; in fact I had no desire to be reminded of them at all. The scars I bore internally and externally were more than I needed for that. 'Soldier X' had become global phenomena and somewhat of an enigma, nobody could agree on what or who he was. Most speculated that he was a US Marine, who had been killed following the exploits that had become the most widely viewed in Internet history, (I'm sure you recall what is now second). Though many had different theories. Some were convinced it was a fraud, different groups of conspiracy theorists insisted the video had been made by one side or another, be it the governments of the west trying to de-stablize 'Bda Nams' followers, or 'Bda Nam' himself trying to fool his enemies so he could relax in his hiding, while planning a gruesome come back act. Luckily, it still seems strange to use that word when reflecting on any of this; my face had never been seen on camera. The shadowy profile and the clear vision of the fresh wounds and scars upon my back, that had created my pseudonym, added more intrigue to the mystery of my identity. 'Soldier X' would be debated for the rest of my days while I feigned ignorance and moved my head in the relevant manner to agree or disagree with theories that would be thrown at me at dinner parties.

Eventually, the man in the cave, as it is no longer I in any way, would become a symbol. Films would be made that speculated his story, students and kids would wear t-shirts with the symbolic scars printed on the back and bumper stickers would state that 'Soldier X guards this car'. Over the years various people would come from the woodwork and claim to be the man who had beheaded 'Bda Nam' in front of a global audience, some even had convincing scars that really had me wondering how far people will go for celebrity. Some would be believed by a selection of people, but most would come and go, while I plodded along in my own world trying to complete my list. On that note, I have not forgotten the title of this chapter, forgive me that it is taking me a while in getting there, there are more blanks to fill than I first realised when I started the new chapter.

"Well!" exclaimed Carl, "I think we are pretty much done here Jean". It was my last morning in Afghanistan but until I received the invite that followed I had no idea where I would be going next. My list had remained on the periphery of my thoughts and a small plan was forming, but I needed to give the logistics more brain time.

"There's just one more thing Jean" Bill interrupted my thoughts, "I'm not sure what your plans are, you are, of course, a free man but, if you can spare us a couple more days, there is someone who would like to meet you". Yeah you got it, now we are back at the point where I said I was going to miss all the boring stuff out, alighting a plane in Washington DC.

A rather beautiful black Mercedes Limousine was parked on the tarmac as I stepped from the plane and took my first lung full of American air. The sky was cloudless and blue, bright sunshine contradicted the chill in the air and I watched that first breath exhale from my mouth in smoky wisps of condensation. I pulled the overcoat that had been provided around the shoulders of my charcoal grey suit which had also been gifted me. The clothes had been there for me on the plane and all fit very well, I had chosen not to wear the tie and my crisp new white shirt was open at the collar. Carl and Bill had protested slightly as I was meeting their Commander-in-Chief, but I pointed out that the new president seemed to be taking the casual route himself when I had seen him on the TV. After the hours of rapid talking and laughter on our flight, it seemed strange that our last hour together, driving toward1600 Pennsylvania Ave, were spent in silence. There was a melancholy wrapped around us in the car, I had enjoyed my time with Carl and Bill following our rocky start, the rapport we had developed reminded me of my first days in the Legion and arriving to meet my new unit in Afghanistan, it was now unlikely I would ever see them again. Between the two agents they had arranged a new identity for me. Well, it was new officially anyway; Jean Ennuyeux was now an actual legal entity with dual citizenship across both the UK and the United States. John Bore had died in action and that statement felt very true. He would not be missed, as nobody knew him and those he loved had also died in action. I wished they were here with me now, deciding what to do with their new lives.

Unfortunately, I did not get a grand view of either the White House or any of the other famous Washington monuments as I arrived for my audience. We seemed to approach through a series of back roads once we left the freeway and, after passing through a set of impressive black iron gates, I found myself in the bowels of the President's home without even knowing I'd got close. Bill, Carl and myself stepped from the car and were met by two further men who were dressed exactly the same as Bill and Carl. In fact, I had to do a double take such was the resemblance, I wondered if my two friends had leapt from the far door and sprinted around to surprise me. The two new comers introduced themselves, I do not recall their names, I doubt I even heard them such was the apprehension I was feeling. They indicated I should follow them and I did so until I realised mine were the only footsteps I could hear in their wake on the concrete floor. I stopped and turned to see Carl and Bill standing by the Mercedes simply watching me.

"What's going on guys?" I asked, I already knew the answer but I was hoping that I was wrong.

"End of the road for us Jean", stated Bill with, I am sure, a small crack in his voice. Carl looked like he couldn't speak at all as I walked back toward them.

"Mr Ennuyeux, the President is waiting" spoke one of the new comers; he then repeated the sentence twice before I gave him a glance over my shoulder.

"Will you just fuck off for a second?" I snapped before watching the speaker and his partner recede into the shadows of the parking garage slightly. I turned back to my friends who were now smiling and suppressing laughter.

"I don't know what to say to you both", I genuinely didn't so while I thought I stepped forward and hugged first Bill and then Carl, they both seemed to find the gesture awkward for a moment before returning my embrace and stepping away, "thank you". This was the last word I spoke to either of them and, turning away, I noticed the look of confusion on the faces of my new agents who had observed the parting act between Carl, Bill and myself. As I got closer to them I spoke again, "you said somebody's waiting for me?" they marched toward a pair of gleaming steel elevator doors and I followed without looking back, those same doors closed behind me as did the doors to another part of my adventure. I always missed Bill and Carl, I still think of them often and admire their professionalism, they knew everything and they must have taken my secrets to their graves.

My dull-as-shit boring new agents escorted me to an office I recognised and I sat on my own in an oval room looking at a dark wooden 'Resolute' desk. I twiddled my thumbs, sat on my hands and then twiddled my thumbs some more. I looked around the room at the various paintings of dead presidents, the embossed golden crest on the royal blue carpet and the matching flags symmetrically placed behind the desk that I mentioned.

When the door to the left of the desk opened, time seemed to linger for a while before the most powerful man in the world entered the room and strode toward me. He thrust out his hand for me to shake and offered a smile so genuine only the finest politician could fake it. I stood, our hands met and mine was shaken up and down vigorously.

"Sir, this is a genuine honour', it took me a while to realise it was him speaking and not myself. Damn, he stole the line I had been rehearsing since I boarded the plane in the Middle East.

"Thank you" I replied rather pathetically, "oh, and same here" I added as a lame afterthought. He laughed a little too much and clamped an arm about my shoulder, guiding me to a door opposite the one he had entered from. This door led to a small snug containing four brown leather sofas symmetrically placed at each point of the compass. The sofas all faced each other surrounding a low mahogany coffee table that carried a decanter of liquid next to two matching brandy balloons; the table sat on a plush crimson carpet. The walls were bare but the beautiful oak panelling was art in itself. The president removed the crystal stopper from the decanter and poured small measures into each of the glasses.

"I understand you like brandy, Jean, it's okay to call you Jean yes?" he was obviously briefed which should not have been a surprise.

"Yes thank you" I smiled, "and yes, of course, Jean is fine Mr President"

"Good, and Earl is fine for me" he replied with an incline of the head, which indicated we should not be so formal. A clock I could not see chimed six times and I realised it was early evening, the President and I began to talk and drink brandy.

During our first two hours we were predominantly pleasant, we had sipped no more than two small brandies each. It's worth a mention that this was not the cheap stuff the good Sergeant and I used to enjoy and I feared it had instantly made a brandy snob of me. Again, the sentimental side of me, that has stayed with me always, wished my old drinking buddy was there sharing it with us. The invisible clock chimed eight times and introduced our fifth and last interruption of the evening, thus far two suited men had made two appearances each to inform the President that he had phone calls from the British Prime Minister, the sultan of Brunei and two from his Vice President who was in Hong Kong. It was the second call from my own Prime Minister that solidified the fact that our fifth interruption would be the last.

"Do I have to start firing people?" was the aggressively asked question that sent the petrified aid running from our sanctuary, no doubt to find his own. "Jesus" exclaimed the distinguished man before me, as he slumped back into the comfort of his chair and loosened the tie I had hoped he wouldn't be wearing. "I'm sorry Jean, I assure you that unless your video is a fake and that fellow pops up again there will be no further interruptions", he laughed and it seemed genuine, before leaning forward and pouring us both a third drink that was each bigger than the two previous ones combined. The mood lightened to a friendly air as we toasted and he locked my gaze with a grin. "You seem to command a certain loyalty Jean, the agents who delivered you held things back from my staff, I can tell" he paused for confirmation which he didn't receive before continuing, "tell me what you want Jean, no more than you are comfortable with but I would love to hear the whole story, I have time", there was a further measured pause during which time I made my decision, before once again starting at the beginning and telling someone of my adventure to date.

The next time Earl spoke, yes, it was definitely Earl now, was when I fell silent, the Brandy bottle was empty and the invisible clock informed us that it was midnight. We were both drunk and exhausted, I drained the last of my glass and the man opposite just glared at me.

"What are you going to do now?" I was eventually asked

"I dunno. I'm pretty drunk to be honest", I answered after some thought

"I don't mean right now, I mean what's next on your list?" he explained

"Oh, an Olympic gold medal", I explained in return. There was another substantial gap in the conversation before Earl brought things toward a close.

"Should be a piece of cake!" we both collapsed into laughter, and then into sleep on our respective sofas. Around three hours later I was awoken and ushered to a plush bedroom by the aide that had been so harshly dismissed hours before, I wondered if he ever slept. I did not wake again until almost noon.

When I did, I found my clothes, which I had left in a pile by the antique oak four-poster bed, cleaned, pressed and hanging on a valet stand by a gold framed ornate mirror. On the opposite side of the mirror, I could see that a door was ajar and led to a rather beautiful looking bathroom. I used the bathroom to freshen up as best I could and, as I fastened the last button on my freshly laundered shirt, another door opened and the ever-awake aide informed me that the President was waiting for me. Washed and dressed, I did a quick inspection in the mirror. I realised I needed a haircut. One of the Nurses had attempted a trim at the hospital in Afghanistan, but I still looked a bit scruffy for my current surroundings. However, the mirror also reminded me of the absence of teeth so I guess the hair was not a huge deal, the least of my problems.

Shortly after this, I entered the infamous Oval Office for the second time to a completely different scene. The President was perched on the front of his desk with a pair of horn rim spectacles sitting on the end of his nose. Both hands were full of papers, those in the left hand been read, those in the right been waved in the air before been snatched away by a man in a suit who looked no more than sixteen. All around him buzzed an absolute cacophony of activity as important looking people vied for his attention or screamed into cellular telephones. Others took notes and one young man passed around what looked like pastries from a cardboard box that was supported in the crook of his left arm. The President acknowledged my arrival with a brief glance and a nod of the head that turned into an indication that I should sit on one of the sofas by the wall, I decided to stand I don't know why. I watched my surroundings for sometime until the President stood to his full height and waved me toward him, each individual in the room fell into his own little world as though they knew the man was out of bounds for a time, I stepped toward him. Everything seemed a lot more formal than the previous day. Meeting in the middle of the floor I realised all eyes were discretely on us as we shook hands as though we'd just met.

"Jean, I wanted to formally thank you for your services to this country and indeed to the world, you are truly a hero", he spoke with a professional sincerity but it seemed like he meant it. Somehow, the leader of the free world confirming my 'hero' status made me feeling better about crossing it from my list, still something about his words and his manner didn't sit well with me.

"Sir, I didn't do it for this country or for any other. I did it for my friends and because I wanted to stay alive". The flinch I caused would be invisible to anyone who wasn't within the arms length proximity that I was, but I knew I hit a nerve at where this might go should he continue.

"I understand Jean" he said as he turned and strode toward his desk where he retrieved a plain manila folder, "but like it or not you helped us end a brutal but essential war and you put a sadistic murderer out of harm's way. Now then, to business, I have here" I just couldn't leave it there.

"Excuse me sir", I interrupted. The eyes on us were no longer discreet as the whole room stared our way, "but it doesn't seem to me it was essential, I know what that man did was evil but 'he' did it, albeit with a small group of deluded followers", nobody, including the President knew what to say, "as I see it we levelled a country and killed God only knows how many, including everyone in the world that I loved. My involvement with that man and with you, my being here now, it was just chance, an egotistical Major with a point to prove put me in that cave, your war, all that pain and death, it did nothing to guide you toward an end. I hope you learn from this I really do, whatever they do to us, however they attack, what was done here can never be the answer". There was a long silent pause that filled the whole room, people looked from the President to me, from me to the President until he offered me a smile that reminded me of the man I had drank brandy with the night before.

"Thank you Jean, I take that on board", I think he meant it and the pause continued until I returned the smile as best I could, allowing myself to relax a little. "Now, here we are", he waved the file he was still holding in front of me, "passports, ID's and bank accounts, you're real now Jean, and nobody outside this room will ever know that you and 'soldier X' are in fact one and the same". I looked around the room concerned at how many people were actually in there. I was amazed to see that with the young individuals gone there were actually only four people standing with us. I took the envelope.

"Why do I need bank accounts?" I had begun to leaf through the documents I had been handed. Receiving no answer I looked up at the man in front of me and then followed his gaze to one of the four, a small man of solid stature with a mop of white hair that framed his round face, he looked at me a little flustered.

"Did you expect cash?" he asked me with a bemused expression that created a mirror image in my expression.

"Cash?" I was clueless so the President helped as the short round man looked flabbergasted.

"Jean, you knew there was a reward for Dba Nam's head right?"

he seemed surprised to be asking the question as I looked at him in shock. A conversation I had had before my capture with Tim and Jay whilst on night watch was beginning to recreate itself in my mind.

"Jean there is half a billion dollars sitting in a bank account in your name at The Bank of America", I dropped the file in my hands and starred at him, my toothless mouth wide open.

"You really didn't know?"

"I..I...I...I" he laughed

"You are a very rich man Jean, and deservedly so", he had rested his rump back on the desk in the same position as when I had arrived that morning, the other four in attendance had joined in his chuckles.

"Sweet Jesus" were the only words I could muster which changed their chuckles to laughter. After a moment the President spoke again and as he did he reached out to shake my hand again, I took it.

"Now, we have to get on with running the country my friend, there is a plane at Dulles that will take you anywhere you want to go. I'm sure you have some thoughts, a vacation would do you good, now is there anything else I can do for you before we part?" I was still in a silent shock and I softly shook my head and turned toward the door, as I did I licked my lips as my mouth was dry and it gave me a thought, I turned back to my audience.

"Some teeth would be good", they all returned to their laughter and the President clamped an arm about my shoulder.

"I'm sure there is something we can do Jean," he said as he ushered me to the door.

Three weeks later I stood looking at the Pacific Ocean from the end of Santa Monica Pier in California. The warm breeze blew through my newly cut hair and the sun was re-kissing my skin back to the mucky brown colour I had acquired in the desert. I drew a deep breath of salty air and ran my tongue across my new set of pearly white teeth. The implants had been painful but I now had a mouth full of permanent teeth that any of the actors in this town would have been proud of.

It struck me as funny how I set my priority of nerves; I had handled my time with the President well I thought, confident and genuine. I had been nervous on arriving at the dentist in Beverly Hills that the White House medical staff had introduced me to , but I had been so scarred on entering the fancy LA hairdressers that I had feared the return of my Prostatitis more than I had in a long time. I am sure my squirming in the seat embarrassed the stylist. However, overall, the results were good.

I was staying in a suite at the Mondrian hotel, which, like the teeth, was courtesy of the US government; I was struggling to spend any of the money that, with interest, was growing daily in my new bank account. That reignited a thought that had been in my head for a few days, I had not looked at my list in weeks, the achievement detailed in the title of this chapter had never been far from my mind but if memory served I was about to once again cross something from my list. I took another breath and simultaneously removed my list from the left pocket of my jeans and a small pencil from the right. I was jumping ahead but right there as I had thought, achievement number four, become a millionaire, I smiled to myself and gently drew a line through the scribbled words so as not to pierce the tatty paper. It occurs to me now that I paid no thought to whatever Mr Newton's comments had been on the goal.

On another note, I was back into my old habits and rose each morning at five. I would use the hotel's gym or maybe drive along Sunset Boulevard to the ocean and run for a couple of hours. All in all, I liked California a lot, but it was time to leave, after all need I remind you, I had a medal to win and I was ready to put my plan into action. I collected my rental car from the vast beach parking lot and decided on the long route back to the hotel, I took the Pacific Coast Highway all the way to the end of Sunset Boulevard, and then let the winding road guide me through mountains and trees and then mansions and gardens, before the shops and restaurants that told me my hotel was close. As I pulled to the centre of the road, with my indicator flashing to let people know I was entering the hotel, I glanced at two men labouring away to change one of the huge billboards that let the ego's of Hollywood know the movies they'd made were in theatres. Traffic as it is in LA, I had time to watch them attach the first half of their poster and once again I was amazed as Gemma's face gradually appeared before me. A horn sounded and the man who had been kind enough to stop the flow of traffic so I could pass in front of him had ceased to be kind, frantically waving his arms at me as I eventually took advantage of his generosity. It was eight in the evening so noon back in England which was perfect as I had one more thing to do with London that day. Both the valet who took my car keys and the lady at reception greeted me like an old friend, which I reciprocated as best I could before heading toward the elevators. As I did this, another face smiled as me as it past, to my absolute astonishment it was the same face that I had just seen unfold on a billboard outside my hotel. It was a slightly older face but it was perfect, it was a slightly worldlier smile but it set me heart on fire, it was Gemma Tsang, Hollywood superstar. Despite the effect it had, the smile was brief and did not even cause her to take pause from the conversation she was having with her companions, two older looking gentlemen who I barely noticed. My head followed them as they passed through the reception and then through a glass door that was held open for them by a man who looked like a mountain in a tuxedo. I slowly wandered back to the reception desk, realising that in her wake everyone in the large white area was still staring at the doors through which Gemma had entered. Back at the desk I poised my question,

"Excuse me but what's through those doors?" the look on the face of the receptionist was somewhere between mocking and astonished. Mocking as she had sussed exactly why I was asking, and astonished that after three weeks at the hotel, I did not know that through those doors was the 'Sky Bar', a notorious A-list hang out which alas was closed tonight for a private party in honour of Gemma Tsang herself. Gemma had just attended the US premiere of her new movie and would be flying to London for the UK premiere the next day; my plan suddenly had a side plan.

Back in my room, I sat at the desk in one of my reception areas and looked at the piles of paper I had printed off, front and centre were the three sets of stapled pages that I had decided were in the final. Estate agents all over London were kissing my arse and no doubt discussing who the hell I was over martinis each evening in certain areas of London. I had given a budget of five million, I was a cash buyer and I wanted to move in quick, I guess that must have been quite rare? I had reached my figure of five million by spending some time on the Internet deciding where and how I wanted to live. I could have course spent ten times the amount and lived as a recluse in a castle in Kent, however this didn't seem to fit. I had finally settled on Chelsea and a town house, I wanted a gym and location to central London, other than that I had simply stated a nice house. The three houses in front of me were certainly nice, no question, this still didn't feel real I mean me, sitting in a five star Los Angeles hotel and trying to choose which house to spend maybe five million on, (a fraction of my fortune), while Gemma Tsang sipped champagne downstairs. Okay the houses, my final three consisted of a seven bedroom place in the network of streets between Kings Road and Knightsbridge, I didn't know the area well and it all looked very residential and strange as it sounds, pompous? This one was almost seven million so I finally dismissed it based on my previous comments and the fact the estate agent had pissed me off by trying to stretch my budget.

Second on the shortlist looked cool, only two million, only? I mean just listen to me. It was close to the middle of the Kings Road on one of the small side streets. The whole street looked lovely and I had always loved the Kings Road, although I'd usually lacked the confidence to walk up and down it like the locals on a weekend for fear I would have been, at best an object of ridicule, and at worst a source of terror for their children. I eventually rejected this property as it seemed small for what I was spending, three bedrooms and the gym looked like a bedroom with a treadmill, I was determined to retain the physical shape the Legion had forced on me. This brought me to Bourne Street, I think I knew from the beginning this was the one for me but when spending such amounts one likes to feel they have put as much thought as possible into it. Five bedrooms and three on-suite, three reception rooms a huge dinning kitchen and a formal dinning room, three terraces as well as a large and private rear garden, a snip at four point eight million. There were two other things that absolutely nailed it for me though. You see, the house had apparently been completely renovated by some Sheik overseas so that his son could live in it while at university, alas his son had promptly got a local girl pregnant and, in disgrace, was staying in Dubai or wherever, to make amends. So to my excitement the five-hundred square feet basement had been converted into a state of the art gymnasium, and secondly the entire place was fully furnished and decorated leaving me with nothing to do but go and live there so I could get on with my list. I called the relevant agent.

"Hello this is Peter at Douglas & Clutton"

"Hello Peter this is Jean Ennuyeux"

"Oh Mr. Ennuyeux, so nice to hear from you, how are you, well I hope? I was just......"

"Peter I want the Bourne Street house, you know I'm paying cash and I want in by the weekend"

"Errr... that's great news Mr Ennuyeux, but... but it's Thursday".

"Best get cracking then Peter, funds will be transferred today to the account you detailed, so you will be making nice interest. If the paper work can't be completed before Saturday I couldn't give a shit, I expect to be living in it until we complete yes?"

"Errr... yes Mr Enn..." I hung up the phone and transferred the money on line. I then called British Airways and booked an open First class ticket to Heathrow, I then called Virgin Atlantic and did the same as I figured Gemma would be using one of the two, hopefully. After packing everything I currently owned into the only luggage I had, a military kit bag that I had been given in Afghanistan' I laid my attire for the next morning on the spare bed and I tried to sleep despite the clink of glasses and the giggles that I could hear from Gemma's party by the pool.

"Milo, I am gonna ask you to do something a little bit weird". Milo was the driver that The Mondrian had provided for me. Despite the fact I had hired a car I had been with him a lot over the last few weeks, back and forth to the dentist and one night getting drunk together in a Mexican bar. Right now we were standing by his limo at the drop off point of one of the LAX terminals.

"Si Senor Enny, anything", he had given up on trying to pronounce my name some time ago and refused to call me Jean.

"Okay, I am gonna get out here at the British Airways terminal, I want you to park up at the Virgin Atlantic terminal and hang around near the first class check in". I received no more than a nod and a confused look, "keep an eye out for Gemma Tsang, the actress you know her, yes?" his confusion only deepened.

"Si Senor, I know who she is?"

'Okay Milo, you keep a sharp eye out, if you see her you call me", we'd exchanged cell numbers on our first outing together. In fact, he was the only person I'd given the number of my pay-as-you-go phone. I really didn't know why I'd bought it but was glad I had at that moment. Having made sure Milo understood what I needed of him and not even trying to explain why; I jumped from the car, threw my hold all across my shoulder and strode into the Tom Brady Terminal to find the first class check-in desk for British Airways. It took me less than five minutes to find but it was a wasted search as the moment I spotted it my cell phone, which was still in my hand, began to ring.

"Senor Enny she is 'ere", Milo screamed down the phone as soon as I answered it.

"Are you sure Milo? How did you even get there so quickly?" I didn't want to run all over LAX for nothing, although it had occurred to me she may be going to London in a private jet and that I was wasting my time anyway.

"Si, Si' insisted Milo, "I didn't even park the car, I see her now walking through the door as I pass, Terminal two Senor"

"Thanks Milo, you are a star". I hung up the phone and quickly asked the first person I saw in any kind of uniform the way to Terminal two, it was not far so I began to sprint and, in no more than four minutes, I was standing in a line of six at the Virgin Atlantic Upper Class Check in. Four of the six crowded the fifth, Gemma at the desk, they were been so helpful I am sure they had become counter productive. I was the sixth, patiently waiting for them to finish as the whole airport stood still, either just staring at or trying to get photos with cameras or cell phones of the famous Hollywood actress. When finished, I watched the group walk away toward the gate. Gemma looked amazing in just skinny jeans and a white v-neck t-shirt worn long with a simple gold belt holding it in at her waist. A modest heel on black ankle boots made her legs look even longer than I'd remembered and, of course, she had on the obligatory over-sized black designer sunglasses and a few simple pieces of gold jewelry. My God she was amazing.

"Excuse me sir' was repeated for the third time and in a slightly irate voice by the gentleman who had just finished tending to Gemma and now wanted to remove me from his queue.

"I'm sorry," I said as I stepped forward and placed my passport and ticket on the desk in front of him, "I have an open ticket and I'd like to be on the next flight to London"

"I see, I'm afraid the next flight is in twenty minutes and now closed, there is one just an hour later?" it was phrased as a question but a rhetorical one.

"No" I exclaimed a little two abruptly making the clerk jump slightly and take a step back, "I'm sorry but I really need to be on that plane." I looked at him imploringly.

"Well, okay sir, I will call the gate and see" with this he picked up the phone and began to wait while looking somewhere a few feet above my head, "it's a pity the next one is no good sir, you'd have been sharing the cabin with a genuine movie star". I reached over the counter and pressed the red button on his phone cutting him off.

"You know what, on second thought, I have some shopping to do and I don't want to cause any trouble, just put me on the next one".

"Of course sir" he replied with a knowing smile.

Shortly afterwards I found myself wandering around the duty free stores of the terminal discreetly trying to spot Gemma, whilst attempting to figure out what the hell I was doing or expecting to happen. At this point in my life I wasn't aware that Gemma would not be wandering around the shops or looking for a spare plastic seat, as there is a secret world of lounges and private areas reserved for those who have paid ridiculous amounts for their tickets. Even now the elitism of the class system, which is magnified tenfold when it comes to travel, does not sit well with me. It has become commonplace for me to anonymously upgrade people who I have seen been treated poorly by airline staff, as they have the cheapest ticket and seem a bit confused by the check in process, not been regular travelers.

The next time I saw Gemma was as she arrogantly, I thought, marched to the front of the lengthy queue as the flight was boarding and got straight on the plane with the remaining two members of her entourage. As with the lounge I was equally ignorant to the fact that Upper Class travelers had their own queue. It was fifteen minutes later when I reached the front of my queue that a hostess informed me I shouldn't have queued so long. On glancing at my ticket, her face positively transformed from that of bored intolerant ticket checker to that of a long lost best friend who was borderline euphoric to see me. My arm was grasped and I was warmly walked onto the plane where we turned left and I was shown to my luxurious seat. Before I sat I risked a quick glance around and noted that all seats seemed empty except four. Gemma and her colleagues, no doubt, though I could only see the tops of heads a few rows in front of me, each in their own spacious pod. The jet-black hair that crowned one of them simply had to belong to Gemma. To my right I was equally impressed to see my only other companion was the media mogul Thomas Beck, however he was so lost in thought he didn't even seem to notice he wasn't alone.

I got myself comfortable, which was incredibly easy and tried not to look shocked when a pretty girl in a red uniform offered me champagne, for free. Once airborne, I tried to formulate some kind of idea as to what I was doing in my head, I decided I just wanted her to talk to me. I didn't want her to know who I was, to think I had done well or pat my back, I just wanted her to look at me and see me as an equal if possible. I wanted to know that, when she was close to me, talking and listening and looking, that there was not a morsel of the old me that she'd recognize. Not a clue in my eyes or my tone or my manner that I was the ridiculous fat guy who worked with her in the bank and seemed to live in the toilet, the one she took pity on and bought a present for the day she had to witness him been fired.

We'd been in the air over an hour and I had still not left my seat, neither had Gemma, though I had seen one of her travelling companions heading forward, I guessed to the toilet. I decided that was a good place to start, at least I'd pass them and we might see each other. As I came level with Gemma's seat, I risked a subtle glance and, sure enough, there she was, albeit with headphones and an eye mask so she could sleep. She still looked amazing though. I guess I let my look linger a little too long as I heard someone clear their throat and noted one of her friends, an elderly grey haired gentleman in a blue blazer with a tailored white shirt and a yellow cravat, a complete wanker it would appear. He looked at me sternly and without needing to speak a word he ushered me on my way. As I entered the restroom, I looked to the end of the cabin and noticed something I had missed that took my 'upper class' travel experience to a new level. There was a bloody bar, a fully stocked genuine bar with a bar tender, stools and everything. Immediately after my restroom visit, I sat myself on one of the leather stools where I could see Gemma from the corner of my eye. I smiled at the bar tender who returned the gesture and asked me in a heavy French accent what I would like to drink, his name tag told me he was Pierre.

"Votre nom est Pierre?" I asked feeling so natural as I returned to French, Pierre positively beamed.

"Oui monsieur, vous êtes Français?" I informed him I wasn't French but had spent a lot of time there and he complimented me on my excellent accent and grammar. We chatted a little more about where he was from and his travels and eventually I ordered a brandy and asked him to have one with me, he declined due to the rules of his job but again seemed delighted by the gesture.

"Bonne santé", I toasted his health as I put the large brandy balloon to my lips and took a sip, allowing the liquid to warm my insides. As I opened my eyes, I involuntarily glanced back down the plane and my eyes connected with the most beautiful pair I believed in, using her left hand she was holding up the mask and staring straight at me. I offered a nod and a smile before she dropped her mask back into place. Then I heard for a second time a cough from the wanker in the cravat. Looking to my other side, he had somehow sneaked up right next to me and Pierre had retreated to cleaning his glasses as far away as the bar allowed.

"Ms Tsang is on a very demanding schedule", his upper class accent suited his appearance, "she needs her rest" he continued as I looked at him, "she is not here to be leered at by any cretin who has been upgraded and gets his thrills from star spotting, do I make my self clear?" He let it linger as if it was a challenge as he glared at me with his lips pursed, so I responded.

"I have absolutely no idea who the hell you or Ms Wang are", I deliberately said her name wrong, "and I don't care. I'm happy to sit here and mind my own business and you should do the same", he made to interrupt so I ever so slightly raised my voice, "BUT….. if you speak to me like that again you'll be getting off the plane before Heathrow, now do I make MYSELF clear?" He looked stunned, offended and shocked, all the emotions I had sought and without a word he huffed and puffed his way past me and back toward his seat. I heard a giggle and looked at Pierre only to find it was not he laughing. Equally as sneaky as her friend, Gemma had managed to get pretty close to me on the opposite side, she was two feet away maximum and I clamped my legs together as nerves reintroduced my old ailment.

"Please excuse Albert" was her opening line. I just stared back at her feeling for the world like a fat, homeless, sweaty bank clerk, I could feel the weight around me and the mole re-growing on my face. I pressed my lips together to hide my rotten teeth. "He's my business manager and he just worries that's all, he's a little over protective". She seemed to blush a little and I realized it was because I'd neglected to respond so I did.

"Well then, he's excused" I tried to say it in a friendly voice with a grin and it seemed to work as she mirrored my smile.

"Your French is excellent by the way, I agree with Pierre I thought you were Parisian when I heard you".

"Err, thank you." What else is there to say to that? "You speak French?" I asked her

"I'm learning for a part," she informed me

"Il va bien?" I asked her if it was going well

"Pas vraiment." Not really she replied, "I'm hopeless to be honest"

"It will come, it just takes practice, whenever you can", I left it there, she looked slightly uncomfortable and just smiled, I was starting to feel a little more confident, "good luck with it anyway" I continued, "it was nice to meet you". I took another sip of my brandy, but she lingered.

"Can I ask you, are you sure we haven't met before?" Shit, shit, shit, right then and there I was right back where I started. No matter what I'd done or how I'd transformed myself, the real me obviously shone out to those who were above me. Then she giggled again, "I'm sorry that was such a corny line." It was? "I know we haven't met before trust me I'd remember." Was she flirting with me? "It's just, well, what does a girl have to do to get a drink around here?" Her blushing and giggling grew a little and I looked to Pierre who was smiling at me and nodded to encourage me, bloody hell that must mean I'd heard her right.

"I'm sorry, please take a seat, can I buy you a drink?" from the corner of my eye I noticed Albert trying to will me to death. Gemma took the stool next to me with a grin.

"Well actually it's a free bar," she pointed out.

"In that case, you can have whatever you want" I offered and her smile broadened.

So there I was with my dream girl in the Upper Class cabin of a Boeing 747, drinking, chatting and giggling away like old friends. Our time together flew by, if you again forgive the pun, under the ever-watchful eye of the disapproving Albert who, on several occasions, approached to whisper what looked like concerns into Gemma's ear. By the time the captain asked us to take to our seats, there had been a million smiles and more than a few friendly touches of the knee or arm. We had talked about almost every subject I can think of and pretty much put the world to rights. Of course, I had had to hold back and miss out an awful lot but, all in all, I was flying higher that the plane and when I buckled myself in for landing I felt confident I had made a connection and that she had in no way at all linked me to the monster from her past. I began to think how I would broach the topic of seeing each other again once we had touched down; alas, I never got the chance.

Stationary at the gate we obediently left our seatbelts on until the captain ordered, but, before he did, there was a commotion behind me. I heard the door open and then a rush of manically organized people entered our cabin and began to coo and fuss around Gemma, Albert and the third companion who had remained silent. Before I could do anything she was ushered off the plane ahead of everyone and she was gone. I didn't even see her leave such was the fuss of the crowd around her. The captain asked that we remain in our seats for a few more minutes and I sat there in a mixture of emotions, between the high I'd just experienced and the low I felt that it was over, she was gone. Albert reappeared and touched my arm.

"Ms Tsang asked me to tell you how nice it was to meet you" he said through a slimy smile, "and, for my part, I apologize for my abruptness when we first spoke." One more greasy press of the lips and he too was gone, running after his charge. I decided not to dwell on this, I would never see her again, save more posters and maybe now I'd even get some pleasure from watching one of her movies? I had passed another test; if it were on my list I would be crossing it off. I had spent several hours in her company and she'd enjoyed it, she'd laughed and smiled and treated me as an equal. She had seen nothing of the former me in there and it made me feel good, it made me feel confident and it made me feel ready to go and win an Olympic gold medal.

A few hours later I left the office of 'Douglas & Clutton' in Chelsea with the keys to my new house and a comfortable feeling all around me. A comfortable feeling with who I was and where I was going, it was alien to me and I liked it. This is not to say that my past was not heavy on me. I would wear it forever like a cape of iron and my dreams would always carry a theme of regret and fear. As well as questions as to what I could have done differently or if I could have broken those handcuffs sooner. The list goes on and on but I was coming to terms with it. I was learning to deal with it and for the first time in an age I felt, well, something good that I can't explain. Over four million pounds arriving in an estate agent's bank account can apparently make things happen quite quickly and the house on Bourne Street was now one hundred percent mine. As I walked across Sloane Square towards it, I wondered if the skin that had been kissed from my ass in 'Douglas and Cluttons' would grow back. Strangely enough, once inside, I didn't spend much time looking around my new home. My first stop was the gym and once I had found the stairs to reach it I was more than happy with what was there. I then did a quick tour of the rest of the house and was frankly too awestruck by where I now lived to take it all seriously. The furnishings, as promised on line, were incredible right down to bedding and towels, all brand new and never touched. I guess if I was to be picky it was all very modern for me but, on the flip side, I would never have had the style or the eye to select this stuff. It was, I think the word is, cool? Once I had selected which of the five bedrooms would be mine, the biggest, comfiest looking one with an en-suite the size of the hospital wing back at the fort, I retrieved another piece of paper from my hold-all that I had printed back in Los Angeles and went in search of a telephone.

The following morning I had made an appointment with the President of the 'Bisely Rifle Club', a Mr Matthew Broadbank. Okay, so maybe you have gathered that we're back on track now, discussing the subject that the chapter's title promised. First I had tossed and turned in my bunk in Afghanistan and then secondly in my luxurious bed at the Mondrian. What event could a guy of my age win an Olympic gold medal in? I was in incredible shape, if I do say so myself, but still I was approaching forty and, tough as I thought I'd become, an eighteen year old well trained boxer was going to knock me on my backside no doubt. It was waking from one of my many nightmares that I had come up with the idea of a shooting medal. In my nightmare, I was back in the desert, shooting at the vehicles as they approached the site where we had been ambushed. My shots were each as true and accurate as they had been on the day but, in my dream, each bullet did not strike 'Bda Nam's' drivers or gunmen. Instead they struck my comrades who were, for some reason, driving towards me. I guess this reflected the fact that I knew I had not saved them despite the lives I had taken.

Despite the horrid context, an idea was lit. I had taken so naturally to shooting and performed under such conditions that I believed I could shine here. It may take years but age would not be a problem with shooting, save my eyesight and incontinence eventually. Facts were that, if I ever got a medal or not, it would be a hobby to fill my time and, at least, I would feel like I was chasing my list. Hell, I had nothing else to do unless I developed a fanaticism with shopping for boats or collecting art.

Mr, (call me Matty) Broadbank was a jovial fellow, dressed in brown corduroys, green Hunter wellington boots and a matching Barbour jacket. He could not have been more what I had imagined, right down to the tweed flat cap that topped off his attire. I was greeted at the reception to the prestigious gun club with all the warmth of a friend arriving for Christmas lunch. There were handshakes and enquiries as to my health and how easily I had found my way to the club and I instantly liked both Matty and his home from home. After my tour which, although impressive, was pretty much like Matty, what I had imagined, we sat in the club house for a cup of tea while Matty quizzed me on my interest in shooting. I decided lying was not necessary. Well, not totally necessary, so I told Matty that I had served in the Legion. He Picardly hid the turn up of his nose when he informed me he had been a Major in the Green Howards, but our meeting went well and we seemed to be becoming friends, however the way this was confirmed was not very satisfying.

"Well Jean, you seem a splendid chap and I am more than happy to put you on the waiting list", he said it with an excited pleasure, as though he was giving a gift to a relative that he knew they'd love.

"List?" I asked looking a little more shocked than I intended.

"Why yes" he explained, "the waiting list for membership is around two years, we're a very popular club".

I paused and looked around trying to think, probably a little too long as Matty began to uncomfortably shuffle his feet and eventually gave a discreet cough.

"Two years is not long really Jean, not many even get on the list" a longer uncomfortable pause, "now I will have to be getting on, you are free to come along as a spectator whenever you would like" another long pause that I eventually ended.

"Of course, I'm sorry." Bugger, what would I do now? There may be shorter lists at other clubs but there was a bigger reason I had selected 'Bisely Rifle Club' one I am yet to share with you. I slowly shook hands with my host and let him follow a pace behind as I headed to the door, then I spotted something on the wall that gave me hope. A giant 'cash thermometer', the kind you see at charity and fund raising events, the temperature gauge only showed around one-tenth full, about ten thousand pounds. The thermometer was surrounded by adverts for coming events to bolster the red line, a raffle, a sponsored walk etc. "What's this?" I indicated the homemade paraphernalia.

"Ah" sighed Matty, "a lengthy task I'm afraid. This place needs a new roof but that's the least of our worries. There's a host of work needs doing to get the club to scratch, even to make some areas safe," he said simultaneously scratching and shaking his head. "Sometimes it's hard to believe we will ever get there and, in truth, I sometimes worry the council will inspect the place and shut us down such is the state of some of the out buildings." The dismay on his face was replaced with complete confusion as I beamed my biggest Hollywood smile at him.

"Matty, it's your lucky day", my membership card was printed within the hour and work started on multiple areas of the club the following Monday, as I arrived for my first lesson.

This first lesson reveals the reason I had selected this particular club in Bisley. To take my lesson a begrudging Trevor Langridge strode toward me as I sat in the reception area of the club. Part of the deal I had struck when agreeing to rebuild the club was that Trevor would be my tutor. Trevor has first popped up when I had researched my new sport on the Internet. He was a former Commonwealth Bronze medalist who had remained close to the sport after losing sight in his left eye, a definite downer when one is a marksman. He now retained two positions within the governing body of the sport, the NSA (National Shooting Association). The first was that of 'Treasurer', the second, and most important, was that of 'Head of the Selection Committee for International Competition', including, you got it, the Olympic Games. He introduced himself politely enough; I knew this was not his ideal Monday morning. He'd not taught in quite sometime and then it had been with those who had amazing potential, not people with too much money and time on their hands seeking a new hobby. I am guessing that is how he viewed me, as I'm sure word of my route to membership must have spread.

To skip ahead, I left my first lesson completely dejected, the words, 'for your first time that was pretty impressive' ringing in my ears. I am not sure what I had expected, I guess that my natural ability would have shone through as it did in the Legion and they would have rushed me to the Olympics as a matter of urgency in order to improve the medal table. Trevor and I had gotten on well, conversation had improved when I had told him of my duties as a marksman in the military, but his long speech about how different this kind of shooting was had been proved correct. For a start I was used to firing much larger bullets from a much heavier gun, the Anschutz rifle that Trevor had loaned me for my first lesson was an impressive piece but weighed under fourteen pounds, my

'M40A3' sniper rifle with all the bells and whistles was nearer twenty and I missed the comfort the extra mass created in my arms. There was also the variation or the monotony depending on how you look at it, my training had consisted of a variety of targets and distances, now I was expected to fire at the same target no bigger than a small saucer with a bulls eye only 10.4 millimeters across. A bull's eye I would have to be constantly in the centre off in order to get anywhere near a domestic competition let alone the Olympics where I would have three hours and fifteen minutes to fire 120 rounds. The biggest differential however dawned on me as my sixtieth shot of the day hit the eight band high above the bull which was worth ten, the best shooting of my life had been when my life depended on it. I guess there was nothing I could do about that, but I definitely had the resources to do something about the rifle

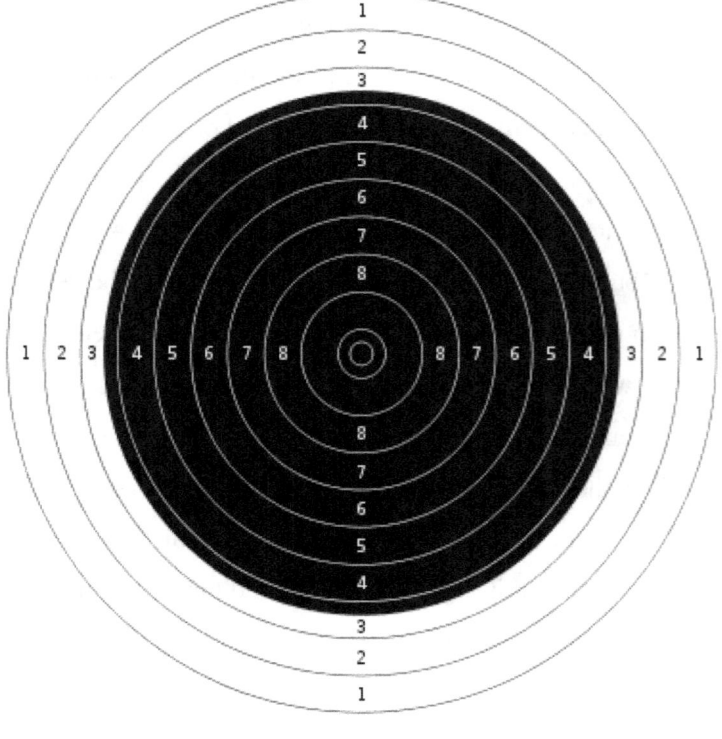

50 METRE RIFLE TARGET

By the time I was back on Bourne Street, I was feeling a little better. I knew what I was going to do about the rifle and I had started to take comfort from some of Trevor's praise and reminded myself that chasing the list was more important than completing it. I casually wandered down my new street toward my front door enjoying my new neighbourhood. The sun was bright in the sky and the air had that crisp fresh feel as I turned through the black iron gate at the front of my house. Whilst fishing around in my jacket pocket for my keys, I suddenly froze in my tracks, my large blue door was sitting ajar. Given my recent history, one might think this situation would not faze me. I think I have sold myself as quite tough, however panic flooded my mind and, of course, my prostate, forcing me to clamp my legs together slightly. Hearing movement beyond the door, I managed to shake off what one may call an irrational amount of fear and I ventured down my short path reaching out with my left hand to push the door further open. An arse that almost equalled the one I had possessed when you first started to read my story confronted me. Okay, probably not that big, but it certainly was a big arse. The arse in question was covered in a blue and white checked dress that covered a rotund body that was topped with a head covered in a mass of curly black hair, bordering on frizzy. I could only see the back of the head as whoever possessed the attributes I have thus far detailed was on her hands and knees scrubbing the black and white mosaic tiles on the floor of my hallway. Next to her was a large plastic bucket that contained a steaming vat of soapy water and she softly sang to herself as her arse and head bobbed up and down in opposite unison like a seesaw. It was the song she was singing that prompted my greeting.

"Excusez-moi, Madame". She was singing a song I recognized from the chefs back in the fort kitchen. They had used it to help me with my pronunciation when I was learning French and some of them had told me it was an old Legion Marching song, it was called 'Allongeons la jambe', roughly translating to 'Let's quicken our pace'. As I interrupted my unexpected houseguest, she was nearing the end of her song, 'Ma poul' n'a plus qu'un seul poussin', roughly translated again, 'her hen had only one chick left'. I won't go into more detail but the song ends when the hen has no chicks, so you see she didn't have long to go. I had tried to make my presence known as gently as possible, speaking softly and in a friendly tone but my attempt failed. With a scream that would have impressed an opera singer, the large lady betrayed her size and, to my amazement, seemed to shoot from her knees almost two feet in the air before landing on her feet facing me having turned 180 degrees whilst in flight. She now glared at me half in shock and half in fear, forcing me to back away as she was heavily armed with scrubbing brush and sponge.

"Qui vous êtes? Que voulez-vous?" She demanded through rasping breaths. I tried to explain who I was and what I wanted, but her breathing became heavier and she dropped her weapons and retreated to the bottom step, where she sat and placing one hand on her chest began to breath even heavier. Not knowing what else to do. I ran past her and down the hall to the kitchen where I filled a glass with water before returning. As rapidly and calmly as I could, I explained, in French, who I was and that I had bought the house. After eventually calming to a point where breathing was possible and having taken several sips of water, the kindly looking lady explained that she had been hired by the estate agent on behalf of the previous owner to keep the house clean until the new tenant took residence and during his tenure. Nobody had explained to her the property's change in circumstance. Following the first glass of water, I ushered the newly introduced 'Madame Tremblay' through to the kitchen and provided her second glass, which she drank heartily, still looking a little disoriented. Eventually calm and actually smiling, Madame Tremblay began to apologize and retrieved a key from a large pocket in the front of her pinafore, with a half smile and a slight inclination of the head she handed it to me but I'd had another thought. On questioning, I discovered that Madame Tremblay was paid ten pounds per hour for one hour a day to keep the house fresh; these hours would likely have been increased once the owner had arrived. I promptly doubled both her hours and her hourly rate and from that day forward Madame Tremblay was my housekeeper and my friend. We quickly fell into a routine; Madame Tremblay was usually there when I returned from my run. I was still up at five each day and had taken to running around Hyde Park. Tea would be in the pot and a continental style breakfast would usually be laid out on the kitchen table. Sometimes she would join me and we would chatter on in French, more often than not she would be tidying, washing or ironing something while I read the morning papers. From late morning she would disappear and return in the afternoon to stock my cupboards and fridge with anything she felt we needed. She would also prepare me something that I could warm up for the evening, she would then leave again to return to wherever she came from. I have now jumped ahead whilst rambling on about the evolution of my relationship with Madame Tremblay. So, back to the day I met her, and when we'd resolved all the issues and she had left to return the following day to begin the new routine, I got back to the issue I had with rifle weights.

On the third floor between the bedroom I had selected as my own and a guest bedroom, was a small office, lovingly furnished with all I could possibly need by the previous owner. My friend Google and I once more commenced on a research project and, in a couple of hours, a sheet of paper to my right hand held the names and addresses of what were considered the best gunsmiths in London. The companies I had listed varied in size and this showed in their promotional material, their corporate identities and, in fact, whether or not they had a website at all. For some reason I was instantly drawn to one gunsmith in particular, probably because he possessed none of the aforementioned paraphernalia. The Name "Colin McAlinden' popped up in various articles as 'from the oldest family of gunsmiths in the UK', going back several generations, gunsmiths to royalty and such. There were however just as many stories as to the people he had refused to make guns for, and this it would appear had alienated him from much of the community, though anyone who mentioned him seemed to concur he was the best.

My plan in place, I went to bed early that evening and, as was the norm, I slept fitfully, my past reinserting itself into my present and getting its timeline confused. In my dreams, I was tied in the cave with my four friends around me in the same state of bondage, two of them dead. Andy had the plastic bag over his head. I was still as fat as I had been at the bank. 'Bda Nam' was sticking my mole back on my face and I had my lips closed to hide my rotting teeth. Then Andy awoke and his ties fell away, he took the bag from his head and walked behind me where he placed the suffocating material over my head. I awoke startled in the half dark of dawn, it was an April and I ran until the images faded enough for me to face the day, returning home my new routine with Madame Tremblay began.

Later on that day, I found myself wandering around the small streets that sit behind Bond Street in Central London. It was not far from my house so I had walked past Buckingham Palace and through Green Park before heading down Piccadilly past the famous Ritz hotel; there I referred to the directions I had scribbled down. I had to check the address several times as there appeared to be no indication that the simple door I stood outside was a gunsmiths or indeed any kind of store at all. The only way to be sure was to knock but, as I stepped forward, I noticed a small plaque on the top of the doorframe. It was no more than an inch deep and maybe six inches long and was made of brass and was engraved with the words 'Mr. Colin McAlinden, Master Gunsmith. By Appointment to her Majesty the Queen'. I'd found him.

As the building was not the commercial outlet I had expected, I was unsure wether I should knock on the door or simply enter. I went for the first option but, after ten minutes of mute reply, I tried the door; it glided open effortlessly. Stepping inside, I was immediately confronted by something that best resembled the office of a professor who had been in residence at the same university for many years and failed to tidy the place, ever. Bookshelves lined two of walls in the large square room, around twenty-five feet square. The wall with the door, where I had entered, also carried a huge curtained window; a long oak dresser ran underneath it, the dresser was decorated with a variety of African and Asian looking effigies. The wall to my right, along with the window wall, was opposite the bookshelves. This contained a mass of various oil paintings jig-sawed together to fill the whole surface of the wall, landscapes, animals of all varieties and a few portraits. The floor was of highly polished dark wood and a large intricate rug covered most of it. On that rug, in the corner where the bookshelves met, was a beautiful mahogany desk topped by a green shaded, brass reading lamp. The lamp was the main light in the room due to the cloudy day that had developed outside. Also on the desk was a further selection of books, files, papers and a French cuffed hand holding a dark Monte Blanc fountain pen. The cuff was held in place by a simple gold stud link and just above that was the start of an expensive looking woolen sleeve. The sleeve led to the rest of an impressive three piece suit which had a rose gold watch chain across the waistcoat, underneath this a crisp white shirt had a plain silk crimson colored tie at the neck, on top of all of this a stern face starred at me imperiously from across the room over a pair of rimless square glasses.

"Some people take the hint when nobody answers the door", was the greeting I received. Despite the stern nature of the face I described, there seemed to be a smile behind both the tone of voice, the eyes and indeed the mouth that was framed by a close cropped, neat grey beard.

"I'm sorry, Mr. McAlindon?" He closed his eyes briefly and nodded by way of confirmation, "I was not sure if you were a shop or a private house". An eyebrow was raised. "I saw the plaque so I tried the door and", I raised my palms and looked around the room indicating my presence as a result of my actions.

"Okay, so now you are here what can I do for you Mr…..?" he left it hanging with an incline of the head and another raised eyebrow that requested an answer.

"Ennuyeux, my name is Ennuyeux but please call me Jean"

"Really", he looked surprised, "you don't seem French, nor do you appear a bore". I smiled both at his knowledge of French and his comment on my translated name. He paused again and I realized it was for an answer to the initial question, what did I want? I had practiced this, knowing that as he had refused to make guns for many society luminaries, I figured I had to catch both his attention and his professional intrigue. I took a breath

"I need you to make me a really heavy gun so I can win an Olympic Gold medal". Not a glimmer of a reaction showed across his face for the next thirty seconds as we just looked at each other.

"Sit down", he pointed at a small wooden chair opposite his desk and he watched me as I lifted a pile of papers from it and looked around for somewhere to place them. I eventually kept them on my knee and he seemed content that they stay there. "I'm listening Mr. Ennuyeux", if you have been told to kill politicians by God, if you are delusional or crazy or simply wasting my time, I will shoot you" he really looked like he meant it, and considering his profession I am guessing he had the necessary tool to carry out the threat. After another one of his wordless pauses that somehow proved I understood, he invited me continue, he did so with just one word and a swish of the hand, "Embellish?"

So I did, as you can imagine, having just met this man, I did not want to tell him my story in full so I skirted around large parts whilst trying to keep his interest and inspiring him to agree to my request. I focused predominantly on reaching the end of my story and detailing my issues with rifle weight, size and those that would restrict me as an Olympian in my chosen field. When I had finished he just looked at me, I almost heard the wheels of his mind turning.

"Let me think about it", was his eventual and rather lack luster response.

"Okay" was my equally dower reaction

"Look Jean", he remembered my name and used it, that was a plus, "I am not saying no, what I need to think about is whether or not what you ask is possible. I need to get my head around the logistics and restraints that are on me. There are some rules as to the weapon you can use in competition". I had never even thought of that. "Give me a week okay? Come back here same time next week. Oh, but before you go, would you mind taking my dog out for a quick walk". It wasn't a question and was immediately followed by a short sharp whistle. At this, a section of the bookshelf behind him swung open and through it padded a boxer dog, an exact duplicate of Sergeant Petit's dog. Shaking off my initial surprise at the request, I smiled broadly and off I went with the newly introduced 'Stan' at my side.

It was not a full week before I saw Colin again, at my request I returned most days to take Stan for a walk. This soon became a run, usually my second of the day as I still used my five a.m. run to shake off the nightmares. I never spoke to Colin beyond pleasantries when I collected or returned the dog and I grew slightly frustrated that he always seemed to be simply sitting at the same desk, apparently doing nothing to research our project. I did not want to shoot any further with a borrowed gun so I avoided the club. To retain favor I had called and explained that I was away on business. Instead, I spent my time researching external ballistics and keeping strong and fit. Shooting is not a strength event but general opinion was that total body control is a key to success and core endurance is essential. Any movement that is not intended can be disastrous; if I am one-thousandth of a millimeter off at my end, I will miss my mark by a tenth of a millimeter, in professional shooting terms that may as well be a meter.

When the end of my seven days was finally up, I again walked from my apartment to the gunsmith's address. At this stage I did not know it was his home as well as his place of business and, indeed, workshop. The door was open as always but Colin was not at his desk for the first time. Stan lay on the edge of the rug and sat up tail wagging at my appearance. He gave one happy bark and almost instantly Colin appeared through the secret door in the bookshelves. As always, he was dapperly dressed in a three-piece suit, shirt and tie. This was the first time I had seen him standing and it surprised me how stocky he was. He had the barrel chest and shoulders of a rugby player, which I was to find he had been for many years at a pretty senior level. The other thing that surprised me was the apparatus that was helping him to stand; both hands were placed on the handles of a black graphite-walking frame. The frame had three wheels and the right handle had a lever-brake with a cable leading to one of the rear wheels, much like a bicycle break. In my mind I was running through the previous week, as I was sure I had seen him moving around unassisted. He had more life in his eyes and his spirit than anyone I'd met and it had never occurred to me he was in anyway disabled. Ironically, as our friendship grew, I felt the same way and forgot all about the frame, except when I was drunk and needed it more than he did. To be honest, on this first day, it registered little in my interest. He was still the same guy and, as yet, I did not know him that well; it didn't seem to register with him either as he didn't mention it,

"Follow me," he instructed with a smile. Stan and I obliged and headed through the secret door. Beyond that door was a short corridor and then another door that was half open. The second door was all together different from the first and although it was regular size it looked more like the door of a vault, made as it was of solid steel with a digital keypad to the right of centre next to a wheel shaped handle. I noticed a large cushion on the floor in the small corridor and Stan obediently curled up on it, not venturing beyond the solid entrance that Colin and I passed through.

As I stepped into this new room following the gunsmith my jaw dropped, the scene before me looked like something one might see in a NASA space centre. The whole room's walls and floor were stainless steel and highly polished, such was the brightness of the place it appeared the whole ceiling was illuminated. A series of work stations made of the same shiny material flanked the walls and each was dominated with a variety of tools in pristine order. What appeared to be the main workstation was situated in the centre of the room and I gawped at what was sitting upon it. Resting on a stand on the far side of the table was the skeleton of a rifle. The barrel was there and part of the stock, but, other than that, a variety of other pieces protruded from it that I could not identify. It looked more like someone was building a satellite for outer space. In front of this was a second stand and resting on this was fully functioning M40A3 sniper's rifle. If I did not know better, I would have sworn it was the very one that I had used in the Middle East.

"Where in the name of Christ did you get that?" was, let's face it, all I could say.

"You don't seriously expect me to answer that?" was, let's face it, all he could say. Colin deftly perched himself on a black leather stool with a high back and with a flick of his ankles sent himself flying around the work station on small black wheels. He was then behind the rifle he appeared to be building. "Now, I wanted to be sure that we were replicating your M40 as closely as possible", he continued, "just the weight is easy, one simply attaches a lump of lead to the stock", he was excited and talking fast, as much to himself as to me. "The distribution is the important thing so I am going to be making it predominantly out of wood. Not the alloys and such that they use these days, that will allow me to stud the length and width with weights in the right places, but I need to see how you position yourself." He looked up at me for the first time as if wondering why I was not reacting, "Well go on, and pick it up" he pointed at the M40, "show me how you stand to shoot. We spent the next hour or more with me holding the sniper rifle in a variety of positions, kneeling standing and laying down and, as I did so, Colin scooted around me on his chair taking endless photographs. Toward the end of the photographic session, I knelt on one knee with the long rifle pulled to my shoulder. After confirming my comfort to Colin, he continued to click away and my mind drifted. The clicking of the camera became deafening and eventually turned into mortar fire surrounding me. The familiar feel of the gun reminded me of the last time I had fired it and, in my head, my friends were again dying all around me. I suddenly realized I could not breathe and, with a gasp, I stood. Placing the gun back on the table, I noticed Colin staring at me, the camera by his side, a confused and maybe concerned look across his face.

"I'm sorry, I..." Truth is I didn't know what to say as I realized there were tears staining my cheeks; I tried to wipe them away unnoticed.

"Let's have a drink". With this, he retrieved his walking frame and headed toward the back of the room where, on pressing a button, to my further surprise, a lift door opened. It was a short journey in the small plain steel lift and it was in silence. When the doors opened, I realized that there were even more surprises to be had in the McAlinden household. I followed Colin from the lift into a room more befitting a stately home. The room seemed to cover most of the first floor above both the office and the workroom, with just one exit in the far right corner, a simple white arch. The room in which I now stood had the same dark, highly polished wooden floorboards as the office. Likewise an antique looking rug predominantly covered it, though this one was huge. On the left wall was a large open granite fireplace stacked with logs and ready to be lit. Somehow Stan the dog had found his own way up there and was curled up in front of said fire waiting for someone to strike a match and warm his shackles. Colin did this as he wheeled himself past before heading toward the arch I mentioned. As I followed him I noted the rest of the room, three dark red leather Chesterfield sofas made a square with the fire as the forth side. Around the walls yet more oil paintings and antiquities were hung or stood on shelves. I stopped and looked at a beautifully made shotgun that hung above the fire; the intricacy of the etching on both the wooden stock and the steel work was amazing.

"First piece I ever made" I was informed over Colin's shoulder, "come on we'll eat in the kitchen".

I followed him through the white arch and found the contrast between the two upstairs rooms almost as dramatic as the two downstairs. The kitchen belonged in a Michelin star restaurant; it was ultra modern with a huge six-ring gas burning oven and an island that was at least ten-feet square sitting in the middle. Copper-bottomed pots and pans hung from a device in the ceiling. Opening a huge double door fridge Colin removed what I was to learn was a Chateaubriand, a large piece of beef, which he was to roast and calve into steaks that we would share. We had this with potatoes and several bottles of red wine, the first of which he told me to retrieve from a large antique oak rack that looked somewhat out of place in the ultra modern room. We sat at the island in the centre of Colin's kitchen and he smiled at me.

"Tell me everything Jean, you've known me a week, you know you can trust me". Despite the joke, somehow I knew I could. I also knew that telling my story again would help, it always did and it was a shame that it was such a rarity when I could allow myself. Two hours later I was opening a third bottle of red and Colin was looking at me mouth agape, we had just reached the part where I was rescued following Bda Nam's death. "Jean, have you told anyone else this story?" At first I wondered if this was because he didn't believe me but I realized he was actually concerned for me.

"Well" I thought, "only the President"

"The President?" repeated Colin, "of the United States?"

"Yeah" I responded, feeling the effects of the alcohol, "he's a nice guy, he got me my new teeth". I pointed at my mouth and grinned like an idiot.

"He and I are the only two people that know of this?" Colin pushed his inquiry.

"Erm. There were a couple of Secret Service agents I befriended, Carl and Bill and I am sure a few of the President's aides know parts but that's pretty much it. Officially I'm dead anyway, or John Bore is". Again, there was a long pause from Colin as I refilled our glasses.

"Okay", he finally spoke, "guess I better carry on with that gun downstairs so you can get on with that list". I nodded both my thanks and agreement and we toasted for the twentieth time that evening, then drank. "Jean?", Colin followed a little timidly as he finished his mouthful of wine, I waited, "can I see it? The famous scar, can I see it?" Without hesitation I pulled my shirt over my head and turned round, "Jesus Christ" was the stunned exclamation I heard from behind me, I am sure it was the sheer magnitude of damage that brought the reaction; the 'X' was far from my only scar.

It took Colin a little under four weeks to complete my gun, during which time I visited every day to walk Stan and see my new friend. Sometimes I would watch him work in awe. Often at the end of the day we would attack the wine rack while he continually demonstrate that his culinary skills equaled his gun making skills. We touched on his frame once, he told me he had fallen off a horse some years ago, but with the exception of one drunken session years later when he told me of the emotional trauma he had been through we never mentioned it. It didn't seem to bother either one of us or affect his life or our relationship so why bother. The day the gun was finished arrived like any other; I walked past Stan in the corridor between the two contrasting rooms on the ground floor, patting his head as I did. On entering the workshop, I encountered Colin, a smug look on his face and a sheet covering a large object in front of him. I knew what it was.

"You finished", there had been fittings as he had gone along, and I had seen a lot of the progress as the weapon evolved, but knowing I was now to see the finished article was beyond exciting.

"Try it out for size," he said as, with a flourish, he whipped away the white cloth. It was amazing. Unexpectedly, the butt and shoulder rest were made of a kind of steel. However the handle where my trigger hand gripped was wood, as was the remainder of the stock where my other hand would support it. Beyond the technical perfection of his work, the engraving on the walnut was as intricate and beautiful as the shotgun over the fire up stairs. The carvings were worked around the chrome studs that I knew were counter weights to emulate my M40. From the end of the wooden stock protruded the long thick barrel, which glinted chrome under the bright halogen lighting. I reached forward and picked it up.

"The trigger pressure is identical to the M40, as will be the weight and the feel when you put these on. He tossed a pair of heavy black fabric gloves across the table. I had secretly thought the gun felt a little light but wondered what the glove could really do. I place the rifle back on the table briefly while I pulled them on, they fit like a second skin, and they were fingerless so I could feel the trigger and stock when I retook the new gun. "The gloves are the weight difference between your gun and Olympic regulation, the balance should be perfect when you wear them". He was right. As I pulled the futuristic looking stock to my shoulder, I closed my eyes and it felt exactly like my old M40.

"It's perfect" I whispered, "let's go shoot it". Two hours later Colin and I arrived at Bisley, his flat had offered one more surprise. We took the small elevator down a floor to a small underground garage that contained a British Racing Green colored Austin Martin. I was past being shocked by Colin, or past mentioning it when I was.

After retrieving Colin's frame and then my gun from a fitted lock box in the back of the prestigious car we entered the club. Matty greeted us, or rather smiled at me and then stood bolt up right looking shocked when Colin walked in behind me.

"Mr McAlinden" he sounded as stunned as he looked, "I... I... errrr"

"You... you... errrr.... What?" Colin snapped back at him in a mock impression, Matty turned and left the room, I looked at Colin for an explanation but didn't get one before Trevor Langridge entered the room closely followed by an obedient Matty.

"Colin, it's good to see you," said Trevor in a quizzical way as he extended his hand,

"Likewise" Colin offered excepting the handshake

"I didn't realize you and Mr. McAlinden were acquainted Jean", attention turned to me.

"Recently" I explained, "he has been kind enough to make me a new rifle".

"What?" Matty practically yelled from the back of the room.

"That will be all thank you Matthew" were the words spoken by Trevor that sent him fleeing from the room in a huff.

"I refused to make his father a gun," explained Colin, Trevor laughed at that

"It was a little more than that if I recall", he followed with. No one explained further and I didn't ask, "you require targets, ammunition?" We were asked.

"Please, and Trevor would you give us an hour of your time" asked Colin

"Of course" Trevor stated as if the question need not have been asked.

On the field, targets set and rifle loaded I settled in and casually took my first five shots with my new rifle. I felt relaxed, calm and confident, my bowels oblivious to my plan and the nerves I possibly should have felt. I think this was just the effect Colin had on me. From fifty meters the target I was shooting at just fit exactly in the middle of the four-millimeter circle that was at the end of my barrel. On each shot I took a breath, I let half of it out and I shot a man that I had shot before in the face. This is how Colin had taught me, we had discussed my reaction when first holding the M40 in front of him and a plan had been formed. I had to harness those emotions, I had to fire in groups of five and each shot had to be a reincarnation of the five shots I had taken to try and save my friends and me in the desert. Unfortunately this meant that every time I pulled the trigger, part of the memories that kept me awake at night had to be relived. Relived and controlled, but it worked. My first five shots fired from Colin's masterpiece struck as centrally as possible, perfect tens. The pattern continued throughout the afternoon to the amazement of all who watched. As with my first encounter with guns, it all just came naturally. I'm sure that the differentials between my military weapon and what I was initially expected to fire at Bisley were psychological blocks, but it didn't matter anymore, I was on fire. The Olympic Games were eighteen months away in Chicago and right then and there, I knew I could make it there, and I was right.

The next year was not all plain sailing; I had days when I could not hit a barn door if I was stood a meter from it. My first competition I retired from as my score after round one left it impossible for me to recover. I had spent most of that day legs crossed with a burning in my prostate. Some days I was perfect and there seemed to be no in-between days, it was one or the other. I shot well when Colin was there, no question of that. Sometimes no matter what, the constant reliving of the five kills I made in Afghanistan was just too much. It magnified the dreams I had each night, dragging them in to my days no matter how early I might rise or how long I might run. However, more often than not, I won and this got me noticed.

By the end of twelve months I was on a shortlist and I found myself at the British National Championships. There is no huge story to tell here as I won and I was on my way to Chicago. The minute I knew this for sure my psychological prostatitis was on fire. I was six-months from the Olympics and it was my thirty-seventh birthday.

I spent the six-months before heading to Chicago practicing, endlessly practicing. I had decided I would not drink and that physically I would train as though I were entering the decathlon. I wanted to leave nothing to chance. I spent a lot of time with Colin in his apartment and, by this stage; he was spending an equal amount of time at my house on Bourne Street where he enjoyed flirting with and embarrassing Madame Tremblay. The two of them seemed to develop a mutual hatred of each other that was completely fake and shrouded in genuine affection and a shared desire to be there for me. Suddenly, I was sitting aboard a plane to Chicago with Colin at my side. It made me recall the last flight I had made and I realized I had never regaled the story to him, so I did. He listened smiling and before he settled in for a nap he spoke just once

"Well Jean, I think that if you knock this medal thing off the list, the next one might just sort itself. Remember though, this Gemma Tsang, no matter how good she looks, some other guy is already sick to death of her". I chuckled at his comment and likewise decided to get some sleep.

This reminds me of something else that occurred during those six-months. In the February of my Olympic year, Gemma Tsang won an Academy Award for Best Supporting Actress. It was a movie about a woman suffering with cancer and defying the odds by outliving doctors' estimates by some seventeen years. Gemma played a Nurse who was encouraging the patient to believe. I had watched the film several times and Gemma was absolutely amazing. On Oscar night, I sat up until three o'clock in the morning to see her receiving her prestigious award live. She was gracious, elegant and still the most beautiful thing I had ever seen.

Like my first visit to the US and subsequent travels, I instantly liked Chicago. The Games had been going for a week and myself and several other members of the shooting team, with family and friends, had flown out to join our competition that started in week two. It was a shame to miss the opening ceremony and enjoy the athletics and such but for me it was all about remaining focused and not being distracted. I had spent the last week at the range in Bisley letting off round after round, each one directed true by the memory of how important a shot can be. On alighting the plane to a beautiful sunny morning at O'Hare International airport, I saw to it that Colin was taken in a cab to his hotel downtown, while I joined my teammates on a coach to the specially built village that was slightly out of town. I was told it was on the shores of Lake Michigan. I had read as much as I could about the area and was quite excited about the trip with or without the Olympics. Actually without the Games, I may have been a lot more relaxed. I had met my teammates briefly before we boarded the plane and had fortunately come to know several of them during competitions over the previous year. There had been a get together which I had missed having spent a long period staying at Colin's house and neglecting to check my mail. I fear that this coupled with my 'new boy' status on the team created a little animosity toward me within the group. This wasn't the best but it wasn't vitally important, the facts are that I had nothing in common with these people. I was used to being an outcast and, once I had had my go at the medal, I doubted I would see any of them again. All except one anyway.

"Hi there, 'am Cammy", the thick Scottish accent, reminded me of my old comrade Andy. It instantly made me smile as a petite Glaswegian introduced himself before sitting beside me on the coach. "'Am told we're gonna be roomies, I hope ya danna snore". He returned my smile with a wide grin, and from that moment when in each other's company we rarely did anything but laugh and smile. He was average in height with the wiry build of a long runner but with a potbelly stuck on the front due to a love of whisky, red meat and chips. Above all, he was constantly happy and it immediately infected anyone around him, myself included.

It was two more days before the shooting competition was due to commence and I spent this relaxing as best I could with the hyper-active Cammy as a room mate. Cammy seemed obsessed with bedding every woman within the village and I have to say he made some progress. The Olympic Village is like any institution of young people. The average age is probably early twenties; the population consists of a the fittest people in the world at the pinnacle of physical ability, effectively on an exciting holiday. Needless to say that hormones and testosterone were rife and for those looking for it there was action to be had. Cammy and I had agreed on a 'sock on the door knob' system should one of us be entertaining and he seemed frustrated that my socks had as yet stayed in my drawer. This is not to say that my head was not turned, my God, some of the women in this place were beyond phenomenal, but I had just five days until my competition was over and I had to be one-hundred-percent focused on my shooting. As Cammy's socks seemed to be on the doorknob more than his feet I spent the next couple of days exploring both the village and down town Chicago, where I would visit Colin for lunch or dinner. The Village was a fun colourful place and always had lots of people in tracksuits walking around and looking excited and happy. It was clean and functional with everything you might need from a few small stores to a state of the art fitness studio. My own obsessive fitness routine continued much to Cammy's disgust, 'complete waste of time' he would say each time he saw me leave for a run or a work out, 'far better ways to get exercise Jean' would be the follow up.

It transpired that when I was at the firing range, practicing or was working out, Colin had been spending time watching the Dressage competitions. You may remember that it was a fall from a horse that had necessitated the walking frame, but he still had a love for all things equestrian. Speaking to Colin on the afternoon before my first day of competition, there were to be two rounds due to the quantity of shooters a first round and the final, I learned that he had quite quickly become friendly with a lady called Julie who trained the British riders. He was to be having dinner with Julie that night so I was left to my own devices.

Cammy's sock was on the door knob, not that I needed it as the screamer he had brought home made Nurse Picard seem like a mute, so I decided to take a walk and try and relax so I could focus on what was expected of me the following day. My prostatitis, although I am sure at this stage psychological, had reared its head and trying not to focus on it seemed impossible. I decided to take a walk to the shores of the famous Lake Michigan and was instantly impressed by the sheer vastness of it. It felt for the world that I was standing at the edge of an ocean or a sea and it was hard to believe this was simply one of three huge lakes, which I came to learn summed up the amazing size of America as a country. I walked a long a sandy stretch of beach and skimmed stones across the gently rolling waves. After half an hour or so, I was no nearer to any kind of peace with my situation and the magnitude of what I was about to attempt weighed heavy on me. Strolling from the shore I came across a large man-made boating pool that was filled by a small inlet that led from the great lake. I found a bench and I sat trying to meditate and re-focus my thinking. I tried to take comfort and confidence from how I happened to be where I was and what I had achieved already to even be here. I had joined the legion, I had become a hero and right now I had a bank account with five-hundred and twenty million dollars in it, that's right the balance was rising, it is surprisingly tough to spend that kind of cash. Still there I was, at that moment in time I was Boring John, I was petrified that I would blow it and fail. I suspected that I had put myself on a global stage inviting the whole world to laugh at me and join in the chorus of chants and taunts at my expense. I had just about decided I was going to hot foot it to the airport when a young boy ran my way with a remote control device in his hands and a heart broken look on his face.

"Mr, Mr" he yelled desperately, I jumped to my feet and put a hand on his small shoulder.

"What is it?" I urged desperate to help the distraught looking lad.

"My boat" he sobbed, "my boat", I followed his out stretched finger and saw that he was pointing at a splendid looking model bloat bobbing around on the man-made pond, I looked at him confused and he waved the remote control console in my face, "it's broken I can't bring it back". That was all I needed to hear, I was going to get this young fellow his boat back. I had cried those desperate tears of a child myself many times, well into my thirties in fact, and I had an opportunity to take them from this boy. The boat was around twelve feet from shore but quickly floating away; with out hesitation I ran and jumped into the water, which to my surprise was a good two feet deeper than the twelve inches it looked. I was to my waist but I waded on and soon had the impressive looking vessel by the stern. I noted a man on the opposite shore screaming at me and realized that being in the water was, no doubt, forbidden, but, as the man began to race around the perimeter, I didn't care, I was going to return this boat to it's rightful owner, or so I thought. Back at the bench the young lad gushed his thanks as he grappled the expensive toy from my arms, before turning and making quick time across a short field toward a small selection of out buildings. He had almost reach them when the yelling man had made his way around the water to where I was, I was in no mood for the 'job's-worth' ranting of a park warden so I held up my hand to still and silence him.

"Look I know I shouldn't be in the water but the young lad had lost control of his boat and.." I was cut short

"That was my boat you stupid bastard!" I noticed a remote control in his hand that looked a lot more complex than the young boy's and I started to question myself. "That was a ten-thousand dollar schooner and you just bloody handed it to some stranger you fucking….." he let the sentence tail off as he shook his head at me in a blazing fury and then began to sprint in the direction that the lad had run. I watched him go feeling like an idiot and wondering if I should help his pursuit. Then I heard laughing somewhere behind me, when I turned my jaw dropped.

"I'm sorry" were the first words she spoke, "but that has to be the funniest thing I have ever seen". I realized my predicament and looked first to the fleeing man trying to retrieve the toy that I had gifted away, and then I looked down to my soaking trousers before re focusing on the dark blonde beauty that was enjoying my situation. Her blue eyes and wide smile left me with nothing to do but join her laughter, "we should get out of here," she continued through her amusement. "No way will that guy catch that kid and I think maybe he'll be back for you when he realizes that." With this she took my hand and led me jogging back toward the lake, we didn't stop until we were a few hundred yards down the beach and a dune had obstructed the pond from our view, we were both still laughing.

"I'm Eva"

"I'm Jean", our laughing gradually subsided and we were left in an awkward silence for a few seconds before she continued.

"Well it's nice to meet you, 'Jean the boat thief'" she giggled again, "are you a competitor at the games? You look like an athlete." The compliment was up there with the President calling me a hero.

"I'm a shooter" I informed her, "fifty-meter rifle", she looked surprised, "and you?" I encouraged.

"Pentathlon" I was informed, she began to look vaguely familiar. Her hair was split into pigtails that gave her a girlish look, but even under her hooded tracksuit top and jogging bottoms her figure showed letting me know she was definitely all woman. My recollection was growing slightly stronger as I looked at her face and its flawless fair skin.

"Didn't the Pentathlon finish yesterday?" she confirmed my observation with a nod of the head as her grin grew wider. "How did you do?" I inquired, though I think I had fathomed the answer, my suspicions were confirmed as she slowly unzipped her top to reveal firstly a magnificent cleavage and secondly her Olympic gold medal. "Eva Novakova right?" again she nodded, "I'm sorry I didn't recognize you, I saw you yesterday you were amazing"

"Why thank you", she giggled with a small mocking curtsy. I remembered that Eva was Czech and I complimented her on her English, assuring her that it was her fluent command of my language that had prevented my immediate recognition. It was seven in the evening and we began to talk. When I walked Eva to the door of her chalet and we kissed goodnight it was midnight and we had covered a hell of a lot of ground, both on foot and in conversation.

Eva had fled the madness of the village and the attention she was receiving at her victory to try and enjoy her success in private. I understood how she must feel and I listened as she told me of her life long journey to the Games. I shared as much of my story as I realistically dared but without the segments that you now know it seemed pretty boring.

"I'd invite you in" she coyly offered, "but I have a room mate and besides, you should sleep if you are going to get one of these for yourself" she gently tapped her chest where the medal rested and like any red blooded male confronted with such a woman, I indiscreetly let my eye fall to the curve of her breasts for a second. "You never know, if you get one of these, you might get your hands on those too", I blushed as her meaning hit me before she kissed me quickly once more, somewhere between my mouth and the scar at my cheek, and disappeared through her blue door.

Unbelievably, I slept that night. I barely thought about where I was or what I was doing there. In the main I thought about Eva, this amazing young Czech woman who already had her gold medal around her neck. In the short time we had spent together she had me completely intoxicated and I was still high on her when I awoke ready to face my first day of competition. As always, I headed out for my run. It was a little before six as I had allowed myself an extra hour so I was totally rested and for some reason I had had no nightmares that night. I gently closed my door behind me so as not to wake Cammy and then stopped in my tracks.

"You lied to me, I've been here nearly an hour", it was Eva; she stood looking breathtaking in the crisp morning air with that trademark smile still illuminating her face. Her hair was tied back in a ponytail and she wore her national tracksuit and trainers, she looked a little concerned at my surprise, "you said you run every day, I thought I'd join you?" My smile seemed to reintroduce hers and off we set. We ran for an hour before a light breakfast together in one of the village canteens. At this stage, I think we were both oblivious to the attention we received though this far I believe it was limited. She was a hero back home and I was nobody anywhere, but people were looking with what appeared to be raised eyebrows of interest. Mainly I suspect due to Eva's enjoyment in public displays of affection, she was constantly holding my hand, stroking my hair or pecking me on the lips and face with kisses, I have to admit, I liked it a lot. After breakfast Eva wished me luck and again kissed my lips before letting me know she'd be watching my competition. For some reason this made me feel good and more confident, I already had a champion in my corner.

After dressing myself in the relevant attire I headed to the shooting range where formalities, rules and etiquette were addressed. Twenty shooters in all were eventually lined up fifty-meters from our respective targets. My God, they looked so small and far away, only five of us would make it to the final which would consist of just ten shooters, my five and five from the other first round to be held that afternoon. The start bell rang and there I was, I had just over three hours to fire one hundred and twenty bullets at these targets. I should have known to be more patient.

I felt good and calm, but I was thinking about Eva and as I prepared for my first shot I was looking around for her in the crowd that was behind me. There was seating stacked up a little further back, only half full, but a small area nearer to us separated by a four feet tall green wooden wall allowed family members, officials and other Olympians to be nearer the action. I noticed Eva watching with what looked like one of her team mates and just to her right I noticed Colin standing next to someone I could only assume was Julie, the Equestrian coach. I nodded and offered Colin a wave, only to receive a stern look and a shake of the head that I could not decipher. I glanced once more at Eva, I turned, took aim and pulled my trigger letting my bullet fly, it was a seven, the ten-minute walk to Eva's apartment to shake of the image of the slight Scotsman with a woman I had to assume was twice his size.

Luckily, Eva had no questions regarding my sudden departure from the shooting competition, or the sombre mood I appeared to have left in. She simply leapt into my arms and began kissing me in her doorway as she congratulated me on my success. I turned my head when I heard a camera clicking but thought little of it as Eva whispered in my ear.

"Lucky you, you're one step closer to a very exciting evening". I looked at her only slightly shocked and then smiled back as she winked at me. A stray thought floated across my mind for the first time, what would I do if it did come to that? I had nerves of course, as Eva would be only the second woman I had ever been with, and the first was not exactly conventional. However the main worry was my physical appearance. Not due to being fat with a horrendous mole and bad teeth this time, my scars especially the infamous and violent 'X' that dominated my back, surely questions and maybe even suspicions would come.

After a couple of hours chatting with Eva, I headed into town and had dinner with Colin. He congratulated me and asked how I was doing before laying down the law as to how lucky I had been with the weather, and that such an error was not acceptable in the final. After this I picked his brain about Julie and he coyly informed me, through a red face, that they had arranged to meet back in London for dinner, I teased him and he flustered before I returned to see course. I saw that after twenty meters it would be blown down and left by a whisker but right before the target a gust would lift it half that distance before it struck. I fired five times in sixty seconds, one each for the men I had murdered. I scored fifty points and I am told that the audience and the media directed interest my way, I noticed nothing as I was at war, fighting to stay free and avoid a torture that still haunted me every night. I fired all my rounds in under half the time allotted and walked back over to Colin's smiling face. I had a score of 3,069 from a maximum of 3,200. All to do now was wait and see if any five men could surpass me and keep me from the final, they would need their own miracles for that and I was not in the mood to wait and see. I embraced Colin and walked straight passed everyone else, spectators, media and Eva, as I headed to my room. I pulled on my trainers and a tracksuit and began to run, desperately trying to take the images I had used to reach victory from my head, I ran for a very long time that day.

I returned to find that nobody else had found their miracle that day and I had finished top of my group. I was two days from the Olympic final. It was Cammy who informed me of the news. He had not made it through his round and would not be with me in the final, though he seemed to care little and was as happy and smiley as ever. He had heard the rumours that I had been seen in the company of a certain Czech lady and, after I informed him I would not need the room that night, he told me not to be home early. He was 'on a promise' with a German shot-putter named Hilda. It took head and you lost track of what you're doing here. It's gonna be tough Jean and it's gonna take a bloody miracle but you've got three hundred and nineteen shots left. You have to get back in that desert, get scared and make sure every bullet nails some bastard so they can't put you back in that cave." I looked at him both shocked and scared by his words, but I began to focus. I knew he was right and I had to put my mind back in hell to do this, but I could do it, then I got my miracle.

I first felt it gently on the back of my neck as Colin was reprimanding me and it barely registered. As I turned and headed back to my stand it was stronger and it ruffled my hair and made me squint slightly. It was wind and it was getting stronger and more erratic by the second as it blew in from Lake Michigan. As I reached my rifle other shooters were letting off shots and then barking their fury as they scored eights and even a couple of sevens, only a small few achieving the nines and tens expected. I picked up my rifle and closed my eyes with my chin to my chest as I slowly dropped to one knee. In my mind I took myself to the desert, I surrounded myself with the images of deceased friends and I magnified the sound of the rifle fire around me to resemble the deafening bombardment that had surrounded me before my capture. I could smell the chaos of battle and all my senses were on fire as I slowly raised my heavy rifle to my shoulder. I turned the small black dot at the end of the range into a man driving toward me wielding a machine gun. Before I pulled the trigger I visualized its journey and noted every wisp of dust and air that might alter its and it was a disaster. My jaw dropped as I lowered my rifle. In a world-class field like this, one would expect everyone to be constantly scoring between nine and ten. Even over the course of three hundred and twenty shots a seven would be so hard to make up, but it was worse than I thought. I leant my rifle against the small stand we were each provided with and made my way over to Colin, as I did I noticed grins on the faces of many of my competitors including my team mates. They were all still simply stretching and getting comfortable with their guns, I was the only stupid rooky who had let off a shot. As I approached Colin I saw Julie step away after he whispered something to her, he just looked at me and we stood eye to eye in silence for a while.

"What the hell was that?" were his eventual first words

"I don't know" was my pathetic response as my head dropped.

"How in the name of Christ do you shoot the wrong target?" I stared at him confused and then quickly looked back over my shoulder, then back to Colin. I had shot the wrong bloody target altogether. At this stage, I was praying I was wrong and begging for my lousy seven. After a few more seconds it was confirmed on the scoreboards that surrounded the area, I registered a no score on my first shot. I had taken aim at the target of a German competitor who was stationed next to me. I should explain that the targets are set just one meter apart and, at fifty meters away, this has been known to happen, but not here not at the `Olympics, Colin continued.

"I'll tell you what it was Jean, it was ego. A pretty girl turned your

Cammy's sock on the door handle, and a sound coming from beyond that made me worry for his safety. Deciding he could look after himself, I headed for a walk along the lake. The next two days were much the same and, in truth, there is little to tell you about the day of the final either. It seems all the drama was to have been in my first round, conditions were perfect; I had my head in the right place, that's to say in hell where it needed to be. The end result was tight but I fired perfectly and calmly, with fifteen shots to go the Gold medal was mine and frustrated competitors were shooting for silver and bronze. As I read this back it seems somewhat of an anti-climax and, in truth, at that moment, it was. On the shot that sealed it for me there was a round of applause from the seats that were now full, and several other shooters shook my hand and patted my back, yet I felt flat. I was mentally exhausted and I was stuck in the world I was forced to recreate for myself. I couldn't even leave the area to try and exercise, I had to respectfully wait for the end of the competition and make all the relevant noises and gestures. I had done it, I had achieved another impossible task and I never wanted to touch a gun again as long as I lived, after my last shot I walked to Colin and handed him my rifle.

"Thank you" was all I said; he simply gave me one of his understanding nods and took the weapon from me. We sat together in silence until the competition was over and, after the aforementioned formalities; we left together, and escaped the media and journalists who were eager to talk to this unknown Gold medal winner from England. We headed to his hotel bar where I had my first drink in a long time. Said media outlets no doubt were already digging around in my past but I wasn't worried as my history was well and truly established. I was assured of it by the President of the country I was currently in. As I was thinking this, Colin seemed to read my mind.

"Are you looking forward to meeting him again?" I was confused by the question and it must have shown on my face, "the President I mean, will it be weird?"

"What makes you think I'll meet him again?" the statement reflected the confusion he had recognized in my expression.

"Jean, he's presenting the medals tomorrow, at your ceremony". My God, I had not even thought about that. Truth was I simply wanted to go home, although Eva had been playing on my mind a little too. "I have to say", continued Colin, "it's crossed my mind that he's arranged to present the medals tomorrow on purpose; he must have been watching you, he'd recognize you, yes?"

"I guess so, it wasn't that long ago and he knew I was going to go for a medal." Colin was about to continue the conversation when a new arrival entered the bar and caught my attention. It was Eva, looking like a super model in a fitted black dress and every pair of eyes in the place was transfixed on her as she strode toward me and kissed me on the cheek, before introducing herself to Colin.

"So this is where you sneak off to huh?" she joked as she turned her attention back to me. The without taking her eyes from mine she spoke to Colin. "Do you mind if I take him off your hands

Colin? I owe him something", a devilish and sexy smile had crept across her face.

"Be my guest," responded Colin giving me a wink over her shoulder. She didn't pause but took my hand and led me from the room still under the observation of all in the bar.

"How did you find me?" I asked simply looking for something to say

"Julie, Colin's friend. I saw them together at your competition so I sought her out today when you disappeared"

"Okay, so where to now?" We were passing a bank of elevators and she suddenly stopped and hit the up button.

"We're staying here tonight, if that's okay with you of course?" She ran a finger along the neckline of her low cut dress.

"Err" was as far as I got before the lift doors opened and I was pulled in side and slammed against the mirrored wall. It occurred to me how strong she was as she began kissing me passionately. She let her hands run down my back to my arse and then around the front to feel my reaction to her. As gripped in the throws of lust as I was, I could not shake the question of how she would react when my shirt came off, and how I would react in turn. I need not have worried. The elevator ride in itself was a pretty explicit sexual experience, and by the time we had made it down the corridor on the top floor and through the door of the suite Eva had booked, she had my cock out of my trousers and her beautiful dress over her hips. We didn't make it to the bed, I was hurled backwards onto a low beige sofa and I was inside her before I knew what was happening. For the next four hours we alternated between the mini-bar and lovemaking, if it could be called that, but she never showed a desire to fully undress either one of us. I think she found the process a waste of time. At two in the morning I was both physically exhausted and a little drunk as Eva began to straighten her ruffled clothing, she kissed me and smiled.

"The room is yours for the night Jean" she said to me "I should get back, my coach is quite strict and my roommate will be wondering where I am. I'll be watching you tomorrow Mr. Gold medal" with this she kissed me again and left the room. I slept right there where I was, somewhere on the floor between the mini-bar and the bed.

There was no run the next morning, I awoke where I had fallen asleep and it was seven o'clock. I dragged myself to the still made luxurious bed and lay for another two hours drifting in and out of sleep, with a huge smile on my face. My award ceremony was at one o'clock so a little after nine I decided to leave the hotel and grab a cab back to the village, in order to ready myself for my second Presidential meeting. As soon as I stepped from the hotel's front door, a barrage of flash photography blinded me. Simultaneously I was deafened as questions about my relationship with Eva Novakova were thrown at me. Not a single question about my Gold medal, it appears my sex life was of much more interest. I managed to get a cab at the curbside without speaking to any of my new entourage and I watched stunned through the rear window as they jumped into cars and onto motorbikes to follow us. Thankfully, they were all stopped at the gates of the village, though I am sure several shots of me were taken as they risked life and limb to snap me in the moving car.

"Where the hell ya been Jean?" Cammy practically yelled as a greeting. At first, I ignored him as I was mesmerized by the sheer size of the body that lay asleep, dominating his bed. I have explained my physical size and height, but even my feet did not hang of the end of the comfortable beds that had been provided for us, as did those of the woman who I was now looking at. "Jean, pal, where have you been?" the words brought me back to Cammy. "What? I spent the night in town why?"

"Why? Why?" Cammy was borderline hysterical, "everyone's lookin' for ya. The Olympic committee, the teams captain, the press. You won a bloody gold medal Jean you canna just disappear y'know?" Cammy was almost instantly proved right as before he could even finish his speech there was a knock at the door. I opened it to a tall brunette lady in a trouser suit carrying a clip board, her hair pulled tightly back into a bun and harsh glasses on top of her pointed nose.

"Mr Ennuyeux, where have you been?" She echoed Cammy's concerns, " you have not spoken to any of the press or the committee and there are things to sort before the ceremony. You have a responsibility as a member of the British Olympic team to.." I smiled and gently closed the door, luckily I heard a huff and the clip of stilettos as she immediately took the hint and paced away.

I spent the rest of the time I had that morning hiding in the room,

Cammy saw off anyone who tried to get to me, and the newly introduced Hilda made tea and smiled a lot. The first cup she brought I assumed was for a child, until I took it in my own hand and realized it was full size, such was the size of her mighty fist it had appeared as a doll's cup when she held it. Again I looked from her to Cammy and back, shaking off mental images.

When it was time to go and collect my medal, I dressed in my team tracksuit and went into the bathroom for some privacy. I sat on the loo with the seat down and my eyes closed. I tried to push away the sensation that, as ever, returned to my loins when I was scared or nervous. I could only imagine the global audience that would be watching this. Yes, a larger audience had seen me behead a man the last time I was on film but that wasn't me. Nobody knew who I was in the cave. Then again, this wasn't me really was it, or was it? I really didn't know anymore, but either way, it felt like this was something else that might change my world. I wasn't sure it would be for the better and so again I experienced regret at one of my achievements.

I left the apartment and made my way to the stadium that was a short car ride away. A car that was provided for me by a throng of people that seemed to appear the minute I left the door. The entire journey I seemed to be receiving instructions on either Olympian or Presidential etiquette, though, in truth, it all merged into one fog inside my head. Before long, I was ushered through a tunnel and walked to stand before a three-tiered podium. I was standing between two other men, a German gentleman that I recognized on my left as the man who's target I had shot accidently in my first round. To my delight, though I don't know why as I had never been shown any affection, one of my teammates was on my right collecting the silver medal. Sixty thousand people sat around me, either watching us in the flesh or on one of the huge screens scattered around the impressive structure. Of course, they were not all here to see us, there were a wealth of other activities taking place, but they all stopped for the medal ceremony and together we awaited the arrival of the President.

When he did walk into the arena, it was with the expected confident air of a politician. He was light on his feet and turned as he walked waving at the cheering crowds. He was coming to the end of his term but there was little doubt he would storm back into power. I am told he had done a wonderful job and the fact that he was a black guy still seemed to excite a lot of people. I was stunned by the sheer quantity of people milling around both the President and the podium. It was a good fifteen minutes before we were ready for the presentation of our medals. During this time, I was sure the President looked my way on a pretty frequent basis and I wondered if he was trying to be sure it was me. It had been a few years but I think I changed little, although the pressures of his role had added a few grey hairs and wrinkles to his appearance.

One by one our names were called out and each of my predecessors received a rapturous round of applause. Suddenly, there I was, standing in front of the President sharing a private smile with him. I gave a quick wave around the stands as that is what the first two guys did and then I turned my attention back to the ruler of the free world. He stepped toward me and I lowered my head so he could place my medal around my neck, as he did he leaned in and whispered very softly in my ear.

"Very well done 'X' I'm impressed and I'm proud of you", he patted my shoulder and stepped back, smiling as 'God Save the Queen' began to play. At the end of the music the three winners waved again at the crowd before walking from the stage so the games could commence. Attention and cameras were still on us when the departing President stopped, and leaving his security detail turned and headed back in my direction. Men that reminded me of Carl and Bill rushed after him speaking into their sleeves, but as the President reached me he waved them back and indicated he needed space, a perimeter was set as they stopped on his command.

"Jean", he began still in a half whisper so nobody else could hear us, "what's next?" He was grinning with curiosity and I knew what he meant. I smiled back at him and reached into my pocket where I retrieved my tatty list and a small pencil. I handed it to him and his face beamed, first into a broader smile and then a laugh that reached me with its contagiousness. "Well good luck with that one!" he joked, "should be easy for you now?" We both reached out, me to retrieve my list but he wanted something from me, he nodded at my pencil, "may I?" He asked in a somewhat humble manner.

"Of course" I handed him my pencil and stepped forward so I

could watch. Before he shook my hand and walked away, once again while waving at the crowds, I watched the President draw a line through the sentence, 'win an Olympic Gold medal' which was near the end of my list, he had a look of sheer glee on his face.

Chapter 5

Everything else

A week later I was back in my Bourne Street house. Departing Chicago had been a little frantic, and I was filled with regret that I had not managed to see Eva again before I left the village. I had received a note via her roommate and then Cammy, and it informed me that her coach had cracked down on her since the tabloids had caught wind of our romance. In honesty, I didn't see the big deal, we were both single people who just met and dated. That was until I reached the part of her note where she informed me that being just twenty years old she really wanted to focus on adding to her gold medal collection, not her love life. As you may also be, I was, at the time, stunned to find how young she was! So, with a nice collection of memories and only a minor aching in my heart, I allowed myself to say goodbye to Eva and I let her go.

Eva was not the only drama to surround my departure from the US, or indeed the journey home and arrival in England. Celebrity was something I had never factored into any of the tasks on my list and I didn't like it one little bit. I was still a very private person in the main. In honesty, I was probably still trying to inflict invisibility on myself as I had way back in the bank. Now, 'Soldier X' was probably the most famous character on the planet at the time but that was okay, as it wasn't me, or at least no one knew it was. This new celebrity was completely different. As an Olympic gold medalist, people want to talk to you, want to ask what drove you, how you felt and what were your plans for the future. To every question asked of me I either did not know, nor dare reveal the answer. Magnifying my problem was the very intimate looking, but very public chat I had had with the President. Everybody wanted to know why he had returned to me, what we had discussed, and what he had written on the piece of paper I handed him that made him smile so much. The speculation almost equaled that surrounding the 'Soldier X' video.

So it was, with an entourage of photographers and journalists, I quietly sneaked home and drew the curtains, where I could hide until the fuss was all over. The truth is, doing that made the whole situation worse and after a few days I feared it would never be over.

Madame Tremblay had continued to keep the house for me since our first meeting and during my time in Chicago. When she first saw me on my return she positively beamed with pride and hugged me like a grizzly bear. The following days she entered each morning past the handful of die-hard photojournalists who refused to give up. On one particular morning Colin, who had come to deliver some advice, accompanied her.

"Just do a Goddamn interview with somebody, please" he exhaled as he wheeled his way into the kitchen and poured a large brandy despite the fact it was only nine o'clock. He offered one to Madame Tremblay who looked at him as though he were insane. I had just returned from my gym in the basement. As I was in hiding, I had taken to running on the treadmill, which was also driving me crazy, I felt caged. Colin ranted on for a while explaining that people were also hounding him at his 'place of work' asking questions about me and how he came to know me. He confirmed my fears, that, by acting like a hermit, I had made things worse. However, Colin was losing my attention as Madame Tremblay had inadvertently started to sow the seeds of another idea in my head. Colin realized I had started to ignore him and turned to see what I was staring at over his shoulder. The robust French lady had ignored our jabbering and set about her daily routine. This started with her flipping on the small television mounted into the kitchen wall above the ample wine rack.

Morning television played on her selected channel and been interviewed was a British comedian who I vaguely recognized. He wore a t-Shirt that advertised a bi-annual event that raised money for charities around the globe. Now I wish I could tell you that my instincts had kicked in here, making me realize I was yet to give any of my new wealth to help others, alas it was something else. As he delivered his narration about what an amazing evening was planned, he began to list the events that would take place both on the evening itself but also on the lead up to it. One thing he mentioned registered and I thought back to my list, that, in honesty, I had thought little of since returning to London. When the article had finished, the couple on the screen began to talk about a man in Cornwall who could sculpt religious figures from cucumbers. I went to the room that I called my office, almost for the first time. Once there I began to dig through papers finding all the paraphernalia I had been given by the Olympic committee before I headed to Chicago. I soon found what I was looking for, the business card of the 'British Olympians Press Officer', an Ms Evelyn Schmidt.

I called the number and held the phone in the crook of my neck, holding the business card with thumb and forefinger of each hand perched on the four corners. It was answered almost immediately in a vaguely familiar harsh voice.

"Evelyn Schmidt" I was informed in a tone that indicated I'd better be quick.

"Ah.. er... Ms Schmidt" I should have rehearsed a script I guess

"I'm quite sure I just said that", she snapped impatiently

"Oh, yes you're right you did." I then, for some reason, paused again.

"Well do you need me to say it again or do you believe me?" she was starting to sound a little pissed off.

"No, no I believe you. Sorry Ms Schmidt this is Jean Ennuyeux" now she paused so I continued, "Ms Schmidt I was just watching the TV and" she cut me off.

"Yes, quite frankly Mr. Ennuyeux we didn't think you'd be interested. You haven't shown your face at any of the official press junkets and, as I recall the last time we met, you slammed the door in my face." It suddenly fell into place and I realized that this was the brunette lady who I had closed the door on the morning of my medal ceremony.

"Oh"

"Yes, oh" she echoed.

"Well look, Ms Schmidt, I am very sorry about that. I was a nervous wreck that morning in honesty. This is all quite new to me but if possible I would love to be involved in the plans for the charity." She paused, no doubt, just to make me sweat a little.

"Okay then" she stated as though doing me a huge favor even though it is impossible for her to know that she was. "I will see what I can do but it's late in the day. If it's possible to include you I'll have something biked over. Thank you for your call Mr. Ennuyeux" I began telling her she should call me Jean before I realized she'd hung up.

I sat and thought about what I had just become involved in and whether or not it counted. I decided it was good enough and certainly as near as I was ever going to get.

In total, with the phone call and the thinking time that had followed it, I guessed I might have been away from the kitchen an hour at most. I was therefore surprised on returning downstairs to see Madame Tremblay, belly up on the leather sofa that sat against the far wall, snoring like Satan with an empty brandy balloon dangling from her fingertips near the floor. I could smell the brandy and, exasperated, I looked to Colin who himself was blurry eyed, though still stationed at the breakfast bar where I had left him. His glass was still half full but the bottle next to him was on its side empty.

"What the hell have you done?" I demanded as I paced over to Madame Tremblay and looked down at her.

"I haven't done anything" Colin defended like a school child with a football by a broken window. I stared at him, "she just can't take her booze," he slurred.

"It half past bloody ten" I snapped. He briefly looked offended and then held his watch inches from his face trying to acquire some evidence with which he could defend himself. He began to lean unnervingly backward and as the doorbell rang, he looked in its direction lost his balance and tumbled from his stool to the kitchen floor. Running around the granite top I saw him on his back smiling in his sleep, he immediately joined Madame Tremblay's chorus of guttural snoring.

"Fell off a horse my arse," I barked at him over my shoulder as I headed to the door, "you were probably plastered you dippy old git"

At the door a man asked me to sign for a parcel and as neither of us had a pen, poor planning on his part I thought, I had him follow me to the kitchen, with hindsight, a mistake. The deliveryman in his pristine uniform looked around the room in shock at the fifty-something couple spread around the floor with empty glasses and bottles. I couldn't think of an excuse so I signed his form and returned it to him; my eyes followed his disgusted gaze.

"Heavy night" I informed him before ushering him back toward the door.

Before returning to the office with my package, I placed a cushion under Colin's head but chose to leave him on the tile floor, he looked comfy enough.

Despite her flippancy Evelyn Schmidt was keener than she let on to have me involved in her charity project, the package was from her. It had taken less time to arrive than it takes a man and a woman to pass out drinking brandy, but only just.

Inside was all I needed to learn, and learn fast as I was expected to do my bit the very next day. It shouldn't be too hard I thought, I already knew the words, it was a very famous song. So I guess I should explain what was going on? You see as part of the charity efforts, the Olympic medalists were to release a single into the music charts. A cover version of the famous, 'One Moment in Time', by Whitney Houston, though I feel I should point out that it was originally sung by a man called 'Albert Hammond' or so the internet told me. Now you may ask, and understandably so, why a self-proclaimed introvert, would put himself up for such a potentially embarrassing showcase. The answer is simple, achievement number five on my list; you got it, a number one record. At the beginning of previous chapters, I have endeavored to entertain by repeating the words of my boyhood nemesis, Mr. Newton. As I have hinted at before I grow bored of relighting his memory, as I feel I have established what a tosser he was and I don't want to dedicate anymore ink to him. The jokes you would think of yourself were the ones he used to draw laughter from my classmates.

You may also be skeptical as to the validity of knocking this off my list should the charity single actually top the charts? Well, as I said earlier, should it happen with me attempting to sing on it, that's good enough, and was as close as I was ever likely to get or indeed ever try and get. I figured it would be easy enough to blend in and hide at the back just to get through it, I was wrong.

The following day I walked into a recording studio somewhere in North London. I was pleased to see there were athletes there en masse so my plan to blend in had legs. Initially, I had the kind of nerves a kid might have joining a new school, in that I thought everyone would know each other and I would be the outsider. I must confess I didn't make a massive effort to mingle while I was at the Olympic village. My fears were unfounded, all those invited to sing were medal winners, and so they were, of course, from a variety of different disciplines. Although I think we were all aware who each other were, there were no strong bonds or cliques.

After a few seconds of handshakes, words of congratulations and a sharing of apprehension at the day's events, none other than Evelyn Schmidt called us to silence. She looked different to how I remembered her. I am guessing she wore contacts, as her sharp glasses were nowhere to be seen and I was surprised to see how blue her eyes were despite the black locks that bounced freely around her shoulders. She was casually dressed in blue jeans and a fitted t-Shirt and I'm sure I was not the only guy in the room that noticed her amazing figure.

"I hope you've all learnt your words" was the opening line she used to shut us all up and have us focus on her. "This should be quite simple, in the studio there are several gospel singers and they should drown out those of you who are particularly tone deaf." A round of sniggers circulated the room. "We are going to be filmed as well and this will be edited into a video along with footage of some of the charities that will be benefiting. Does anyone have any questions?" I don't know if anyone else did but, if they did, then, like me, they kept their mouths shut. We were gonna be videoed, I wasn't happy about that for starters, this may make hiding at the back a little harder. "Okay", she said, "could those of you who are going to be wearing costumes follow me, the rest of you can follow Pete." Pete was pointed out and waved, "Pete is the sound engineer, please put your medals on now". I fished my medal from my pocket, I had been instructed to bring it in the package received the previous day; I then began to follow the crowd. "Mr. Ennuyeux, where are you going?" It took a second to realize the voice was talking to me; it was Evelyn with a broad grin across what I realized was a beautiful face.

"Me?" I asked

"I see you are no more articulate in person than you are on the phone" on this occasion she said it with such warmth I had to smile back at her.

"I'm afraid not," I offered, "I was following Pete," I stated pointing my finger in his general direction.

"Oh, we have something special planned for you Jean." I liked that she called me Jean for the first time. Standing around her were another three bashful looking guys all at least my height and all thicker set. I recognized them all as medal winners but with the exception of Bruce Gold, who ironically I knew took decathlon silver, I could not place the other two. "Come and meet your rapping buddies", Evelyn followed with, I didn't like the sound of this at all.

All my initial fears on hearing this piece of information were confirmed as we were told that to modernize the song a rap chorus was to be added. Myself, Bruce and the other two men would be performing this section. My other two allies transpired to be weightlifting medalists. I wanted to run, right then and there. This was more terrifying than the Games, than the cave and than sitting in a theatre watching Gemma Tsang whilst smelling like a toilet, literally.

The four of us looked at each other with mirrored faces of fear, which, I have to say, helped a little, and then someone else was introduced to our group.

"This" announced Evelyn as a small black guy in sunglasses entered the room, "is MC BallistiX" he paused in a stance ready to receive our adulation. He received four blank faces each around three feet above his. Realizing that not one of us knew who the hell he was, he smiled uncomfortably blinding us with a huge set of jewel-encrusted teeth. He couldn't have been more than nineteen and I wondered if the jewelry that dominated his neck, wrists and earlobes could be real. After a few awkward seconds he eventually spoke

"Yo, I'm gonna make rappers out y'all", he almost yelled in an American drawl. He turned and walked into the next room where, after been ushered to follow by Evelyn, we were dressed up to look like bigger versions of MC BallistiX. Our humiliation was complete.

So it was that in a gold tracksuit, a black fur hat and a pair of thick sunglasses I entered the recording studio. I was walking in the way MC BallistiX had taught me, which was like I had shit my pants. The rest of the Olympians, who were lucky enough to simply be in the choir hooted with laughter as my three 'homies' and I stood around a separate microphone at the front of the room, our medals buried under a mass of further fake 'bling'.

If I am honest, though it was something that haunted me forever amongst family and friends, the day itself turned into an absolute blast. Possibly helped by the fact that my new friend 'BallistiX' started to lay on the champagne within the hour. The entire Olympic medal contingency was blotto by the third take. To magnify my embarrassment and, in fairness, all of BallistiX's new 'crew', we really got into it. Before long I was throwing moves, hugging myself and making flamboyant gestures with my new 'bling' while clicking my fingers. As I remember it, the rap element itself went something like this

"We'd like a lotta moments but we only get's one
a second to show you our skills in the sun
y'all saw us in Chicago and no one was quicker
now y'all hears us rap ain't nobody's sicker
it might sound cocky we're fly and we're bold
but that's what happens when y'all wearing our Gold"

My God, it's still humiliating as I look back now. Though thinking of the day we recorded it, I still find myself laughing out loud. The day turned into evening and long after the hilarities of our singing had ended we were drinking BallistiX's booze and new friendships were been formed. Not least of all with BallistiX himself who, as well as been an amazing host, proved to be a very interesting and intelligent guy from the West Midlands.

As the night wore on, I decided it was time for me to leave, not least of all as I saw Evelyn heading for the door. I was hoping to head off at the same time and maybe suggest sharing a taxi or even a nightcap. As I headed into the night I was more than a little smug to see her leaning against the wall outside with her coat wrapped around her as if waiting for someone, I hoped it was I.

"Hi" I said trying to sound as surprised as I could yet receiving a knowing smile.

"Hi back" she giggled at me. I was about to make one of my suggestions when the door behind me swung open and another party-goer headed into the night. It was Patsy Smith who had won us a Silver medal in the pool, I'm not sure which discipline. Patsy pecked a good night kiss on my cheek and then seemed to loiter around between Evelyn and myself, we all fell into an awkward silence before Evelyn laughed out loud and walked toward me, repeating Patsy's kiss on my cheek she smiled at me and spoke

"I'm afraid someone beat you too it lover boy." She turned and, taking Patsy by the hand looked back over her shoulder and said, "beside, you're not my type". I reached the street just in time to see Patsy stumble into a cab whilst Evelyn attacked her in a manner that reminded me of Eva in the hotel lift back in Chicago. Seven cabs ignored me that night before I realized I was still dressed like a cross between a ghetto rapper and gold souk. I finally stumbled home around four o'clock in the morning and having sobered up wandered straight to my gym. Don't be too impressed; I quickly fell asleep on the bench press.

The next three weeks I did little. I exercised a lot, mainly in my gym as I still received a lot of attention outside, though at last it was wearing off. I had figured out a route I could walk to see Colin and Stan the dog that was pretty inconspicuous, mainly down leafy streets though it did start with me hopping over my garden wall into a small ally that took me half way down Sloane Street. At some time during those three weeks, Colin's equestrian friend Julie arrived and she never left. It was wonderful to see my friend so happy, she was an amazing woman, and I soon realized why Colin had fallen so quickly and so hard. It was during one of my visits, on a Sunday night towards the end of those three weeks, that the three of us sat in Colin's plush living room with the radio playing in the background. I should say the four of us as Stan was obediently lying on his mattress by the fire. We chatted and sipped wine until nearly nine o'clock and then Colin hushed us and turned up the radio. It was then that I realized what I was listening to, the weekly chart show on Radio One, the DJ was almost at the end of his shift and we all leaned closer to the radio.

"Okay then", announced the DJ in typically irritating over the top DJ fashion, "we're down to the last two, what will be the new number one single?" There was a countdown and a drum roll but no surprise that 'One Moment in Time' by the British Olympians and MC BallistiX was top of the charts, charity singles usually are. Colin and I laughed and clinked glasses while Julie looked at us puzzled.

"May I?" asked Colin

"You may," I confirmed as I handed him an aging piece of paper that contained a diminishing list. I smiled at him as he drew a line through the sentence that read, 'have a number one record'.

"What is this thing" Julie frowned reaching out for the paper; Colin kept it from her and gave me a look which received a shake of the head from me. As I said, Julie was amazing she and Colin would always be in my life. However, at this stage, she was just a new girlfriend and, although she would learn my story in time, I was not ready to impart it to her at that stage.

Any justification I needed in crossing this achievement from my list was validated for me a couple of days later. Madame Tremblay answered a knock at the door and before heading upstairs with her vacuum cleaner she yelled down the corridor to tell me that I had a guest. I was surprised to see it was Evelyn Schmidt, looking as casual and gorgeous as she had done at the recoding studio. She offered me a dazzling smile and held up a square, flat package. I beckoned her in and led her to the kitchen where she accepted my offer of tea.

"So what's in the package?" I enquired as I sat opposite her with my own tea at the breakfast bar.

"Jean this is quite a place" she observed looking around her as she ignored my question, "what the hell do you do for a living when you're not shooting things?" I was not prepared for questions as to the source of my wealth and I flustered a little. Luckily I did not have to come up with an answer, "I'm sorry" she blushed, "that's so rude of me." I shook my head to dismiss it and again pointed at the package. "Ah' she continued, "this is for you" she handed me the package and I discarding my tea and tore of the brown paper to reveal a beautifully mounted CD in a teak looking frame. Below the CD of the Olympian single was a small plaque that read;

"Presented to Mr Jean Ennuyeux.
For his success in reaching the top of the UK singles chart with
the recording of 'One Moment in Time."
Performed with The British Olympians and MC BallistiX"

I laughed out loud as I read it.

"This is great" I managed between smiles, "it really was a fun day, I didn't expect it to be"

"I guessed as much, you should let your hair down more often you were quite the gangster rapper" she teased

"That's not even on the list," I half whispered to myself, prompting her to raise an eyebrow and look at me quizzically

"List?"

"Nothing"

"Well, everyone got one of these but I wanted to drop yours off and apologize for the other night", she played with her teacup and looked down.

"Apologize?" I really didn't think it was necessary.

"Yeah, I guess I tried to lead you on a little because you pissed me off in Chicago. Maybe I wanted to blow you out,. Stupid really, Patsy and I had a hell of a row about it"

"Hey, don't worry about it, we were all a bit drunk by the end of the night, otherwise I'd never have had the courage to follow you out." She shrugged at my offer. "Anyway, I knew you were gay", I followed with flippantly, this got a reaction and she sat bolt upright and stared at me.

"You did not!" she exclaimed

"Of course I did, otherwise you'd have jumped on me as soon as I opened the door in Chicago", I gave a wink just in case, but she didn't take me seriously and wacked my arm with a tut.

"Typical guy" there was a pause, "look, there's another reason I visited, I wanted to ask a favor." Again she paused so I ushered her on. "I know you are not a fan of the limelight and such but as you had so much fun at the studio I thought maybe you'd change your mind? Maybe you'd think about doing an interview, this week?" She bit her bottom lip and looked at me as if she had anticipated my reaction.

"Evelyn I don't know", I stood and began to pace.

"Look just one, it's a biggy and then everyone will leave you alone I'm sure." she also stood and began to pace the room beside me.

"Biggy, what do you mean a biggy?" She could not know it but this made everything worse, and an all too familiar sensation began to return right in the pit of my stomach.

"It's 'The Saturday Night Show, with Michael Ross", I turned and looked at her stunned. This was the biggest chat show on television at the time and attracted global stars when they had something to sell. I had been hounded by a plethora of newspaper journalists and a few magazines, local TV stations even but nothing like this, twenty million viewers each week.

"Why in the name of Christ would Michael Ross want to interview me?"

"I'll be honest Jean it was a cancellation, some A-Lister can't make it and it airs tomorrow night. Besides people are interested, your first Olympics, you haven't been shooting long and everyone wants to know what that chat with the President was about." As a side note she said, almost to herself, "including me actually".

"I've never done anything like that"

"Jean, a few weeks ago you dressed like an idiot and did a rap on a record that has sold millions." It was intended to sway me but it fell on deaf ears.

"That was different, this is, well all those people watching me in the studio and at home" I had pretty much made up my mind there was no way I was doing this.

"It's not really live, there's a fifteen minute delay in case anyone swears or anything, and they edit it to make you look cool. This would really be good for me too, the committee are sulking that you're in hiding and it would win me a lot of brownie points" I thought that was her final argument

"Evelyn I'm sorry, I just" she interrupted me.

"I know you'll enjoy it, you'll meet some great people, the other two guests are Gemma Tsang the actress and…"

"Okay I'll do it!" I cut her off and said it with such enthusiasm that Evelyn froze in shock for a second or two.

"Wow, I mean the girl's hot but Jesus Jean," we both laughed again and then Evelyn jumped forward and wrapping her arms around my neck kissing my cheek.

"Thank you so much, you won't regret it" she turned and almost skipped down the corridor, "I'll call later today with all the details" were the last words she yelled over her shoulder.

I sat back down and allowed what I had just committed to marinate in my mind for a while. The panic came and went in waves that almost caused nausea at times. I allowed myself to contemplate the things I had done over the last several years and almost convinced myself that, compared to those things; the TV appearance would be nothing. Then reality knocked and I found myself sat on the toilet biting my fingernails at the thought of all those people watching. Whilst sitting there unable to do anything that one is supposed to be doing on the toilet, more practical concerns hit me. John Bore was officially killed in action. I had no worries that anyone from before the Legion would recognize me but I had met a lot of people before I was murdered in that cave. I worried that someone might start to put pieces together. After too much time worrying about this, I realized how unlikely and redundant it was. There was nobody that knew the old me dead or alive, no family had received a message of my death, nobody was missing John Bore. On the redundancy side it occurred to me that my Olympic achievement had been televised globally and these concerns had never occurred to me before. I was still sitting on the lid of my loo when the phone rang and I reluctantly and nervously made my way to and picked up the receiver. It was Evelyn and I screwed up my eyes and prayed that she was calling to cancel, that they had found someone more befitting the show, they hadn't.

"Great news Jean, we're good to go", she continued to rattle off the information I would need. I had to be at BBC Television

Centre at eight o'clock the following evening and I was to be emailed a list of likely questions so I could rehearse some answers. The format of the show was that Gemma Tsang, as the most important guest, would come out first so as to benefit from the full hour's publicity. The second guest, who I had never learned the identity of, would join her after twenty minutes and then I would join the group for the last twenty minutes. I would therefore be expected to chat and interact with a group of people who were no doubt a lot more used to this than me. I was also told to, 'Look sharp' as 'the country will be watching'. Bloody marvelous, I had no idea what 'sharp' meant. I needed help. So it was that, as the twenty-four hour threshold passed, I found myself on Colin's doorstep.

"Where do you get your suits?" was the greeting that awaited him when I entered his house.

"My suits? Sit down Jean, what's going on?" so I told him. He sat opposite me on a sofa with Julie, the pair of them offering me annoyingly patronizing smiles until I finished. When my dilemma was explained there was a silence that I soon filled

"Guys" I was desperate, "what the hell am I gonna do?"

"Don't worry Jean" announced Colin confidently, meet me here first thing in the morning and we'll have you looking like Mr. GQ long before your big performance". He reached for his frame and headed to the phone.

"Gemma Tsang is not going to know what hit her" added Julie with a motherly pat on my hand.

That night I slept in a similar fashion to the night before my story started, in that I didn't sleep at all. I paced around, I shaved, I sat on the loo, I did anything to fill time and tried not to think about what I would be doing the following day. So it was that my run started very early that morning, by half past three I was running down Kings Road having decided to try a more urban route at this hour. I ran until five and was outside Colin and Julie's by six. They were not happy. Despite my protests, a breakfast that I could not touch was made and coffee was drunk. As with the breakfast, I did not touch the coffee, as I recalled it had been the worst instigator of my prostatitis. Instead and to the bemusement of my hosts, I found some broccoli in the fridge, boiled it up and drank the water. I did this a little too hastily and I burned my mouth causing my first, but by no means last, swearing fit of the day.

When the lazy clock dragged it's ass around to nine-thirty, Colin had had enough of my impatience and, grabbing a coat, he threw me the keys to his car and told me he would give me directions.

On his instruction, we headed to Bond Street. It was not far and, if not for Colin's frame, we would have walked, but I have to say I absolutely loved driving the Austin Martin. Colin smiled broadly when I mentioned that I'd like to get myself a car, he expressed surprise that I had not bought one, but he nearly choked as I told him I would as soon as I passed my driving test. We switched seats while holding up all the traffic on Piccadilly and Colin had his first swearing fit of the day, amidst the sounding horns and road rage screams.

Once surrounded by the prestigious stores of Bond Street, I instantly felt intimidated. Colin informed me that his suits were made at a tailor named 'Kilgour'. Although I was told I should invest in one, they could not make one by that afternoon and their 'off the peg' stuff was new, not great and, in Colin's opinion, should never have been allowed to tarnish the 'Kilgour' name. He led me into a store called 'Canali' where, to my surprise, I was greeted like a regular and, to my amazement I was offered a glass of champagne, which I readily accepted. As Colin explained what we needed, the sales assistant, who was a slim young man that looked like he belonged on a catwalk, seemed to recognize me, then he confirmed his observation.

"You're the guy with the rifle that shot the wrong target?" he was three feet from me but pointing at me as if there could be some confusion as to whom he meant. I nodded to concede his point and withheld the desire to point out that I had missed one in two hundred and forty shots and I'd won a bloody gold medal.

"So you're gonna be on Michael Ross? That is so cool!" With a brood of assistants helping, they set about dressing me in a variety of outfits from the surreal to the ridiculous. We were under Colin's supervision, but eventually his patience ran out.

"Look, we just want a slim fitting grey suit." In a sulky manner, this was provided along with shoes, a crisp white shirt and a slim, black, knitted silk tie. The jacket fit me perfectly but the trousers were unfinished and flapped over my feet, I was assured this could be altered and delivered to my home by lunchtime. I actually felt a slight pang of pride and confidence, as I looked at myself in the full-length mirror. I'm tall, as you know, but, at this stage, I was lean having lost a lot of my Legion bulk as I ran more than I lifted weights now. My skin was still dark from all the sun exposure and my scar had settled to a jagged trench that was almost the same color as the rest of my skin, just slightly lighter. I reached to touch it as memories came rushing back and I thought how farcical this all really was. Why in the name of hell was I nervous about this, sitting in a room with some 'lovies' and talking for twenty minutes? Nothing would change; when I left the studio tonight I'd be the same insecure guy with a list of dead loved ones that was far too long. An older gentleman who introduced himself as the store manager interrupted my thoughts; he informed me that should I mention I was wearing 'Canali' on the television show they would happily provide all the clothes for free. Typical I thought to myself, I finally get some cash and no bugger wants it.

As promised by twelve thirty, I had a delivery to my house on Bourne Street. They'd actually sent the suit in two colors, the grey and a navy both altered to fit. There were two pairs of shoes and a belt to match each pair and three ties, the black one I had tried, a burgundy one and a gold one, all in knitted silk.

As my thoughts from the shop continued to echo, I focused too much on the past but it helped me dismiss any nerves I was having about something as trivial as what I would be doing that evening. Saying this when I arrived at Television centre just before four o'clock the nerves were back and my stomach was doing somersaults, I'd not eaten the whole day. Evelyn met me in the reception area and gave me a mock wolf whistle as she walked toward me.

"Wow Jean, Patsy had better watch out with you looking like this", she winked at me.

"Very funny" I blushed at her. I had worn the navy suit as I still had hang-ups about what would happen if I had an accident in a grey suit. Can you believe I was going on national television and worrying about how it might show on my clothes should I piss my pants? I wore the gold tie, as it seemed fitting for the occasion. She flashed a card that she was wearing on a chain around her neck at a guy in a uniform and we passed through what looked like a metal detector. She informed me that filming would commence in an hour and the other guest and I were to meet Michael Ross in the Green Room as soon as we arrived. I was informed that a Green Room is a waiting area for guests to wait pre show. The audience was in place and currently been warmed up by a comedian.

After been ushered into the Green Room, I was a little surprised to realize Evelyn did not follow me in. She simply wished me luck, told me I'd be great and kissed my cheek. Michael Ross was the first to greet me, shaking my hand warmly and introducing himself. He was almost as tall as me, which I hadn't expected, and he had a genuine looking smile.

"It's so good to meet you Jean, and get the chance to congratulate you on your win. I watched it all, simply an astonishing performance" I wondered if this was true or he was just buttering me up? Either way, I was flattered. "You look fabulous as well, great suit and love the tie!" Okay he was defiantly buttering me up. "Thanks", I replied anyway, "it's all from 'Canals' and if you don't mind, they've asked me to mention that on the show?" He seemed confused, "because they gave me all the clothes for free" I explained. His confusion seemed to be replaced with a little shock, but this soon turned into gentle laughter while he figured out if I was joking or not.

"I think you mean 'Canali', Jean, and, of course you should mention it. Listen carefully and I think you'll be amazed how many names we all drop across the night. It's a perk of the job." With this, he placed an arm around my shoulder and turned me to face the only other person in the room, it wasn't Gemma.

"This is Rage Miller." He introduced me to the famous old rocker who had been lead guitarist of the legendry 'Kings Destiny". This guy was a genuine rock star. He must have been at least sixty-five at this stage, but he radiated an energy that instantly let you know why he had been at the top of his game as long as he had. He had the contradiction in appearance that many of his kind do. He looked haggard due to years of drug and alcohol abuse but he also looked healthy, as he'd not touched anything for the last fifteen years. I remembered reading recently that he had married for the fourth time to a twenty-four year old lingerie model. As I looked at the scrawny leathery arms that hung from his sleeveless torn t-shirt, I couldn't help but think he may not have been as lucky in love, had his career not had such a wonderful effect on his bank balance? To complete the rock and roll look, he had skinny blue jeans painted on to his matchstick thin legs, again with a variety of tears. His mop of dyed black hair was topped with a traditional bowler hat. His nose was pierced on both sides and his wrists were covered in beads and leather bangles. Most of his skin that I could see was tattooed from the neck down including his feet that were on show as he wore flip-flops. All in all, he looked like a granddad at a fancy dress party but he carried it as well as he could and he seemed like a really nice guy so what the hell. He was also, as I have said but will repeat, a legend. Like Michael, he shook my hand.

"Just call me Rage," he instructed.

There was a tap at the door and a young girl in a head set informed Michael that Ms. Tsang was arriving, and, without giving either of us a second look, he ran from the room, neatening his hair with his hands as he went.

"Lady Muck's here and we suddenly don't exist huh?" I realized it was Rage talking and I turned and looked at him having not yet registered what he had said.

"The actress, the other guest is Gemma Tsang", he continued

"Oh yeah, I heard. Have you met her before?" I wanted to know if I was the odd one out among friends.

"No never, but there all the same. She won't come in here they never do, she'll go straight to the set and then vanish straight after the show, stuck up bitch", he seemed to sigh at the thought and I almost expected him to say something like 'kids today, don't know they're born'. I made a kind of head gesture to indicate some sort of understanding and he looked at me like I was an idiot before suggesting that we sit.

"How are you feeling?" was the next thing he said and I again created the 'you're an idiot' look as I stared at him confused. "Don't know about you, but I'm a nervous wreck." My confusion deepened, "Jesus man, I know you can speak I've heard you", he continued in exasperation.

"I, I'm sorry" I eventually stammered, "you're nervous?"

"Yeah man, this is live fuckin' telly" his original Birmingham accent surfaced ever so slightly. "You know how many people are gonna watch this? There's a bloody studio full of them as well!" He was shaking his head with his fingers interlocked behind his neck, while he massaged the wrinkly skin with his palms.

"But, you're Rage Miller?" He grinned, "I've seen you perform in front of a hundred thousand people in Paris!" How could this guy be nervous?

"You were at 'Band Relief'?" he asked referring to the charity concert I had mentioned in Paris.

"Well no, I saw it on TV" I said.

"That's different anyway, I didn't have to speak, just play the guitar. Besides, I was throwing up with nerves for two days before that gig". My God it helped to hear that, if this guy was nervous despite all he'd done in life, I had nothing to worry about. Nobody even gave a shit I was there. I was a filler for someone who had cancelled and I was flanked by two of the biggest stars in the world. My nerves all but calmed and I breathed easier. Then the door opened and Gemma Tsang walked into my life again.

"Sorry I'm late guys", her face was alight with a beautiful smile that lit the room, 'Mr. Miller' it's great to meet you" he accepted the out stretched hand and shook it.

"Err, I think I owe you an apology", it was said in a surprised but half mocking tone.

"Sorry?" asked Gemma

"Nothing" he allowed himself a small laugh as he stood and kissed her cheek. "Lovely to meet you too, young lady", the rock star had gone and a Picard elderly gentleman replaced him as her charm and presence captured him. I had already joined him on my feet.

"And you must be our great Olympian?" She turned to me and began to extend her hand. "It's so nice to…" both the sentence and the advancing hand stopped and Rage looked from one of us to the other and back. "It's you?"

Bollocks, bollocks, bollocks. How in the name of all that is holy did she recognize me now? I was convinced I was about to piss my pants, I had to try and bluff through this.

"I don't think we've met?" I don't think I sounded convincing. Gemma withdrew her hand and tried to hide the frosty look that could not be hidden.

"Like that huh? Did we not meet on a flight from Los Angeles a few years ago", Christ of course the bloody plane, thank God.

"Oh, of course, I'm so sorry I thought you meant before and…. err, nothing, Again, I'm sorry, of course I remember, I think of it often.

I had a wonderful time on that flight!" I was over compensating but it seemed to work.

"Well, I'm not sure what you meant by 'before' but you're forgiven, almost? I saw you win your medal but I never linked the two until I just saw your eyes again right now", she was teasing and flirting again I thought. She smiled again and stepping forward she kissed my cheek. Her lips landed right on my scar and for a heartbeat the touch seemed to linger, my heart seemed to explode.

"I was just telling my new friend here how nervous I get at these things" the silence was broken by Rage.

"Oh my God, me too" Gemma opened her mouth and put her hand to her chest. Her as well, this was all helping a lot and I was calming further.

Suddenly the girl in the headset returned and informed 'Ms Tsang' that they were ready for her.

"Good luck guys, see you out there!" I watched her leave. She wore a yellow sleeveless dress that looked like silk and hung to the floor. It was held at the waist by a simple gold belt, it was cut low but classy, letting you know something was there but not showing it to you. She seemed taller so I guest the dress was hiding heels and her hair flowed freely, black and straight down her back.

"What an amazing young woman" Rage distracted my thoughts again. "How do you know her again?" I spent the next twenty minutes talking to Rage who, like his musical brother 'MC BallistiX', turned out to be a thoroughly pleasant guy. When the headphone-wearing girl arrived for Rage he slapped my back, repeated Gemma's wishes of good luck and I was left alone to gather my thoughts. For the first time I noticed a TV playing on the opposite wall and realized that the recording outside was being played through. I turned up the volume and watched Gemma and Rage talking with Michael Ross. She was truly amazing. The room was captivated as she took them under her spell making them laugh, at times sigh and often burst into rounds of applause. I listened as she was asked about her late break into acting and what she had done before that. They talked about her opening night, when I had watched her on stage as she made her debut to the waiting world. She talked about working in the bank and how lucky she had been to get the break that had allowed her to achieve the things she had wanted to do all her life. As she did this, something changed in me; I suddenly wanted her to know who I was. I realized we had things in common. Okay, she'd not had the initial problems that I'd had in terms of appearance and health, but I couldn't begrudge her that. She had, however, been a person with dreams, still was, and she was not yet where she wanted to be or who she wanted to be. Written down or not, she had a list of things she wanted to achieve and she was out there achieving them. The only things she could ever really know were that I had joined the Legion and that I'd won the medal. Alone these were amazing accomplishments anyway, but more so if one knew where I had started, I wanted her to know.

I had been toying with an additional accessory to my wardrobe and I then decided I should add it. From my pocket I took the bracelet Gemma had given me years before, and rolled it onto my right wrist, I knew I would be sitting to her left. I glanced at the card I kept with it, and read again the words I had memorized so long ago.

I was also surprised at the amount of names that were dropped on screen. As the host had assured me, everything from soft drink brands to luxury cars were thrown into conversation, no doubt to give thanks for or to generate freebies. I reminded myself to mention my suit.

On the screen Rage was talking now, he was telling a story about a time he'd tried to throw a 'Toshiba' TV from a hotel window, 'The Hilton'', but he'd stayed at that hotel before. 'The Hilton' and the management had installed plexi-glass. The TV had bounced back into the room knocking him out cold for over three hours; the crowd was in hysteria as 'headphones' came to collect me.

Suddenly, I was standing behind a flimsy looking wall where I could hear Michael Ross narrating a brief introduction for his final guest. The applause began and music played as I walked around the screen out onto the stage. I felt good, I felt calm and confident, I felt ready. After shaking Michael's hand I introduced myself to Gemma and Rage again for the cameras and took my seat. Gemma was to my right next to Rage and Michael was opposite me at an angle so we were all on show to the audience.

The applause ended having lasted slightly longer than I expected, even interspersed with a few cheers, all very good to keep my nerves calm.

"What a reception" announced Michael, as he prepared to begin the interview, "there must be a few 'Czech' girls in here tonight" the audience laughed again and I felt myself blush. I had not expected any references to Eva and I didn't want to talk about her. I laughed along in an obviously fake manner. "Are you still in touch with the lovely Eva?" I shook my head.

"No, but I am sure if I am in Prague or if she's in London, we'll grab a coffee, we became good friends". To my surprise a picture of Eva looking ridiculously sexy from a swimsuit calendar she had done appeared on a screen behind us.

"Very nice", stated Gemma and I looked at her as I seemed to hear a sarcastic undertone. I must have imagined it, surely.

"Just friends huh?" continued the host.

"Just friends" I confirmed, "She's a lovely girl and an amazing athlete"

"Okay Jean, we'll take your word for it." He leant forward and patted my knee in his trademark fashion. "Now, let's talk about that medal of yours, an amazing performance." He continued and we chatted about the competition and the lead up to it. I managed to draw a few giggles at the right places and my host was amazing at making me feel relaxed and comfortable. We interacted as a group and Gemma and Rage both asked questions and shared relevant stories of their own that linked to my tales. After maybe ten minutes the interview moved away from the Olympics slightly and interest was expressed in my past and how I got to the Olympics, how I learned to shoot and such.

"Like Gemma with acting" I looked to her to express the point and make eye contact, "I came to shooting late, I also worked at a high street bank until just around six-years ago and it was only after that when I first picked up a rifle".

"That's astonishing" encouraged the interviewer, "what made you suddenly leave the bank, I'm guessing in your thirties, and decide to learn to shoot?"

"Well, I didn't decide to leave the bank. I was made redundant" again I gave Gemma a glance and noted ever so slightly that her brow was furrowed. I continued, "I didn't know what else to do, I was hugely overweight." The furrows in her brow deepened. "So I joined the French Foreign Legion at 'Fort de Nogent' outside Paris and I learned to shoot there." There were a few muted gasps from the audience and those alongside me on the stage went quiet. Nobody knew this about me and I could see in Michael's eyes that the boring athlete who was there as a filler just got interesting.

"That's truly a fantastic story Jean. Is that where you received the scar on your face? If you don't mind me asking?" Involuntarily I touched the wound with my right hand and I noted Gemma looking at the gemstones around my wrist.

"Kind of, it was actually a mole I had removed" I replied. Gemma looked like she was trying to solve a 'Rubik's Cube', her eyes flicking from side to side in their sockets.

"They remove moles in the Foreign Legion?" the audience laughed with me at the question.

"Well, it was no surgeon, my Sergeant did it with a bayonet, he thought I had a turd on my face" the audience laughter doubled, "it was a pretty big mole" I added.

"So" the follow up questions began, "you were fired from the bank? You were over-weight and sound like you looked gorgeous" more laughter, "and you just decide to up and off to France and become a soldier?"

"Well, there was a little more to it than that. It was a particularly shit day. I lost my job and my landlord evicted me from my flat" I didn't want to mention my list. Luckily my revelations had taken us from the Olympics and I had not been asked any questions about my chat with the President or the piece of paper we had exchanged. If we could stay away from that subject then great.

"So having lost your job" my statements were repeated to me for clarity, "you get home and your landlord has kicked you out? So off you go and join the Foreign Legion"

"That's about it yeah?" I laughed and the audience laughed with me.

"Wow, I guess you owe this landlord a thank you in a weird way, can you remember his name?"

"I can, ironically it was Mr. Tsang just like Gemma here" I didn't look directly at her but I felt her chair move as I saw her sit bolt upright with my peripheral vision. She looked at me still confused and unsure.

"Wow Jean. I'm actually lost for words, we obviously do research for the show and someone is gonna get fired I can tell you". There was more laughter, amplified again when I stated that 'I doubt the research is as extensive when a guest is filling in for a cancellation last minute'.

"Maybe so" concurred Michael, "but again, they really are incredible achievements".

"Well maybe, but someone once told me, I think it was my thirty-second birthday actually, the day I was fired. Anything is possible with courage and confidence" I let it hang and Michael turned a question to his first guest.

"That's exactly what you said I think Gemma, at the beginning of the show? Gemma? Gemma?" he got no reply from her.

I turned to look at her along with the entire audience and saw Gemma Tsang starring at me. Her mouth was hanging wide open and a look on her face that could only be described as complete and utter astonishment. Her silence was an awkward length, though eventually as she composed herself, some of the frostiness I had experienced earlier seemed to have returned. I began to question and even regret my grand unveiling. The rest of the interview was fun but underlying it was a panic at what would happen afterwards when the cameras stopped rolling. Before the show finished Michael did me the favor of reminding me of another obligation I had.

"By the way Jean, I have to say you look very dapper tonight, where is the suit from" thank God he remembered but it didn't really matter, surprised by the reminder my head began to spin and my brain decided not to confer with my mouth.

"Oh thanks," I babbled, "it's made of Candles", what the? He stared at me for a second with that 'you're an idiot' look on his face, then he thanked his guests and said goodnight, the show was over.

As the final applause subsided a team of technicians and floor staff swarmed the studio. They disconnected microphones and started to usher out the audience whilst dismantling equipment and such. Gemma had yet to speak to me directly but had not taken her eyes off me since reality had dawned on her; she had a look on her face that said she just couldn't believe something she knew to be true. Michael shook hands with each of us again, me, Rage and lastly Gemma who he lingered around in his suave manner. 'Headphones' was suddenly by my side and informed me 'I was done' and could leave at my convenience. I shook hands with Rage but declined his offer to join him for a drink, promising a rain check. I gave Gemma another glance and decided it might be best if I just left, I hoped she'd follow but she only did so with her eyes. Backstage Evelyn grabbed me in a hug and told me how well I'd done. She asked if I was okay, as I seemed suddenly somber, I told her I was fine and continued my exit. Under an hour later, I alighted a cab on Bourne Street, wandered into my kitchen and selected a bottle of red wine from my ample rack, which Madame Tremblay always kept full. I felt low. I don't know what I had expected from Gemma. Well, I guess I expected the reaction I got but I mean after that. I mean what could she say really? She didn't really know John Bore, she certainly didn't know he was madly in love with her; she had just felt sorry for him. She definitely didn't know Jean Ennuyeux, who did. She was now one of the most famous women in the world so, other than surprise at the fact that someone she worked with once had changed quite dramatically, what would she care? I threw my jacket and tie onto the back of a chair and poured myself a large glass of the fragrant crimson liquid I was craving. It was a warm night and I decided to drink my wine in the garden, finding the key for the rear patio doors in a kitchen draw I opened them and breathed in the fresh night air. The smells of all the flowers in my garden filled my nostrils and I thought at some point I should learn their names, I never did. As I was about to sit in one of the teak chairs that were beside the small pond with the fountain, I thought I heard a knocking. Convinced I must be wrong; I headed to the front door? Surely if it was anyone they would have used the bell and at this hour it could only be Colin, maybe come to congratulate me on the show?

I opened the door to the most beautiful girl in the world, still in her yellow dress but with a sleek beige raincoat over her shoulders, her arms not in the sleeves, I just stared at her.

"Are you going to invite me in John?" I could not decipher her tone.

"Of course, I'm so sorry, I was just surprised, how did you?" She cut me off

"Evelyn. I saw you talk before you left and it wasn't hard to get your address out of her" she smiled, "in fact, I'm not sure I actually got as far as asking for it." She followed me down the corridor to the kitchen and accepted my offer of a glass of wine;

she placed her raincoat on the same chair as my coat and tie. She looked around the room before she spoke again, "well, I have to say I am just dying to hear this story". I shrugged at her.

"You pretty much heard it tonight. When I left the bank that day, I got home, your uncle had kicked me out and dumped all my stuff in the bins", she blushed at this.

"I am so sorry about him, he's..." I now interrupted her

"Hey, it's fine, I owed him rent and, well, never mind" I decided to provide a little more information than I had on the show, so I told her about my stepmum and what she'd said to me before passing away. I told her about my list, but flippantly declined to show her it, and then I told her that I had seen the first ten minutes of her play." She just sat and listened while sipping her wine, I told her about my prostatitis problem which explained my behavior at the bank, I told her about the legion, the training and how all my comrades had rallied around to get me fit. I told her about the Sergeant and walking his dog, about Andy and Ivan and all the other guys. I covered Afghanistan off by saying it was mostly boring foot patrols, but I'd learned to shoot, so when I came out I focused on the Olympics.

"That's it" I eventually finished with.

"That's it? I hardly think that's it John", I frowned at her trying to establish her point, "what about this place John, I'm sitting in your bloody Chelsea mansion drinking a £1000 bottle of Château Petrus. Where the hell did all this come from?" She paused, when I did not respond and then urged me on, but I was just staring at the bottle of wine

"£1000? For a bottle of bloody wine?" She laughed at my apparent naivety

"John?"

"I've been Jean for some time now, it's what they called me in the legion and I stuck with it." My mind was racing to come up with an answer. "When I won the lottery I figured a new start and all that?" I was a bloody genius.

"You won the lottery?" she asked looking for the world like she didn't believe me for a minute, "okay if that's your story let's stick with it. So Ennuyeux or whatever it is, where does that come from?"

"It's French" I informed her, "it means boring" I followed in a half whisper. She froze with the glass to her lips and stared at me again, I tried to change the subject. "Anyway what about you?" I took the seat opposite her at the breakfast bar where she had come to sit when I was speaking. "What a rollercoaster you've been on, what happened after that first night when I saw your debut?" After a brief thoughtful look she seemed to relax and decided to let me off the hook for a while.

"Okay 'Jean'" she emphasized the name, "Only fair I guess?" so she began, I listened to her story mesmerized. I found her adventures more than equalled mine and I marvelled at her bravery in going to Los Angeles alone and the stature of people she had met, impressed and worked with. She talked with an enthusiasm I could only aspire to when we reached her Oscar win, but none of it was vain or conceited; she still carried a humble air about her albeit surrounded with a calm confidence. It was not so much the Oscar that generated such passion in her but the part she had played to win it. Again I drew comparisons between our situations, on a regular basis she had to pretend to be someone else, to such an extent that she almost became that person. I guess that is what I had been doing for six years now; I guessed it is what I would do forever.

This was, and, in my memory, still is an absolutely amazing night. Before we knew what was happening the sun was peeping through the windows and our second bottle of ridiculously expensive wine was empty on the table. We were actually laughing after she confirmed she had heard my ill-timed fart at the bank all those years ago, then the mood seemed to turn a little melancholy.

"Jean, I hope you don't judge me on how things were for you at the bank back then?" she was staring at the empty glass in her hand.

"Judge you? You were the only person who was nice to me", I was not trying to make her feel better, it really was the case.

"But I was nice to you in private, when I let you in and when nobody was looking. Looking back it seems pathetic, childish", I was not sure what she wanted to hear.

"Gemma, it was more than most and more than I ever expected. I never thought anyone like you would notice me or want to be my friend. Back then I lived for the few kind words I could steal from you. I always wished I could steal them without you actually looking at my appearance though, without you seeing me." Now I was staring at my glass.

"Is that why you never got in touch after we met on the plane? Is that what that was about? Just proving that you could impress me with your physical appearance now?" Now she was looking at me and I made eye contact in confusion.

"What? Not at all, Jesus I booked a ticket on every plane to London just so I could see you, I didn't even think we'd speak. If there had been a way to contact you or any indication you wanted me to then, well of course I would have". She dropped her head and began to shake it.

"Albert" she said almost to herself, "typical"

"Albert?" I asked

"My manager, you met him on the plane. I sent him back with my number after I left the plane. When we landed there was such a ridiculous welcoming committee that I didn't get chance and I asked him to sneak back and talk to you", she sighed heavily, "he's a good man, a great manager, but a little over protective".

"Yeah the posh guy in the cravat, I remember. He did come back but just told me you'd said it was 'nice to meet me'", for some reason I did that inverted comma's thing with my fingers.

"I'll bloody kill him," she half laughed and half snapped the sentence.

"It's not his fault" I offered to try and excuse him, "I was pretty rude to him on the plane"

"I'm sure he deserved it, he has that way about him until you get to know him". We sat in silence for a few seconds before I worked up a little more courage. I placed my hand on hers before I spoke.

"You're here now." She didn't move her hand, but focused on me again. "I'm really glad you are." The next pause was too long as she bit her bottom lip and grinned.

"So am I Jean, I really have had a lovely night. I hope we can be friends." Friends I thought, oh well, more than I ever dreamed of, "for now at least" she added with a blush.

"I'd like that a lot," I managed to it say without whooping for joy.

Two hours later Albert arrived at my front door following a call Gemma had made from her mobile. I was still ushering him through the door when Madame Tremblay arrived at the gate looking concerned at the stranger before her. In his typical fashion Albert neither exchanged pleasantries with me or introduced himself to Madame Tremblay. She pulled a snooty face behind his back as he headed down the corridor. I suggested she start at the top of the house on the third floor while I sorted things down here, I didn't detail the things that required sorting.

Rejoining Gemma and Albert in my kitchen they suddenly both fell silent as no doubt the unsuitability of Gemma's conduct was been preached to her. She snatched a small holdall from Albert's hand and asked if there was somewhere she might change, as she was still wearing the same beautiful yellow dress from the previous night; I was still wearing the same suit trousers and dress shirt. I directed her to my bedroom on the first floor; confident it would look immaculate having not been visited since Madame

Tremblay's last blitz. As soon as she had left the room Albert turned his guns on me.

"Do you know how dangerous this could be for her", spittle was flying from his lips and his face was the color of a ripe tomato.

"Dangerous?" I said it sarcastically to magnify his obvious exaggeration.

"All it takes is one slimy journalist to follow her back here and get a picture of us leaving and all her hard work is over, people will be more interested in her sexual exploits with a nobody" he turned up his nose and waved his hand in my direction, "than all she has achieved and is capable of as an artist".

"Albert" I said it as harshly as I could to ensure he'd shut up and listen, "I know you believe what you are saying and I am sure you have nothing but Gemma's best interests at heart", he nodded as if obvious, "but you are an arrogant bastard and you really need to stop talking to me like this, it's starting to piss me off." He began to fluster almost to the point of hyperventilating as he tried to form words, but he was prevented from forming a sentence by a blood-curdling scream that echoed through the house from above.

By the time Albert and I reached the foot of the stairs Madame Tremblay was already near the end of her decent and met us in the hallway. Her face was sheet white and she was physically shaking.

"Monsieur Jean" as she had taken to calling me, "there is a naked lady in your bedroom", I have to be honest it struck me as sad that it was such a huge shock to find a woman in my bedroom.

"It's okay Madame Tremblay" I tried to explain as Albert was shaking his head in disgust.

"No Monsieur Jean you don't understand" she tried to explain, "I think it is Gemma Tsang, the actress". Albert just grunted.

Gemma and I had already exchanged numbers and agreed to meet for dinner that evening. She was due to be in London for the next month or so during which time she had several more interviews to promote her new film, before heading on a world tour of premiere appearances for the same movie.

What a month it was. Gemma had laughed with a little blush, when I had asked what the likelihood was of us getting a table at the exclusive 'Nobu' restaurant for our first date

"Don't worry, it's a perk of the job," she explained. That night over dinner I experienced true, overbearing attention, all eyes were on us. Who was the tall guy with the girl who was fast becoming a Hollywood icon.

"How will you explain me?" an eyebrow was raised at my question, as an invitation to explain it, "I mean, this is pretty public, people are going to ask how we know each other". There was a pause while we ordered water from a striking waitress.

"Tap is fine," replied Gemma to the baffling list of options we were given. Alone again, albeit with an audience Gemma continued, "I'm assuming that you have an objection to me saying we're old colleagues from the bank?"

"Yes" I replied a little to hastily.

"Jean, I am not going to ask why, well not yet, but one day. I'm also going to want to see that list", I received a wink with the sentence.

"One day I'll tell and maybe one day I'll show you," I promised with a wink in return. From that point the night got better and better and, as I have already indicated, the following weeks continued in that vein. We ate together every night and several lunchtimes, we saw a movie, we walked round first Hyde Park, then Regents and then Green. We visited almost every museum in London where Gemma both amazed and educated me with her knowledge of art and it's history. Although Gemma had learned a lot of tricks to disguise her self with sunglasses and hats, our time together was not unnoticed. Several people approached her for autographs and she always obliged with a smile. A couple of pictures taken by either eager paparazzi, or gold digging, camera phone wielding, members of the public, appeared in magazines. All in all however we were not that exciting a story, we were both single, calm and drug free so many of our counterparts across the pond were a lot more interesting and financially viable. As Gemma was now an 'English treasure' and I had brought home a gold medal, all in all people seemed to smile on us and what our relationship may or may not be.

Before Gemma was whisked away to Europe on her whirlwind tour she invited me to the London Premiere of her new movie. So it was that on a chilly Friday evening I, Boring John, found myself walking down a red carpet in Leicester Square. I was wearing a tuxedo that a nice man called 'Giorgio' had, for some reason, sent me. It fit like it was made for me, and I had Gemma Tsang on my arm. I stood back and watched her chat with fans, sign autographs and pose for pictures. All in all, she spent over two hours in the cold conducting herself with a grace and class that one can only be born with. I was in heaven, it was my thirty-eighth birthday, and the fact that nobody else knew it meant nothing.

We didn't actually watch the movie, we spent the time with a bunch of Gemma's peers in what appeared to be a specially built bar. That experience is a whole other book, *'Strange People Actors'*. Later in the evening, having spent an hour shaking all the necessary hands at an after party, Gemma invited me back to her hotel for a nightcap. She was leaving the next day. I was as terrified as I had ever been at what the invite might lead to but my excitement was palpable and possibly visible should one take a look at the crotch area of Giorgio's suit. I again became nervous about Gemma's reaction should she see my scars.

I suddenly found myself sitting on a sofa opposite Gemma in a hotel suite that seemed bigger than Bourne Street. We sipped champagne, I really didn't like it but thought I'd best not say anything. We made small talk and both professed what an amazing time we had had over the last month. The conversation became whispers and eventually came to an awkward silence, our first and last.

"I'm tired Jean" she leaned forward and placed her glass on a low ornate coffee table, kicking off her shoes at the same time and curling her feet up under her legs. She let her head fall sideways to the back of the sofa and gazed at me with a half smile, "I should get an early night, I fly to New York tomorrow."

"Oh, of course, I see", I instantly felt like a visitor who had outstayed their welcome. I placed my glass next to hers and stood up, she frowned at me but said nothing. "Well, I'll be off then, again it's really been great and if you are in London again, well, you know?" Looking back I realize she was looking at me like I was a moron, but, at the time, I didn't see it. She didn't speak so I gave a wave and turned to leave, yes, I actually waved.

"JEAN!" I had never heard my name in such a shrill voice and I froze half way to the door and turned to see she had stood and taken a few steps after me, "you have got to be kidding me right?"

"I…" That was as far as I got.

"Don't you like me Jean" she sounded like a shy teenager all of a sudden and I took a step in her direction.

"Of course I like you I…" Cut off again

"I know you like me Jean, I mean do you 'LIKE' me', she did that inverted comma thing with her fingers as she said 'like' the second time. I figured I was running out of time and chances here and decided to go for it.

"You're wondering why I haven't tried to kiss you?" Okay I didn't so much go for it but this was a brave sentence for me. She laughed out loud and let her head fall back, now I frowned.

"Kiss me? Kiss me? What is wrong with you?" she seemed really mad now, "Jean, I'm completely in love with you I'm wondering why you haven't ripped my dress off and thrown me around the bloody bedroom!" She instantly blushed and fell silent but she stood her ground and we looked at each other. My mouth was half open; did she just say she was in love with me? She bloody well did you know. I walked toward her and handed her a piece of paper that I took from my inside pocket. "What's this?" she took it from me and looked exasperated at me, as though she thought I was trying to change the subject.

"It's my list. I said I'd let you see it one day"

"Now? Is this what you want to do now?" I think she was about to tell me to 'just go', I had decided I wasn't going anywhere.

"You need to see it, there are things you need to know, things I need to tell." This changed the mood completely and she appeared concerned before she gently unfolded the infamous piece of paper.

"You only have a few left," she whispered so softly I could barely hear her, "this is the piece of paper the President took from you at the Olympics?" She'd told me many times that she'd watched my medal ceremony but then I was just some guy, she'd not even made the link to me on the plane, I nodded. "How did the President know about your list, I mean he came back and asked you for it, or that's how it looked on TV?"

"He'd seen it before Gemma", I don't know why I was expecting her to figure it out, how could she? How could anyone?

"I don't understand Jean, what are you trying to tell me? You're being a bit weird." The last statement was said with a smile and I could tell she was trying to defuse what felt like a slightly tense situation. She looked back to the list. "Okay so I know you've done this stuff, I guess the 'hero' and the 'gold medal' was two birds, one stone?"

"No, it was something different"

"Come on Jean what is it, what do I need to know?" I took off my jacket and let it fall to the floor. Then I began to undo the black stud buttons of my evening shirt. Now this sounds cool, but the buttons were really fiddly and when I tried to undo my bow tie, which took two hours to tie, it knotted and began to choke me. Eventually I got everything undone and Gemma's giggles turned to a look of sheer horror as the shirt joined the jacket on the floor and the mass of scar tissue across my chest, arms and torso were revealed for the first time. "Oh my God Jean, what the hell happened to you?" Tears began to roll down her face but I was committed now, so I slowly turned around revealing the scars that were more famous than even Gemma Tsang. "No" she sobbed, "it's not possible. I knew you only six years ago, it just isn't possible." I kept my back to her to hide my own tears that memories were forcing into my eyes. 'How is this possible' and 'I don't understand' she repeated several more times before falling quite. I heard nothing but felt her approaching me. Then I felt her finger touch the tip of the scar at my right shoulder, she traced it gently down to my left hip and then did the reverse on the second scar. She stepped forward and I felt her breath on the skin between my shoulder blades, then her lips. Her arms crept around my waist, she held me "You've been working out, soldier" she whispered.

In the early hours of the morning we lay tangled in the bed sheets looking at each other, smug post-sex smiles painted across our faces. All the conversations had been had and she now knew everything. She still loved me and knew that I had loved her, well, forever. The next few hours were pretty much equally divided between sleep, sex and the mindlessness of new love as we explored each other. During the course of the night, my every scar was 'kissed better', and we did other such soppy things that you do when you're at this stage of a relationship. At around nine o'clock, we awoke from the last of our slumbers and Gemma rolled over placing her chin on her hands on my chest.

"About this list?" I raised an eyebrow as a question, "I think I can maybe help you out with the next two but only on the condition you promise me you are willing to forget about the last one" she smiled at me mischievously.

"We'll see" I teased her

"Come on Jean, you were a kid, it's official I am banning you from the last thing on your list!" I threw a pillow at her as she pranced toward the kitchen. The thin cotton sheet she was wrapped in was doing nothing to hide her figure so I paced after her. Feeling passion worm its way back into my system I decided I might like to break-in the kitchen. When I arrived Gemma had flicked on the small flat screen TV on the wall and was taking a small bottle of orange juice from the well-stocked fridge. She giggled and dodged away as I kissed the back of her neck. I decided to check the fridge myself and I took a bottle of still water.

"I've been thinking", she said coyly, I turned to look at her but, over her shoulder, I saw the TV and instantly recognized another face. "Maybe you could come to New York with me and, Jean are you okay?" The plastic bottle dropped from my hand and bounced across the tiles spreading it's contents everywhere, "Jean what is it?" She followed my gaze and with a concerned expression focused on the man on the screen. A man I had last seen in the dessert shaking his head at me in terror as he lay underneath the corpse of Tim, the British Commando who had been my friend. It was Major French.

Gemma continued to ask me what the problem was and who the man on the television was but she was a blurred voice barely reaching me through a foggy haze. Likewise the words that the Major spoke were unclear. I thought I was dreaming but a tickertape system across the bottom of the screen simply read, 'former Major plans to reveal the identity of Soldier 'X' in a tell-all book'.

Reality eventually struck and I focused on the TV. An hour later, introductions made, Gemma and I sat with Colin in the workshop where he had built my medal-winning rifle, I noted it taking pride of place mounted on the wall.

"He knows who I am," I confessed to my audience. I told them everything about the day of capture and the last time I had seen the Major.

"But are you sure Jean" asked Colin, "I saw the interview and he didn't give anything away, maybe he is just trying to make some cash and he'll just use a name?"

"Maybe he's not sure, but he knows where we were captured and he knows 'X' was obviously my size and build. My scar, I guess he could have recognized me".

"Because it is you," Gemma offered with a shrug that made me smile.

"I know Sergeant Petit wasn't clear in the video, but again to someone who knew he was with me it could be figured out I guess. I just can't take the risk". I simply couldn't believe either what was happening, or the front of the Major himself. In the interview he had gone on to explain how he had hand picked and trained 'Soldier X' for a mission across enemy lines and he was heartbroken that after the assassination of 'Bda Nam' we had not managed to reconnect. Jesus, everything had been going so well, I was with Gemma, she was with me, and now this.

"I need to talk to him, convince him not to do this. If it is about money I can give him more than he'll make from a book, can't I?" I think it was a rhetorical question.

"Jean I'm not sure there's anything you can do", Colin was not helping but he was trying to give me a dose of reality. "He seems pretty determined and how would you even find the guy, he could be anywhere". My head dropped as the truth of his words hit. Then Gemma spoke again.

"I know where he is", it was said in such a matter of fact manner that I had to request clarification.

"What?"

"I know where he is," she confirmed with a confident air, and then she went silent which seemed ridiculous.

"Well?" I asked, obviously in the wrong tone.

"Well if you are going to be like that"

"Gemma please?" I pleaded. She shrugged and pouted a little before resigning herself to delivering her information.

"Okay he's at the Lancaster hotel in Paris", she offered no explanation but the expressions on the faces of Colin and myself indicated we needed one.

"I've stayed there many times, that interview was in the forecourt at the centre of the hotel, I'd recognize it anywhere. I'll be staying there soon for the Parisian premiere.' We just stared at her in shock. "It's on the 'Rue de Berri', just off the Champs Elysées" she finished with, as if that made it all clear.

Moments later it was decided, I would not be joining Gemma in New York and I would miss that premiere the next night. I was shattered but secretly ecstatic that she also seemed so disappointed. I was to head to Paris where I would try and 'talk' to Major French. Upon the results of my efforts, I may then fly on to Los Angeles and join Gemma there.

Less than twelve hours later, I stepped of the Eurostar train at Guard Du Nord in Paris for the second time in my life. I could not help but reflect upon the last time I had taken that journey, terrified, obese and embarrassed as my fellow passengers had boarded to see my underwear scattered across the seats to dry. I dozed off in my first class seat and, thinking of the Major and the past, I had my first nightmare since I had begun spending time with Gemma. I woke in a sheen of panic-induced sweat when the train pulled into Paris.

It was not until I was sitting in a taxi heading to the 'Hotel Lancaster' that I realized I had no plan whatsoever. What would I say or do? At the last minute, I told the driver to continue past the hotel and drop me at the end of the street. In typical French fashion, he began to protest at the change of instructions and as I calmly told him to 'shut the fuck up', to my amazement I recognized my driver. I was leaning through the window to hand him his fare when it struck me, it was the exact same driver who had taken me to the Legion Fort all those years before. He was older, he was fatter, but his eyes and his voice left me in no doubt. That same arrogant prick was the one who had laughed at me so hard when realizing I was planning to be a Legionnaire all that time ago. I smiled at him broadly which shut him up far quicker than my barked demand had. Laughing I threw his fare into his lap and headed to a bench opposite the Major's hotel, where I took a seat and waited. I tried to figure out what the hell I was going to do now. I had reached no answer, when, after less than ten minutes sitting at my new station, my mind was made up for me.

I don't know why but, for some reason when, I saw Major French leave the hotel opposite me, I was in shock. He was right there in front of me. As you know, the last time I had seen him he was cowering to save his own hide in the desert. Now, I kind of understood that, had he made his presence known at the ambush would likely be dead as well. But that is not why he had stayed silent, he had not fathomed that, how could he? He had simply cowered there and abandoned us and now he was trying to make himself a hero based on the lives and the blood that had been lost. I gathered up my small leather overnight bag and I followed him at a safe distance.

He was pristinely dressed, it was a chilly day and a heavy overcoat covered his smart suit, his brogue shoes shone as only former soldiers shoes do. He looked older though, tired, almost haggard, I hated him and it was doubling by the second. I walked behind the man who, if not responsible for, had certainly delivered my friends to their death. He seemed small and, as my anger grew, he shrunk even more, by the time he walked into 'St Philippe du Roule' church after just five minutes on foot, he looked like a miniscule Satan in my eyes. Before I followed him in, I looked up at the impressive Catholic structure, one of a million in Paris. I had no idea he was a religious man, why would I? One of the last times I saw him he was masturbating over fetish pornography whilst choking himself with a dog collar.

When I did enter the building, I once again homed in on the Major. He was on one knee at the front of the central aisle at the front of the main altar. He crossed himself as I've seen people do in movies. Immediately after this, he turned to his left and, after a few short yards, walked straight into something that I could only assume, again from movies, was a confessional. I instantly knew what I was going to do. I picked up my pace and within a second I was seated within inches of the man I had come to see, separated by a small ornate wooden screen in the priest's side of the Catholic 'forgive me box'. He almost immediately registered my presence "Forgive me Father, for I have sinned" he opened with, obviously in French.

"Go on" I instructed, "my son" I awkwardly added as an after thought. I guess my response was not 'text book' as he paused before he continued. I saw him shuffle in his seat through the intricately carved wooden screen. I couldn't make out his actual features but even his profile was familiar and made me grimace with anger.

"I think I have killed men father." Think? Damn right you did. I didn't speak and after a pause he continued. "I don't know if my main sin is that I am a coward, or that I let my cowardice control me." Again I was silent and he took this as an invitation to carry on. "I fear I led men into danger to prove my bravery and then allowed my lack of bravery to abandon them".

"All these men were killed?"

"Yes Father, except one I think?"

"This was recently?" I enquired and I heard a sniff as though he was crying.

"It was several years ago Father, but it still haunts me"

"And what have you done to make amends thus far my son?" I was getting into character and had developed an idea as to where I might take this.

"Father?" he seemed confused.

"Have you honored the memory of these men and explained to the survivor what happened?" This actually seemed to cheer him up slightly.

"No Father, but I intend to. I have written what happened and intend to make it available to the world?"

"And have you been completely honest in these writings as to the part you played?" unbelievably he didn't even pause.

"Absolutely Father", the lying son of a bitch and to a bloody Priest as well, or, at least, as far as he knew.

"So this book may cause you further pain?"

"Errr... I don't understand Father?"

"If you are to publish a book in which you admit you are a coward who led men to hell and left them to die, the world will judge you on that yes?"

"Well I". As we were speaking I was looking at the partition that separated us and realized it was held in place by four simple wooden pegs. They were nailed in the middle so they could rotate from the frame and hold the carved wood panel in place, I slowly opened all four and interrupted him.

"Or have you actually written a book of bloody lies and painted yourself as a hero who trained and led men?" When he next spoke he sounded somewhere between shocked and scared, which was perfect

"Father?"

"Have you written that 'WE' were close and that 'YOU' trained

'ME' and even tried to save 'ME', that 'YOU' tried to find 'ME' when I didn't return and that 'YOU were my mentor, that I was your protégé?" I spoke fast and violently, I heard his tears increase to sobs and I could see him shaking through the screen as he tried to stare through at me.

"W..w..what?" he managed to stammer. I let the screen drop and for several seconds I stared at him, he was paralyzed with fear, "NO" he eventually managed to utter. All the blood had gone from his face and his breathing was coming in short shallow gasps.

"All my friends are dead. I'm dead" I raged, "and it's your fucking fault you son of a bitch. We're all gonna be visiting you a lot if you publish that book, me, the Sergeant, even 'Bda Nam' wants to meet you headless as he is now. We'll be seeing you a lot". As I slammed the panel back in place I was not sure whether or not he had died on the spot, though the stench that quickly surrounded me confirmed he had soiled himself. I left the confessional as quietly as possible and headed to the exit quickly. He was still in the confessional as I left and I noted a real priest enter the side I had left just seconds before.

I took the first taxi I saw to 'Charles de Gaulle airport.' I had been in Paris less than two hours. As you know, I planned to join Gemma in Los Angeles. Her New York Premiere had been the previous evening, and, looking at the digital clock in the taxi, I realized that she would be on a plane to the West Coast at that time. We had spoken while I was still on the train from London and she had told me that I should be careful and that she loved me, yep it had not been a dream, Gemma loved me.

I booked a first class 'LA Premiere ticket' at the 'Air France' desk on a plane that would be leaving at four-thirty; I had three hours to kill so I sat in the lounge with a large brandy and allowed myself to think. My thoughts spun around my head until I boarded the plane and then continued for the entire flight. I had no idea if my charade would have the desired effect in silencing the Major. I had acted on impulse and improvised with the cards I was dealt. He had been beyond terrified, no doubt, and I knew he could be unbalanced from his ranting in the desert before our capture. I did not know if that was a good thing or a bad thing for me. All I could do now was wait and hope.

I landed in LA at around seven in the evening local time, and memories prompted me to lick the teeth I had received on my last visit. As soon as I was past the strict customs officers, I switched on my phone and called Gemma, things did not sound good.

"You're here already?" Not the warm welcome I'd hoped for.

"Yeah, it took less time than I thought. Is that okay?" There was a silence on the other end of the phone. "Gemma is something wrong?"

"You tell me?" It was said in a soft tone of voice but I didn't like it and a little panic set in. "Look come over", she added before I had chance to respond, she gave me the address and informed me it would probably take around an hour to get to her in the Hollywood Hills at that time of day. I took a cab and arrived in two hours.

I pressed a button set into the wall besides a pair of huge wooden gates and was greeted by the all too familiar voice of Albert, Gemma's manager. I was curtly informed I should follow the driveway and I was awestruck by the length of the walk from the grand gates to Gemma's even grander home. I didn't have long to admire Gemma's home, once I reached the large wooden front door, it was held open by my number one fan, Albert.

"She is waiting for you on the veranda" he informed me. "Leave your bag here if you like, I doubt you'll be staying". This wasn't sounding good, as I mentioned Gemma had been frosty on the phone, and Albert's smug confidence that I would not be hanging around made me nervous. I followed Albert's outstretched finger and walked through a large hallway, then a kitchen and eventually onto a vast balcony that gave me panoramic views of Los Angeles. Gemma stood with her back to me talking into a mobile phone. She looked amazing in blue jeans and flip-flops with a simple white t-shirt. She turned and looked at me coldly before informing whoever was on the other end of the phone she had to go. After hanging up she offered me a half smile that broke my heart, she made no move to touch me after our time apart and the mood was uncomfortable.

"Just tell me the truth Jean", she eventually murmured without making eye contact, "did you do it?" She finally looked directly at me, her head held high in a confident stance.

"Gemma, I have absolutely know idea what you are talking about, what is going on?" Her body seemed to physically relax but her gaze stayed on me, she was unsure of something.

"Come with me" she instructed, and like a reprimanded school boy I followed her as she strode past me and headed back into the plush kitchen. Once there she retrieved a remote control from the counter and flicked on a flat screen television that was attached to the wall. She got a little frustrated trying to find the channel she was looking for and then together we stood in silence watching a European news channel called BSkyB. After just a couple of minutes the story she was waiting for came around, a news anchor in a pristine jacket, shirt and tie began to speak

> *"Within the last couple of hours reports are in that a Major Reginald French, the man who claimed to know, and planned to reveal, the identity of 'Soldier X' has committed suicide by throwing himself from Le viaduc d'Austerlitz bridge in Paris. Police say they have no reason to suspect foul play, but they are hoping to talk to tall man who was seen in the vicinity, purely for questioning. You can imagine that conspiracy theorists are all ready saying that 'Soldier X' himself was responsible for the Major's demise in order to protect his identity."*

The newsreader went on to state that the Major had a history of depression and a drinking problem, neither of which I new about. As the words from the screen sank in I realized that Gemma was staring at me not the TV, I met her gaze.

"Did you do this?" she asked again.

"Yes, I think I did", my head dropped to my chest and began to feel weak.

"Think! Think? Jean did you throw that man off the bridge or not?" She was crying now, though if I hadn't been able to see the tears I would not have known, her voice was like stone.

"God no, of course not" my mind was in turmoil as I tried to think.

"Then what did you do in Paris" Gemma demanded.

"I...I talked to him, in a church. I just talked to him". Gemma stepped towards me and took my hands in hers.

"Look at me Jean!" I did, we were inches apart and she looked desperate. "Just tell me exactly what happened". So I did, I told her how I had followed the Major to the church, the confessional, my performance on the other side of the screen and then my journey to the airport and onward to be with her. When I had finished my chin was on my chest ad I was struggling for breath. I felt desperate for the toilet but that was impossible, I had drunk nothing for some time. A few seconds after I had finished she stepped forward and held me. "It wasn't your fault Jean, he was obviously troubled. I just needed to know that you" she let it linger.

"That I'm not a killer anymore." I finished her sentence.

"No it's not that, it's just..." again she left an unfinished sentence.

"Would you like me to leave?" I asked in the most normal voice I could, I was terrified what her answer might be.

"No Jean I wouldn't." Thank the Lord above, "look this is hard.

Since we parted in London I've been nosey I admit. I wasn't really aware of 'Soldier X', well I was, of course, aware, but I've been reading about you and I must have watched that video on the Internet a thousand times. Eventually it was just like watching you" she paused and bit her bottom lip. "I know you've killed Jean, and I understand why, but the fact that you are here now must mean that you killed a lot more than the three men on that clip. That's just a little scary for me, do you understand?" I nodded that I did as she looked into my eyes. "When I saw the news about the Major I just panicked, but Jean I believe you and this is not you fault". When she had finished she continued to stare at me, I didn't know what to say. "I love you Jean and I'm sorry, I love you so much".

"I love you too Gemma". We kissed and I was back in heaven. I was in heaven with a burden.

The following weeks my journey into heaven continued. I stayed with Gemma in the Hollywood Hills mansion. A mansion, she informed me was rented for her by a studio she had signed to for her next three movies. We ran together each morning in Runyon Canyon, I was constantly amazed by the number of Gemma's A-list peers that we saw running by us, they would simply wave and smile at us. During our time in London we had been so absorbed in each other that I had forgotten to exercise, it was such a pleasant discovery to find that like me Gemma rose early and needed to run. I knew though that I was possibly running from something, I think she just enjoyed it.

We attended the LA premiere of her latest film together. As with London we didn't watch it and I let her know that at some point I would actually like to sit through it, she gave me a DVD and I did. She was amazing. I was in LA a full three months in Gemma's rented home before I felt the need for new scenery. I broached the subject cautiously with Gemma over breakfast on her veranda one morning, I was cautious for a very specific reason.

'I'd quite like to spend some time back in London" was my opening gambit which backfired big time. Gemma looked crestfallen.

"Oh, I see. You're bored here? I thought we, well I hoped we, well, oh never mind, of course you should spend some time at home. I mean maybe a break would be good, I mean…" I couldn't help but smile, she sounded like me on that distant day in the bank, all she needed to do was accidently fart and she was me at age thirty-two.

"Gemma", I interrupted her, "I meant the two of us. You don't start filming again for two months and it's in Prague", we had talked about her next role together and even read scripts with each other. "I thought we could go back to my house on Bourne Street, maybe spend some time around Europe and then find somewhere we both like to get married before you have to work again".

"Oh, okay I guess that could work", she was so casual it seemed weird considering what I had just said. She was spreading strawberry jam on a slice of brown toast, and then she froze, glaring at the bread in her hand. "Did you just say 'get married?'" she positively stammered.

"God no" I exclaimed, "why would I say anything like that, yuk", I pulled a face to confirm my distaste.

"Yes you bloody did" she laughed out loud and physically threw first her toast and then the entire table that separated us across the patio. She jumped forward and straddled me on my chair before kissing my face a million times.

"Is that a yes?" I managed to ask between laughter and kisses.

"It's a yes," she eventually giggled. I stood with her still in my arms, her legs now wrapped around me. As I smiled to myself over her shoulder I noticed Albert in the kitchen window, he appeared to be in tears and as our eyes locked he smiled and gave me a thumbs up, I returned it behind Gemma's back.

We married in France, it was my fortieth birthday, and it was the happiest day of my life. Even as I look back now that day outshines everything, the births of all four of our children, every anniversary, every holiday, every award ceremony, the school plays, the births of our grandchildren and all the joy that comes with these things. I know I am running ahead now, my friends, but I need to explain this to you, all the events I have mentioned were amazing in their way but that day, that was the day when it all came together, when it was all worthwhile and when it all made sense. It was a day that was a catalyst for all those other joys; it was the day that the nightmares stopped, it was the day I started to feel safe.

It was purely chance that we ended up marrying in France. We had spent only a week back in Bourne Street before we had one night, over a bottle of wine, decided to go on a wine tasting holiday. It was simply a tipsy conversation in my kitchen when Gemma had admired the label on a particular bottle of wine we were drinking, 'Louis Jardot', it was a sepia colored label depicting an angelic face set at the top of a stone arch. When we arrived at the actual vineyard we were pleased to see that the entrance to the actual vintners was a real live replica of the very label. It made up one of the thousand and twelve pictures we took on that eight-day trip.

We left this vineyard with our rental car boot almost full and headed toward the town of Beaune which was the source of another of the wines we had come to love. Lost while en route in the Burgundy region we noticed the village of Vezeley sitting atop a hill in the distance. It looked amazing with its gothic looking church that was visible for miles so we decided to stop there for lunch, maybe even the night. It was still light when we drove up the winding road and parked close to the Basilica of Mary Magdalene, that we learned was one of Europe's largest and best-preserved Romanesque churches. The view from the town of Vezeley was breathtaking, offering heart-fluttering views of valleys, hills and vineyards that reflected the suns rays with such natural beauty that one could believe the religious tales that surrounded this area.

"Lets look inside", Gemma was tugging my hand like an excited child on a school trip and she tried to drag me toward the wooden doors of the vast church.

"Hang on, I need to find a toilet" I said pulling away, don't worry I really did need the toilet, my prostatitis had not bothered me for a while, even in it's fake psychological way.

"Okay, I'll meet you inside" she stood on tiptoes to kiss me and I watched her walking away with a spring in her step. I smiled at the happiness I felt and then let out a lung full of air as, I confess, as I looked at her amazing ass in her jeans.

It took me a while to find a loo and when I did it was in a small café just off the main church square. I felt obliged to buy something as I'd used their facilities, so I was heading out of the door with a bottle of water and an apple when I saw Gemma urgently wandering around the square looking for me. When I was spotted she came running over.

"Jean it's an amazing place", Jean just came naturally to her now, Boring John it would appear was as dead to her as he was to me, and in fact the world. "I met the priest, he's lovely and he said he would marry us now if we can get back there quick!" She was speaking fast and her words did not register at first. She looked a little embarrassed that I did not respond to her enthusiasm and excitement. "What are you thinking?" she added sheepishly. I answered honestly.

"I'm wondering where we can get you a dress?" Her smile returned and she kissed me.

"Leave that to me" she grabbed my hand and led me down one of the cobbled streets. Let's check into a hotel and then I'll start looking for a dress and you can try and find a suit, I'll meet you in the church in an hour tops, okay?" She led and I followed.

Once we had a room secured, I left Gemma searching for a wedding dress and headed off in search of my own attire for the ceremony. It proved harder than I had imagined. After forty minutes of running around I had found no store where I could purchase, rent or steal anything that one would traditionally want to get married in. I found myself back in the square outside the church wearing my jeans and trainers coupled with a white polo shirt that had been given to me as I left the hospital in Afghanistan. As my situation played through my head, I noted an elderly gentlemen heading toward me, as he passed by he touched the brim of his trilby hat and nodded to me, I smiled back and secretly wished he had been twice the size so I could have asked to borrow his beautiful three-piece suit. At his waist was a handsome rose gold watch chain, his white shirt was pressed to perfection and his navy tie looked...... it looked like I could use it. He seemed a little uncomfortable as he noted over his shoulder that I had followed him but he seemed to relax when I began to speak to him in French. I explained the bizarre situation as accurately as possible as he studied me intently.

"Un soldat?" he asked. Appearing to look at the scar on my face.

"Oui" I replied, "I was a soldier" He smiled at me and slowly removed his tie which he handed to me refusing to take any money from me despite my initial insistence. I thanked him and then tied his tie the best I could underneath the collar of my old polo shirt. I found my reflection in the window of a small bakery and suspected Gemma would not be happy with my efforts. I decided to go for brownie points and get her some flowers to form a bouquet. Alas, a florist proved as difficult to find as a clothes shop in this small town, so I headed to a field I had seen behind the hotel having convinced myself that handpicked wild flowers would be even more romantic. I froze as I reached the end of the dry stonewall that bordered the field. Framed in the beauty of the flowers and blowing grass was my bride to be, outshining all the beauty around her she was smiling broadly, crouched collecting her own bouquet of flowers having obviously shared my thought. I watched her for a few seconds lost in the magnificence my life was becoming, before sneaking away unnoticed wondering to myself, 'was she wrapped in a bed sheet?' I made my way to the church. I introduced myself to the bewildered priest who shook my hand while ogling my improvised wedding attire. I didn't wait long. Hearing the door behind me open and close, I turned around and saw the love of my life looking more beautiful than ever. As I had suspected, she, like I, had struggled to find traditional garb and was wearing an improvised wedding dress made up of a bed sheet, pinned in the right places to give it some shape and hold it steady. Noticing my efforts, a tie added to what I was already wearing, she laughed and I joined in, the priest did not, but he cracked a smile when we embraced in front of him after her lonely walk down the isle.

Ten minutes later we were Mr. and Mrs. Ennuyeux, although the actress Gemma would always be Tsang. After kissing on the priest's instruction, we laughed again and Gemma reached inside the folds of her dress/ sheets and removed a familiar piece of paper and a small pencil,

"There you go" she smiled at me as she drew a line through the sentence, 'Marry a famous actress'. I thought about apologizing, explaining that this was not why I had pursued her, but she knew and her smile confirmed it. We kissed again and headed for the door, but not before the blushing priest asked Gemma for an autograph. I was slowly getting used to that.

The fact that we were in the church a total of twenty minutes made the sight outside even more amazing. At the front of a veritable hoard of people, stood the man who had provided me with my tie. As we appeared at the steps, he lead his neighbors in a chorus of cheers, before stepping aside to reveal three rows of tables laden with food and wine of such proportions one would think they had been planning the party for months. What a party it was! Over one hundred people I have never before met before ate with us, drank with us and danced with us until the small hours of the morning. Such was our love for Vezeley, the surrounding area and the people after that night, we bought a modest villa just a mile from the town centre, and spent at least a month out of every following year in the company of our new friends. As the sun began to crash our party, I swept my new, drunk wife, up in my arms and carried her to our small room in the hotel down the lane. I lay her on the bed that had no sheet, because she was wearing it, and sat on a wooden stool looking at her in ecstatic disbelief. She briefly opened her eyes and slurred that she loved me. Her eyes reopened to twice the size and her face flushed with embarrassment, as to my never-ending amusement, she accidently let out a little fart.

It was forty-five years later when Gemma was presented with her sixth Academy Award, a lifetime achievement award for her contribution to theatre, film and the arts. It was my eighty-fifth birthday. The sixth Oscar came on top of, five Golden Globes, eight BAFTA wins, three Olivier Awards and an Emmy Award she received for a guest appearance in a popular US comedy. My marriage to Gemma continued to be the crowning glory of my life from that distant day in Vezeley and onward. We travelled the world; we raised perfect children and helped them to raise perfect grandchildren. Every day I told Gemma that I loved her more than the previous day and she returned the sentiment. Despite her job we made a pact that we would never spend more than a week apart and we stuck to it, even if it meant me flying fourteen hours to spend just two hours with her, as happened on one occasion.

Now, I am aware that I have taken a huge leap in time. This is pretty much because the day I married her nothing else mattered. It was as good as anything could ever be and, the story I was trying to portray in this book had pretty much concluded. There were a few things left on my list but I didn't care, I had nothing left to prove to anyone anymore. The book would be far too long if I continued with all the tales of what Gemma and I did over those forty-five years, and it may start to sound a little wet and sappy, I am a little concerned that it already has. Saying this, I suppose there are a few things I should tell, things that definitely had a great impact on me and on my story.

One pivotal thing occurred the very next day after our wedding, the party and Gemma's fart. It's a small thing that started with the flirtations of a newly wed, slightly hung-over couple. We were wrapped up in Gemma's old wedding dress sipping a shared bottle of water as I doted on my bride.

"I can't believe I'm married to you," I rather lamely stated. Gemma giggled at me.

"Why so, you know how much I love you", I did know that, I felt it with every fiber of me, I still do.

"I know and it's amazing" I continued, "but you could have anyone in the world, better looking, smarter, richer". Her face turned serious and she leant forward placing her hand on my cheek.

"Jean I love you, to me you are the smartest, most handsome man in the world", she held by gaze for a moment before falling back to the bed, again laughing, "and I'm pretty sure there aren't many richer", she instantly came bolt upright back in front of me, "oh

God, I didn't mean that to sound, I mean I don't want you to think I, I mean…" She stammered, it was my turn to laugh.

"Gemma I don't think anything of the sort" I tried to pacify her. "Truth is, I completely forget I have any money, it still doesn't seem real". This was completely true, of course I had the house and a few nice things but I had never really spent anything else, and I didn't feel any different despite the growing balance in my accounts. Gemma and I had never really talked about it, but of course she knew the reward on Bda Nams head. She dropped her head in thought and then without looking up at me continued.

"What have you done with it?"

"The money?" I asked, she confirmed with a nod, "Nothing really, the house and a few bits and pieces but it's pretty much all sitting in the bank I guess?" Gemma looked no less than shocked, borderline offended in fact, I was nervous, what had I done wrong so early in my marriage.

During the next hour I was reprimanded for my lack of passion, vision and charity. There was, apparently, so much I could do with all that money to make things better in the world and help others. Now, it's not that I lacked generosity or a 'do good' attitude, I had simply never thought about it. Until very recently I had been pretty much 'a charity case' myself and again, the receiving of all that money had never really computed at all. It wasn't that I never intended to do good things with it; I had simply not given a thought as to what to do with it at all?

So it was that during the rest of the vacation, that had suddenly become our honeymoon, my future career was decided. I was to be the founder and president of what would become one of the world's largest charitable organizations. The World Institute for Kids of Exciting Disposition, W.I.K.I.D., as we are known. I confess, the short name came first and we played around to find the words to make it up. My charity would be dedicated to taking underprivileged kids, from all countries around the world, and making their lives better, more exciting. This in the most dramatic cases, involved getting food to children, so close to death, that it could not be described to me, had I not seen it on my many visits to Africa, Asia and South America with my work. In the more fun situations we took inner-city kids for camping holidays, often supported by the military to install a sense of discipline and self-respect.

We started the charity, much harder than one might think with all the legal ramifications, with $200,000,000 of my own money. I had told Gemma I was happy to give it all away such was her frustration at my lack of vision; she had coyly suggested we should keep some. The facts are my funding soon paled into insignificance. We received extra funding from Governments and many private contributors. As the years passed these increased tenfold when we were proved to be completely transparent as to every penny, all of which went to the benefit of the charity and it's recipients. Each year Gemma and I hosted a Gala Dinner in Los Angeles, even at a million dollars each the hundred tables we offered were snapped up as the hottest on the social calendar. Soon we were auctioning them for up to ten million a table. By the end of each night after the collections, sales and auctions of signed merchandise, dinners with movie stars and a raft of donated prizes our record was $175,000,000, that's in one night.

I confess that, partly for selfish reasons, there were other fund raising events that took place throughout the years. Four years after my marriage I swam the English Chanel with a famous British comedian and two members of my former Olympic team. With a small pencil I scratched a line through that achievement on my infamous list. The crowning glory of my charitable tasks was on my first son's twentieth birthday, my sixty-first birthday, when with a team of British Paratroopers we reached the summit of Mount Everest, this also was scratched from my list.

On my return from Nepal, I sat with my wife in the house we had always kept on Bourne Street, marveling at the inconceivable fact that she was more beautiful now than the day we married.

"Just two left", I grinned at her knowing the response to come.

"Jean, I love you, but for the last time, if you go anywhere near that last thing on your bloody list I will leave you in a heartbeat. I'll take all the bloody kids as well she added!" I laughed as she crossed the floor and sat on my knee, and added. "Seriously Jean it's enough yeah? It's you and me right? You have nothing to prove, you never did and you know that now". I smiled and began to kiss her, then our youngest daughter returned home with friends and yelled at us from the hallway to, 'seriously, get a bloody room!' as we were, 'so embarrassing', she was at that age.

Gemma's last comment about having nothing to prove brings us to the second event that I should fill you in on, arguably the most important, certainly to me.

It was two years after our impromptu wedding that Gemma won her second Oscar Award. I had walked the red carpet with my wife in another suit provided by the elusive 'Georgio'. Over the years since Gemma and I became a couple, I was often sent clothes from this benefactor, even underwear but I never wore that, it had his name on it which just seemed weird.

I had become close to Gemma's parents as well, despite their initial misgivings about me. I guess children build bridges and, although Gemma was an only child, there were a raft of cousins who completed my newly extended family. To celebrate her new award, the family had decided to throw a party for Gemma and, as she was never one for large events, it was further decided it would be a small affair at the Bourne Street house once we returned from the Los Angeles ceremony. Knowing how much Gemma would hate it, I had let her know about the 'surprise party' on our way from the airport. On entering the house she acted suitably surprised, as one would expect from a double Oscar winning actress.

After the initial cheers, the night was pleasant enough. People mingled and chatted, children eventually fell asleep under coats with the exception of my son, who as always slept in the crook of my arm with his head on my shoulder.

Having been encouraged to make more of an effort mingling. I kissed my wife and begrudgingly left the kitchen coming instantly face to face with an all too familiar face. He was older, much older than the time lapse should really have dictated, but the pile of free food he had managed to cram onto his small plate and the embittered grin made my old landlord unmistakable.

"Mr. Tsang", I said it with surprise and this, in turn, created surprise in him. Gemma's uncle had become something of the family's' black sheep and this was the first time I had encountered him. Well, the first time since he had evicted me from my home leaving all my belongings in the bin. Gemma appeared at my side in a heartbeat with a cloak of concern that was so obvious to me; I wrongly assumed everyone would see it.

"Jean, this is my uncle, I don't think you've met?" I was still processing. "Hello Uncle" she added leaning in and kissing his greasy face before wiping her lips discretely on a napkin. Of course, he had no idea who I was, why would he? I calmed and allowed myself to smile, what did I care anyway?

"Oh that explains it," I offered. "I thought you were Gemma's dad", he frowned but should have taken it as a compliment; he could only wish to look as well as his distinguished younger brother. I offered my hand whilst grasping my son firmly with the other, and he shook it with his soggy grip. As well as his over advanced years, he had gained weight and lost his hair. All in all, he was a bitter looking little man, all of which added to the lack of care I had regarding our past. That was until I noticed his wrist; I held his hand a little firmer and pulled it toward me twisting it slightly. For reasons she could not possibly know Gemma's cloak of concern grew heavier.

"That's an interesting watch Mr. Tsang." He glanced at his watch, and then back and me again. "Where does someone get a watch like that?" What I was thinking was actually illogical, even impossible. Mr. Tsang was wearing a slim, very old looking Seiko watch, probably not hugely rare but this particular one sat on something called a flex-o-fix strap. I have subsequently learned that these are also not rare but at the time I had only ever seen one before. I had seen that actual watch before. It was my father's, but again that was impossible.

The old man looked at me quizzically but why would he worry, why would he lie?

"Actually long story", he began to smile at the thought of it, "I have property, I'm landlord" he informed me pointing at himself with the hand I was not hanging on to. "Many years ago I evict useless tenant, fat man not pay rent", Gemma linked my arm and tried to drag me away.

"Come on Jean lets put the baby to bed", no way I thought.

"And the watch?" I encouraged the uncle to continue with his story.

"Oh yes" his smile broadened, "after fat man go, box arrive from solicitor. His mother or someone, she die and belongings sent to my address". He paused and took a mouthful of wine before finishing, "mostly rubbish but watch cover some of fat boy's rent".

I handed the baby to Gemma in a manner that dictated she could not refuse him, before I practically tore my father's watch over Mr. Tsangs hand. A few people near us had started to watch and Gemma began to circulate using the baby as a distraction. I leaned into the sweaty face that was wincing at the scuffs I had caused removing the watch.

"This belongs to me old man, now what else was in that box?" At that moment in time he looked for all intents and purposes like a ghost had materialized and I suppose it had. He could not conceive that I was the 'fat boy' who he had rendered homeless all those years ago, how could he I was the Olympic gold medal winning millionaire who had married his niece.

"Not much" he eventually stammered, "bits, pieces, books and maybe diary?"

"A diary?" I demanded, "what kind of diary?" Okay, it was a stupid question.

"Dunno?" He shrugged, "just diary".

"Show me." I took his arm and throwing fake smiles at our guests I all but carried him from the house, where I hailed a passing cab. Half throwing him into the back, I climbed in after him and, on assumption; I gave the address of my squalid former apartment in Islington. I was guessing he had never evolved from there. I was about to pull the door closed behind me when, Gemma grasped the handle stopping me; jumping in after us she joined the confused faces of her uncle and the stunned taxi driver.

"What the hell is going on Jean, where are we going?" she grasped my hand trying to be calming.

"Your uncle is gonna show me what my father left me." There was anger in my voice that Gemma had never heard and I could see she didn't like it. Her uncle didn't like it either and, beneath the bewilderment of who he was discovering I really was, there was fear. The cab slowly pulled from the curb heading north. Save the briefest of explanations to Gemma, the journey from my new life to the old one was in an uncomfortable silence.

In under half an hour I found myself standing on the exact spot where I had rediscovered my list, having salvaged my meager belongings from Mr. Tsang's dustbins. Gemma took my hand but I barely felt it, so absorbed was I by the memories of Jean Ennuyeux's beginnings. I could still hear the group of mothers ushering their children away from me. I could vividly recall the panic I was feeling as to my future and the dogged determination created by my list. It was Mr. Tsang who broke the silence; he had thought of a new angle and spoke in a Picard helpful tone.

"I was just saving, knew you come back one day." What a crock of shit I thought.

"Where is it?" With open palm he gestured that we should follow him but I shook my head and told him we'd wait where we were. I was as close as I ever wanted to be to that part of my story. I was staring at the window that I knew to be from the bathroom I had woken in when you started reading my words. In an attempt to remind myself there was some good in my past, I began to play with the black bracelet that Gemma had gifted me on that same fateful day.

Ten minutes later, and still in silence, Gemma and I were returning to Bourne Street in the cab that I had instructed to wait for us. I had simply snatched the disappointingly small, but impressively carved, wooden box from Mr. Tsang's clutches and, with Gemma on my heels, marched back to our ride.

When we arrived home, our party had dwindled out, no doubt due to the absence of the hosts. Colin and Julie were helping Madame Tremblay clear things away but all knew me well enough to see that this was not a time for conversation. Colin simply nodded and Gemma and I headed upstairs to the room that had become my office. I sat with my new box of historic belongings on my lap and for some time just stared at them. As an inheritance, there wasn't much there and I wondered briefly what had happened to the rest of his things. I surmised there had been quite a gap between the deaths of my father and that of his second wife, so most would have filtered off to her family; I recalled she had sisters.

I started to sift through a selection of letters and postcards, none really note worthy, I then found a stack of pictures. It became immediately apparent why my stepmother or any of her relatives had not wanted these; they were all of my father and I. As I looked down at the first of these the air left my lungs, it was so long since I had seen my father's face. I felt Gemma's arm come around my shoulder but for the first time since I had been with her, I wanted to be alone.

"Could you please get me some tea?" I asked trying to sound as genuine as I could. Her smile confirmed she understood, she kissed my cheek and left the room, she brought the tea two hours later.

When Gemma returned I was just finishing the pages of my father's diary. I had looked through the pictures one by one and marveled at how happy I had been as a child, and how slim, fit and full of life I had been. The diary that I had devoured twice while Gemma made tea, covered just the four months that led up to my father's death in early May. When my wife walked into my office she smiled like only she could, despite the tears in my eyes. She knew they were tears of joy.

"Happy?" she asked me

"Happy" I confirmed.

The contents of those pages changed everything again. They were wonderful. I don't want to bore you with this, so below I have included just one extract to give you a feel for what I had read.

"29th April

My John never ceases to amaze me, he is by far the brightest child I have ever met and I am confident this is a true observation and not just the biased pride of a doting father. The activity of his mind shines through his eyes, he has his mother's eyes. I do wish my new wife could see this in him, the facts are I'm sure she does and I have to forgive her jealousy, and just hope she comes to love John for the amazing boy he is. I tell her time and time again what a wonderful young boy he is, and the excitement he brings to my life and all he touches, maybe I have over done it. I suspect she knows that as much as I love her, it could never compare to the love I have for my beautiful boy. I genuinely believe my son could achieve anything he wanted in life"

Wherever I was mentioned it was in a similar vein and my thoughts catapulted around my mind. I understood why my stepmother had said those things on her deathbed. I found it contemptible and evil but I knew why she had done it. I began to think how proud my father would be if he could see me now and all that I had achieved. The dilemma that hit me was regarding those achievements. If I had known the content of those pages, would my journey have ever started? The driving force behind my achievements was my hope in somehow proving something to my dad. Would I still be where I was had I known this, had he not died, but would I trade all I had for him not to have died? It took Gemma just ten minutes to realize the folly of such thoughts, we got on with our life together, and that night I'm pretty sure we conceived our next child.

You know, that's almost it. Oh, there is just one other thing that always makes me smile. I think you'll remember there were only two more things on my list. Well, this was reduced to one, albeit a little cheekily, when Gemma received her last Oscar. With a pride I had never become accustomed to, due to its sheer magnitude, I watched Gemma in her senior years glide onto the stage of the Kodak theatre. She remained the most beautiful sight I had ever seen. Her speech that year was short and after the obligatory, though heartfelt, thanks to peers and friends she turned her attention to me. She informed the global and enthralled audience that one man had been with her since the very beginning of her career. A man who had watched her first stage performance in London over forty years ago and, since becoming her husband, had read every script with her, shared every laugh and smile and kept her feet on the ground when the industry dictated she should be a diva. She finished by telling all that this Oscar really belongs to that man, to me. On her invitation, I joined her on stage to a thunderous applause that became a standing ovation. I knew many in the crowd by this stage. Despite my age, it was my eighty-fifth birthday, and the fact that I was standing next to an angel from heaven, I felt confident and, I thought, all in all, I looked pretty damn good. Gemma passed me the award, which I reluctantly took. I leaned in to kiss her and, as I did, she slipped a familiar piece of paper into my hand. I looked down to see my ancient list with a line through the sentence 'win an Oscar'.

"Good enough?" she beamed up at me

"Good enough", I confirmed with a smile. She began to laugh and for the millionth time whispered to me

"Now you forget that bloody last one old man, right?" I smiled and kissed her again before we left the stage together hand in hand.

As any father will know, and I ended up the father of four, there were of course a million more mini-adventures from the fearful to the joyous. My married life was beyond magical from the day we were wed in our second home of Vezeley, until the day Gemma passed away. It was quietly in her sleep in our bed on Bourne Street, two days after she received her lifetime achievement Oscar and gave it to me for my list.

We had an amazing life together; it was long and full of love. Many may suggest that we 'had a good innings'. However, the blow that Gemma's parting struck me was beyond the measure of anything that had happened in my life. I would gladly have returned to that cave in Pakistan, for a thousand years, if it meant one more day with my Gemma. The visitor that came to my dreams the night after I had buried my soul mate, my wife, and my reason, multiplied the pain I endured. Gemma's funeral was almost a state affair; the great and the good were in attendance and a crowd of hundreds gathered outside the small church in South London. I have to confess that I was surprised to see the Prime Minister there, as well as the American Secretary of State, who passed on the apologies of the President who could not make it. During my marriage there had been seven Presidents of the United States and I had met them all, each knowing from his predecessor who I really was and offering me anything I needed. I never needed anything; I had everything anyone could want. There was a small wake after the funeral at which time I found out that the Presidential information flow had extended to my own Government. As the Prime Minister was making ready to leave I was invited to join him in a small side room by an aid of his.

"I am so sorry for your loss sir," said the suave politician as I entered the room.

"Thank you" was all I could think to say.

"Jean" he continued, "I'm sorry to make this introduction now, I know today is tough for you". He paused as if expecting some acknowledgment that it was okay to be addressing me in this way, on that day. Not receiving one he cleared his throat before he continued. He basically detailed the 'special relationship' that he had, note 'he', not 'the country', with the United States. I watched this man who in his early forties was a boy to me then. I had not voted for him because I found him to be arrogant and full of his own self-importance and he was confirming my theory with every word. He informed me that due to this 'special relationship' there was certain information that was passed from President to Prime Minister and vice-versa as time past by. My identity was one of those things that helped to cement the relationship in question, as I had performed 'the ultimate service as an ally'. If this was the case, I disliked the young man in front of me even more, none of his predecessors had ever felt the need to confront me and show off this knowledge, which, as a side note, amazed me, or would have any other day.

"What do you want?" He looked a little offended that this was all I had to say after his little speech, what did I care? I had buried my wife that day and I was consumed by a grief that I knew would never leave. I also desperately needed a piss, or felt that way, yes, that was back too. However like any good politician he composed himself quickly.

"I wanted to extend the gratitude of the country Jean, I feel it is long over due and today of all days it may give you some comfort", he smiled in self-pleasure again.

"Well, it doesn't Prime Minister, but I appreciate the gesture", I made to leave with a nod of my head.

"Come now Jean, I also wanted to meet you properly, you and I have a lot in common", his smile intensified as my raised eyebrow confirmed he had my interest. "Like you Jean with Bda Nam, I took charge when it was needed, I stepped up for the better good. I did it because no one else was up to the job", the sanctimonious little shit.

"Well Prime Minister, I just did it because everyone else was dead", he had nothing to say and I left the room.

I blame that conversation for what happened later that night at home; Bda Nam remained on my mind the whole day and in my head he spoke to me. As he was only in my mind he of course knew every button to push, how to taunt me and how to drive me to distraction. It was no surprise that when sleep finally came he was there waiting for me. He was surprisingly Picard.

"Hello again my old comrade, or should I say executioner?" He was sitting in one of two leather armchairs that had spent twenty years on the wall facing our bed, serving no purpose but to collect clothes until they disappeared, when I insist Gemma put some things back in her wardrobe. I sat up in bed.

"That's really distracting," I pointed to his head that was still decapitated and sitting in the second of the two leather chairs.

"Oh, how rude of me, I am sorry", he genuinely seemed embarrassed as the arms attached to the body reached over and retrieved the head, before placing it back where it belonged. It seemed to sit unsteadily, just a jagged red line showing where my blade had struck. "You look well" he offered.

"As do you" I smiled, "I mean considering", he chuckled and his loose head wobbled slightly atop his neck, he corrected it and his expression gradually became somber.

"You killed me" it was a flat statement almost to himself.

"I did" I confirmed, "I'm not sorry"

"I understand, we have very different views and, in fairness, my intentions were not all that friendly when it came to you", he again allowed himself a slight smile. "I feel conflicted in thought now though"; I frowned by way of requesting an explanation. "You see, I understand that you thought killing me was necessary, even essential or noble. That is simply the beliefs of an infidel who has been raised by dogs to understand nothing but his own evil views." Ah, this was the Bda Nam I had remembered. "But I'm not the only man you murdered am I?" He continued. His words struck like a bullet. Even though I knew what he meant, I tried to play dumb.

"Everyone that died in that desert knew why they were there, and the risks. I was fighting for my life, for the lives of my friends". He had began to chuckle long before I finished the sentence and his morbidly perched head wobbled on the stump of his neck again.

"Why waste your breath lying to me, I'm dead Jean, I know everything", I looked down as his words swirled around me, "the point is Jean, soon your gorgeous bride will know too", my eyes flashed back to him. "She'll know what you did and that her entire life with you was based around a lie". He was now leaning toward me for all intents looking like Satan himself, one hand atop his turbaned head to hold it in place, "welcome to hell, my murderer".

The chairs were of course empty as I suddenly sat up right sweating in bed, wide-awake. I stared at the spot where he had been sitting and allowing myself to realize the truth of his words. I began to cry, my first tears not born of joy in over forty years had been cried that week and I could not imagine a time when they would ever stop. I guess I know that Bda Nam was never in my room, that my own fears and self-judgment was simply been projected through the most evil thing I had ever come close to. To explain this to you I need to take you back to the months before my beautiful wedding, waiting outside a church on a Parisian street. You see dear reader, I'm afraid I have lied to you too.

You recall my meeting with Major French when the revelations had been made about his plans to identify me. What I told you about the hotel, following him to the church and confronting him in the confessional, this all happened as I said.

However, my journey to the airport was not as direct as I implied.

Leaving the church, a panic struck me. Could I really rely on him to be scared enough to keep quite forever. I recalled his face in the desert as he left us to be dragged away, that was fear I had never witnessed before, yet here he was hoping to profiteer on his courage. In truth, I think he believed his own fantasy of events. He may be scared again right now, having thought my dead comrades and I would haunt him, but it would pass. The defence mechanism that protected him from the knowledge of his own cowardice would kick in, and he would begin to believe a different version of events again.

After I left the confessional, I found a seat on a wall across the street from the church and sat there letting these thoughts and fears run around my head. This guy was going to destroy everything, and probably with venom once he decided he was a victim again. Hours seem to pass and dusk was settling before I saw the Major leave the small church. I had not really been waiting for him. I didn't have any plan. I was just sitting there thinking; afraid of the future once again. I watched him heading down the street still looking shaky and I followed. I had to speak to him again. I followed at a distance not wanting to shock him into a scene on the street.

Clouds began to gather as we walked, hastening the coming night.

It grew dark quickly and I found myself following the Major along the banks of the Seine, until after almost an hour we reached a large stone bridge. I followed him up an iron staircase that took us to the street level, and then into the fog over the dark river. For a second I lost him, so quickly had the ghostly mist emerged with the returning tide. I reached the centre of the bridge and he was gone, yet I could hear gentle sobs, I spun around trying to focus and then I saw him. He was standing by the grey brick wall hanging onto one of the black lampposts that cast a slight yellow hue across him. He was on the opposite side of the wall, slowly allowing himself to lean further and further into the abyss.

"Major don't, please", he spun around grasping the lamppost with both hands and stared at me in terror as I emerged toward him.

"P..p..please leave me alone" he sobbed, "I'm sorry, I'm so sorry".

"It's okay Major, I'm here", I tried to sound reassuring, "come back over the wall". He seemed to sag slightly and stared at me, letting go of the lamp with one hand and placing it on the wall in front of him. I stepped forward, "it's ok Major".

"Truly, it's you? How did you find me, it was your dead friends". I was now close enough for him to take his free hand from the wall and touch my face like a blind person might, I let him assure himself, "but in the church, you said", he let it hang.

"I'm sorry, I just didn't want anyone to know about me, I was trying to scare you. I need you to keep my secret." He was now looking confused but the emotion was quickly evolving into something else, it was anger. He let out a genuine scream and looked enraged.

"Why? Why do you have to humiliate me again", I noted the drying patch at his crotch as his overcoat blew open in the wind.

"I'm sorry, I…" He didn't let me finish.

"I am going to tell, everyone, I'm going to tell the world that you are a coward and a bully", he was looking and sounding insane, spittle flying from his gnarled mouth. "It was me that led you into the desert, I made you the hero and you just embarrassed me and took all the glory, and the money"

"Major you can have the money if that's it, just leave me be" this seemed to fuel his anger.

"I don't want your fucking money, I'll make my own by telling everyone who you are and what you are. I'm going to ruin your life like you did mine!" With this, he placed the flat of his hand on my chest and tried to push me away. He underestimated my mass and the slippery surface he was on, his foot slipped and his own force sent him backward. His free hand flayed freely and losing his grip with the other he took it from the post and managed to grasp the lapel of my coat. He was overstretched and, as his weight pulled me forward, he was at a precarious point of balance on the edge of the ledge.

"Help me, Jean! I'm sorry, I was angry", he was gasping for breath and life. My mind worked at lightening speed. This guy was never gonna let me go, he was going to take everything from me, my life as I knew it. All I'd been through would be on show to be judged and studied, or hunted down by Bda Nam believers. His grip was slipping and he continued to beg. I drifted into a trancelike state, I saw his lips moving in slow motion but I did not hear anything. I had never seen a face so desperate, and as I lifted my arm and used the back of my hand to knock his grip from my coat, that face was imprinted on my mind forever as it disappeared backward to the murky water, and to death. Then I flew to America and I lied to Gemma, I lied to everyone who knew me and I lied to you.

The Bda Nam of my dreams was right; this was murder for my own gain, nothing more. If he was also right that the love of my life would soon know this, she had to hear it from me, I wanted to tell her myself.

I don't know what comes next, if anything at all, but a black void of nothingness is better than been here without her. So this is it, I'm finished and you can judge me as you see fit. There are a few things I must do now so I will write just a few more words. I have to write some letters and sort some things and then I am going to go and finally finish my list. If I do see my Gemma again, she will go crazy with me, but there is method in my madness, it seems as good a way as any and, as always, I will be thinking of her.

I was thinking of her everyday when I was forced to sleep in the bath and spent my days being bullied and harassed. I was thinking of her when I was training to be a soldier around the world and, when a mad man brought me to the deserts of the Middle East by trying to destroy that world. As the same man broke me again and again she was on my mind and as I escaped and continued my adventures she was with me in a way. It all started with her and it will finish with her and I, it's the only way I know. I love her, more today than I did yesterday. Thank you for reading my story, goodbye.

Epilogue
Written by Michael Ennuyeux

I am very proud to tell you that my name is Michael Ennuyeux, I am even prouder to tell you that my father was Jean Ennuyeux, and lest we forget my amazing mother, Gemma.

I, like you, have just read the preceding pages; it is hard to explain all the emotions that are surrounding my family and I right now. Confused emotions that we find difficult to categorize or understand. I want to first tell you a little about myself. I don't do this to boast, but to let you know the man my father raised. First and foremost, nobody has ever called me boring. You already know that on my twenty-first birthday I reached the peak of

Everest with my father. Although this was one of my most amazing experiences, it is one of many. With the love and support of my family, I was consistently encouraged, not pushed, to challenge myself and believe I could achieve anything I put my mind to. In my second year at Oxford, I skippered the rowing team to beat Cambridge in the boat race. I graduated top of my class with a law degree that placed me instantly within the top firm in London. Within ten years I was Managing Partner, five years later I had left and started my own firm, five years after that my firm was the top firm in London. I replaced my father as CEO of W.I.K.E.D. where fifty percent of my companies' profits still go. On top of this, we raise half a billion pounds a year through a chain of events and a non-profit clothing line sold through my wife's stores. I have three beautiful children.

My siblings, the rest of my father's children, have equally excelled under our parents' support and encouragement. My youngest sister is a doctor specializing in pediatrics at a leading hospital in Genève. She lives there with her Swiss husband, also a doctor, and their two children. My brother works with me and is a partner in the firm with the best track record in the company; he has yet to marry but is enjoying the search, a little too much we tease him. My eldest sister followed in our mother's footsteps and is a hot favorite for her first Oscar next year. She lives in LA with her husband of eight years and the newest additions to our family, the twins. We have always been and remain a very close family, this was always so important to my father. Despite this, most of the things you have learned in the previous chapters were a mystery to all of us when we first came across my father's memoirs.

Of course we knew about my father's Gold medal, we had also teased him constantly about his attempt as a rap star. These things were part of family banter at every gathering. We did not know of our father's beginnings, his situation with his father, the condition he was in both mentally and physically when he started his adventures, or the sheer suffering he had been through in every possible connotation of the word. We only knew our father as a happy, loving successful man and doting husband and father. Over the years as I watched my parents, my observations changed, they were the apple of my eye and I loved them, for a period in my teens they were annoying and embarrassing as all parents seem. Then they were the benchmark by which I would measure any relationship I entered. They were in short, amazing.

It seems unbelievable that we had no idea our father was 'Soldier X'. This, above all, took the wind from us when, as a family, we shared the words he had written. I was always aware but, in a weird way not aware, of my father's physical scars. They were just always there, in hindsight I saw them little so maybe he was consciously hiding them, and in fairness the famous ones on his back had settled dramatically differently to how they looked on the tape that we had all seen, where they openly bled.

The day we found my father's 'memoirs', for want of a better description, was just four days after my mother's funeral. He had asked for time alone and we reluctantly gave it, he was still a very fit and active, self-sufficient man. As well as all their active holidays and travels, he and my mother had continued morning runs until well into his sixties, before they had gradually been replaced with brisk walks and bicycle rides. It was day three when I picked up the phone, it had been the longest time I had ever not spoken with my father, and it had been hard for me, especially given recent events. So, on that fateful morning, it was decided that my wife and I would gather up the kids, collect Uncle Colin and head around to Bourne Street, where we would force some company and some love on my father. After repeated knocks I gave in to Uncle Colin's demands and used my key to let us into the house. Uncle quickly scooted past us to the kitchen where he poured himself a brandy and sighed with pleasure after his first mouthful. Although this is two months after Uncle Colin's one hundred and first birthday, he is as active as ever. He is gradually becoming more and more eccentric since Auntie Julie's death, allowing his grey hair to grow into a long mop atop his head. He still wears his three-piece suits but, had opted for large check patterns over his previous plain flannel materials. He talks to himself out loud and often follows this with out bursts of laughter. I personally remain convinced it is all an act, a privilege of age he feels he has and I tend to agree. The facts are, that whenever I need him he remains the best source of rational and intelligent advice I have in my life, beyond the professional advisors and consultants I employ, his is the final word in many of my personal dilemmas.

As the kids set about destroying the place in their usual manner, jumping on furniture and chasing each other around their great uncle, my wife gave me a concerned look that I'm sure I mirrored. Beyond the invasion that we represented it was too quiet in the house, which was completely alien. Everything was in order and tidy. No used cups littered the kitchen tops, no magazines strewn across the coffee tables or sofas. In proof of his clear thinking, Uncle Colin opened the patio doors and led the kids outside leaving my wife and I alone.

"What are you thinking?" she asked when we were alone, the kids now just distant backing noise.

"I don't know. I guess we should look upstairs". Obvious concerns spun around my head as I climbed the stairs in front of my wife, the silence now engulfing me seemed to magnify. On the first floor, I walked into my father's study, glancing around the room as I entered. Just a few short hours later all the paraphernalia that decorated the place would make a lot more sense. I had loved to play in this room as a child but, as I had grown, I had never really questioned any of the contents. Some were obvious, the framed Gold Medal on it's ribbon hanging next to the gold disc for a number one song. Other things needed the detail that you and I have now read to understand their significance. There was a deliberately blunted French bayonet on top of the large oak desk; it was used as a letter opener. An equally French 'Kepi' hat sat on a bookshelf behind the desk, as did a smaller frame, which held the tickets to my mother's debut Shakespearian performance. Various maps in frames hung on the rest of the walls, but all of this was dwarfed by the sheer mass of framed photographs of our family, spanning decades, one never removed, to be replaced by another. Every achievement that the members of my family had ever made immortalized in my fathers pride and love.

For some reason, I focused on the formerly lethal blade that decorated the desk. I suspect because at that stage it seemed the strangest object in the room. It was several seconds before I focused on the large pile of paper next to it. Somehow I knew my wife was staring at it to. There was an envelope on top and as I approached I noted the addressee, 'My Beautiful Children'.

I've no wish to divulge the full content of the letter, it was personal and it was obviously intended purely for the eyes of his 'beautiful children'. Otherwise, no doubt, he would have added it to the end of the chapters you have read. As would be expected, it expressed again his love and pride. He offered a lot of needless apologies and he provided some logistical details that he wished to be carried out. All in all it was written as he spoke to us, which was as if he lived purely for us. After I read it I looked to my wife with a tear-suppressing smile.

"Well?" She smiled back, "where is he?"

"I don't know?" I said it with a shrug, despite the magnitude of the note, at no point had he said what he planned to do, where he was going or where he would be. He simply invited me to read the manuscript we had found. When asked I handed my wife the envelope and letter so she could read it. She did this and then began to look around the room as though hunting for clues. I settled down to read my father's words, within moments I found I was reading out loud to my captivated wife, who sat opposite me enthralled.

Together we followed the journey you have just followed, of course, a lot closer to it than you. There were times when my wife comforted me as tears streamed down my face, sometimes with heartbreak and sometimes laughing at things that were so reflective of the man I knew. Sometimes, a man I didn't know. More often than not the emotions were mixed. The idea of a fat man washing himself in a theatre toilet made me laugh, the fact that man was my desperate father choked me. Likewise, when my father was been trained by a band of Legionnaires and his dear Sergeant I welled with pride, though his reasons and what was in his mind, again destroyed me emotionally. I judge my father on nothing he did, in my mind what happened in the desert made him a hero, and what he did on that bridge in Paris, I am sure I would have done myself. The self-torture he secretly inflicted on himself for that one act, despite all the other amazing things he did for others in his life, speaks volumes as to the very rare and special kind of man he was.

Our full emotional rollercoaster took maybe four hours, when we read of my father's escape from 'Bda Nam', we took an exhausted break and made tea. Uncle Colin had exhausted the kids and they all lay asleep on the chairs and sofas around the living room. We gently covered them all with blankets before we went back upstairs and found out how Uncle Colin actually came into our lives and, the fact that we were also reading many secrets he had kept to himself for decades.

Our second sitting was just as exhausting, and as I came to the final pages the sleeping beauties downstairs had woken and joined us sleepily around the office. Uncle Colin had a fresh brandy and a knowing smile. 'Thank you for reading my story, goodbye', the last words my father had written, less our wonderful letter of course. I looked around the room, my wife was now stood by my side with her head down, one hand on my shoulder which she removed and used to retrieve a previously missed tatty piece of paper from the envelope that had contained our letter. My beloved Uncle sat in the recently vacated chair opposite me, his jaw set, trying to suppress the liquid that was gathering at the bottom of his eyes.

"Where's Granddad?" asked my youngest, who unnoticed had woken from her slumber and waddled across the floor where she began to climb onto her Great Uncle's knee, whilst rubbing her eyes with her tiny fist. Colin looked at me as if repeating the child's question. I again shrugged and simply mouthed the words, 'I don't know'.

"I think I know where he is", the emotion in my wife's voice was hard to describe, shock, surprise, devastation even maybe a hint of humor. I starred at her desperate to find the solution she'd found to our puzzle.

Without another word she dropped the tatty piece of paper in front of me. I studied it without reading it and realized it was my father's list. A shabby scrap torn from a textbook, retrieved from the bins of an evicted, jobless tenant. The scrawl of a ten-year-old boy, it detailed all his dreams and ambitions. All but one of these dreams had a line drawn through it, one of these lines I now know to have been drawn by a president, and one by a famous actress, my mother. Sensing her movement I turned to see my wife bend and retrieve a further piece of paper, from a small, wire waste paper basket on the floor, this she laid next to the list in front of me. I stared at it, a contrasting crisp, and white piece of A4 neatly typed with a blue and red airline logo emblazoned across the top. I read it three times before its contents and then its relevance struck me.

"Oh my God", I half whispered. My wife again squeezed my shoulder and I felt her tears land on my neck. The sheet, taken from the bin, was a printout of an airline ticket receipt for a flight to Vancouver in Canada, and a subsequent charter booking to a small airport in the heart of British Columbia. When it registered fully, I looked back to the piece of paper where all this had started, gradually scrolling down my father's list until I reached the last unchecked task. The only words without a line drawn through them on my father's list, in his dreamer's, ten-year-old writing, read, 'wrestle a bear'. We never saw our father again.

THE END

'THE INCREDIBLE ACHIEVEMENTS OF BORING JOHN'

Aka

'Réalisation incroyable de Ennuyeux Jean'

Michael J. Cooper